SPI
EGE
L&G
RAU

ALSO BY EDWARD CONLON

Blue Blood

RED
ON
RED

RED
ON
RED

A NOVEL

———

EDWARD CONLON

Spiegel & Grau

New York

2011

Published in the United States by Spiegel & Grau, an imprint of
The Random House Publishing Group, a division of Random House, Inc., New York.

SPIEGEL & GRAU and Design is a registered
trademark of Random House, Inc.

Library of Congress Cataloging-in-Publication Data
Conlon, Edward.
Red on red: a novel / Edward Conlon.
p. cm.
ISBN 978-0-385-51917-5
eBook ISBN 978-0-679-60441-9
1. Detectives—New York (State)—New York—Fiction.
2. Criminal investigation—New York (State)—New York—Fiction.
3. Male friendship—Fiction. 4. New York (N.Y.)—Fiction. I. Title.
PS3603.O5413R43 2011
813'.6—dc22   2010017534

Printed in the United States of America on acid-free paper

www.spiegelandgrau.com

2 4 6 8 9 7 5 3 1

First Edition

Title page photograph by Kevin Brainard

To the memories of

TED PHILLIPS
&
VAL MARGOLIS

We might wish that policemen would not act with impure plots in mind, but I do not believe that wish a sufficient basis for excluding . . . probative evidence. . . . In addition, sending state and federal courts on an expedition into the minds of police officers would produce a grave and fruitless misallocation of judicial resources.

—Justice Byron White, in a dissenting opinion

Nature loves to hide.

—Herakleitos

AUTHOR'S NOTE

As of this writing, I am a New York City detective. I was born in Manhattan, but I have never worked or lived there. While pains have been taken to produce an effect of surface realism—many features of the landscape and much police procedure are described substantially as they are—all has been seized, as by eminent domain, and remade to fit the needs of the story. Mother Cabrini is a high school for girls in Washington Heights, but its role in this book is wholly imagined. No character corresponds to any real person. Facts end where this story begins. None of this is true.

RED
ON
RED

ONE

Nick Meehan knew there was more to every story, but he usually didn't want to hear it. He was in the woods, at a presumed suicide, and it was raining. There had to be limits, even if it seemed cold-blooded to set them. If, say, he asked a young man if he'd hit his girlfriend, a "No" might not mean anything, but a "Yes" always did, and Nick wouldn't have to listen much longer. The story would be worth hearing if she'd chased him with a hatchet, but there was no point listening to his sad proofs and sorry protests about how she'd never really loved him. That was another story, maybe true, but what mattered was how the man put his belief into action with a roundhouse right, chipping her tooth with the gold ring she'd bought him for his birthday. She might then wonder whether she had ever loved him, doubting why she'd stolen the money for the ring from her mother's new boyfriend, who tended to walk into the bathroom when she was in the shower. You needed to contain a story like a disease, before it spread. Nick was at a suicide in the park, and it was raining.

What happened was this: The rain had let up in the early evening, and Ivan Lopez had been walking through Inwood Hill Park when the shoe had dropped on him. Inwood, the stalagmite tip of Manhattan, where the Dutch had bought the wild island from the Indians, green since the beginning of time. The shoe, an open sandal with a low heel, had fallen from the foot of a woman who was hanging from a tree. She was half-hidden amid the lower branches of an old oak whose leaves had just begun to turn gold and red. Lopez had given a little shout—"Oho!"—but had regained his breath a moment later and called the police. He had done nothing wrong, he knew, aside from wandering in the woods after dark. He told the first cops that he'd gone there to walk his dog. Lopez didn't see the problem with his story, but even when it was pointed out that he didn't have a dog, he clung to the tale like a child clings to a toy, fearful that if it were taken, nothing would be the same.

Lopez was a slight man, with a put-upon air that made him look older than his thirty-odd years. He would not have agreed with any suggestion that his was a dishonest face, despite his worried, furtive manner. He had other burdens, other troubles. He'd had little experience with the police, but he knew at once that he shouldn't have begun by telling them, "You're not going to believe this, but . . ." Those first seven words were the only ones they seemed to accept, as he stumbled and jumped through his version of events, further jarred by the skeptical questions that seemed to presume he knew the woman's name, where she lived. Two cops had arrived, and then two more, in cars that had rambled over the muddy fields between the street and the woods, with stops and starts and shifts in direction, as if they'd been following a scent. The cops were all larger than Lopez, younger than him, and both facts rubbed against his dignity. He reminded them angrily that he'd tried to be a good citizen in a neighborhood where that quality was not always apparent. The rebuke seemed to have some modest effect on the cops, who withdrew and asked him to wait to speak with the detectives. No one was wrong—not yet, not terribly—but neither side credited the other with good sense or good faith. No one knew what had happened, and as more was said, less was believed.

That was the scene of stalemate the detectives took in when they arrived. One of them was physically robust, emphatic in manner, ready for conflict, the other spare and withholding. More of one, less of the other. The second one, the lesser—Meehan—seemed more sympathetic, and Lopez chose to focus on him when he repeated his account. The audience-shopping instinct was noted with suspicion, and it was the first detective, Esposito, who asked the first question, taking control of the conversation and returning to the earlier sticking point.

"So, where's the dog?"

Lopez exhaled heavily and said he did not know. He knew how it made him sound, but he didn't see the point—or rather, he didn't like it. He didn't like the next question any better, or the man—Esposito—who asked it.

"What kind of dog was it?"

"A brown one," he said, after some hesitation.

"What was the dog's name?"

"Brownie."

That answer came too quickly, and seemed anticipated rather than re-membered. Esposito pressed ahead, testy.

" 'Brownie.' Where's the leash?"

"I don't have one. What does this have to do with anything? I was walking by and I got hit, out of nowhere—I could have lost an eye or something—and I try to do the right thing, and I get my balls busted by guys who—"

"By guys who what?"

Nick Meehan intruded with a mild and slightly sideways follow-up, and Lopez couldn't tell whether he cared more or less than the first de-tective, if he were signaling that he shared the joke with Lopez or was playing a new one on him: "You could get a ticket for not having a leash for the dog."

"But you don't believe the dog," countered Lopez, with a jubilant smirk. "You can't write the ticket if you don't believe the dog."

"Touché."

"Qué?"

"Exactly!"

Nick didn't believe Lopez, but he was delighted by the oddly theo-logical detour of the conversation. He didn't pretend to be useful, and didn't always want to be. Nick preferred cases that went nowhere, or rather, he was drawn to mysteries that were not resolved with a name typed on an arrest report—funny things or lucky things, glimpses of ar-chaic wonder and terror, where life seemed to have a hidden order, a rhyme. Here, a witness was hanging himself in his story about a hanging woman, and the detectives were becoming entangled.

Esposito stepped heavily through the mud to borrow a flashlight from one of the uniformed cops. When he returned, he shone it back and forth between Lopez's face and the suspended woman, which somehow suggested a line drawn between them, connecting the dots.

"Do you have identification?"

Lopez handed Esposito a driver's license, which Esposito put in his pocket without looking at it. One of the cops began talking to another about the Yankees game, and Lopez looked over at them, irritated. Nick escorted Lopez to the back of their unmarked car, suggesting it might be more comfortable, more private, and situated him in the backseat. Nick sat beside him, not too close, and Esposito took the front passenger seat, leaning back. Nick put a hand on Lopez's shoulder, in a gesture that might have seemed more friendly, had the space not been so confined.

"Thank you. Thank you for calling us," Nick said. "Nobody should end up like that."

"I try to do the right thing."

"You did. Tell me, I'm not much of a dog person myself, just because you gotta walk 'em all the time. How often do you gotta take him out?"

"Three, maybe five times a day."

"That's a lot. How do you have the time? Are you working now?"

"I manage a shoe store. My daughter takes him out, too."

Esposito leaned in, as if he disbelieved that Lopez had much acquaintance with either work or women, and looked down. Lopez's boots were mucked over, like everything else, making it hard to tell much about them. Esposito did not relent. "What's your kid's name?"

"Grace."

The response came without hesitation, as did Esposito's follow-up. "What's your dog's name again?"

The seconds that passed before Lopez spoke were few—three or four—but painful to endure. "Lucky," he said, which was not true in either sense. He squirmed and pleaded, "Can I have my ID back now?"

"Yeah, sure," said Esposito, blithe for a moment before becoming abrupt and demanding again. "Let me see your hands."

"What? My God, this is a bad dream. . . ."

"Wake up, then. The hands. Now."

Lopez looked to Nick for support, but found none. The detectives did not feign anything in their hoary old binary roles—each hard look and kind word was authentic, heartfelt—but all of it was nonetheless deployed for effect, joined to a purpose. Nick took the flashlight from Esposito and turned it on—"Just procedure. Don't worry. Relax."—as Lopez raised his palms for examination, turning them over slowly, to show unblemished, unmarked skin. That, at least, did not lie. He might as well have slept in mittens and kept them on all day. Esposito grunted, noncommittal. Lopez shook his hands as if they'd been dirtied, then pointed outside.

"See? I told you—this is not me! I'm just here, same as you. It was already over, finished, done! This is just this. I don't know why you keep trying to put me in the picture. . . . This is simple—"

Esposito cut him off as he climbed out of the car, disdaining even to look at him as he left. "The funny part is, it coulda been."

Nick thanked Lopez again and asked him to wait there—"It won't be too much longer"—before joining Esposito outside, where they continued their conference beneath the tree. He understood what Esposito had been doing and why, respected its necessity. It wasn't as if Esposito were a bully demanding lunch money. Still, there was something unappealing in the unfairness of the contest, which bothered Nick, and he saw little to be gained from regarding Lopez as an adversary instead of a distraction.

"Lighten up a little on him, would you?"

The request was amiably offered, received with an obliging shrug.

"Whose is this, anyway?" asked Esposito. "Whose turn is it for what?"

"If it's a homicide, it's yours. If it's a suicide, it's mine. And it's a suicide."

"Good. I mean—you know what I mean. This is not my cup of shit. Your case, your call."

Nick did know what he meant. Esposito disliked noncriminal investigations, the runaways and accidental deaths; they could be almost as much work as murders, but there was no contest, no opponent—no bad man to put in handcuffs at the end. Esposito was a fighter, and this fight had already been lost. For him, the dead woman in the tree might as well have been a live cat, a sad situation but not an urgent problem, not one that made his neck stiffen or his heart soften. Lopez was the only figure of interest for him, and only because of a professional aversion to certain forms of deceit. Nick could see the impatience gather again in Esposito's face and then recede.

"However you wanna handle it, Nick. But tell me, you don't have a problem with a guy standing by a dead body, telling you lies?"

Nick took the flashlight and shone it upward. The midair fixity of the woman, taut on the tentative line, reminded him of a dog straining against a leash. The rope held, but would not for long. He didn't want to think of dogs, and he contemplated pointing the light accusingly at Lopez, as Esposito had. He pictured holding it under his own chin, as if to tell a campfire story. Which is what Nick was convinced that Lopez had done, making up nonsense because he had been caught sneaking out in the dark. Still, Lopez didn't matter; the woman did. He shut off the light and turned to Esposito to work through the practicalities.

"Say you got a guy, he's on his way to a whorehouse when he witnesses a bank robbery. He's a good witness, your only good witness, but he tells you he was going to church. Do you use him?"

Esposito smiled, taken by the fable, even more appreciative that Nick could disagree with him without argument. "That's why you gotta break him. You get in there and straighten him out. You let him know how it's gotta go. You break him, you avoid the whole problem."

"All right, but you know, it's my analogy here, and you don't get to change it. In my story, he won't break. And my story isn't this story— nobody robbed a bank. I mean, we'll cover the bases, but this guy didn't kill her. Nobody did. Come on. If this guy confessed to killing her, here and now, you'd kick him in the ass, tell him to go home and sleep it off."

"You're right. But his story still matters. It changes things, even if it's not true. And I still might kick him."

"Do me a favor and don't," said Nick, almost sure Esposito was joking about the kick, unready to consider the full meaning of the other remark. "Let's look at this, run through it, worst-case. How did she get up there? She climbed or someone took her. Say it's a homicide. He killed her there? Alive? Not even leopards on the nature shows do that. They kill them first, then they hide the food in the tree, so the lions don't steal it. That didn't happen here."

"Was that on the other night?"

"Yeah."

"I saw that. Not bad. Still, you can't beat Shark Week. . . . I'm glad she's not a floater. They're a pain. You never know with them."

Esposito was right about floaters. They were far worse. You rarely could establish whether they'd jumped, fallen, or been pushed into the water. He and Nick had only worked with each other for a few months, but Nick had learned to follow his partner's trains of thought. Esposito had begun to shift from anger to boredom, disengaging—not that he was often or especially angry, but when he was in the game, he was all in, with all emotional color on display like a peacock's tail. If they'd been at a bar, leaning over drinks, it might have been interesting to puzzle over the situation, to spitball and tease the possibilities among the four categories: homicide, suicide, accident, and natural. They'd talk as if they were playing themselves on TV, looking for the odd detail, the brilliant twist. As it was, the case had the fascination of a flat tire for Esposito.

Floaters, leopards, bank robberies—the comparisons had become a way of avoiding the subject instead of illuminating it.

"Anyway. The crime scene is the body, the tree, the ground," Nick reasoned. "The ground's already gone, with the rain, all of us here. The body's the main thing. We'll check it out as best we can. In theory, the tree should have scuff marks from the climb, bits of clothing, whatever trace evidence."

Things rub off on each other. The woman had a bit of tree on her, the tree a bit of woman, commingling in constant, invisible transactions. The oak seemed mournful and uneasy, as the branches shifted and the raindrops splatted from leaf to leaf with a staticky whoosh, a radio station that didn't quite come in. Nick looked at Esposito, and Esposito looked at his watch. They hadn't rubbed off on each other so much just yet.

Both of them glanced up at the sky to see whether more rain threatened, but night had already fallen. The breeze was heavy with September weather, the edge of a hurricane that had blown out to sea lower down on the coast. Their shoes were muddy, as were the cuffs of their pants, which bothered Esposito especially. He was strongly built, with a bit of a belly on him that he would slap after meals; he had thick black hair and fair skin, and though he was not a particularly handsome man, he carried himself like one, and women responded. He had his vanities, many of them only half-serious, most well earned. Lately, he seemed to be taken with his own nose; Nick had made offhand mention that it was a Roman nose, and Esposito had been delighted, as if he'd won it at a raffle. He worked the subject into interviews: "The guy who robbed you, tell me about his face. Was his nose flat, or upturned, or was it . . . a Roman nose, like mine?" Tonight, Esposito had walked into the office looking like a mob lawyer, in a blue pinstripe suit and flowered tie; now, from the knees down, he could have been mistaken for a zoo janitor on elephant detail. Nick noticed a great deal about Esposito, not only because they were partners, but because he had agreed to keep an eye on him. Esposito didn't know that. He knew only that he was appreciated, and he was grateful. Nick dressed in the G-man standard—dark suit, white shirt, dark tie—but his vanity was grandiose in comparison. He thought he could betray his partner, just a little, and they could still be friends. He was like Lopez, he thought, in his desperate insistence that only his better motives mattered.

Nick thought about the cold and then felt it, shivering a little. The wind rose again, and the branches shook, and the red and gold oak leaves fell around them, landing on their shoulders like tame birds. The smell of the body, faint but foul, crept through the wet leaves. Esposito wrinkled his nose in disgust and moved away. "You mind going up?"

"No. It's my case. You won't have to worry about your manicure."

"All yours. Go ahead, work your magic."

"I will. I'm going to make it all disappear."

"Let's do it, then."

When they returned to the little crowd of cops, Esposito put his hands on his hips and announced the course of action, "Okay. We're gonna need to take the tree down. Where's your sergeant? I need you to get Emergency Services here with a chain saw, cut it down, pack the whole thing up—with the body—for the medical examiner. You'll need a flatbed truck, a lot of plastic tarps. What else, Nick?"

Nick's mouth tightened. Even though Lopez was probably out of earshot, Nick thought this was disrespectful. There were mysteries to be preserved here as well as mysteries to be explored. Still, he had his partner to consider, his part to uphold. To hell with it, he thought. He'd take the low road, too, and make up for it later.

"Strobe lights," he deadpanned. "Generator."

"Right, strobes. All right, guys, it looks like it's gonna be a long night for you. Maybe you can ask the guys for coffee when they bring the lights."

With another gust of wind, the black sky emptied rain onto them again. Nick saw two of the cops' faces. One was blank and sorrowful, as if he'd learned he'd been drafted; the other looked to be near tears, though the weather made that hard to tell. Only a guffaw from one of the older ones, who held back for a moment, broke the scene of perfect misery.

"All right, but you know I had three of you," said Esposito, to their general relief. "Anyway, let's get hold of a ladder. Maybe two of you drive over to a building, borrow a ladder from a super. The other two, you might as well wait in the car."

The cops agreed gladly, retreating to the warmth and dryness. One car drove off, sending a spray of mud from beneath its wheels. The detectives took shelter beneath the tree, keeping a wary distance from the potential drop zone. Neither detective wanted to join Lopez in the car, to ask him more questions or even to pass the time out of the elements. As they waited, the conversation dwindled, and their moods turned as gloomy and autumnal as the landscape. Esposito inclined his head up toward the woman and frowned.

"What kind of grown woman climbs a tree?"

Nick imagined her pursued by a pack of hounds, even imaginary ones, like Lopez's. "Treed," that was the word, in hunting. The dogs couldn't follow, but the chase was over. Nick knew that feeling, knew this place.

"I might have climbed this tree, when I was a kid."

"That's right, you're a native. I forget, when you don't wear the war paint and carry the tomahawk."

Before Nick could dwell too much on his childhood, still less his recent return to Inwood, the wind shifted the branches, and the body swung gently, a movement that suggested a plea—*Please*—and a threat—*Don't make me*. They moved farther out of range. Suicides intrigued Nick, or they at least held out the possibility of interest. Most cases had a distraught or demented aspect, bad guesses by bad gamblers. With other cases, though, there was a hint of chill insight, like that of a cardsharp who cheats to lose rather than prolong a game he cannot win. Nick hoped that she had left a note. In his worst moments, Nick didn't understand why more people didn't kill themselves, as they seemed to take so little pleasure in life, served such scarce purpose. Why wasn't there a forest of suicides, a body hanging in every tree of the park, from every branch of every tree, dangling like morbid ornaments? Nick added that thought to the long list of those he'd never share.

Esposito fidgeted, wiped his mouth, rubbed his temple. Nick couldn't tell if he was bothered or just bored, ready to move on, out of the rain. Esposito shook his head; he was more than bored.

"And what kind of grown man walks in the woods at night?"

"Some people just like walking, you know."

"Whatever."

Over the summer, Nick had seen a pheasant in the park, strutting across a meadow clearing on the wooded ridge, a brilliant thing of crimson and copper, tail feathers long and jaunty, and it had seemed less out of place than out of time, a figure from heraldry. It had been a ceremony in itself, and he'd found that he could not move until it had passed. Neither Lopez nor the woman shared his reasons for wandering here, he guessed; other people are just that, otherwise haunted, otherwise hopeful. Again, Esposito pulled him back from his reverie.

"You'd have to be crazy to kill yourself. Do you think she was crazy, Nick?"

"No."

The almost pensive tone of the question troubled Nick, as did the casual certainty of his own answer. Other people—Esposito was one of them. Nick recalled that one of Esposito's old partners had killed himself, though the two men had never spoken of it. The partners were not supposed to have been close, and there had been other problems—a divorce, some drinking. Esposito was begrudged his failure to see it coming or to stop it, all the more so because he was so richly gifted in his vocation, in which perception was the means, and protection the end. When Nick had first started working with Esposito, two or three detectives had told him about it, in hurried and stagy whispers, as if warning him that a house he was about to buy had a reputation, a history. The insinuating manner had made Nick defensive of Esposito, though he'd known that other aspects of that history, that reputation, were the reasons they had come together. Esposito had been wrong, then, in his last words to Lopez: The situation here never could have been simple.

The other patrol car returned, ambling over the field, and Esposito directed both cars to face the tree, shining the headlights against it. The borrowed ladder was set up, and Nick took out a camera from the trunk of their car, as well as a pair of latex gloves from a box borrowed from an ambulance. Lopez stepped out from the backseat as Nick did so, and Nick, seeing his pained—though still dishonest—expression, did not instruct him to return. Nick slung the camera around his neck by the strap, and as he ascended the ladder, the camera bumped against the rungs. The flashlight beam chanced upon a spot on the trunk where it illuminated a blockily carved heart. The narrow, trembling focus and yellow warmth gave the light the look of a drama club spotlight, and within the valentine were the initials MR, a plus sign, the number four. An unfinished equation, lacking whoever, forever.

The knots, Nick remembered. He should save the knots in the rope. As he climbed up, he took in the woman's form, slight and almost childlike—the one shod foot; the jeans, stained at the seat; the black winter jacket worn before the season, most likely because it was that jacket or none; the purse, still over the shoulder. The body didn't smell as bad as it might have, a day old at most. She had gone out when the storm had been heavy, the wild weather matching her mind. He looked at one of the hands, the fingers dark and thick with lividity. Shining the light on the fingers, he saw a ring, barely visible, as the swollen skin had begun to push around it, nearly covering the stone. Engagement? No, the wrong finger, a red stone. He snapped a few pictures of the hand. The bare foot would show the lividity, too, but it was a little farther away, and he didn't want to turn the body.

"How's it going up there?"

"Great, fine, beautiful. Wish you were here."

"How are we gonna get it down?"

Nick didn't answer. Up another rung, and another, as the ladder angled in closer to the wet bark. He reached over to the woman's head, flashlight in one hand, clasping a branch with the other. She had long black hair, loose, wavy, and luxurious, and the strangled grimace made the woman look put together from two different dolls, a princess wig on a monster face. She looked Mexican. Immigrants didn't kill themselves. Not often, Nick had found, which he assumed had to do with them being accustomed to struggle. A note would be helpful, but only one in four suicides left them, that was the statistic. Who knew if she had been able to write? There were Mexicans here who didn't even speak Spanish, Indians from the in-country hills who picked up how to *hablar en español* on Amsterdam Avenue. Nick pictured a graph of the trajectory of this woman's journey from Mexico to this tree: three thousand horizontal miles, fifteen vertical feet. Moving up, moving out. It didn't fit, but there it was.

Poor girl, poor girl. God have mercy. . . . Nick's father would have said that. It sounded like him even as Nick said it to himself. A brogue in the mind; he heard it more often since he'd moved back home. The girl was poorer now. She was the poorest, by the old precepts. Despair was the only unforgivable sin, a kind of heresy, holding that the clock was stuck on this hopeless hour, and God had lost track of time. Then again, maybe suicide was unforgivable just because you quit, chucked it in, game over. Forgiveness was for the living, when you could raise your hand to ask for it, when the possible is still possible. Stupid girl, he thought, with unexpected harshness. That didn't sound like himself, either.

Nick took a few more pictures. The ligature had yanked the head to the side, creasing the neck with a sharp upright line, dark above and light below. The rope was white wool, wrapped round and round a branch above, like a cat's cradle. She had unspooled a ball of yarn into a noose, and dangled gently less than a foot below a branch. It didn't seem strong enough, and yet it held, and the physics-problem curiosity took Nick away from the grimace and the smell for a moment to consider the logistics. Her hip was beside another branch, and she must have sat there and slipped off—a few inches, no more—so that the force of the drop didn't break the yarn. She must not have struggled, which could suggest drugs or drink, a sedative to edge her beyond second thoughts. There were so many better ways to do this; its difficulty was impressive, and he caught himself thinking that she was lucky that it had worked out. What was the Sinatra song? "I've got the world on a string . . ."

The tactlessness made Nick look away from her, as if he'd sung it aloud and she'd caught him making fun. Just above her, to the side, there was a plastic bag tangled in a branch—in color somewhere between water and white—that must have been hanging there for some days. It had frayed at the handles, and dank water that had collected inside made it swell like a belly. Nick wondered if she were pregnant, if that had been her reason, and his stomach tightened for the first time. The sight of the bag bothered him more than the body. Reckoning that it was not part of the crime scene—if there even was a crime, which there wasn't—and that it could leak down on cops or the ME later, he pinched a corner and tore it. He hadn't thought about what it might look like, from another point of view. As the fluid gurgled and streamed down, there were stifled cries from below—"Ugh!"—from less familiar voices, and a concerned query from a familiar one.

"Nick? You okay, buddy?"

"Yeah—don't worry. It's not me. Not her, either. It's just water from—never mind. Don't worry about it."

Tactless again, not just in his imagination. Was he himself tonight? Yes, unfortunately. Nick resumed his task, shining his light on the body, determined to finish, to see whatever had to be seen. It was his case, and it wouldn't take any magic to make it disappear. If this was a staged crime scene, the killer deserved an award. The hands were Nick's main concern, to check if they were dirty but undamaged; the rest would have to wait for the autopsy. He stepped down a rung, leaning out slightly.

The woman was facing him, her arms barely bent at the elbows; the left hand was practically pressed against the coat, palm-in, but the right was slightly askew. The body swayed gently. Nick leaned out farther, and as far as he could make out, her hands were dirty but undamaged, streaked by rain. As he pondered his next step, weighing the available science against the sadness, he heard Ivan Lopez begin to screech from below.

"There you are! Here! C'mere, boy! C'mere, Brownie! I told you, I told you!"

Nick frowned at the bad showmanship from his perch in the dark, the sheer and callous conceit of the performance. It was a profanity, almost as bad as the one beside him. And then he heard the dog barking, coming closer. He didn't believe, but he had to see.

As Nick shifted his stance on the ladder, he slipped on the rung; as he lurched to regain balance, he shoved the body. It swung like a pendulum. The noose shredded, a few strands, and then a few more. Nick scrambled on the ladder, and it began to slide from the trunk. As he tipped forward, crashing through the branches, he grabbed the woman, maybe from a reflex to protect her, or maybe to break the fall, but even the instant of contact with the stiff, sour, oddly heavy mass prompted him to shove her away. They broke through the branches, side by side, one flailing, the other as poised as a diver, arms behind her as she fell. Two of the cops jumped back, hitting the mud with a dull splatter; a third held his arms open for the calm female form, and she met him like a lover stepping off a train. The ladder struck Lopez, first on the weak hand that tried to block it, and then on the nose. He howled as he fell, bleeding, his DNA flooding into the ground, connecting him to a scene that wasn't a crime but was becoming a disaster.

Nick landed on all fours, grateful, after a stunned moment, that he had not hit face-first, that he had not broken anything. He was grateful again as he watched the cop fling the corpse to the side and fall down, retching. Esposito began to laugh with a violence that threatened to knock him over. The little brown mutt ran over to the circle, barking. The dog approached the body, sniffing, until a cop pushed it away. Esposito stepped back a few paces; he didn't like dogs at all. The mutt loped over to Nick, as he crouched in a like posture, and met him, eye to eye. As the dog licked his face, Nick imagined in the canine grin a consciousness that he was not just some nighttime stray but proof of Lopez's story. This was no mutt, but the rarest of breeds, a corroboration hound. The dog barked, twice. What instinct possessed Nick then, he did not know, but he said to the dog, not loudly but with utter sincerity, "You're a liar, too."

Nick stood up and took in the spectacle of fallen men and falling ones, illuminated by the car headlights. A bad dream, dreamt by all. The older cop went over to help his vomiting partner. Lopez wailed in the mud, holding his face. "My finger, my nose, they're broken." Not dreamt by all. Esposito laughed helplessly, holding the tree for support. The dog wandered off, into the dark.

Esposito called out, still laughing, "Look! Get up! Your dog is running away again!"

"I hate that dog! I hate you!"

As Esposito fell back against the tree, Nick leaned down to fish the flashlight out from the mud. He walked back to the car, and replaced his gloves with a clean pair. He returned to the woman to collect her purse, pressing on with his task as if nothing had happened. As if he hadn't just vandalized a cadaver. Could he make it up to her somehow? He'd think about that later. Let the other ones curse, cry, puke, or laugh; he still had work to do. *Work to do here. Move along. Nothing to see here, ma'am. Go about your business.*

The purse was still around her shoulder, and he slipped it off and took it back to the car, where he could examine it on the dry seat, in better light. He slammed the door shut behind him, wiped his hands, and dumped the contents out. Woman things: a brush, compact, hair band, lipstick. Knitting needles. No surprise there, but a reminder of how the fall could have been worse. A little Spanish bible, *El Nuevo Testamento y Salmos.* Here it was—an address book and wallet. No, not so fast. The address book had two numbers. The wallet—new pink plastic, what a child would pick—no ID. Not even a fake ID, and the cardboard square where she might have written a name and address had been left blank. She had left him with nothing, no information, which meant she hadn't left him. She was his responsibility until he could find next of kin. Until the bad news was broken to someone who mattered, maybe who cared, the book could not be closed. He felt self-pity gather in his mind, plumping up like a teardrop—Not your night, is it?—when he caught himself, cut it off quickly. There was sufficient illustration of worse luck in the vicinity, should he care to look. Other people, they did come in handy sometimes.

Nick scooped the contents back into the purse and returned to the scene. Esposito had recovered somewhat and was talking to the older cop—the last man standing—telling him what needed to be done with the body, the paperwork. Lopez was on his knees, holding his face and moaning, "Hospital. I need to go to the hospital. . . ."

Nick turned to him and began to approach, when he was halted by Lopez's furious objection. "Not you! Stay away from me! You've done enough!"

Nick raised his hands and retreated as Esposito finished his instructions.

"Yeah, and one of you oughta take this guy to the hospital. Maybe the pound, after. I think he needs a new dog."

"What should I tell them when I get there? The hospital, I mean?" the older cop asked.

Esposito paused, pursed his lips. "Say he was a victim of a self-inflicted injury committed during an offense against my giving a shit."

Nick appreciated the aptness of the summary, but instead he suggested that the cop write it up as a "city-involved accident," so at least Lopez would not get the hospital bill.

"Fine, have it your way, Nick," Esposito replied. "How are we doing?"

"I'd say we're finished."

"Right. We're out of here," said Esposito to the cops. "Me and Nick, we're the only ones on tonight in the squad, if something heavy—something real—happens. The night's young. And I'm an optimist."

As the detectives departed for their car, Nick thought that this qualified as something heavy, something real. He was also inclined to believe they should do something, stay to help clean up the mess—bring the ladder back, say—but he held his tongue, unwilling to delay their leaving. Inside the car, he was about to tell Esposito that he was right about Lopez, that his story mattered, that it changed things, even if it hadn't been true—when Esposito brought up something in the same vein first.

"You were wrong about Lopez, Nick."

"How?"

"You broke him."

Nick wasn't quite ready to laugh about that yet, though it was clear that their thoughts had further commingled. Not a successful containment under any terms, not between him and his partner, not between yesterday's mess and tomorrow's. All of the bad stuff should have been stopped in a bottle, corked, and put away in the basement. Instead, he'd christened a ship with it. Not a wise act, not safe, not one associated with good fortune. Nothing gained here—a presumed suicide, still, in the woods, in the rain. What else had he failed to.do, failed to learn? Nick surveyed the wreckage as they left the park: a suicidal death, an accidental injury, homicidal feelings. Was there anything natural here, to complete the last category? God help them if any of it was natural.

TWO

Esposito's optimism had been well founded. Nick had halfheartedly half-cleaned his shoes, but Esposito had changed his, as well as his suit, from abundant spares he kept in his locker, when the next call came. The crime scene had been taped off when the detectives arrived on the project grounds, the yellow plastic strip marking the area like a construction site. Which it was, in reverse. A dozen cops were there, and the bosses had begun to arrive, their white uniform shirts setting them apart from the patrolmen's dark blue. There were never just the right amount of cops—either not enough to contain an angry crowd, or more than was needed to block the door of a rented basement room. Here, on the path by a playground, a young black man lay on the ground, his face largely gone, from a shotgun blast. The rain kept all but a few of the onlookers away, the hard-core fans of uptown drama, and the cops mulled and muttered like they were at the wake of a distant in-law. The yellow tape threaded through fence and trees to mark an irregular square twenty yards on each side of the body, and an orange traffic cone was placed beside the shotgun shell. A young cop was bringing over a black plastic tarp to protect the corpse from the elements. Esposito held up a hand, motioning for the cop to wait.

"Relax. He ain't gonna catch a cold."

"The sergeant said—"

"Don't worry what he said. Worry what I say." Esposito smiled. "Nah, don't worry, just listen."

Nick followed his partner into the crime scene. Lifting up the yellow tape always felt like passing the velvet rope at a nightclub, and the little thrill of that moment never paled for Nick—the looks from the crowd, from cops and bosses, rookies and veterans alike, greeting the squad's arrival as if they were VIPs at a premiere. It was good to be on the list, but never as the guest of honor. Or should the victim be called the host? The star of the show? This one was dressed for the part—expensive sneakers, black and red, and a sweat suit of a shiny material, in the same colors; on his chest a necklace of heavy gold Cuban link chain, and diamond-studded initials in florid script: MC. A white wire led up from the digital music player tucked in the slim waist, splitting by the neck for each ear-bud. One was still in place, snug in the ear. The other lay beside him, tapping out a hip-hop beat. It was unlikely that the victim had seen it coming, but he definitely hadn't heard it. Millions of soft kids dreamt of seeing this, of being this, in suburbs from Scarsdale to Tokyo, scribbling rhymes in notebooks: "rich-bitch," "fat-gat." What face remained was ragged meat.

A sergeant near the cop with the tarp seemed to be in control, and Esposito put a hand on his shoulder, commanding despite the show of deference.

"What's up, boss? Whadda we got here?"

"Half hour ago, we got two calls for 'shots fired,' then one witness—not really a witness—he comes by later, sees the guy on the ground."

Esposito looked up and around. The projects were more than fifty yards away, and the view was blocked by sycamores. The calls had likely come from there, and the callers likely had nothing more to say than that they'd heard a shot. A homicide case breaks because of statements and substances, things seen, said, and left. Shotgun cartridges were not traceable in the way bullets could be, which left Esposito nothing physical to work with. None of the revolutionary technologies of digital databases and cellular signatures would make a bit of difference. This would be all story, no science. It was the kind of case Esposito thrived on, and its meager potential, its difficulty, brought out in him the ferocious focus that made part of his reputation so enviable.

Nick was relieved that it wasn't his homicide. He hated them, the thug-on-thug blast-'em-ups, the victims who were no better than their killers, only a little slower. Even in the newly safe new-millennium city, this slaughter still happened, the retrograde ghetto shoot-outs, the street gang drug-driven turf war hits that were exhausting and depressing to work, thankless if not exactly pointless. Territory, discipline, retaliation—those were the rational ones; there were also the ridiculous ones, over a look, a remark, a move on a girl, but for men who killed for business, the killings for pride or pleasure worked as exercise and good advertising. It was a radicalism without politics, rage as a style or sport. Mostly, you found out what happened; often, nothing could be done. The neighbors were glad the guy was dead; the witnesses—if you found them—were terrified; the friends hated cops more than the killers; and the relatives thought him an angel, now in heaven. Nature—or was it history?—sometimes intervened before the police could, when the killer was killed. "Exceptional clearances," as they were known. Nothing was righted, as such, but something was resolved. In the military, when the enemy turned on the enemy, they called it "red on red." Soldiers didn't have to pretend to be sad about it.

Esposito thrived here in the red zone, more than he should have. Maybe he had some thug in him, too. He crouched down by the body. He didn't want to be too close, but he knew he was under reverent observation. The cop with the tarp leaned in, to watch him watch. Esposito feigned dipping a hand into the blood pool and tasting a finger.

"B-positive. As I expected."

There was a convention of jokes among cops at scenes like these that worked equally well at covering whether you were bothered by the dead body or you weren't. You didn't want to admit the first to other cops, and you didn't want to admit the second to yourself. Nick was in the second group. The cop with the tarp thought for a moment, then smiled. This was drama, and Esposito was a showman.

This was the other part of Esposito's reputation, Nick knew, the need to be envied. It was the engine that drove him, or at least a rich strain in its fuel. Nick did not know how far, how fast this need could take him—take them—and whether his own genuine admiration could get them to slow down at the sharper curves.

The cop asked, "What do you think happened?"

"I think somebody didn't like him."

Esposito winked at the cop, then stared at the medallion, at what was left of the face. The showmanship was forgotten. Esposito began to think, to work, to realize. "I think I don't like him, either. Lemme just check one thing."

He shuffled back half a foot, then picked up one of the arms, pinching a bit of the sleeve, to examine the hand. The nails were long enough to hold skin if there had been a fight, but they looked clean, and there were no scratches or bruises; the same for the other hand.

"These are not a workingman's hands. The ME's not gonna get anything off this body. And you know what? I think I know this sonofabitch. I think I just closed a homicide, or somebody closed it for me."

He lightly patted down the pockets, the jacket and then the pants, and then pulled out a driver's license from beside the right hip. He handed it to Nick without looking.

"Tell me it doesn't say Malcolm Cole."

As Nick read the name on the license, he felt light-headed, for reasons that had little to do with Esposito's uncanny prediction. He struggled to regain enough composure to toss off a weak wisecrack. "If it does say Malcolm Cole, do you still want me to not tell you?"

"Sonofabitch."

Malcolm Cole was a drug dealer who had killed another dealer named Jose Babenco a year before. It was Esposito's case. Cole and Babenco had worked different corners that had seemed to grow closer over the years, and as the crack market had dwindled, the corners had grown closer still, until the dealers had been stepping on each other's feet. Malcolm made a little room one night, slipping behind Babenco in line at the window of an all-night bodega as Babenco bought cigarettes. He put a hole in the back of Babenco's head and caught the pack of Newports as they dropped. There had been one weak and ambivalent eyewitness—the bodega worker, looking through scuffed Plexiglas—and some suggestive phone records, but little else. Esposito would have had to take a crack at Malcolm to try to get a confession, but Malcolm, rumor had it, had struck out for the Carolinas. Another exceptional clearance, it seemed.

What Esposito didn't know was that both Babenco and Malcolm Cole, despite their divisions, had each made accusations against him to the Internal Affairs Bureau. Sometime in the past, Babenco had claimed that Esposito had taken money from him, that Babenco had paid Esposito a thousand dollars a week to leave him alone. Babenco had made several allegations while under several indictments, so the story had been regarded as somewhat dubious—for one, Esposito didn't work in Narcotics; for another, the price had been exorbitant—and Babenco's death had closed the IAB case. When Malcolm Cole had been on the run from the Babenco murder, he'd called Internal Affairs to say that Esposito had fired a shot at him when he'd seen him on the street. They'd been acquainted with each other, though most of the better troublemakers in the precinct had crossed paths with Esposito at some point. Downtown, at Internal Affairs, there were those who saw Malcolm's fugitive status as proof of his credibility, that he was afraid to come in, and the more streetwise among them, who saw Malcolm's story as the scam of a killer laying the muddy groundwork for his defense. Still, there were two major allegations, and in some minds, two lies added up to at least a half-truth. Skeptics and believers concurred that Esposito should be watched, and Nick had agreed to do the watching. He'd been desperate for a transfer at work, any kind of change, and he'd traipsed into the situation as Lopez had, with a kind of dishonest innocence, a narrow selection of his better intentions. He was not a traitor at heart, Nick told himself, but he'd managed well enough, so far.

Nick indulged himself for a wishful millisecond that Malcolm Cole's death would end the investigation of Esposito, too. After all, he would be his partner's alibi for tonight. He savored the delusion, its sweetness and neatness, as if the issue were now closed, the story successfully contained. More likely, IAB would look at Esposito as Esposito had looked at Ivan Lopez, dirty per se, with the ultimate particulars of his guilt to be determined at leisure. Esposito leaned over the body again.

"Wait! Did you hear that?"

They leaned in, the three of them—Nick, cop, sergeant—all attention on Esposito's earnest face.

"There it is again! 'I killed Jose Babenco. I gotta clear my conscience before I meet my Maker.'"

Esposito was trying too hard. The sergeant didn't laugh; the cop did, a little forcibly. The sergeant walked away, and the cop hung in close.

"A 'dying declaration'?" Nick asked, still dutiful in his sideman role.

"You know, in the old days, it would have been," said Esposito, eyeing the young cop. "Some of those detectives, they had incredible hearing back then. A guy like this, a couple of bad cases would be buried with him."

"I got a few of those," Nick muttered.

"Everybody does. Well, Officer, those bad days are behind us. So stay in school, brush your teeth, and always remember, crack is wack."

Esposito liked playing the grand old man, and the young cop liked seeing it.

"Nick, let's get to it. Malcolm, we hardly knew ye."

Esposito walked back to find the witness, an elderly man who'd been returning from church. As expected, his statement regarding how he'd found the body was that he'd been walking past and found the body. He saw nothing else, and his hearing was poor, so he didn't recall any gunfire. Nick took down the uniformed cops' information, the smaller, duller facts that had to be collected for the report—shield numbers, assignments for the day, the time they responded.

Esposito told the young cop to take out more tape, to make the crime scene bigger, not twenty yards but fifty to circumscribe the scene. His case, his call. Not a nightclub rope, Nick thought, but an *eruv*, like the Jews made, an imaginary boundary that made the larger world your home. And Nick knew why Esposito did it. There wasn't any more evidence to be found in the wider area, but enlarging the space would make it seem more important, giving the cops more to consider, more to protect. Though Esposito clowned around as if the situation didn't matter, it mattered more than anything to him. He'd circle the world like Magellan, yellow ribbon unspooling behind him, until the perp was trapped inside. One day, Malcolm was Esposito's sworn adversary; the next, Esposito was Malcolm's last champion. The terms could change, but the contest went on.

At the far side of the tape, a man rode up on a bicycle and lifted it, ducking under, and managed to get five or six feet before a burly cop spotted him. The cop charged over to block him, barking out, "Hey! You!"

"Who?"

"You, asshole! Who do you think?"

"What?"

"What the hell are you doing?"

"Gotta get through!"

"Do you see the yellow tape? What do you think it's there for?"

"You don't gotta talk like that to me."

"If you listened, I wouldn't have to. Go around. What's the matter with you?"

"It's muddy over there. I don't wanna mess up my bike."

"You gotta be kiddin' me. Get out of here. Beat it!"

The man walked off, taking his bike and wounded dignity, shaking his head. "You don't gotta be like that. . . ."

The man had begun to rewrite the story in his head to recast himself as the injured party. *Mindin' my own business, doin' nothin' wrong, when all of a sudden this cop starts screamin'* . . . Sometimes you had to freeze a lobby for hours for a crime scene, and the inconvenience was real—especially for the mother with her arms laden with laundry, groceries, three kids in tow—but it had to be done. Most waited with some semblance of patience, but a few always tried to push through, or screamed as if the cops had lost sight of the real victim—Me!—who risked dinner getting cold, or having to use an unfamiliar bathroom. The man with the bicycle broke from his ruminations to look back and ask, "Who died?"

The cop stared at him coldly. "Who cares?"

The man got on his bike and rode off, muttering curses. Esposito walked over to Nick, slipping his notebook back into his pocket.

"We good here?"

"We're not making any friends."

"We're not in the friends business. Let's do the notification, pay a visit to Momma Cole. I was there a couple of times, after the Babenco homicide. And before, for an older brother. I wanted him for a shooting, when he got killed. Stabbed, at a club downtown. You know, Nick, these things have a way of working out. Anyway, she's not the friendliest lady. Not that I blame her. Whaddaya think I should I go with, 'You want the good news, or the bad news?' "

"It's a classic, but maybe not this time."

"Whatever. You're the diplomat. Let's go."

The drive to the Cole residence would be a short one. The apartment was beneath the elevated subway, in the same projects, at the northern end. News would travel fast, and they had to get there first. The weather had slowed down the ghetto grapevine, but time was limited. They had to deliver the shock, to watch the responses and gather what they could before the defenses went back up. The rain had eased again, and the hustlers had begun to creep back out onto the corners, ready for the night. Esposito scanned the landscape from behind the wheel—he always drove, by mutual preference—as the wipers cleared the fat, irregular splashes that fell from the elevated train above them. On one corner, five or six young men, one or two women, had gathered on the far side of the street beneath a bodega awning. As the car approached, Esposito grabbed Nick by the biceps.

"Watch this."

The car swerved across the street, screeching, and the gang half-froze, half-started to scatter, all of them too late as the car struck the puddle by the curb. The puddle was wide and deep, and sent a cascade of filthy rainwater over them, staining their baggy pants and doo-rags and three-hundred-dollar sneakers. The car was half a block away before they recovered enough to throw beer cans and shout empty threats. Esposito bellowed with laughter and grabbed Nick again.

"Hah! Nicky! See 'em? Did you see their faces? God, this is fun sometimes. . . ."

Nick cringed, even as he caught himself laughing, too. Were they all perps and hangers-on? Or had the youngest one's big sister just marched over to tell him, *Cut this out and get home. You can make a life if you work hard and play by the rules.* Still, it was funny, as long as it happened to someone else, as long as you could imagine that they deserved it.

"Did you know them?" Nick asked.

"Probably. I couldn't see. But it's a crack spot. One of Babenco's."

"So that was kind of a tip of the hat to Malcolm Cole."

"You might say."

That was the kind of thing Esposito did often, a little reckless and almost righteous, and Nick wondered if he would have enjoyed it more if he could know for sure he wouldn't be asked about it, later on, under oath. Nick grimaced at the thought, and Esposito smiled at what he mistook for a smile, for Nick's appreciation.

When they arrived at their destination, they straightened their ties and tucked in their shirts, checking themselves in the rearview mirror. The messengers should be respectable even if the message is not, and they headed into the projects. From the outside, the housing complex looked much as it might have on the drawing board in the late 1950s, the model modern city of redbrick towers grouped amid playgrounds and tree-lined lawns. Once the door of the Coles' building was yanked open, however—the lock was broken, again—the lobby looked like a set from a 1970s movie, Gotham bankrupt and at bay. By Sunday night, the porters hadn't cleaned in two days, the yellowed tiles had a urinal smell, and the floor was littered with trash. As they stepped in, three kids tossed their blunt—a cheap cigar stuffed with marijuana—and froze a moment, ready to run. Esposito raised his hands. "At ease, men. Smoke 'em if you got 'em."

They relaxed, and one giggled, while another bent to fetch the blunt.

"Yo! You cops is all right!"

"They not cops, dummy. They DTs."

"Homicide? Shit! Who got it?"

Esposito stepped toward them and handed out his card to each, correctly estimating they would be more intrigued than repelled by his combination of real conversation and official status.

"You'll find out soon enough, guys. When you do, if you hear something, give me a call."

"Nah, man, we ain't snitches."

"Snitches get stitches."

But even as they mouthed the slogans of defiance, each of them stared at their card as if it were a map to buried treasure, contact with a world they'd only seen on television.

"I ain't talking about snitching," Esposito went on. "I'm going upstairs to tell somebody's moms some bad news, and if you guys help me, I won't have to tell somebody else's moms the same thing next week."

Nick was intrigued by the way it was said here—"moms." Plural or possessive? Neither, just slang, words thrown around. Nick didn't speak the lingo. Best to say nothing. Snitches get stitches.

"Also, there's money in it."

"How much?"

"You call me with something good, I'll let you know."

The elevator opened, and the detectives stepped inside. Nick pressed the button for fourteen, blocking the panel with his body so the kids couldn't see which floor he'd selected; they would know the family. They might be the family. As the doors shut and the elevator rose with a jerk, Nick asked Esposito how many Coles were left.

"God knows. There's a pack of 'em, mostly older. As far as I remember, some went straight, and some went straight to the streets. There's two younger brothers. I think they've never been in trouble, grandkids, whatever. Malcolm, though—he was one tough kid, a real hard case."

There were families here that were inmate dynasties, generation after generation of wards of the state—killer, crackhead, whore, thief; the slow girl who got fat on paint chips; the lucky one in the wheelchair, with a settlement from when he was hit by a car. The clustered disasters made a certain grim sense: bad inputs and bad outputs. Other families were dizzyingly split—dead, jail, army major; dead, plumber, custodian, jail; jail, jail, hospital administrator. Most tragic were the families where the failures were harder to explain than the successes—two parents, churchgoers and job-holders, with four daughters who made six figures apiece, two sons who made their sneaker money sticking up old ladies in elevators. There were good people here, too—more than the other kind—but detectives ran into them less often. These people . . . Nick stopped the thought before he could be sure what he meant.

At the fourteenth floor, a different music thumped through each door—R&B, salsa, reggaeton, until they came to a door marked with bumper stickers for a rap station. There was no sound inside, at least none they could hear, when they pressed an ear against the frame. Esposito hit the door with his fist a few times, waited, then turned around and gave it a few solid kicks with his heel.

"Who?"

"Police."

"Who?"

"Police! Open up!"

They could hear shuffling footsteps approaching. An eye appeared at the peephole, and a wary male voiced called out, "Nobody called the cops here."

"I know. We gotta talk to you."

"You got a warrant?"

"Shut up and get your mother."

There was no contempt in the tone, only a blunt indifference to a junior player trying to buy time he could not afford. The force of it, and the absence of anger, had a confusing effect on the other side of the door.

"She can't . . . I can't . . . She's sleeping."

"Wake her up."

The footsteps trudged away. Esposito muttered, "If she can sleep through this racket, God bless her." Just when they were about to start pounding again, the footsteps returned, and the door unlocked. A wiry young man in pajama bottoms opened it with obvious reluctance. How many times had cops come to his door? He was brown skinned, and though he must have been at least twenty, his faint, fuzzy mustache looked like it could have been the first he'd tried to grow. A disdainful stare met their faces, turning to disgust as he looked them up and down. Nick noted the condition of his own shoes.

"Wipe your feet."

The young man turned away before the detectives entered, to show that they were not worth his consideration.

"She says to have a seat, she'll be out in a minute."

They followed him down the hall, past a kitchen with a pot of rice on the stove, to a living room with two couches, one pulled out into a bed. On the walls were taped various certificates, attesting to attendance at drug awareness and parenting classes, a program called Positivity and Peer Pressure. The tattered curl of the edges added to the faintness of the praise. Two infants lay there; another toddler in diapers scrambled on the floor nearby. The uniform for a fast-food restaurant hung neatly on a closet door. The lights were dim, but the television was big and bright, with a video game paused; it showed a car chase on a city street, with gang members in an alley and snipers on a roof. Disapproving thoughts began to form in Nick's mind as the toddler rushed over to him and hugged his leg. The young man leaned down and snatched him up.

"No, Daquan, no. They ain't your friend."

Nick stiffened at the child's touch, but when the boy was taken away, he felt a twinge of regret. The hostile pomp showed the Cole kid had never been in trouble before—a real criminal knew to avoid needless provocation—but the act was aggravating. So it was going to be that way, was it? In the end, the undisguised enmity might make it easier; who wouldn't rather break the heart of a bastard? No, it wouldn't; the room wasn't big enough to hold the hate as it was, and it was better not to add any more. Nick felt tired, and knew the pressure at the back of his neck would be a headache within the hour. He caught himself scowling, and made himself stop. Esposito maintained a tone of agreeable calm, as if they'd been offered tea on the verandah. The baby said the name Michael, and Esposito picked up on it.

"Michael, is Daquan your boy? I got a two-year-old at home, a girl. It's a tough age."

The young man kissed the child, but pointedly watched the frozen TV screen instead of looking at Esposito. "He's only one. He's big. He's my sister's. She's out . . . like always . . ."

As Nick recalled, Esposito had three sons. He could have said so. He'd lied because he didn't want to bring them into this, he didn't want to think of this, with them. Still, he'd put out something of himself, connected on human terms. And the move had worked. The anger seemed to ebb slightly. The young man put the toddler down, collected the infants from the pullout couch, and brought them to a back room. He looked as if he suspected the detectives might take the children, as if Esposito might distract him with a comment—*Hey, nice TV!*—and slip a kid into a pocket like a shoplifter. And then Nick realized, they *were* there to take a child from this house, or at least tell of his taking. Go ahead, stay angry, and hide your babies. Keep away from the police. They bring no good news.

A moment later, Michael Cole returned with his mother on his arm, shuffling out from the dark hall in a worn blue flannel robe. She was a heavy woman, breathing heavily, who carried herself as if she were getting tired of the weight. She settled into her seat with a long exhalation. She patted one arm of the couch as if it were a friend, and mopped her brow with a damp washcloth. Little Daquan ran to her and held her leg, before waddling over to the TV to slap the screen.

"There, now. My pressure's no good. I had a stroke since I seen you last, Detective. I'm sorry I can't help you. I haven't seen Malcolm."

Esposito leaned down and touched her hand.

"I'm sorry Miz Cole, it's not that. I got some bad news."

"He was arrested?"

Michael broke in abruptly. "They don't come to tell you that, Mama. They ain't that nice—"

"Quiet now, Michael. Go get me some water. Let these gentlemen get to the business they come for. What is it?"

She looked up, wide-eyed and ready for the blow.

"There's been a shooting. . . ."

And then she looked down, mopping her brow again, shaking her head. "Malcolm?"

Esposito nodded and looked to Nick. His fumbling in his pockets for the license provoked a scowl from Michael, and it was a long minute before Nick found it and handed it over. Miz Cole glanced at it, like it was a receipt. She had gotten one before, at least once; she thought the bill had been paid.

"Is he . . . ?"

"It doesn't look good."

Michael left for the kitchen and returned with the water. He sat beside his mother, holding her as she sobbed, and placed the glass of water on the arm of the couch. Daquan turned from the television and ran to her, stumbling after three steps to fall on his face. His piercing screech joined his grandmother's low moan. Michael leaned over and scooped him up, and Miz Cole clutched him to her chest.

"My baby . . . poor baby . . . My Lord . . ."

The three generations huddled as one on the couch, woeful arms entangled, and grief seemed to flow through the bodies. Esposito picked up the license and stepped back a few paces. Nick had already given them room. The apartment was hot, and it felt like their wailing was using up all the air. Esposito waited for a minute, and then another, but no more. The Coles had lifetimes to mourn; the detectives did not.

"Miz Cole, when's the last time you saw him?"

"Only yesterday."

The disclosure struck Michael like cold water, and he sat up straight. "Ma, don't tell 'em nothin'! They don't care. They ain't here to help us! They glad Malcolm's dead! Shit, I bet they killed him!"

That was a turn that Esposito was not willing to let the conversation take; he didn't expect to get much from them, but he would not allow Michael to open another front of the war.

"Easy now, Michael. We are here to help. And you gotta help us find out what happened, because whatever Malcolm did or didn't do— I don't know, I wasn't there—it ain't right what happened to him."

Michael shook his head but fell quiet again, and the family slid back into grief. The glass toppled from the arm of the couch and broke on the floor. Nick picked up the bigger pieces and left for the kitchen.

"Let me get you some more water."

The kitchen was narrow, and even though Nick was alone there, it felt crowded. A frying pan with a turkey leg sat on the stove, the grease congealing; the pot of rice was crusty at the edges. There was a clean glass in a cabinet and several dirty ones in the sink. He didn't think Michael would take anything from him, not even a glass of water from his own house, but he washed an extra glass and filled up two. Nick was about to step out of the kitchen when the front door opened, and another young man walked in.

"Mama? What happen? What's goin' on?"

Though Nick had only seen his picture on the license, he knew it was Malcolm Cole. The air seemed to thicken now to a viscous gel, and no one could move through it; if any of them had tipped over, it would have taken half a minute to hit the ground. Malcolm looked ahead, at his mother and Esposito, then to Nick, a few paces away in the kitchen, close enough to cut off his escape. The possibilities played across his face, the simple switches clicking in his mind. *Yes or no? In or out? Fight or flight?*

Miz Cole made the decision for him, in a weak, high, curiously singsonging voice: "Malcolm, these men . . ." Every Sunday of her life, she had raised her hands to attest to the resurrection. Now she saw but could not believe. "These men told me that you was dead!"

"I'm all right, Ma."

"But they said—"

Esposito took the ID and held it up. "Who did you give this to, Malcolm?"

Malcolm thought with effort, as if his mind now had to move through the sticky stuff that held their bodies. It was not a hard thing to remember, but he didn't want to succeed with the recollection. He looked down at the floor.

"My brother Milton. To Milton, Ma. He wanted to go out tonight, to a club."

"Oh . . . now . . . no."

What sense it must have seemed to switch. Malcolm as Malcolm was a wanted man. Milton as Malcolm was a grown man. Stay out of jail, get into the bar. A win-win.

Miz Cole looked at Malcolm and smiled, as if determined to relish this one moment of the miraculous before she was subsumed by the next waves of grief. No, this would be all for today. Her eyes fluttered and then her head sank to her chest. Her arms loosened and the baby slipped down to her lap.

Nick picked up his radio. "We need an ambulance here, Central, forthwith . . . and send another couple of units for backup."

"What's your condition there?"

What was the condition here? Head-on collision of two tractor trailers loaded with bad karma? He didn't want a hundred cops barreling in, but they might need reinforcements. Malcolm had rushed to his mother on the couch. He didn't need to hear that he would be coming with the detectives, though he had to know it. Nick stepped back and muttered into the radio, "Cardiac, plus one under."

"Can you repeat that?" Nick did not want to announce to the room that Malcolm was under arrest.

"Negative. Two units and an ambulance."

Nick lowered the radio and checked his watch—11:35. A bad time, the shift change. The four-to-twelves had gone into the precinct, but the midnights had not yet come out. They had a few minutes, at least. Esposito helped the Cole brothers lay the mother on the floor, and said to Nick, "Stay back. Give us some air." He meant for Nick to block the door. "Go get a pillow," he told Michael, which sent him to the back. Malcolm fanned his mother with a little towel. He looked up at Esposito and asked, in a jarringly plaintive voice, "Can I stay with my moms?"

Possessive now, not plural.

"Sure, yeah. Of course."

Michael returned with the pillow, and they gingerly lifted the head. She wasn't breathing. The Coles looked on helplessly.

"All right, you guys. Your moms needs your help and I'm going to tell you how to do CPR. One of you has to breathe for her, and one has to press down on her chest. Five short pushes—lock your arms out, hands together—then one breath. Okay now. Ready?"

Esposito took Malcolm and had him crouch beside her. Esposito put an arm around Malcolm's shoulder, then patted his back, his flanks, a friendly gesture that also felt for a gun. He guided Malcolm through the chest compressions, then told Michael to hold her nose for the breaths.

"Good. Let's go now. One, two, three, four, five. Now a breath. One, two, three, four, five, breath. Good. Keep going. Michael, count out loud."

Esposito stepped back to let the resuscitation proceed, despite its lack of promise. The Coles worked with visible anxiety and little aptitude. Malcolm's compressions were jerky and light, and Michael's breaths were shallow. Michael counted with hesitation, trying to follow his brother's rhythm but throwing him off and being thrown off in turn. He called out each number with a soft uncertainty, as if he were taking a stab at a math problem. "Three . . . four? Five?" Malcolm stopped when the baby let out a wail and fell onto his grandmother's breast. He picked up the child and laid him on the couch, returning to the compressions with still less enthusiasm. He stopped again when he knelt on a shard of glass—"Shit!"—and did not rush to return after he brushed it out. Nick checked his watch. Four minutes had passed. She was past saving, and they now operated purely on pretense, giving the Coles busywork until backup could arrive. Esposito would have told them to do calisthenics or a rain dance if he'd thought they would fall for it. His mission remained fixed, even as the Coles' world changed as if struck by a meteor, with extinctions and evolutions proceeding with unreal speed.

The baby began to scream, and Malcolm stood to walk over, casting a last glance down, shaking his head. But whatever belligerent spirit left him did not linger long without a new host. Michael looked up from his mother, his eyes hardening. He was angry again, and Nick could tell that Michael liked the feeling. Nick envied him, thinking back to his own apartment, his own mother, decades ago but just blocks away. Last breaths, but here a son held on, fighting, as if she would not go if he did not quit. Was love a gift of sight, or the refusal to see?

"Where you going? Get back here! Let's go!"

Malcolm sat heavily down on the couch, picking up the boy to nuzzle his neck, burying his face in him. He seemed less like an adult with a child than a child with a doll. He closed his eyes, and Nick closed his, too, just for a second, to picture it—mother dead, brother dead, his own life a life sentence. Nick opened his eyes to see Malcolm lifting the boy, his nephew, to kiss him on the lips. This was all he had, this baby, this moment; he chose what he could hold, whom he might help, here, now.

"She gone, yo. In God's hands. She gone."

Michael breathed again into his mother, heavily this time, and moved around to press down on the chest. The compressions now were forceful and precise, and gave a drill sergeant's percussive punch to his speech. "We don't stop! Get over here! Now!" He was no longer sidelined by circumstance; he was suddenly in command. The walls could crack and shudder, the roof could buckle down on him, but he would not be kept from his purpose. His life did not matter, and even his mother's mattered less than the stand he had taken—"Get up! Get over here!"—to hold fast without breaking against any disease, despair, or white boys the dirty world could send against him. Malcolm seemed shaken by the new man beside him, and stood up as summoned. He knelt beside his mother's face to offer empty breath.

There was a knock at the door, and Nick opened it for two paramedics. A man and a woman, both young, one white, one Spanish. The woman was small and certain in her movements; the man less so, accepting her guidance as to the placement of the stretcher and oxygen. She stepped aside to let her partner and the Coles lift the old woman onto the stretcher. "Who lives here with her? You? Go get her meds."

Malcolm went to the back, and Esposito followed him. Michael tensed visibly, and relaxed only a little when they returned with fistfuls of pill bottles. The female took them to study the labels as the male put an oxygen mask on Miz Cole. The male paramedic looked at the opposing pairs of men, taking in that this was not an ordinary ambulance run, that the detectives were not there merely or even mainly to help.

"So . . . who's gonna ride with us to the hospital? Both of you?"

Michael answered, "Both of us."

Esposito said, "Malcolm's gonna come with us, try to help with Milton."

"No. No he ain't," said Michael. "You took enough of my family today."

Nick went to the door and held it for the paramedics, waving them on. They moved forward, pushing the gurney. Malcolm hesitated; he was past fighting, but he could not lose face in front of his younger brother. It was a deadlock, for the moment, but it could have been worse. Nick ran through the possibilities: The detectives could stay with Malcolm until the paramedics left, and bring him to the precinct later; they could bring both Coles in and leave Michael outside while they talked to Malcolm, all night if necessary. They could not let them both go to the hospital, and they were not staying here with them. If they went outside, there was a chance Malcolm would run; he had run before, and they were low on living Coles to draw him back uptown.

"Go on, Mike," said Esposito. "Go ahead with your moms."

"The name is Michael."

"Okay, Michael."

Michael stepped in front of his brother, hands on hips. The male paramedic paused near the door, where he was leading the stretcher—"Well, who's going with us? We can't wait!"—until the female shoved him ahead with an audible thud. Nick was beside them as the stretcher slipped past, clearing the door. As the wheels bumped over the threshold, Miz Cole's arm slipped off and dangled. Esposito stepped between the Coles, one arm holding Malcolm, the other guiding Michael forward.

"Look! Your mom! She moved her hand, she waved!"

Nick was taken too by the unreasonably hopeful turn, reaching down to the wrist to feel for warmth, a pulse. He didn't think it was possible, and knew at once that it wasn't. As Nick tucked the hand back onto the gurney, Michael spat at him, "Don't touch her! Get your hands off her!"

Nick stepped back. They were at the elevator, and one of the paramedics had already hit the button. Michael was losing control, his facial muscles electrified with twitchy anger. Nick tried a line that Esposito might have ventured, though it had the disadvantage of being true.

"Michael, I'm sorry. I know—I lost my mother—"

"Fuck your mother."

"Fuck yours."

Though Nick regretted it the instant he said it, the insult lifted him to a higher level of animal readiness. Michael's eyes did not leave his own; they were radiant with hate, and Nick could picture them blazing in the dark. Was hate a way of seeing, or not-seeing? Michael whirled and threw a punch, wide and weak. Nick caught it with both hands as if it were a tossed softball, twisting Michael's arm, lowering him to the floor.

"You muthafuckin' cops! I will kill you! Dead men! Dead! Dead!"

"Stop. I'm sorry. I shouldn't have said that."

The ease of his takedown was a further indignity, and Nick held the arm firm, letting Michael feel how easily it could break. He felt the breathing slow, the rage abate. Or maybe it was just better controlled.

"You can go with your mother, or you can go to jail," Nick said, with civil indifference. "It won't be with your brother. You can do some good for your family, or you can screw up everything for yourself. Go on now. Your mom's at the elevator. Don't leave her alone."

Michael twisted his head and glared at Nick. The hatred in his face was no less, but it was cold instead of hot; Nick took it as a cease-fire and released him. Michael shuddered and rolled over, stood and stared again at Nick. He would never be frightened again, he knew, but he had learned that he could be fooled. The paramedics were at the elevator door, which thankfully opened. Michael looked at them, at Nick. Michael began to walk to them, still fixing Nick's eyes.

"No way this is over. No way."

Nick looked at him without answering and withdrew back toward the Cole apartment, trusting that Esposito could handle whatever went on inside. Michael knocked at the apartment door next to the elevator, and when an old woman answered, he told her she had to take care of the babies, he had to go. The woman stared at the stretcher, at him, at Nick, and nodded. When Michael Cole turned away, Nick waved on the female paramedic, who patted Miz Cole's arm, offering soft assurances that from now on, all things would be good.

Nick could only guess at what oaths Michael uttered in the next hours of his vigil, as grief seeped from him to harden into tougher, stranger stuff. But Nick was reminded of his own agreements, sometime before dawn. They were back at the squad, and Nick had stepped out of the interrogation room to get coffee, when his cellphone unexpectedly rang. The number was blocked. His wife's office line was blocked, but it couldn't be her, not now, not from there. Nick hesitated, then decided to answer. The caller did not identify himself. Nick did not know him, nor did he need to ask.

"Meehan?"

"Yes."

"Can you talk?"

"Yes."

"The Milton Cole homicide, the woman's death."

"Yes."

"Well? What happened?"

"The report's in the system. You don't have access?"

"I've seen it. And?"

"What happened is what's in the report."

"Are you sure?"

There was guile in the question, and Nick waited for the next.

"The other brother wasn't assaulted? We have a witness that will testify that Esposito assaulted the other one. That the bastard actually told a young man who had just lost his mother, and I'm quoting here, 'Go fuck your mother, you asshole.'"

Nick had to think about that, about who had been there in the hallway—Michael, the EMTs . . . and the woman Michael summoned to take care of the children. No, she was later. Anyone else, looking out their peephole? Still, he had to agree that no decent man could ever utter such words in such a circumstance.

"That was me."

"What?"

"And the kid tried to hit me, not the other way around. The quote's not exact, either, but it's not that far off, I guess."

Now there was a pause on the other side of the line, disappointed, then accusatory.

"Then, why didn't you arrest him?"

"Half his family had just died. I wasn't hurt. I didn't think it was worth it."

"This is not about you, Detective. We'll be in touch."

THREE

Mornings, Nick woke to the thought that waking was a mistake. Not that he wasn't glad to—he just didn't believe it, didn't believe that what he woke to wasn't some devious subconscious subterfuge, some dream within a dream. It was not just the ashy light in the alley outside the window, the aged creak of the springs in the bed, or that his feet dangled off the lower end. Nor was it the fact that he slept in a bunk bed, even though he was an adult man and had been an only child. A large neighbor family had outgrown it decades ago, and his father had accepted the hand-me-down with the remark, "You never know," which of course is what you always think before you know.

At the head of the bed, there were water pipes, and sound traveled down them sometimes, with passages of uncanny clarity broken by schlock-horror sound effects, reverbs and echoes, muddy slow fades. The voice was male, usually calm, never happy. It didn't happen every day. It didn't happen most days, but Nick didn't remember it at all from when he was young. The pipes, the pipes are calling . . . He wondered if it would have bothered him more or less if it had been a female voice—it had been a house without women for a long time—and he decided that the malcontent manner made the gender immaterial. There was no good company to be had. After a few minutes, he threw back the thin sheets and rough wool blanket, and began to shake off sleep to figure out what day it was, whether he was late for work or could just lie there for a while. He'd stretch and scratch, like he was sloughing off skin, as the exhalation of warmth left the bed. When he was married, he would walk to the kitchen without a cleanup stop in the bathroom, at home in his home. He was still married, he remembered, but often he'd have to remember.

Here, which was also his home, and had been at all states and stages of his life, he was newly self-conscious. He'd wash his face, brush his teeth, run a comb through his hair, and examine the mirror for a moment, half-expecting to be met with the reflection of a pensive child, or an aged man, blinking through milky eyes. He'd then go out to see his father, who was almost always there, whatever the time. It was nearly ten in the morning; Nick had slept for three hours.

Since he'd come home some six months before, his mother had been more in his thoughts. She had been a shy woman, never at home in the world. There had been an awkwardness to her that he'd noted even as a young child—at the grocery checkout, the rapidly downcast eyes, the slight fumble with the change purse—that had had little to do with being an immigrant, or a country girl come to the city. Early on, she would give Nick the money to pay at stores, thinking it educational for him and a relief for herself. "You're a powerful help," she'd say, and Nick loved how she said it. She and his father were from "the other side," a phrase meant to convey a family sameness of Irish wherever they scattered, but for Nick it was suggestive of otherworldliness. The fact that she'd died when he was twelve carried the phrase deeper into that sense. The other side was a kind of intersection between Galway and heaven, foreign and familiar. "Don't go," were her last words to him, as if he were the one who was leaving.

Nick was with his mother when she was struck by a car, crossing the street at a distracted moment, when she remembered she had forgotten to buy stamps. Though she suffered no more than a bad bruise to the hip, he was horrified by her lurching, unnatural movement, by her being taken unwillingly from one place to another—five feet, maybe, but a mile, it seemed—and by the sight of the bulky plaid purse that shot away, dumping its contents as if in a rush to escape, dollars and coupons and rosary beads spilling onto the street. It was seconds before the look of raw mammalian fear left her eyes for an expression of twice-tearful pity, because of the pain and because her son had seen the accident. Nick could never decide whether it had been the fear or the pity that had told him, but he'd known then that she would die. He was likewise unresolved to the nature of her death, when the subsequent hospital visit—pro forma, it was thought, protested against but insisted on by the apologetic driver—led to the discovery of the cancer that killed her in a month. A brute accident, but also a cabal in her blood. Nick learned that there could be knowledge without profit, and that other, larger forces were always at work, no matter whether you slept or kept watch. Still, vigilance seemed the better stance.

After she died, his father drank a bit more for a while, then less, and now hardly at all. It was the better way, Nick knew, but there was something pointlessly thrifty about the way he took care of himself, the small portions and boiled vegetables and brisk walks. To what end? That was the way the old man would phrase it, were the question turned around, something from catechism, the first principles. But Nick never asked him that, in part because he couldn't answer the question himself, and in part because he was fond of his father. He'd asked the question in interrogations, and had drawn baffled looks from both crooks and cops. "Why are you here? Not in this room, in handcuffs. Why are you here in the world?" The cops thought it was a trick, and wondered where he'd go with it. Nick honestly hoped to learn something.

Before he became a cop, there was some time in the service, some time in college. He worked on Wall Street for a while, married. Allison was a kind of athlete, driven but unhurried, and she rose steadily as an analyst at her brokerage. They had known each other in grammar school, but her family had moved. It was a dozen years later when they ran into each other again, downtown, at a restaurant. The transformation was storybook, from the spectacled twig of a kid, studious and awkward, to full-blossomed beauty with a sly, kind smile. She knew the probabilities but called it destiny, just to be sweet. Nick said he didn't know what the chances were, but he'd take them. They trusted each other, seemed to fit; Nick moved in within months, and they married a year later. They could talk or not talk, take hold of each other or leave each other alone, and each felt natural and apt. When he joined the police department, Allison thought it would be better for him, for them, and she was half-right, which was a low percentage for her. They were in no hurry to have children, but when they decided it was time, it didn't happen. A year of kamikaze lovemaking followed—in the park, in the back of a car, once in a stuck elevator—when they joined forces as much as bodies, it felt, delighting in the cause, determined for the effect. After several false starts, you might call them, sex became part of a regimen that included vitamins and calendar markings and thermometers, undertaken with the eye-rolling good sportsmanship of office mates during a fire drill. Pleasure gradually became duty, and both of them became increasingly derelict. Management terms popped up in Nick's mind as he tried to see it as Allison might—results and goals, returns on investment, viability. As their confidence in each other, in what they had together, slowly dwindled, both of them fell back into their jobs. With her long hours and his odd ones, their easy drift became an empty one.

Together they kept each other company for the off hours, which meant a little food in front of the television, a few nights a week. Sundays were a slight confusion for them. She liked tennis, or games with a purpose; he preferred pastimes without one. He liked to go for walks, looking up at the windows of the tenements and towers, catching a face here and there, and picturing the rest of the story—in one, the old man yelling at the television; in another, the young woman weeping by a phone that doesn't ring; in a third, the couple shocked with love, leaning over the crib of their newborn. He thought she liked these walks too until one week she twisted her ankle and didn't come out again. That was her excuse, at first, until she realized she didn't need one, telling him with a note of touching embarrassment that she'd rather lie in bed and read the papers. The walks got longer, and in time, more and more often, Nick found himself heading from where they lived on the Upper West Side to Inwood, back home.

Earlier in the year, his father had felt dizzy and had fallen, breaking his collarbone. It had been some kind of spell, he'd said. Nick had stayed with him in the hospital for three days of tests, and then had gone back home with him for a while. The doctors had agreed, it had been some kind of spell. Bit by bit, and then more and more, Nick had left Allison, but they still spoke, still met, when they found the time. What had begun as a rescue had become a retreat; both of them knew it, but neither brought it up. It would have felt like fighting to talk about it, and they hated to fight. Tonight, in fact. He would see her tonight—some sort of company dinner—and the venue would keep their conversation from straying beyond public-room limits. Still, there would be a pull toward the subject of themselves, whether from gravity or curiosity. Unwatched words had a way of going where they are warned not to stray. Words were like children, just like them. Nick decided to stick to conversation about the weather and work.

When he'd first moved back, his father had asked him if he would be staying. Nick had nodded, and his father had said it was a shame. Nick's father spoke his mind without restraint or thought of consequence. Not loudly, not often—but when you asked his opinion, it was like picking his pocket. What was there came out, and if you didn't like it, you shouldn't have reached. Days later, he'd felt obliged to clarify, to say that it didn't mean he wasn't glad to see Nick, didn't mean Nick wasn't welcome. No offense had been taken, Nick had assured him. He had understood the first time around. There really wasn't a question of hurt feelings, Nick had realized later, only that the old man said so little that he had time to dwell on the ramifications of each word. There was a luxury to that way of living, and a poverty, depending on whether the man in the cell was an inmate or a monk. His father didn't seem like either, very much. His range seemed limited to slight bemusements and mild regrets. Five years ago—longer?—Nick had bought him a recliner, which had inspired the sole evidence of his father's capacity for fascination and delight: "What an astonishing thing, to invent such a great machine, just for sitting on!" This morning, when Nick went into the kitchen, he was met with a question in the more accustomed range. His father had clearly put some thought into it.

"There was a dollar on the table. Did you leave one?"

"Maybe, Da . . . it's not yours?"

"I don't think so. I empty my pockets in here, but I just leave the keys. Still . . ."

"Tell you what, why don't we split it."

"That's the lad." The old man pocketed the dollar and counted out five dimes, sliding them across the table. "Coffee?"

"Yes, but not instant."

A look of mild distress crossed his face. Nick had introduced a note of disorder into the little room.

"I had mine already. . . . It seems a waste to make the whole pot."

"Make half, then."

"Aha!"

He smiled and turned to the percolator on the counter, measuring out careful spoons of coffee. From the sink, the water flowed brown a moment, then clear.

"You had a long day at work?"

"All through the night."

"That is a long day. Someone died?"

"A couple of people. Three."

"All murdered? God bless us."

"One murder, one suicide, and one . . . accident, I guess."

The old man paused from his task a moment, and his tone was cautious. "Black people?"

"Two out of three. Not the suicide."

"Ah. They have their troubles, don't they?"

"Yes."

"Drugs, is it? They're mad for them, aren't they?"

"Some of them, I guess. But look at Jamie Barry. The other day, I saw him nodding off in the lobby. He's on the needle."

"Is it the drugs, then? Hadn't he a good job, with the computers? I thought he'd too much to drink."

The old man shook his head, not so much to disagree as to dislodge the thought from his mind. Jamie Barry was the superintendent's son, and Ms. Barry was also from the other side. Jamie and Nick had known each other for the entirety of their lives, which was an indifferent matter to both of them. Nick had tried to avoid him at each phase of his life, from the mousy, cosseted, and complaining child to the hard-drinking, hard-talking, hard-puking young man. He was an only child as well, and his mother had died when he was in his late teens, which had sped him into dopeland. After a few lost years, he'd cleaned up, moved to Long Island and Christianity, which was not how he referred to the religion of their fathers. Still, Jamie had been doing well, Nick had heard—his father was right, it had been something high-tech—until somewhat recently, when something had slipped. He'd returned home not long before Nick had, and when Nick had run into him, the bleary look of kinship Jamie had offered, the bond of brotherly failure, had made Nick want to kick his teeth down his throat.

As the coffeepot gave up its last sputter and gurgle, his father's thoughts continued to meander.

"Still, it seems it's the black ones who are just mad for the drugs. Not all of them, of course. Look at Mr. Williams, from the third floor—what a nice man! A bus driver, like I was, married. Two children, very polite, both of them in Good Shepherd. I wonder what he thinks of all of this. . . . I might ask him one day."

That was a little too much for Nick before coffee, but he didn't say anything. His father was fully capable of asking Mr. Williams what he thought about the Negro Question; for all Nick knew, Mr. Williams had the Negro Answer. Nick was afraid sometimes he would end up like his father, without even an acquaintance to share his benignly boorish small talk across the breakfast table. As the coffeepot emitted a final hiss, Nick shifted the topic to an old favorite.

"How is Mrs. O'Beirne feeling? Did they find out what was wrong with her?"

"Ahh," Nick's father replied, standing and turning to fill the cup, then looking back, as if to check if there were listeners in the room. "She's not well at all. It was . . . the cancer." He said it in a hissed whisper not unlike the sound from the coffeepot. He sat back down and slid the coffee across the table, anxious to begin.

The brokerage of bits of bad news was the great pastime of the neighborhood and one of the few pleasures that his father did not deny himself. There was a comfort in misfortune that fell elsewhere, as if there were then a little less left to go around. Three years ago, he had considered joining a parish trip to Lourdes; Allison and Nick had both urged him to go, had offered to pay. A dozen men and women had signed on, mostly his age, mostly out of a sense of devotion, a hope to witness the miraculous rather than any particular need for a miracle. He'd decided to stay home, alluding to various inconveniences. When the tour bus had collided with a milk truck, and the pilgrims who had left in robust health had then returned with crutches and neck braces, his father had felt not merely spared but somehow vindicated. He'd visited the injured at every opportunity.

"She has months left, at most, poor woman. Did you know her nephew, her brother's boy, Mannion the name was, and what happened to him? It was on his honeymoon. He went rock climbing, of all things. He broke his neck. Now he's a paraplegic, God bless him. On his honeymoon! Who would ever go to a place where you could get hurt on your honeymoon?"

"People used to go to Niagara Falls."

"Not to jump, though. I'm sure Niagara Falls has had its share of jumpers and honeymooners both, but they were rarely the same crowd." He let out a small, satisfied breath, looking ahead and slightly upward, as if to picture the separate lines of lovers and leapers, each in their rightful place. "I'm not the type to say they were asking for it, but God knows what put it in his mind to climb a cliff when he had a woman at the bottom waiting for him."

Nick remembered the woman in the tree. Knocked a dead body down last night, Nick had, like the special boy at a Spanish birthday party, too enthused by the piñata. He felt bad enough to resolve to put extra effort into that one, to find out who she was, where she belonged. That way, there would be fewer questions, all around. She was like his mother—immigrant, and emigrant—on the other side.

"Where'd you go on your honeymoon?" Nick asked.

His father looked perplexed, as if he were disappointed to see that his son was capable of such a stupid question.

"To bed, of course."

Nick walked away, laughing, tramping back down the old hallway to finish getting ready for work. As his father watched him recede, he didn't get what the joke was, but even when he did, he felt sorrier for his son for missing the larger point of it, for fixing on what might have seemed backward or out of touch. He'd gone where he'd wanted, with the one he'd wanted with him, and he didn't think it was a bad thing at all.

FOUR

Nick walked across the aged linoleum of the lobby, down the concrete steps onto Broadway. The air was cold and lively, taking up stray leaves and old newspapers in vigorous, jerky gusts. The storm had torn down branches, with green leaves along with the yellow and brown. There was no sign of Jamie Barry, and Nick was glad to be spared his reminiscence of how Mike Diskin hid the erasers on Father Callahan in the third grade before asking for spare change. When Nick saw the bus slow down, he half-jogged toward the stop on the corner. This was a day for walking to work, but he hadn't the time. Yes, he did. Today was for autopsies and arraignments, reports and notifications, plus whatever fresh calamity awaited, the hell of the day. Still, the prospects did not weigh on him as they might have, did not seem more than he could bear. A little sunlight, a little sleep—was that all it took to make it all seem workable, worthwhile?

The bus stopped for him, the pneumatic brakes shifting with a whoosh, and he waved it on. Today was a day for walking. Below Dyckman Street, the west side of Broadway framed another park, Fort Tryon Park, a hillside rising up the spine of Manhattan, up and over to the Hudson. He loved this time of year, when the woods started to turn the color of lions and tigers, and the distant views were no longer hidden beneath the heedless green. The blocks of six-story prewar apartments gave way ahead to the patchy commercial strip above the George Washington Bridge, the gas stations and storage spaces near the precinct. Too short a walk, coming down.

When he was married to Allison, Nick would begin his walks on the Upper West Side, full of new strivers, people who came here for the money and freedom. Sunday was brunch and the *Times*. On Sundays, you saw white women pushing their children in strollers. During the week, you saw the same white children, pushed by black women. Following Broadway north, you came upon a ten-block stretch of no-man's-land, of winos and bums selling old porno magazines on blankets on the street, men who stared through you, with the sour, goatish smell of schizophrenia. The fleabag hotels then gave way to Columbia University, fortress and factory, that sent a lot of strivers and a few schizophrenics to the neighborhoods below. In Harlem on Sunday mornings, you heard gospel bursting from storefront churches, and saw the women in their hallelujah hats, dressed up to meet Jesus for a date.

As you crossed the border to Washington Heights, on 155th Street, you passed the most melancholy landmark in the city, which Nick thought of as the museum of museums. Even the graveyard across the street was less desolate, with its sign that warned, *Activo Cementerio,* promising at least the company of ghosts. The same couldn't be said for the museums, which comprised an entire city block of stately old beaux arts buildings, surrounding a plaza of herringbone brick. Two of the institutions were definitely gone. The Museum of the American Indian, the American Geographical Society—these had moved elsewhere; as for the American Numismatic Society, it was hard to tell if it had been abandoned or just ignored, a penny dropped in an old pocket. The illustrious names were engraved just below the rooflines—the now-lost tribes, like the Eskimo, the Salish, the Algonquin, and the now-lost explorers, such as Livingstone and Magellan. As you read around the plaza, it had the look of old ticker tape, of data you no longer needed to know. The motto of the Geographical Society was carved above the door: *Ubique,* Latin for "everywhere." Nick wasn't sure if the word was ill chosen or the loss was in everything but the translation. How could it be everywhere if it wasn't even here?

The Hispanic Society shared the same air of desertion. The section of plaza before it was sunken and walled, which trapped leaves and newspapers in eddying off-river breezes; the fountain was dry and its two flagpoles were bare. But while the other places were sites of double erasure—no more Iroquois, and no more Iroquois exhibit—the Hispanic Society was in the middle of a thriving Hispanic society, which had pushed the edges of the older black neighborhood farther south. An equestrian statue of El Cid dominated the section of plaza. He was a champion of the Reconquista in the eleventh century, who helped drive the Moors from Spain. Legend had it that when he died, his wife strapped his body upright on his horse, to lead his troops in one last battle. A thousand years ago, he helped kick out the new people; now his monument stood in an immigrant neighborhood, whom half the country thought of as invaders. That was the difference between history and a joke; you could kill a joke if you repeated it.

In Washington Heights, on four Sunday walks, Nick saw four different fights—a cock fight in an alley; a dogfight on a roof, from which the loser was thrown, yelping, to the sidewalk ten feet from Nick; a catfight between the prettiest girls he'd ever seen, tearing each other's shirts and screaming, "Puta! Puta, puta!"; and then a gunfight, as shooters from a passing car let loose at three guys on a corner, who emptied their own guns back at them. After the gunfight, Nick ran to Riverside Drive, where the old Jews still lived, from before the war and after, and he saw a pair of old hands close a window, muffling a piano concerto on the record player. When you crossed Dyckman Street, to Inwood, the last Irish bit of Manhattan, there were games in the park and beers in the bar, after Mass at Good Shepherd, the gray stone church where stony old monsignors gave stony sermons about what would not last, which was everything, almost.

The monsignors were right about the neighborhood, at least, about the good times and the bad. Inwood was disappearing and had been since Nick's childhood, as the working classes worked hardest at leaving. In the seventies, the city was a cesspool, bankrupt and flooded with heroin, but it was a golden playground for Nick and his friends. They would run across rooftops and hide in the park, Inwood Hill Park, green since the beginning of time. For a decade, the city was on the mend, until crack hit in the mid-eighties, and the Heights were narco central for the entire northeast. The Colombians brought in cocaine, and the Dominicans moved it, cut it, and cooked it into the little rocks that burnt people alive. For a time, the precinct that covered the Heights and Inwood logged a homicide every three days, and shootings, robberies, and break-ins beyond counting. But through the nineties and after, crime began to fall, and then to free-fall, so quickly it seemed like a stock market collapse—*Murder is now at two thousand . . . fifteen hundred . . . twelve . . . closing this year at less than a thousand . . . eight hundred, seven. We are now approaching six. . . . Sell, sell, sell!* Young people with money started to move to Inwood, consultant types and creative types who didn't dress for work, and worked not at jobs but in "fields" like software and graphic design. The newcomers were in the main thoughtful, respectful, and tasteful, and a lot of the old-timers liked them even less than they'd liked the Dominicans. They baffled bartenders with requests for wine lists. There goes the neighborhood. . . .

And then the apocalypse downtown, on a morning that began with the bluest of skies. For hours, it seemed that history had ended, that Manhattan would join the list of ancient lost places—Babylon, Byzantium, Troy. The two towers had possessed a flat magnitude that had made them seem ageless, though they'd been no older than the men who'd destroyed them. The cataclysm felt like a natural disaster or even a supernatural one, visited as it was by demonologies of the air, but it was history, its return and not its ending. The city had been built by foreign hatreds, after all. It had taken in throngs of exiles to such extravagant benefit. And New York was never more splendid than in the grieving season that followed, abundant in dignity and decency, even as cops and firemen fought with gulls in the rubble piles for fragments of what once had been friends. There were no unknown soldiers here—wakes were held for scraps of skin, funerals for bits of bone. For a while, if you got a bad feeling, a sudden intuition of fear, you looked up instead of over your shoulder. What to make of it all? What warnings and amends? Was it a singularity, a rogue wave, or just the first to break?

But nothing else happened; nothing like it, not here, not yet. History departed for its old hunting grounds. Shopping resumed, at first under patriotic pretense. The anniversary ritual of listed names, flowers tossed into the still-gaping pits, grew more modest and peripheral to the public mind, and it was a matter of time before the event would be marked by department store specials: dinette sets, sectional couches, and throw pillows—everything must go!

People did keep on buying things, until the economy collapsed. Trillions of dollars disappeared, too much to contemplate, let alone count. Nick could picture his father asking, *Where was the last place you left it?* Though the statements from his retirement fund did not make for pleasant reading, Nick had far more troubling deficits, and he was struck by the economy's lack of impact on him, on anyone he knew very well, even on the city as he knew it. No epidemic of boarded-up storefronts, and the men who loitered on corners were the ones who always had. Allison had prospered. She'd convinced her firm to make a big bet on a bad future, and Nick wondered whether he flattered himself to think he may have played a part in her inspiration. When Nick arrived at the precinct, he cast these thoughts from his mind like evil spirits.

The precinct building was of recent construction, a box of cinder block three stories tall. It was built of the cheapest material by the lowest bidder, at the cost of a palace. On sconces beside the front door were two green lights, the centuries-old marker of a New York City police station; one cop in ten might have known what they meant, or noticed that they were green. Inside, a lieutenant stood before a desk that extended from one end of the room to the other, like a bar, and two cops and a prisoner stood before him, awaiting service. Nick slipped up a stairway beside them, half-nodding to two more cops, and walked into the squad.

The room was long and rectangular, with a central island of desks doubled up, face-to-face. It would have taken great effort to make an impression of order here, and little effort was made. Each desk had both a computer terminal and a typewriter, and a few had electric fans; all were littered with reports. Wanted posters lined the walls of the waiting area, some yellowing with age, others covered with more recent posters of more local priority, so that the posters formed sedimentary layers of newer and nearer crimes. Inside the squad, the posters were for their own consumption, warning against corruption and sexual harassment, although money and women were both in short supply. Fluorescent lights flickered over scuffed tile floors, and the air was filled with broken phrases of cop talk, as they hustled the phones.

"Like I said, I don't know if it's true. She said you hit her. I'm not here to judge, but come on in and tell me your side. . . ."

"This is the police. *Sí, la policía.* Is Reuben Alvarez at home?"

"I need to know if the kid goes to school there, if he's there today. . . . Yeah, I can get a subpoena, but that'll just waste everybody's time. . . ."

"No, this is the detective squad, not the hospital. You got the wrong number. . . . No, I don't know why he's not getting better, lady. Ask the doctor."

"No, but you gotta come in to talk to me. That's how it's done. . . ."

"Does anybody there speak English? No, you don't speak English, believe me. Stop kidding yourself, you don't. Get me somebody who does."

"Tell you what, let me talk to your supervisor. . . . No, I don't need a subpoena to talk to your supervisor. Just put him on the phone. . . ."

"Like I said, lady, you got the wrong number. . . ."

Napolitano, Garelick, Perez, Smith, Valentini, Crimmins. There were no strangers. Good. The phones kept ringing, and almost half the time, they were answered this way:

"Detective squad. Detective McCann. Can I help you?"

"Detective McCann. How can I help you?"

"McCann . . ."

There was no Detective McCann. He was a figment used to dodge wives or girlfriends, pesty complainants, or demands for administrative arcana from headquarters. Several angry letters had been sent to the squad accusing McCann of incompetence; one, which was framed and hung up on a wall, thanked him for talking a runaway son into coming home. Nick was never McCann, and neither was Esposito. Nick disliked lying altogether—almost altogether—and Esposito never felt the need for that kind of evasion. Garelick was McCann most often; he may have invented him. Garelick also minted any number of Jewish holidays when he wanted to take off, and though the boss was suspicious, he rarely denied him.

Nick signed in and went to his desk. There was a mild apprehension as he checked his new cases, the fresh feuds and afflictions. None would be heavy ones, since on-duty detectives would have been called out to the scene, but the little cases were frustrating, all the effort spent on petty disputes. Three cases today. Not too bad. A missing teenager, described as a chronic runaway; a fistfight between neighbors; a series of threatening phone calls, made from tenant to landlord over a leaky sink. The advantage to the sluggishness of the system was that the day or two the report took to make it to the squad often acted as a cooling-off period. Three phone calls closed all three cases. The runaway girl had returned, the neighbors had sobered up and shaken hands, and the tenant had gotten his sink fixed and had sent an apology along with the rent check. As Nick hung up the phone, relieved, there was a rap at the glass that separated the lieutenant's corner office from the main room.

Lieutenant Ortiz was a veteran of thirty years on the Job, most of them with the Detective Bureau. He hadn't spoken with a criminal in nearly two decades and hoped never to do so again. His battles were fought entirely within the police department, in his office and the slightly larger offices belonging to the captains, inspectors, and chiefs he had to answer to; they would drop by in the middle of a shooting and complain that the desks were messy, or too much overtime was being made, or the vehicle inspection logs were not up to date. For his subordinates, the lieutenant's management skills consisted entirely of a determination to make miserable those who caused him misery. It was rumored that his wife cut his hair, an irregular brush cut, and he expected that someone else should make coffee, even if he was the only one who wanted a cup, and his smoking was so constant that it even bothered the smokers in the office. He also treated the men with a kind of mock belligerence that Nick found in the long run was better to feed than fight. Nick now stood before the lieutenant's desk, allowing his moment-ago calm to sustain him through the impending interrogation.

"What the hell happened last night? I heard you and Esposito killed an old lady!"

"We did, more or less."

"What?"

"Well, we did. Not on purpose. But—well, there you go."

The lieutenant seemed slightly deflated at the lost opportunity to argue. "Don't take it so hard, Meehan. I mean, don't be so hard on yourself."

"Okay."

"Esposito . . . he didn't do anything I should know about, did he? You guys seem to get along. I'm glad about that. You got a level head, Nick. Esposito—you know how he gets . . . a little enthusiastic sometimes."

The question troubled Nick; he was briefly worried that the lieutenant was aware of his status. No, he couldn't know. They were careful about these things downtown. As for enthusiasm, Esposito had once chased a perp with a gun down an alley, breaking his ankle just as he closed in. He tackled the perp and cuffed him, then ordered the perp to carry him on his back to the street. Nick shrugged. "It was a disaster, but everything was by the book."

The lieutenant seemed satisfied by the response. He put out a cigarette solely for the purpose of lighting another, pausing to think.

"The guy you locked up last night, did you get a statement out of him?"

"Yes."

"And how— Never mind, I don't want to know. Where's your partner?"

"I don't know. I'll take a look for him. He's probably in the dorm. I went home for a bit. He kept rolling."

"All right, let him rest a little. So, basically, with last night's scorecard, we closed an old homicide, but the new one's still open, with nothing on it, right?"

"Right. Plus, the suicide's still unidentified, and there's the old lady. I don't think the ME is gonna do anything crazy like make her a homicide. Do you?"

The medical examiner could theoretically determine that the death had been caused by another person, and it was not a bad theory. It didn't seem right to call it natural. Nick believed Miz Cole would have lived had they not done what they'd done. Even if her heart had had only one more day of beating in it, another hour, another single beat, and they'd deprived her of it, it was in that sense a homicide. The ending is all that counts. But in practice, it put too great a burden on the bearer of bad news. In fact, Nick had already called the ME. They'd done the autopsy first thing in the morning, and had deemed the death natural. Miz Cole and Milton had already been shipped to the funeral home. The suicide hadn't been examined; she was scheduled for later in the day. The lieutenant didn't know any of that yet, and Nick did not feel the need to enlighten him.

"How could they?"

"When the old lady in Harlem with the heart condition died after the cops knocked her door down, they made it a homicide."

Lieutenant Ortiz pressed his hand across his temple and brow.

"Don't try to cheer me up. Go. Some days, this is not my cup of shit."

That was Esposito's phrase, Nick thought, and he wondered who'd copied it from whom. As Nick left the lieutenant's office, Esposito entered the squad, his hair wet from the shower, freshly shaved, in yet another clean suit, though the tiredness told in his eyes. He began to rummage through papers on his desk, then stopped and shook his head before turning away and walking to the meal room for coffee. Nick followed him.

Nick asked, "What do you need?"

"I started to look, but then couldn't remember what I was looking for."

"Can't be important, then. We gotta go."

"Yeah. You hungry?"

"I am. Let's get some breakfast first. We got a little time."

There were three or four diners they went to for breakfast, on a sporadic circuit motivated by obscure grudges. The bacon was chewy in one, the owner was rude in another, and they only had milk instead of half-and-half for coffee in a third. Otherwise, there was not an iota of difference among them. The detectives only sat down for breakfast on occasion, weekends mostly, and so they were somewhat familiar faces in each of the diners, rather than regulars in any. When Nick proposed breakfast to Esposito, Garelick announced that he was hungry, too, and within a few minutes, there was an outbreak of sympathetic pangs. Napolitano suggested the Athena, because the last time he'd gone to Joe's, there'd been a scattering of white pellets in the bathroom that he'd thought was rat poison, and he didn't want to think about it while he ate. Perez seconded the motion, on the grounds that the Washington had an inferior grade of pancake syrup, and it was thus decided.

Napolitano was dapper and stout, all sharp creases and round curves, with a deliberateness of movement that made him seem as if he might be more at home in the water. He had a genial demeanor and a stubborn streak, which suited his role as the union delegate. Though he had an Italian name and African skin, he was of indeterminate Caribbean origin, and on the phone, he was adept at making residents of most continents believe he was a cousin. Garelick was the oldest man on the squad, nearing sixty. He was thin and pale, with fine wild white hair and baleful eyes. He had decades of experience, keen powers of observation, and a chess player's intellect, strategic and roving. None of these abilities were dedicated in the slightest to police work. Office politics were his sole concern, and he was a vigilant guardian of custom and tradition. He didn't retire, he admitted frankly, because he couldn't stand his wife. Garelick couldn't stand Perez either, but to Perez's credit, he didn't seem to notice. Perez was the youngest of them, and though he had a menacing aspect, with his shaved head and fixed stare, in truth he was sweet-natured and considerate, anxious to please. He should have been a natural fit for Garelick, as Perez endorsed Garelick's every opinion, but Garelick was unused to a steady diet of respect, and it disagreed with him, like rich food. The five of them took two cars to the diner, so they could proceed afterward to their separate errands.

As they walked in, they met two detectives coming out. In the customary split, there was a younger and an older one, the first fit, the other thick. Esposito and Napolitano recognized them, and Garelick pretended not to. Hearty handshakes were exchanged.

"Hey!"

"How you doin'?"

"You look good!"

"It's been a while! You're still at . . ."

"Special Victims?"

"Yeah."

"Whadda you guys got, way up here?"

"The pattern rape, the guy who pretends to be the plumber's helper, with the old ladies and kids. A bullshit lead. This wacko says his neighbor keeps askin' where he can buy Girl Scout cookies—but we gotta talk to everybody. It's a phenomenal operation—three twenty-four-hour surveillance vans, we're up on wiretaps, they got the youngest-looking hottest female undercovers on the Job, playing jump rope next to whorehouses. Every chief calls every day, has to know the latest. Not bad, though. We make our own hours, weekends off, unless something happens. Tons of overtime. What about you guys?"

Death by rope, gun, and misinformation.

"Ah, the usual shit."

"Anyway, gotta go. Good to see you."

"Likewise. Good luck."

"Yeah, stay safe."

"Take care."

They found a corner booth and slid inside. Esposito, Napolitano, and Garelick exchanged testimonies of grievance and outrage.

"Can you believe those guys?"

"So fucking full of themselves. Can you believe that?"

"Unbelievable."

"They get three vans and cheerleaders."

"We're lucky we don't have to pay for gas for the squad cars."

"The other day, I had to."

"Some people, they got it easy," said Garelick, as if he'd spent his morning splitting timber. "The one, though—Paulie—I knew him as a cop. He was good. Two shoot-outs."

"The other guy, Johnny T, he was no slouch, either," added Napolitano. "A lot of gun collars. Good guy, too."

"Fuck 'em both," said Esposito, to general assent.

Nick thought about the codes of the place, like with the bedouins—my brother is my brother, and my cousin is my enemy, unless another tribe makes a claim on the well. The five men at the table would have gladly given blood for the two who had left, but Nick doubted that they could have sat together for fifteen minutes without an argument.

"Do you want menus?"

The waitress was in her early twenties, with a sweet, plain face and a top-heavy figure. Napolitano made a pretense of looking at her name tag—Marina—and Esposito didn't bother with the pretense. The menus offered what they'd seen at every diner they'd ever gone to and ever would: eggs, pancakes, french toast; bacon, sausage, ham; orange juice and coffee. There was little else available, and nothing else was desired. There was no more need for menus than there was to pass out the lyric sheets to "Happy Birthday" before the cake arrived at a party.

"Yeah, we need menus."

"Please."

"Sure, we'll have a look."

Marina nodded and turned, and ten eyeballs took note of her retreat.

"Wouldja?"

"Oh, yeah."

"Yeah."

"No question."

Nick looked around the table at the yearning gazes. As far as he knew, Napolitano was happy at home, and faithful to his wife; Esposito professed contentment but cheated at will; Garelick's marriage was a prison from which he made no effort to escape, in either the short or long term. Perez was unattached, as far as Nick knew. It occurred to Nick that he understood nothing of human nature and relationships.

After Marina returned, the orders were placed, and she collected the menus. Garelick noticed the momentary lag in the palaver and took action. "She should have brought coffee, without asking. Anticipating needs is at the heart of all of the service professions. I didn't get a real night's sleep last night. Nine hours—I know, it isn't bad—but I still think I'm owed, from past aggravations. How about you, Nick? You need coffee?"

The question was baited, all at the table knew, though it was unclear whether its intent was playful or pointed. Garelick had been one of the cavilers who'd warned Nick about Esposito at the beginning.

"Yeah, coffee. A lot, a helmet full of it."

Garelick was pleased at the response. "A helmet isn't such a bad idea for you, in and of itself."

Esposito caught something of the implication and directed his own question to Perez. "How about you, Ralph? You got your helmet on, for the game? Or do you just carry around a pillow, for when you can't stay awake?"

Conflict was constant, the "them" a given, sliding in scope and scale from the hordes on the horizon to the man across the table, next to you on the bench. The "us" was variable, but Napolitano had hoped to maintain solidarity at least through breakfast.

"Remember, Espo, when I had that shooting, what's-his-name, the guy's shot right in the balls? He was mistaken for his brother, who'd shot somebody else. Completely innocent, this guy, but it turns out he was a rapist. DNA hit, a month later—he was jumping out on joggers in Prospect Park. I was sure he knew who shot him, and he was holding back. You know, the usual thing, all lies and 'Fuck yous.' Fact was, he was blindsided. He wouldn't have told us if he did know, but he didn't. Remember, Espo?"

"I remember," said Esposito, nodding with vigor, evidently seeing other relevance to the recollection. "You remember, Nap, how that ended, in the hospital?"

Napolitano's smile was more rueful than Esposito's. "Oh, yeah, now I do. Walking out—"

"Yeah, walking out, I ask the guy—remember, Nap?"

"God knows I do. I had a few meetings about it, was getting ready for a sit-down with the good people at the Civilian Complaint Review Board, until the DNA hit. When we're leaving the hospital room, Espo turns to the guy and says, 'I just got one more question for ya.' The guy makes a face, like he's gonna answer this one after all the others. Espo says, 'Does it whistle when you piss?'"

Napolitano laughed almost as much as Esposito did, but Nick knew that if their satisfaction had been the same, they would have still been working together, as regular partners, and Nick would have been the odd man out. Perez laughed the hardest, glad to be included, and Garelick shook his head. "If they locked you in a room with a mirror," said Garelick to Esposito, "it'd be half a day before you found out you were locked in a room."

The food arrived, and conversation became desultory before falling off altogether. Near the end of the meal, Garelick suddenly took on an animated look, and he finished quickly. He was more indulgent toward Perez than usual, in that he had so far refrained from any direct criticism during the course of the meal. When Perez had mopped the last bit of egg from his plate, he got up from the booth, took a newspaper from the counter, and headed to the bathroom. Garelick summoned Marina in some haste, for the check.

"As soon as you can, we gotta go," he said to her.

"No problem."

Napolitano pushed his plate back and smiled. "Are you new here? I haven't seen you before."

"Yeah, I'm new, but this is my last day. I'm just filling in for my sister. I'm going back to Greece tomorrow. I'm going back to college."

"Really! My grandfather was Greek," Napolitano said, perhaps truthfully. "All I remember, though, is 'kale nita'—'good night'!"

Marina nodded in appreciation. Garelick was oddly excited by her news, as if he had been relieved of the responsibility of paying her tuition. Nick knew he had some stratagem in mind.

"Well, good luck to you!"

Marina accepted Garelick's vehement benediction with a slight blush, and when she left, the remainder of the party looked at Garelick, wondering what was afoot. He had a cunning expression as he took out a pad from his pocket.

"If I can prove that Perez is completely out of his mind, will you guys work with him, take him off my hands?"

"No."

"Why would we do that? You want me to buy a car, if you can show it doesn't run?"

"Would you lay off him? He's a decent guy!"

Garelick was undeterred by the responses, and indifferent to the practical result of his experiment. He coughed and slid the notebook to the center of the table. "All of you are witnesses. I have written down a phone number that a complainant gave me. It's disconnected. Nick, would you call, please, to confirm this?"

Garelick slid the pad over. Nick called and got a recorded message—not in service. He held the phone up for the table to hear, like a magician's assistant.

"And we have our statement from Marina, a person whose credibility we have no reason to doubt, that she will not be in this hemisphere by tomorrow. Are you with me so far?"

"So far."

"You want to show something about the mental health of somebody at this table," observed Esposito, "not including yourself."

"Watch, listen, learn. I take out a new piece of paper." He tore out a half-sheet from his pad. "We provide a name and a phone number, which we have demonstrated to be nonworking."

He wrote in a bouncy cursive, attempting to seem feminine. After a pause, he changed the dot of the *i* in Marina to a heart.

"That's it. Watch. Wait. Observe."

Marina returned to place the check on the table, but Garelick took hold of it—"Hang on, wait"—and slipped a few bills inside the brown vinyl folder.

"We don't need change."

"Thank you!"

"Best of luck, Marina. We're on our way here, too. Duty calls. The other guy, in the bathroom? He'll be out in a minute, but we have to go. He dropped this piece of paper, from a homicide case, I think it is. Would you mind giving it to him?"

"No, not at all."

The four of them slipped out of the booth, taking care not to appear desperate to leave, as Perez came out of the bathroom. He viewed the empty booth with dismay, but was reassured at the sight of Garelick waving to him from outside. As he walked toward the door, Marina intercepted him.

"You dropped something."

Marina beamed so brightly that Nick wondered how much Garelick had tipped her. Perez opened the folded note and smiled at her. He winked at her as he left.

"Good thing you caught it," Perez said.

Perez touched her shoulder as he left, with a lightness in his step. The joy in his face was so contagious that the other four detectives were nearly as childishly elated. As they drove off, Nick knew that he'd never feel sorry enough for Perez to risk spoiling the scheme, or rather—in this instance, at least—his conscience was no match for his curiosity. Sunlight, sleep, and whatever this was, Nick was glad to have started the day with them.

FIVE

On the drive downtown, little was said; the meal had been heavy, the night long. Esposito said that driving helped to wake him up, and as much as Nick didn't want to think about that, he didn't like to drive. The wind took up the gray surface of the Harlem River in feathery ruffles, and the Bronx projects and apartments lined the palisade on the far side, like sentry towers. Nick saw Esposito regarding the projects darkly, as if there were a mile-long BEWARE OF DOG sign along the shoreline, warning trespassers of all kinds. When any ghetto cop got a glimpse of some other rough stretch of town—the South Bronx, Bed-Stuy, forget about Newark—they thought, *Now, this place is baaaaddd!* And all of a sudden Spanish Harlem or East New York seemed easy, like home. Highbridge rose above to the left, with its rocky slopes and hardy oaks. Allison used to say that she couldn't believe Nick was a city kid, because what he liked best about the city was the country. Ah, the green woods of Gotham, sweet home.

Across the water were the East River islands, Randall's, Wards, Roosevelt, adrift in history. No one had ever really figured out what to do with them. They had been workhouses, poorhouses, madhouses, places of quarantine. The names changed, following their shifting purposes—Blackwell's Island became Welfare Island before it became Roosevelt Island. Though the lighthouse at the northern tip still stood, a haphazard bar graph horizon of concrete housing towers had taken the place of the Idiot Asylum and the Inebriate Asylum. At the southern end, the ruins of the smallpox hospital were lit up at night, the grand shell of a chateau, fenced off to keep tourists from being crushed by falling stone. It was the problem with islands—everyone wanted to get on them or no one did. To the right, where the skyscrapers of Manhattan rose, a square foot of

space might cost more than a square mile in Texas. On the little river islands, ideas went wrong, and money fell short, and then interest dwindled. But when they lit up the smallpox hospital at night, it looked like a
palace.

"Why have you been staring at me?"

Nick laughed so hard he choked. "I was looking at Roosevelt Island."

"Nobody ever looks at Roosevelt Island."

"That's true, but I was looking at Roosevelt Island."

"It's okay to admit it," Esposito continued, the attention working
through his system like caffeine. "As Garelick says, 'Watch, listen,
learn.'"

Esposito smiled with a theatrical self-satisfaction, raising an eyebrow,
letting slip an amused sigh. It was an act and it wasn't; he wouldn't have
joked like that a month ago. Nick tried to think how long had they
worked together—was it five months? Esposito fished for a piece of gum
from his pocket, and Nick knew he wanted a cigar. Espo knew himself
well enough to laugh at his vanity, and he trusted Nick enough to show
him that he wasn't entirely kidding. Friendship can begin with likeness,
a shared past, a shared taste—*You're from Brooklyn? You like Sinatra?*—or
it can begin with unlikeness, a thrilling difference. You think, *I'd never
have thought of that joke. I could never sing like that, or have figured that out.
Not only couldn't I have done that, I wouldn't have known how to begin.* A
stranger can almost become a brother through a handful of these little
epiphanies. They began to hit it off after one visit to an apartment where
they'd heard a perp from a shooting might be staying. It was a cousin living there, with the name Garces, uncommon enough to have promise.
There was no answer at the door, or at the neighbors', or at the super's.
There were no names by the doorbells, or the mailboxes, a two–tiered
row of them at the side of the lobby. Nick and Esposito strolled over,
glancing around to see if anyone was watching, and Nick pried back one
of the mailbox covers half an inch with his house key. He took the chewing gum out of his mouth, wadded it to the end of a pen, and slid it inside the little gap. With a quick pluck, out came a phone bill, addressed
to a Fernando Garces. He slipped it back inside.

"This is the right place," Nick said.

"That was a federal offense," remarked Espo approvingly. "Did you
make that up yourself?"

The other thing that warmed Espo to the partnership was a chance remark. Nick had asked him where he was from in Italy, and he'd said Sicily, two generations back. Nick told him that his name was for foundlings, a name given to children abandoned at hospitals and churches. It meant "exposed." Others in the tradition tended to be prettified, puffed into euphemism—D'Amico was "from love," Donodeo meant "gift of God." There was an unpainted plainness to Esposito's version, a factory flatness that appealed to him.

"No kidding!" he said, beaming. "My name means something!"

Never was someone prouder to learn of a bastard ancestor. But Nick understood that what appealed to Esposito was the idea that he was self-made, self-invented. He had no brothers, and his father was not loved and long gone. His life was the work of his own hands, he felt, and so the fortune-cookie factoid took on an oracular depth.

As it was, neither had shown any particular gift for friendship before then. Nick was too self-contained, Esposito too competitive for lasting fellowship of any depth. Nick knew that his own unmoored state played some part, how he was both sinking and floating, and the greater effect of his betrayal, his pre-betrayal, had been to inspire in him a dedication to ensure there would be no need for further betrayal to occur. He stuck close to Esposito, listened and learned with true esteem, and his cautious counsel was accepted more often than not. He didn't know why Esposito had taken to him, but he was glad for it. They pulled off the highway at Twenty-third and headed back up First. Here they were, in the city.

"Why don't you ever work down here, Espo?"

"The city? Didn't you hear, they made crime against the law down here. Nothing happens. And if it does, the butler did it. What fun is that? I mean, I know shit happens sometimes, but half the time you're running around because some millionaire, some politician, their silverware was stolen. What I like about uptown is nobody's important. Nobody's important until they kill somebody or get killed."

Though Nick dismissed the casual slander of their downtown colleagues, the last assessment had a measure of cruel truth. Still, Esposito's contentment was not absolute.

"You think it'll be in the papers, last night?" he asked. "My homicide, I mean."

"I don't know, maybe a line or two."

"Amazing, isn't it? We have three dead last night, and there wasn't one reporter. Not a single picture that wasn't taken as evidence."

Nick struggled to frame his comment so he wouldn't snap under the weight of its irony. "No pictures? Not a single snapshot of me knocking a body out of a tree, you splashing the mud puddle on the hustlers, the old lady's face before she died? That's fine by me. You know the deal—you're out of the limelight, but you're also off the radar. It's the better way."

Esposito grunted, unwilling to concede that he couldn't have both privacy and publicity but he didn't bring it up again.

At the medical examiner's, the lobby had a security desk in front of a marble wall inscribed with an ominous Latin quotation: TACEANT COL- LOQUIA. EFFUGIAT RISUS. HIC LOCUS EST UBI MORS GAUDET SUCCURRERE VITAE. They both stared at it for a moment, as they grasped for ID to show the guard, who nodded them past. Nick had looked up the quote before and memorized it. There was a dignity here that was lacking in the Bronx morgue, where you went in the back of the building, through the loading dock. In the elevator, Esposito scratched himself as they waited for it to go downstairs; he seemed somewhat discomfited. Nick had never been to an autopsy with him, and quite a few detectives, even veterans, tried to avoid the procedure. More were troubled by the gore than the ghosts, he guessed, and Esposito seemed immune to haunting.

"I wonder what the hell that means, on the wall there."

"It's Latin."

"Duh."

"Do you want to know?"

"I got a feeling you're about to tell me."

" 'Let conversation cease. Laughter, take flight. This place is where death delights to help the living.' "

The elevator stopped, and Esposito pursed his lips. "What's the first bit again?"

" 'Let conversation cease.' "

"In other words, 'Shut up already.' "

Nick had fallen for it. His own vanities had not passed completely un- noticed. Esposito began to shake with laughter, and made little effort to control himself as they walked out into the basement corridor.

"Bite me," Nick said.

"Itebay emay, in the Latin. This place skeeves me."

But Nick had been right about the squeamishness—"skeeve," from the Italian "schifo," "disgust." Esposito wasn't the only detective who had fallen out of the habit of going to autopsies. It was true that in out-door gunshot cases, which are the benchmark murders of bad neighbor-hoods, you usually learned little from autopsies—whether Milton Cole's liver had been otherwise healthy was as relevant as his sixth-grade re-port card. But Nick felt that you connected in a way that you would not if you only saw a rap sheet—and it was a rare man on the slab who didn't have a criminal record. You might see abrasions on the knuckles, from the effort to do a hundred push-ups a day, or the waistline that told of fast food and video games. There was history in the skin. You might not have known he was a Latin King until you saw *"Amor de Rey"* tattooed on his back; you might have forgotten he had a mother until you read it on his shoulder. And you met the customer, who you now worked for, which was always a good idea. Esposito didn't need to make the effort to connect, but Nick did.

Esposito started to say that he'd go out for coffee if nothing looked too bad, when Tully, the detective liaison at the ME, caught them in the hall. Tully helped fill in the story when the pathologist had a question. Was there diabetes medication found at the scene? Was there any history of domestic violence? Was the body found in the bathtub or next to it? He helped negotiate the minefield of theoreticals—Why? Why not? What if? All the anal whatiffery that annoyed you most times—and embarrassed you on occasion, when they came upon the puncture from the ice pick that no one noticed at the scene. Tully took hold of Esposito's arm and whispered that Internal Affairs was in the room—an old junkie locked up for shoplifting the night before had expired quietly in a midtown precinct holding cell. There was nothing suspicious about the death, but since he'd died in police custody, they were obliged to investigate. Esposito reacted as if he'd been told there was a gas leak.

"Dead bodies, and now rats," he muttered, glowering. "It's like a hor-ror movie."

Nick shuddered, and his discomfort was unfeigned. He had rational-ized his decision to work for IAB by deciding he didn't really work for them. They had a doubly bad reputation, for both credulous malice and incompetence. If there was an accusation that a cop was robbing banks, they'd blunder around ATMs for a month and then write up everyone in the precinct who came in ten minutes late. In-house justice for the NYPD was a Wizard of Oz affair, booming and arbitrary pronouncements from behind a curtain—five days for failure to wear a seat belt in a car crash;

thirty for being out of residence while on sick leave; ten for felony assault, off-duty. Failure to comply with a lawful order, five days or sixty. There were stories behind all of the cases, Nick knew—Al Capone went down for the taxes, not the murders—and he hoped every hard hit on technicalities compensated for something rotten but unprovable. Still, the numbers were baffling, the charges relentlessly inventive—unauthorized sexual conduct while on duty, fifteen days. He'd never seen the on-duty sex authorization form. He'd have to check around the office. Could a sergeant sign it, or did you need a chief?

Technically, Nick was an IAB "field associate," a kind of informal informant, someone in the neighborhood who would pass on word, gossip more than hard news. If he saw a cop do wrong—real wrong—his obligation was no different from any other cop, which was to tell the truth. No different from any other person, really, though perjury was apparently a crime only for policemen, not politicians. Nick himself was in daily violation of department regulations by living in the same precinct where he worked, but he had been assured that petty stuff was not what IAB was looking for. What they were looking for was Esposito, though Nick didn't know until later how hard they were trying.

There had been nothing especially wrong with the squad where Nick had started his detective career, but it had not been in the same Bronx precinct where he had worked as a cop and had expected to go when promoted. He'd been moved because of manpower issues, it had been explained, due to retirements, resignations, and promotions. It was temporary, he'd been assured, and he'd believed them. That belief may have figured into why he'd never settled in, never connected to the people and place as he might have, and his sense of transience and separation, made emphatic by the same qualities in his off-duty life, had begun to corrode the sense of fulfillment and fun he'd come to depend on. No matter its burdens, work had been a refuge, his last one of late, and Nick had not wanted to test his capacity to withstand the equal aversions he'd felt for going to the office and coming home. He had not wanted to be at either, and he had not known where else to go. When he'd judged that he had done his time, he'd put in for a transfer to Manhattan.

But months passed without even the rumor of movement, and Nick could foresee the months turning into years. He had no significant friends or relatives to intercede for him; his personnel file would molder and yellow in a cabinet downtown. He could picture it, and he knew how it felt. As he waited, one less-than-stellar colleague was transferred to a suburban corner of Queens because he couldn't keep up with his cases; another, notoriously abrasive, found himself reassigned to Manhattan overnight when a chief didn't like how he answered the phone—"What do you want?" Nick had no desire to be as incompetent as the one or as impolitic as the other, but when they called to crow variously about the better restaurants, the lighter workload, the ease of the commute, he left the office in a foul temper. Hours were spent in acrid speculation over whether he was being refused or merely ignored, and which was the preferred insult. When he asked for a robbery assignment with steady tours, he was passed over for a junior man, the sergeant's favorite. His considerate treatment of a tearful perp he locked up for a fight—ex-wife, hooking up with the ex–best friend—led to what should have been a professional coup, a data dump on a gang of home invaders—names, addresses, phone numbers, past and planned jobs. Kilos and machine guns were ultimately recovered, but Nick wasn't there for the takedown. It happened on his day off, and the sergeant had forgotten to call him in. Junior took the collars. Nick had always had his bleak side, but after this, he was becoming bitter.

On his next day back, he confided his frustration to one of the veteran detectives, a shrewd and decent old Barbadian. What Nick took at first to be magnificently sympathetic indignation proved to be the onset of a stroke. At the emergency room, he met a neighborhood acquaintance from Inwood, a former partner of the ailing man, now a lieutenant at IAB. "Don't hold that against me," he joked, and Nick didn't. The man had always been affably unserious, almost boldly so, noted mostly in his youth for running naked through a church picnic on a twenty-dollar dare. They went out for a beer and had at least eight, at which point the offer was casually tendered, impetuously accepted.

"What do I do?"

"Nothing, really. Just keep your eyes open. Some of the shitheads I work with have a real hard-on for some guy," he said, laying out the allegations by Malcolm Cole and Babenco, hinting he didn't take them at face value. "Who knows? You don't have to be best friends with the guy. Nick, I never worked really hard at anything, but I never did less than what I do here. . . ."

Nick told himself that if the claims were false, it would be an easy task, and if they were true, it would be an important one, but he knew that he was lying to himself to think that the assignment was his main concern. He wanted to move, and he did what was necessary to do it. He might as well have been one of those wrong-turn pioneers, starving and snowbound in a mountain pass, praying that his companions survived the ordeal but wondering how they would taste if they didn't. The lieutenant said he'd arrange everything, that Nick should call only if he changed his mind. Nick didn't, and he was in Manhattan within the week. He never spoke with the lieutenant again. Nick's first official contact with IAB had been the late call after the Cole homicide, the final crossed wire of the night. Nick did not look forward to meeting the man.

On Nick's first day at the squad, Esposito approached him about working together, sensing another odd man out. Esposito had made a few calls, and had learned that Nick was a man who knew how to keep his mouth shut. *He got a rough deal and he didn't even complain once.* The Barbadian was in no position to contradict. Nick dreaded the prospect of working with Esposito, but no one else in the squad was unpaired, and it would have raised alarms to refuse. So it was from the outset that it went perfectly right, perfectly wrong. As Nick liked Esposito more, he liked himself less, but he started to look forward to going to work again, was eager to see what the day would bring. Almost at once, Nick was dismissive of the Cole and Babenco accusations—even the cops who carped most about Esposito never suggested that he was corrupt—but he also grasped that the view of Esposito as a dangerous man was not confined to his enemies.

Esposito told Nick about old allegations that he was shaking down drug dealers. "I never shook anybody down," he explained, soon after they had settled in with each other. "These guys, though, I was shaking them up pretty good." He would visit them at their clubs and stores, and their furniture would break. One crew went through several pool tables at their favorite bar before they had to give up the pastime altogether. Esposito caught IAB following him early on and made a game of that, too. When they parked on a corner to watch him, he would slip away and call 911, telling the operator in a cartoony Spanish accent that there were two men masturbating in a car near a school yard. If there was a male-female surveillance team, Espo would call to say they were having sex, and go on about how well-endowed the woman was—"*Ai, papi,* she beeg!"—which tended to speed up the police response to the scene. They had their revenge when they watched him fight two dealers in an alley, breaking a total of three of their arms; he had his, when in the trial room on charges of brutality, he faced his accusers and said, "You witnessed a police officer being assaulted and did nothing about it? I want these men charged with cowardice and dereliction of duty." The slate was wiped clean on both counts. "Things have a way of working out for me," he observed. When Nick pointed out that IAB's spite about his triumph might provoke their continued and not entirely professional interest, Esposito laughed and said, "These guys couldn't catch a cold in a leper colony."

In the morgue basement, there were four IAB men in the room, bunched into a corner, in full hazmat gear—white jumpsuits, masks, booties, and hair covers. The dress code at the core of a nuclear plant was more casual, and Nick almost expected to see them clutching one another's hands. The gauntlet had been laid down for Esposito; he couldn't be weaker than them. There was some distance between the two stainless steel autopsy tables, which was a relief, and the ME who had their suicide was cute, which was a welcome distraction. She had short, spiky hair, and wore a low-cut T-shirt and jeans. Her protective gear consisted of latex gloves. Esposito moved ahead of Nick to take a place by the table, giving the IAB detectives his back. The body was covered by a sheet. Esposito put on gloves, giving the wrist a loud snap on each; he raised his hands and limbered his fingers, as if an orchestra awaited his signal. He gave a curt bow to the ME. "Pleased to meet you, Doctor. Detective Esposito."

"Likewise, Detective. Is this your case?"

"No, it's my partner's, Detective Meehan. Doctor . . ."

"Pryor. Pleased to meet you."

"Dr. Pryor, Detective Meehan. I'm merely consulting in this matter. Shall we proceed?"

Esposito put his hands together and cracked his knuckles. Dr. Pryor raised her eyebrows and looked back and forth between them; Nick was not inclined to give anything away. He shrugged, and she picked up her scalpel. Esposito never looked at the table, never took his eyes off the doctor; his repulsion and attraction were dueling and profound. A glance in the wrong direction, and his breakfast would erupt from him like a geyser, over the living and the dead. Dr. Pryor seemed almost amused. She had work to do, and even if Esposito was being ridiculous, he was not getting in the way.

"What do you think of this, Detective?" she asked demurely.

Esposito refused to lower his glance and declaimed, "Ah, typical . . . liver specimen . . . touch of fever, maybe." His voice dropped to a more intimate timbre. "Are your eyes green or brown? Do they change in the light?"

Dr. Pryor smiled, though it was hard to tell whether it was because of the compliment, or the fact that it was not the liver but an elbow to which she had directed his attention. Nick had never been to an autopsy so rife with sexual tension, and hoped he never would again. He put it out of his mind once the doctor cut the Y incision into the chest of the Mexican girl, who seemed smaller now, dark and pale in marked zones, where the blood had settled. Dr. Pryor didn't look up when she asked questions, and Nick didn't look up when he answered. The Mexican woman seemed so much younger than she had in the park, in the night and the rain. There were bruises on her arms and legs.

Behind them, another assistant sawed through the breastbone of the other body, cracking open the rib cage. Gloppy handfuls of organs— liver, heart—were lifted out and weighed, and blood samples were scooped up from the abdominal cavity with a stainless steel ladle. The IA crew clustered still tighter. When Nick turned around, he could smell that the other assistant had moved on to the bowel.

Dr. Pryor continued to cut. "So, what's the story?" she asked.

"Weird one. Hung herself in a tree, with yarn."

"Any note?"

"No."

"Background?"

"What you see is what you get. No ID. Mexican, I guess. Ever see this kind of suicide before?"

"No."

She kept on cutting, and Esposito averted his gaze as high as he could. Dr. Pryor laid the scalpel down, and traced her hands down the lifeless arm, tenderly, it seemed.

"Look at this poor girl. She went through a lot. Took a few lumps. Somebody beat her up, not just once. The bruises look older, and there's no broken bones in the X-ray. No defensive wounds, no skin under the nails. We'll clip them, but they looked clean. The ligature, it's classic, suspended vertically. There's violence here, probably domestic violence, but I bet nothing on record. Nobody beat her to death. It's more like she quit fighting. It's a suicide. Just because I've never seen it before doesn't mean anything. I don't know of any documented history of yarn-related suicidal asphyxia, but I bet there's not much yarn-related homicidal asphyxia, either. On her jeans, on the inside of her knees, there's dirt, decayed vegetable matter from the bark, like she humped her way up the tree. Shoes, too—the soles and insteps. And on her hands, the same stuff. Nothing's final until the toxicology comes back, but I don't think there's anything for you guys here."

Esposito stared with determination at the ceiling as he announced, "Doctor! I concur!"

Dr. Pryor either coughed or laughed, turning quickly away, but when she faced Nick again there was no trace of a smile. He was caught up by the hand closer to him, the pale band of flesh where the ring had been, and the smudged abrasions on the fingertips, as the doctor had pointed out; the color of the palm was muddled, bricky purples and browns. There were marks there, black script, that had nothing to do with the patchy lividity. He tried to make it out, the bad handwriting on the bad hand: *E-S-P-E-R-? N?*

"Doc, have a look at this."

She came around to the other side, and lifted the wrist. It was loose, long past rigor mortis. Esposito stepped aside, quickly. The letters were legible, and she called for an assistant to come over. The back of the hand was laid flat on the table, as the assistant put a four-inch ruler on the fingers to show the scale, snapping pictures from several angles. Dr. Pryor leaned in to study the hand, and Esposito inclined his head delicately, so he could see Nick and not the cadaver, and winked. Nick heard the whine of the saw again and turned around. They had cut through the skull of the other body and popped it off like a bottle cap; the face was peeled down like a rubber mask. The corner foursome packed in still tighter—they could have fit into a phone booth now—and it was hard for Nick not to give the high sign for Esposito to look at them.

Dr. Pryor was nose-close to the hand. Nick told her what he thought. "Doctor? Do you speak Spanish? I think it says 'esperan,' and I don't know what that means. 'Esperar' is 'to hope.' It seems like the last thing you'd say in a suicide note, talking about hope, but maybe she hopes for better in the next life, hopes her family understands, that kind of thing."

"Mmm."

"Huh?"

"No, that's good, that's interesting," said the doctor, laying the hand back down, gently, as she straightened up. She spoke quietly, for only her detectives to hear, as if she had an inkling there were two dramas taking place. "But I do speak Spanish, and that's not what it says."

"Oh?"

"It doesn't say 'esperar,' or 'esperan.' It says 'aspirina.'"

"What does that mean?"

"'Aspirin.' Underneath, you can almost make out the word for 'tampons.' I think it's a shopping list."

"Oh."

No hope, only a headache. Nick knew the feeling, but he was chagrined that his insight had proved a false start.

"If you have other things you have to do, I can handle it from here. Detective? Detectives? I'll give you a call if there's any other questions."

"Doctor, I do have one last question."

"Yes . . . Detective Esposito?"

"Is that paper cup on the counter there full of water, or . . . yucky stuff?"

"Water. Yucky stuff is not kept in paper cups."

"Thank you, Doctor. Detective? Shall we go?"

"Yes, Detective. Thank you, Doctor."

"Thank you both."

"The pleasure has been mine," Esposito said.

As they walked out, Esposito snatched up the paper cup. The brain had been lifted from the second body, and after the other pathologist gave it a few earnest glances, it was plopped without ceremony onto the hanging scale. Nick didn't think any of the IA people were mindful of the direction from which the splash came, as Esposito tossed the water at them. There was a gagging sound from one, then another, and there may have been a third, but Nick did not wait to see how many of his colleagues Esposito had taken down.

SIX

When the Brooklyn Bridge loomed up, they left the highway again for downtown, passing the squat cube of police headquarters to cut behind the court building. Esposito parked the car next to a fire hydrant, and they stepped up to a nondescript steel door on the side of the court. They were buzzed into the cages where they had dropped off Malcolm Cole the night before. Central Booking had always had its own brand of air, sometimes stronger and sometimes milder but always the same blend of resentment and despair and days-old underwear funk. It smelled better when they let the prisoners smoke. The light was oily and yellow, somehow congealed but weak, as if it came out of a can. Nick looked around at the cops and was reminded that this was a place where it was not possible to look forward to work. They would search prisoners and subdue them when necessary, shuffling the paperwork for the hours or days before the defendants were brought upstairs to see the judge, where a new round of chances awaited them. For a cop, it was like being the attendant of a broken elevator, forever getting stuck between floors. Someone had scrawled on the wall, "Thank you for not caring!" The sergeant behind the desk didn't look up when they approached. "What's up, Sarge?" Esposito asked.

The sergeant continued to cross-check lists of names. "Prisoner?"

"Malcolm Cole."

"Tier three. Purpose?"

"We need to take him out for lineups."

That wasn't true, Nick knew, and it troubled him briefly to consider that if Esposito ever lied to him, he was unlikely to catch him in it.

"ID?"

Esposito produced his ID card, which the sergeant did not pretend to examine, and they left. Esposito gave Nick his gun to hold, and he walked to the back, past the first holding cells. Plastic crates held sweating half-pint cartons of skim milk and stacks of tongue-pink baloney sandwiches on industrial white bread, packed in wax paper. Most of the perps had settled in, had found a spot where they could sit and wait in a half-daze, metabolic rates winding down to the lowest setting—breathe and fart. "Ooohh . . . Yo!" "Sorry . . ." "Yo! That's not funny, that's nasty!" "Sorry, yo, can't help it." A few others waited by the bars, alert, ready to argue, ready for anything, anyone, for a sympathetic judge that might happen by, a radical minister, for a drunken workman to drop a steel file; they reminded Nick of the liveliest puppies in the pet store window, desperate to be noticed, to be the first to go home. It didn't work that way here.

One called out to Esposito as he passed the cell, "Yo, you a lawyer?"

Esposito didn't stop, but held up his cuffs, giving them a jingle.

"Damn!"

As Esposito and Malcolm returned from the passage a few minutes later, the same voice called out, joined by a few others. "Be strong!"

"Be cool!"

"Don't say nothin'!"

Good advice, all in all, late as it was. Malcolm had made his statement hours before, on video, at the precinct. Three minutes with a tech guy who was text-messaging during the confession and a DA with a bad head cold, sneezing through the monosyllables of how Malcolm had shot Babenco and why. "Anything further you'd like to add?"

"I'm sorry, I guess."

Now the door buzzed again and they stepped out into the city air, and you could catch hints of ocean and hot dogs, freedom and home. Nick had been inside for less than ten minutes, and the wind on his face felt like a governor's reprieve; for Malcolm, he couldn't guess how it felt. Malcolm looked both more tired and better rested than when they'd left him last. He stretched his lanky frame and unkinked his neck. His eyes scanned the street, wary and wistful, and he stood still for a moment, before he looked at the detectives and smiled.

"This feels nice. Even a day like today, thank God. You know?"

Nick was impressed. He remembered the day after his own mother had died; his prayers had not been ones of gratitude. And he had not spent the night before on a cell bench. Was it a gift, to be able to switch like that, from here to there, from now to the next thing? Esposito had other concerns. "Yo, Malcolm, you got some serious jail breath! We gotta get you some mouthwash or something, man. You're taking the curl outta my hair."

"Let's do it. Believe me, I know."

They got into the car and headed uptown, snaking through the Chinatown streets. Nick sat in the back, behind Esposito and beside Malcolm. Esposito rolled up onto the sidewalk and stepped out, the keys still in the engine. He ducked into one store, then another, returning with arms laden with bags. He tossed them onto the passenger seat and headed back into the street, demanding a place in traffic with a long blare on the horn. Malcolm seemed intrigued by the sudden stop, seemed taken by the fraternal tone, as Esposito had intended.

"That's the problem with Chinatown. I could tell the best stories, tell the best lies, say why I need a discount, government discount—it's for an orphan, it's an emergency—and they don't understand a thing I say. Plus, there's no time . . ."

They cut onto Canal Street, with the markets and stores full of alien fruits and vegetables, barrels on the sidewalk with live carp, turtle, and eel, the windows crowded with ducks hung upside down. Esposito shook his head.

"How am I gonna explain I need an emergency government discount for mouthwash to people who eat eel heads for lunch?"

Malcolm snorted with laughter. "Dogs and cats, man! They eat dogs and cats!"

"You know what I'm sayin'!"

There was a kind of beauty to the moment, the bond of prejudice, and Nick nodded along. Inside the store, Esposito had probably told the Chinese merchant he needed free deodorant to get a black murderer out of the neighborhood.

"I couldn't even get into it, showing the guy the shield and telling the story, whatever story, without him thinking I was just some cop shaking him down for free underwear."

"You got me underwear?"

"C'mon, man. I told you I'd look out for you."

"I appreciate that, I do."

"Anyway, there's no way this guy's gonna take this the right way, and there's no way I can explain, and he can't understand me, and I don't got time."

"So you didn't say you was a cop?"

"Detective, Malcolm. I said I was a detective. And of course I did. I took what I needed, threw down what I figured was the right amount of money, and walked out. I ain't a thief, but I ain't stupid, either. I work with people, I really do, and the hell with 'em if they don't realize it at the time."

Malcolm nodded, and so did Nick. There was a logic to it, and cops heard it every day, usually from the other side of the cell bars. Nick didn't fully appreciate Esposito's notion of his own privileges, and Nick wasn't sure if he'd agree when he did. A lot of it was for show. All of it was. The hours down here were pure gesture, a display. But Esposito was not the kind of performer who relied much on research. He made the left, rolling up to First Avenue. It wasn't the fastest way to Harlem. Nick guessed that there might be a deviation from the plan, an improvised detour, but he was not in on it; he didn't like that, either, but there was nothing to be done. He didn't force any small talk. Esposito knew how much they could try to build trust without hitting false notes, that this was fun, and they were friends.

Nick leaned forward to take the bags from the passenger seat, showing them to Malcolm as he opened them for inspection. Nick only looked at the price tags—ten dollars, ten again, then a half-dozen dollar items. Thirty dollars, at most. They pulled over suddenly, rubbing right up against the curb. Nick tensed a moment, looking at Malcolm, then Esposito, then at what had drawn Esposito's attention—a woman, striding down the sidewalk like it was a runway, in a short skirt, tall boots, and a loose, light coat that flowed behind her. She had a Somali look—long, lean, and elegant, with light-brown skin and a tangle of black hair held back in a yellow band. Esposito leaned out the window.

"Excuse me, miss? Police. Can I talk to you a minute?"

She paused, hesitant. She wore sunglasses, which made it hard to read her, whether she was suspicious or merely surprised.

"Police. C'mere a sec. I just want to show you a picture."

Holding up his shield, he leaned over to the passenger seat and fished a random mug shot from the glove compartment. The woman approached slowly at first, before her curiosity got the better of her. She leaned over to the car and looked at the photo intently.

"What did he do?"

"Have you seen him?"

"I think . . . in the area. Is he dangerous?"

"Very."

"Should I be careful?"

"Somebody like you should always be."

A smile broke on her face and she laughed, tossing back her glossy tumble of hair. Malcolm and Nick both leaned forward, to see her better.

"I should be careful of you, especially."

Esposito took a card from his jacket and handed it to her.

"If you see any bad guys out there, or if you'd like to meet some, call me."

She held up the card for a second, reading it, then waving it like a fan. For a moment, it looked like she might throw it away, but then she slipped it into her pocket. She touched his shoulder and then glanced into the backseat, waving before walking away. Esposito gently put the car back into drive, casting a few backward looks out the window.

Malcolm laughed, impressed. "Man, you beastin'!"

"You like that, huh?"

"Not bad," said Malcolm, appraising. "Too skinny."

"You're out of your mind."

"No, I ain't—what's it, what they say? 'Meat for the man, bone for the dog.' "

"You're crazy," said Esposito, looking at her dwindling image in the rearview mirror. "She was perfect."

Nick thought so, too, but Esposito never saw a woman who wasn't beautiful, or ate a meal that wasn't exactly what he wanted. Enthusiasm, which once was considered a disease; still was, sometimes. Animal and tactical, for Esposito to think of women, to make Malcolm think of them, remind him of outside. They settled back into traffic. Nick considered the word, the verb, "to beast"—a little monstrous, all natural. It fit. As they drove, Nick looked ahead, so he could keep an eye on Malcolm without staring at him.

Nick's phone rang, but the call was from a blocked number. Allison, from her office, or Internal Affairs. He didn't want to talk to either, and he resented how they had become associated, the overlap of fraying claims on him. He waited to see if a message was left, but there was none. Maybe a wrong number. He fretted over it until he heard Esposito, with his own cellphone to his ear.

"Hey. It's me. . . . Yeah, you know . . . Right. . . . Well, when you're right, you're right. . . . Right. . . . So, anyway, I need a favor. Government emergency, police emergency. It's for an orphan, believe me. . . . You wouldn't believe me if I told you. Just trust me, I need you, I need this. There's nobody else I can call. . . . Yeah? Beautiful! Five minutes."

He clicked the phone shut on his chin and tossed it onto the seat. He glanced backward, gladness in his face, even as he gunned the engine, sending them shooting up the street.

"This is gonna work out all around."

The brick towers of Stuyvesant Town cropped up, and Esposito parked the car and took off his jacket. When Malcolm got out, Esposito threw his jacket around Malcolm's shoulders, so his rear-cuffed hands wouldn't be obvious, then pulled his shield from his belt and stuck it into his pants pocket. Nick picked up the bags, and the detectives walked on either side of Malcolm, close in, swaying a little, as if they were three jolly executives coming home from a multiple-martini lunch. Esposito guided them to one of the buildings, and caught the lobby door as an old woman left, frowning at their overindulgence. He caught the drift and played it up, staggering, keeping close enough to Malcolm so that she could not see the gun on his hip, holding Malcolm's cuffs so he could not reach for the gun.

"Shank you, ma'am!"

They stayed close inside the lobby, waiting for an empty elevator. It looked like the projects, but it wasn't. Esposito pressed the button for the tenth floor. Malcolm and Nick both looked at him, differently confused. He declined to enlighten them until they reached their stop.

"I got a friend here. Like I said, it works out all around."

At the end of the hall, he rang a doorbell. A woman answered, olive-skinned and dark-haired, in a T-shirt and jeans. She smiled but waited at the doorstep for a moment, unsure whether to let her curiosity get the better of her. Esposito scooped her up in a hug, lifting her and twirling her around.

"Baby! So good to see you! I can't tell you how good! You look great. I ain't kiddin'! You did me a big, big favor, lemme tell you. Wait, I will—this is Nick and Malcolm. And this is Donna, guys."

"Hey, Donna."

Nick shook her hand and Malcolm nodded, having no hands to offer. She held the door for them, and they walked in. Esposito led the other two to the bathroom, plainly familiar with the route. He took the shopping bags and set toiletries in the sink, a dress shirt, pants, socks, and underwear on the toilet. He stood close to Malcolm, smiling and putting a hand on his shoulder.

"Here you go. You're all set. I forgot shoes, but I didn't know your size, and what you got looks okay anyway. So clean up, we'll get goin'. I'm gonna uncuff you and give you privacy. I think we respect each other, we got something working here, but, hey—let's be real. I don't think I gotta remind you, we're on the tenth floor, no fire escape. We're working on a handshake. Both of us can back out, take the other road. We understand each other?"

"Yeah. You been cool."

"Good. Now go ahead in. We'll be right here if you need something."

Esposito uncuffed Malcolm, who went into the bathroom and shut the door. Esposito turned to Nick as he headed back down the hall to another room in the apartment.

"You wanna wait here? Knock on the bathroom door in ten minutes if he's not done. Hell, I feel good. Matter of fact, make it twelve. . . . Believe me, Nick, it's all good."

He turned the corner and disappeared. Nick checked his watch, to make sure ten minutes would be the most either of them got. "Believe me, Nick . . ." Nick wanted to, he was working on it. New York was for believers, he knew, and he opened the hallway doors—closet on the left, bedroom on the right, with a narrow view of the water, the harbor flooding up beneath the bridges. Downtown, the old island, the lowest tip settled first, by the Battery. On the Feast of the Epiphany, Greek boys dove into the harbor to retrieve a golden cross flung into the waters; on Rosh Hashanah, Hasidim gathered by the shore in their beards and black hats for *tashlich,* a prayer of atonement, and cast their sins into the river with crumbs of bread. It was an island littered with enchantments, the buildings freaks of steel that made you agnostic about gravity, the people a wandering carnival, all of it lit like a forest of Christmas trees. He checked his watch again—a little more than five minutes left. He didn't have an on-duty sexual authorization form with him.

The toilet flushed, and the shower went on inside the bathroom. Four and a half minutes. Nick made a note to himself. Next time, he gets the girl, Esposito guards the bathroom. Nick imagined what would happen if he did this to Allison, stopping by with a perp, five minutes' warning. A visit like that would have ended the marriage right there. Or not. It would have given them something to talk about, decades from now. Would he tell her about this at dinner? Would he tell her friends? Work and weather, that's what he'd talk about. Maybe just the weather. This was not the kind of story he could tell in public, and, even with Allison, it could easily come across wrong. Too much time had passed for them, or not enough. The thought of him and Allison, old together and laughing, made Nick forget his watch. The shower went off, and Malcolm was out shortly, in a crisp white polyester shirt and black pants that made him look like a waiter.

Esposito appeared, straightening his tie, recently dressed as well.

"You look sharp," Esposito said to Malcolm.

"C'mon."

"All right. You do look better, though. Let's get going."

"Do you gotta cuff me again?"

"Yeah, for now."

Donna called out her goodbye, unseen in another room, as they headed back to the car, in the same drunken musketeer formation. The histrionics were less, because they cared less about being noticed, and the destination loomed closer. There was little conversation as they headed through midtown, the Upper East Side, toward Harlem. The Northwest Passage, Mannahatta version. The streets were less packed here, but the people seemed to move more slowly; in midtown, downtown, no one stood still. Here, they stood on corners, in front of bodegas and project lobbies, as if assigned to their spots. Nick glanced over to Malcolm and saw how he watched the streets as they did; he was a stranger here, too. There were no familiar faces for him; he was an immigrant, a tourist, though he was a black man born here, sixty blocks up. He leaned up against Esposito's seat.

"You know where we're goin'?"

"Yeah, I got it."

One-two-five, 125th Street, was the hypertensive heart of Harlem—

fat, fast, and ready to pop. With its new superstores and theaters, its traffic and lights, its shoppers, strutters, and ranters, it was like a jukebox playing every song at once. A single turn and a few blocks uptown, and they were in a 1970s ghetto, with boarded-up buildings and empty storefronts. Another turn, a few blocks more, and there were rows of old brownstones with flower boxes in the windows, maple-shaded sidewalks swept twice a day, beside which you could imagine the clip-clop of carriage horses. The world changed so much with each corner, it was like switching channels. Harlem: hell-bent and bound for glory, minding its own business and moving on. They rolled up to a funeral home and parked the car.

Esposito spotted a side door and rang the bell. A young man in a dark blue suit opened the door, his mortician's poise momentarily broken by the unlikely sight. Now that Malcolm was cleaned up, the detectives could have been mistaken for his bodyguards instead of his captors.

"We're here for the Coles—Miz Cole and Milton."

"I'm sorry, but I believe her viewing is scheduled for tomorrow."

"We're here for a private viewing. I'm Detective Esposito, and this is Malcolm Cole. I called early this morning. I spoke with Mr. Pendleton."

It occurred to Nick that the side trip to Stuyvesant Town had been necessary to waste an hour, as much as it had been for sex or showers. Things did have a way of working out for Esposito, or maybe he had a knack for taking advantage of them. The young man appeared to appreciate the situation and nodded, opening the door.

"I see. Come in, and let me find out what arrangements have been made."

Inside, they waited as the man disappeared into an office down the hall. When he returned, he led them in the opposite direction down the corridor to a modest room, and ushered them inside.

"The public viewing will be in a larger venue," he said, an apologetic note in his voice. The room was a mix of the once-deluxe and the office functional, red velvet and black leather below, fluorescent lights and acoustic tile above. "I could show it to you, if you have time."

"That's all right," said Esposito. "We appreciate it."

The man shut the door as he left. Esposito took the cuffs off Malcolm. Nick scanned the room to make sure there were no other exits, and then stepped back, leaving Malcolm to say his goodbyes.

There were two coffins, both dark wood, one half-open, which showed Miz Cole in a bright patterned dress of blue and yellow checks. Her hands were clasped piously, resting high on the breast, and here the pose seemed real, seemed right, and not model number three from the undertaker's handbook. A poster of Milton was set on an easel beside his closed coffin, a blowup of a school photo. Malcolm stood, his head hanging down. A minute passed, and another, and Nick heard him mutter something, maybe a prayer. He seemed to have little to say, but he was unwilling to go. Nick turned away, and his eyes came upon a large gilt-framed *Last Supper* on the wall. Who painted that, Leonardo da Vinci? Nick looked closer, scanning the faces, the twelve around the one. When he painted it, did his Jesus have such a big Afro? Did the prophet not say, *Yea, shall ye not know him, by his funkadelic halo of hair?*

It was a kind of disease, Nick thought, the sudden laughter that overtook him sometimes. The susceptibility struck him after long exhaustion, like the flu, and when you looked back after a good night's sleep at what had been so hysterical, it was as funny as a foreign cartoon. *I guess . . . I get it.* Nick had seen black Christs before, and though they had seemed odd at first, he realized they were no more fantastic than blond ones. This should have been no different, really. Really. Jesus at the center, surrounded by . . . his point guards and power forwards. Nick coughed to cover up the laugh that seized him like a hiccup, and then he lowered his head, as Malcolm and Esposito turned to look. Nick rubbed his brow. Esposito moved in, picking up a folding chair and setting it beside the coffin.

"All right, Malcolm. If you wanna sit for a while, we wanna pay our respects, too."

Malcolm took the chair, and the detectives knelt at the rail, heads bowed, and Nick didn't look over at Esposito, even though he knew Esposito was sneaking a peek at him. Nick had almost been caught, and he knew he would be, unless he played it straight all the way to the end. The words of the Hail Mary and the Our Father escaped him, scrambled like puzzle pieces dumped from the box. He counted backward from fifty, slowly, eyes shut tight. Malcolm might have taken the larger view and decided that they had not killed his mother. Still, there really was no good way to get around the sight of a cop laughing at his mother's corpse.

Yes, there was. Nick stood and rose, looked over the body, and shook his head. Nick went over to Malcolm and rested a hand on his shoulder, letting him see the redness in his eyes.

"Sorry, Malcolm. My mother died, too. I have a tough time with this."

Malcolm looked up, seemingly touched. "S'arright."

Nick took a deep breath and walked to the back. Esposito got up and stood beside him, but Nick avoided eye contact. Malcolm walked over to the coffin. He leaned in and kissed his mother on the cheek. Whatever his regrets were, he seemed to leave them there as he turned around and approached the detectives, offering his hands to be re-cuffed.

"All right, then. Let's do it."

SEVEN

That was the deal—a chance to say goodbye, in exchange for a confession. Malcolm hadn't known that the sole witness to the murder, the grocery clerk, had been hesitant with the identification, and had since returned to Yemen. Maybe he would have come back, and maybe he'd have been willing to look at a lineup, and maybe he would have picked him out; otherwise, Malcolm Cole had no idea how close he had been to freedom. And yet it wasn't freedom, never would be, as long as he was on the run. Every knock at the door made the hair on your neck stand up; every tap on your shoulder felt like a hand at your throat. Malcolm was here to settle his accounts and move on. He was going to break his life in half like a wishbone, and hope the bigger part was not behind him.

The ride downtown was somber. Malcolm looked out the window, his face brushing occasionally on the glass. The detectives did not want to disturb him. When they arrived back at Central Booking, Esposito parked the car and led Malcolm out from the back like a chauffeur. Before they went back into the jail, with its skim milk and baloney sandwiches, its denials and excuses and indigestion, Malcolm looked over at Esposito, tipping up his chin—*Wait.* He had what Nick first thought was a plaintive look, but it began to shift—or Nick did—even before Malcolm spoke. It was weary but didn't ask for pity or anything else. Malcolm was slightly taller than Esposito, and looking down to him, he spoke without ego and from strength.

"This worked out with us, today. I did what I needed to do, said what you needed me to say. What's done is done. I'm gonna pay and move on. Where we go from here, I don't know—but this don't got to be over, between us. I know a lot. I know about a lot more than just the thing I did, a lot worse. I wanna help myself. You interested?"

"Oh, yeah."

"How do I get ahold of you?"

Esposito stuck a card into Malcolm's pocket.

"You call me. You need to sleep, to clear your head. If we're gonna do this, you gotta be all in. Don't even answer me now. Tell me tomorrow, the next day."

"Answer's not gonna change. Everything else got to."

"I believe you," said Esposito, as he took hold of Malcolm's shoulder. "Tell me about Milton. Who killed your brother? Did someone want to kill him, or did they think it was you?"

"If they thought it was me, it was Babenco's cousin Kiko. If they knew it was my brother, it was Kiko. If they didn't care, it was Kiko. You follow me? It was Kiko."

Esposito couldn't shake Malcolm's hand just then, but he did as soon as he uncuffed him inside, before leading him down to the cells. The detectives headed back uptown.

Traffic was heavy and conversation was brief until the road cleared above the bridge, when Esposito stepped on the gas. He seemed to open up with the engine.

"That was great. It went perfect! The video, he gave up everything! His clothes. Didja see the look on him when I gave him the clothes? It was like he was meeting Santa Claus. And that girl, Donna—was she hot, or what? I hadn't seen her in years. I can't believe I still had her number, and she was game, ready to go. And, and—wait a second, what was up with you? In the funeral home, when you made it look like you broke down? You cracked up, didn't you? What was it that was so funny you almost laughed my homicide—two cases, two homicides—straight down the toilet?"

Nick started to laugh again, at the memory and in relief.

"There was a picture there, a painting of Jesus and the apostles. Everybody was black in it. It looked like an old commercial for something, an ad for menthol cigarettes. It just hit me."

"Well, it was a nice save. The thing about your mother—is it true?"

Nick had to think for a moment. "Yeah, it is true. She died when I was a kid."

"Sorry. . . . Like I said, it was a nice save."

Esposito looked over to him with an appreciative eye—a man who would take advantage of his own mother's death to salvage an interrogation was clearly someone he could work with. Nick didn't think of it that way. He was neither as bad as that nor as good—and the gambit had failed as solidly the night before, with Michael, as it had succeeded with Malcolm. For Malcolm it had been a poignant gesture; for the other, an appalling presumption. Who knew how these things would go over? Still, if he couldn't cry on cue, he could think on his feet, and he was glad for the compliment. He and Esposito were still in the testing phase.

"Hey, let me cover half of Malcolm's stuff, the underwear and toothbrush and whatever. What did you pay?"

"Don't worry about it. Buy me a beer next time."

"What was it?"

"Forty bucks. The guy made some noise about it, but I didn't understand him, and I didn't have time."

"He might have been trying to tell you it only cost thirty."

Esposito laughed. "See? I told you it worked out, all around."

At the precinct, they went to their desks. Esposito was eager to begin work on the next thing—Kiko—and Nick was anxious to finish up the last, yesterday's suicide. The fingerprints had not matched anyone in the database, as expected, so she was still a missing/unidentified person. The case would be reassigned to Missing Persons in a week if he couldn't find a family member to notify, and she would be buried—physically in Potter's Field, on Hart Island in the Bronx, statistically in a folder downtown. Nick had tasted of both fates, and he didn't care for them. He took her to be Central American and illegal, someone who had slipped over the border or had missed a flight home, looking for work and finding it by the end of the day. She would not have gotten in trouble, at least not with cops, though she was no stranger to misfortune. Beyond those loose ideas, Nick had two phone numbers. Nick called the first—disconnected. The second was a beeper, and he punched in his number for the return call. When his phone rang, he snatched it up.

"*Sí?*"

"*Sí?*"

"You speak English?"

"*Un poco . . .*"

"*Soy policía, soy detectivo, es muy importante que tu a la precincto immedi-amente venir*. Understand? You gotta come to the precinct. You talk to me, *a hablar con mijo*, right away. *Tu nombre?* Your name?"

There was a pause on the other end. Nick's Spanish was poor, and he didn't know for whose benefit he repeated himself, in simultaneous pid-gin. He wanted to make the other man feel uncomfortable trying to speak English, wanted to make him work at understanding, but the mes-sage had to be clear. Nick didn't want to threaten him, whoever he was, but he had to let the situation seem threatening to him, to impress that his involvement couldn't be sidestepped. That kind of blame-spreading was one of the primary skills of a cop, to make one person's problems be-long to someone else, to as many people as possible. *Mi casa es su casa*, and my problems are yours.

"*Mi nombre es Jose.*"

"*Jose qué?* Last name, papi, *también*."

"Jose Rodriguez."

"Okay, Señor Rodriguez, you come now?"

"No, no, *trabajando*. Maybe tomorrow."

"No, not tomorrow. Now. How do you work, what kind—*qué tipo tra-bajar?*"

"Taxi."

"Good. Taxi up here, drive up here, now. Five minutes."

"No, I in Bronx. Fifteen minutes, I go there."

"Good."

Nick didn't necessarily believe that Jose Rodriguez had found his inner citizen, but he believed he'd show up. Nick took out the Polaroids of the woman in the park and laid them across the desk. Her black hair blended with the black night, and the flash had given the skin a bluish tint, a cool, almost underwater pallor, so that her face looked like a mask. There is something deforming about the official camera, for passport, li-cense, or yearbook, that makes people go stiff and flat. Most mug shots are more natural; hostility and fear photograph better than a fake smile. The woman looked better than Nick remembered, less afflicted than she had seemed in the tree, less pitiful than she had seemed in the morgue. If only the same lying kindness that the camera had shown had found her before yesterday.

When the cabdriver came, Nick put him in the interview room and pointed to a seat. He was young and looked Mexican, like the woman, which was good. He seemed nervous, and Nick encouraged it, leaving the room briefly—"*Momento, señor.*"—closing the door and sliding the bolt shut with an audible click. Nick went around to the side to have another look at him through the one-way mirror. The man's left leg jackhammered under the table, and his fingers twisted and untwisted into cat's cradles. These little lab rat experiments said so little. Rodriguez was afraid because he was her lover who had left her; because he was illegal; because he had speeding tickets, a bloody machete under the driver's seat from the last guy who'd tried to rob him; because he was a decent and hardworking man who had never even spoken with the cops before. You watched what he did, wondering what it meant; the only true proof of guilt was sleep. If he had killed someone, he'd have been slumped over, snoring, as Malcolm had the night before, in any two-minute break. A nightmare to be caught, but also a relief; fear had held the body rigid for so long that when it passed, it was like the bones turned to butter. Then again, if Jose Rodriguez had anything heavy on his conscience, he wouldn't have come. Nick went back in and set the pictures on the table. Rodriguez glanced at them and looked up, offering dim and pointless observations.

"A lady?"

"Yes, a lady."

"She dead?"

"Yes, she dead."

"Who?"

"You tell me."

Nick let the silence weigh on him. Rodriguez's eyes were on Nick, not the pictures, and Nick tapped on the table to return his attention to them.

"Oh, I don' know. . . ."

"Yes, you do. Look again. I'll give you time to think, to remember."

Nick abruptly stood up and walked out. The door shut and the bolt locked with a bit more force. Esposito looked up from his desk.

"Does he know her?"

"Beats me. He's playing dumb, though, so he gets the dummy treatment."

"You want me to talk to him?"

"Why? Your Spanish is worse than mine."

"Yeah, but I'm fluent in Stupid."

"Fine. Let's get some coffee first."

Nick followed Esposito into the meal room. Esposito rummaged through the drawer below the coffeemaker: ketchup packets, duck sauce, hot sauce, salt and pepper, but no sugar. The coffee club had been run by an elderly and meticulous detective named Gerhard who had taken great pride in it. Every morning, there had been bagels and rolls, and on Sundays, fresh Italian pastry from Arthur Avenue. Since his recent retirement, three successors had quit amid constant insults to their efforts; as a result, the position was vacant, and the squad had degenerated into barbarism, sneaking and pilfering private pints of milk. Esposito unstuck a sugar packet from between two mustards, muttering in disgust.

"If Gerhard could see this, he'd be rolling in his grave."

"Is he dead?"

"Beats me. As far as the coffee club goes, he might as well be. Do you want to do it?"

"God, no. Somebody should, though."

"Yeah."

Esposito took a carton of milk out of the refrigerator furtively, casting a glance out across the squad room, and poured the last of it into their cups. They drank them quickly.

"How's the hunt for Kiko?"

"I got him. Name's Babenco, too, might even be a real cousin. He's got a couple of collars, drugs, a gun. He beat a shooting last year, on Amsterdam. I remember it. He shot a bum in the foot. Uncooperative. He shouldn't be too hard to find. Wanna go out now?"

Nick could see that Esposito was impatient, anxious to move. Nick wasn't. If they caught up with Kiko tonight, it would be another twenty-four hours before they were done, straight through, at a minimum. Nick knew he had something to do tonight; it escaped him at the moment, but it would come. And he wanted to finish up the case at hand. Esposito took all of it in with a look, and resigned himself to respite. "All right. We'll get going on that tomorrow. Now's not good anyway. He's probably out and about. Let's finish up with your guy there."

Rodriguez was hunched over the pictures, twitching, and didn't look up when the detectives walked in. That was good; it meant that he was concentrating.

"Okay, Jose. Who is she?"

"The lady . . . maybe I drive her?"

Rodriguez shrugged and looked at them weakly. Esposito leaned in to face him, elbows on the table, gathering himself. He repeated the response slowly, as if it were unbelievable, offensive, painful to speak. "The lady. Maybe I drive her." This is how he would spend the energy that would have gone into chasing Kiko. They tag-teamed, hitting Rodriguez with questions before he could think.

"Not good enough. What do you mean, you drove her?"

"She had your number. Your personal number, not your cab company."

"I don't got cab company. . . . I got me. I drive Mexican people. They call me, I drive them."

"Let me see your livery license."

He gave them a fearful look.

"Let me see your driver's license."

His eyes widened further, and he began to fish through his pockets.

"I no got it with me. . . . My name, Jose Rodriguez. You check on computer. I got license."

Esposito grabbed his arm and gripped it tightly. " 'You check on computer. I got license.' Guy! Listen to me! I can play dumb with the best of them, but you're reachin' here! You're pushin' it! This is box-of-rocks dumb. This is Forrest Gump dumb. This is Polish-joke dumb. And I don't like Polish jokes! My partner here is Polish. On his behalf, I find them offensive! You know how many Polacks it takes to screw in a lightbulb? 'I don't know, I'm a Polack!' What are jokes? What are numbers? Who am I? Am I talking now? I'm so dumb, I don't know! That's what you're doing now, Jose Rodriguez! You gotta tell me who she is, or where she's from, or where she works, or lives, or I'm so stupid I might try to call my wife and get Immigration instead! I might try to throw you across the room and miss! You'd land clear out of the country, in Mexico!"

Jose Rodriguez shrunk back in his seat and blinked. Nick, too, was startled by the force of it, was disquieted by the genuine aggression that had inspired the cockeyed harangue. He doubted Rodriguez understood one word out of ten, but one of those words had to be "Immigration." Still, it seemed to work. When he sat up straight again, his memory had been refreshed. "Okay . . . maybe . . . maybe, I think, I think I know where I see her before."

"Fine, good, let's go," said Esposito, cheerful again. He had sent out his bad mood to do good work. Nick wished he could master the same trick.

"You . . . drive me?"

"The hell with that. Drive yourself. We'll follow. I ain't the driving police. I don't care if you're running a submarine service up and down the river."

Esposito stood up and extended a hand, indicating the way out. Nick scooped up the photos and pocketed them. Outside, Rodriguez headed tentatively to a beat-up old Lincoln and waited for the detectives to get into their car. Esposito kept his eyes on him as he started the engine. He asked Nick, "How much do you think he understood?"

"Bits and pieces. Enough, I guess."

"Yeah. Hey, you're not Polish, are you?"

"I have my moments."

"Don't we all. See, Nick? I told you I was fluent in Stupid."

"We all have our moments."

Rodriguez pulled out cautiously, and drove south on Broadway at a geriatric pace. His brake lights were off only for seconds at a time. Nick took the license plate down, as if it might have mattered; the car wouldn't be his. Nick had to remind himself that he was not investigating any crime. The case was a tragedy, nothing else. There were facts he had to find out, but if he didn't find them, the only difference would be that she'd be buried in Potter's Field instead of some dusty corner of Mexico. Still, Nick felt his duty to the dead, a notion as old as the fear of fire. He had been bound to her when he'd knocked her down. When Rodriguez made a right on 181st Street and pulled over at a store, they parked behind him. Nick walked up beside the driver's window. Rodriguez gestured to a florist shop, the gates half-down over the windows, covering a climbing bank of yellow roses, white lilies.

"Here. She work here, sometimes."

"Okay, you wait, one minute."

Esposito waited beside the cab, blocking Rodriguez's exit, as Nick went to the store. He tended to believe Rodriguez, or at least believed that this was the best they would get from him. Nick could pick up a wreath, if nothing else. The door was locked, and he tapped on the glass, drawing an older Spanish woman to shake her head and point to the clock. Nick shook his head in return and showed his shield. She nodded and approached to let him in, offering a quick, reflexive smile. She waved Nick in and walked to the back.

"Un momento, señor."

"Sí, señora."

Another woman came out from the back, in a white dress, summery as she strode down the green aisle. She was younger than Nick by a few years, but not young in her eyes, which were strikingly green and, he somehow felt, always open. Her hair was tawny blond and lighter than her skin, and her smile was bright and easy; the mix of dark and fair in unexpected mixture caught him up for a moment.

"Yes, Detective?"

"Yes."

She extended her hand, and Nick took it, and he could smell her perfume amid the flowers.

"Can I help you?"

"I hope so."

Nick withdrew his hand and fished in a pocket for the Polaroids.

"A woman died yesterday, and we don't know who she is. Someone told us you might know her. Would you mind looking at some pictures? They're not pretty, but it's important we find out who she is, so her family knows. Would you mind?"

"No, not at all."

The older woman came out from the back as he spread out the pictures on the edge of a counter that held bouquets of fall flowers, yellow and red, with autumn leaves scattered amid the petals. She clutched the younger woman's arm and leaned in, both women looking at once. The older woman gasped—*"Ay, dios mío!"*—even before she took in the face, but the younger looked closely, carefully, before they leaned back and conferred.

"Es Maria, de Mexico?"

"Sí, es Maria, pobra niña. Ay, dios mío, pobra mujer . . ."

The older shook her head, crossed herself, and stepped back. The younger looked down for a moment, and was about to speak, before there was another tap on the glass door. It was Esposito. The older woman opened the door for him, and he half-stepped in, looking for the nod from Nick. When he got it, he tossed a set of keys back out toward the street, so Rodriguez was free to leave. As Esposito sized up the scene inside, Nick could see he reckoned several kinds of luck had been hit upon at once. Nick touched the pictures to return attention to them as Esposito joined in.

"So, you know her as Maria?"

"Yes, she used to come around at the end of the day, buy the older inventory to sell on street corners."

No one had ever made the word "inventory" sound so sensual.

"And she was Mexican?"

"I think so. It's a Mexican business, the street vendors, anyway. Her accent, her look, everything about her was Mexican. But I'm just assuming."

"You didn't know her last name, did you?"

"No, I'm sorry . . . but there are other girls who come in. I've seen her with them. They're Mexicans, too. I don't know if they're family, but I bet they know who she is. They're a little standoffish with you gentlemen, but I'll ask. Do you have a card?"

Nick had already taken one out, but Esposito beat him to the punch, offering his own.

"I'm Detective Esposito, by the way. Pleased to meet you, and you, señora. Are you sisters? *Sorores?* No? *Madre? No creo!* It's Detective Meehan's case, but you can ask for either of us. And you are . . ."

She handed out two cards of her own: ORTEGA FLORIST, DAYSI ORTEGA, PROPRIETOR. They were simple, in black italic script, with red and green vines making neat columns on each side. They were understated, elegant, like the word "proprietor."

"So, a florist named Daysi. Does that mean the same in English?"

"Yes, we just spell it differently in Dominican, in Spanish."

"Somebody's pointed that out before, haven't they?"

"You're not the first."

Nick enjoyed Esposito's stumble more than he should have, but she seemed to take no offense. Esposito was undeterred. "The first detective, though, right? The first to notice it right away?"

"The garbageman noticed it, too. And the super, and half the bums on the block."

Esposito laughed again, because he knew it was no stumble. Even to step on her toes was a kind of touch, and Nick hadn't touched her. He'd only thought about it.

"The name comes from 'day's eye,' like the sun, because the flower looks like the sun," Nick said. Daysi looked at him and smiled.

"This is not a detective who just notices," she said. "This is one who knows."

If only that were true! Because the pleasure of that moment was so intense, Nick knew he wasn't having a seizure but what could be considered a cardiac episode—a minute bodily mutiny as his heartbeat upticked from one-two, one-two to waltz time. Esposito laughed again and put a hand on Nick's shoulder. Nick wondered if his partner had seen that he might need steadying.

"He knows a lot, my friend Nicky does, and what he doesn't, he wants to find out. Which means we gotta come back to see you. Do you need anything? Can we bring anything?"

"What would I need?"

"I don't know," he mused, looking around. "Dirt?"

"No, I think I'm fine, dirt-wise. . . . Nicky? I should have something for you in the next day or two."

" 'Nick' is fine, Ms. Ortega. I'll stop by."

"Nicky, please, call her Daysi," Esposito said.

"You can."

"Thanks, Daysi. I'll see you."

They shook hands, and Nick turned away, Esposito a half-step behind. At the door, Esposito stopped and turned again.

"There's just one more thing, Ms. Ortega . . ."

"Yes, Detective?"

"Don't leave town."

Her laugh was easy and musical, and began even before he finished his fake tough-guy admonition. Nick laughed, too, as they walked back to the car.

"I've always wanted to say that," Nick said.

"I say it all the time."

"To who? I've never heard you."

"I say it to my wife and kids whenever I'm mad at them."

"Does it work?"

"They haven't left yet."

"She was something, huh? Daysi?"

" 'Like the sun, the day's eye.' I could have cried."

"She liked it."

"Hey, and you thought you had that useless bullshit in your head for no reason, right? Little did you know, right? It makes you think, there's gotta be some kind of plan. . . ."

"That's a little deep for you, Espo, isn't it?"

"Yeah, probably I should stick with bad movie lines. What next?"

"I dunno. My mind's not exactly in the game right now. Gimme a minute."

"I'm not talking about work. Daysi! C'mon, man, you gotta get in there! This is the game! Don't walk away from this, don't let this drop!"

"Yeah . . . well . . ."

" 'Yeah, well'? That's what you got for me? C'mon, Nick, you gotta go for this, or I'm gonna be back at that store tomorrow. I'm gonna buy so many flowers for my wife, she's gonna think I'm cheating on her, and she better be right. You're lucky you saw her first."

As they drove off, Nick looked at his phone—a missed call, another blocked number, no message. The semi-police or the semi-wife? Yes, that was it. He remembered what he had tonight. He snapped the phone shut. He'd made a deal, too. As they turned off 181st, he saw a small, dark figure on the far corner, near the turn for the highway, with armfuls of flowers for sale. She would be back tomorrow, here or somewhere else. As Nick had said, his mind was not in the game.

"Listen, can you run me to midtown?" Nick said.

"Yeah, no problem. What is it?"

"Dinner with my wife."

EIGHT

The last message she'd left, a day or two ago, had been that she'd be happy to see him but it would be okay if he couldn't make it. She'd only asked that he call if he wasn't coming. They had reached the point where civility masked regret, which masked things they were unwilling to consider. It was a point past the point. Esposito had noted how Nick had replayed the message several times, probing it for codes. Come, go; stay, don't. Esposito didn't ask questions, even when Nick asked him to drop him on a corner in Hell's Kitchen where no restaurant was immediately apparent.

"See you tomorrow?" Esposito asked.

"See you tomorrow."

Nick found the restaurant midblock, a small French place. There was a crowd inside, and Nick scanned them through the plate glass window—no Allison. Her company had closed some kind of deal, and this was a celebration. That was all Nick knew, all he needed to. Single women, divorced women, were not an exotic species in the twenty-first-century New York workforce, not even on Wall Street. At Allison's level, though, it was still a men's club, and he suspected she wanted cover as much as company. It would make it easier for her if he were there. That was fair, because she had made it easy for him, or at least she had not made it as hard as it could have been. The restaurant was cozy and old, paneled in wide dark planks, with antique brass lamps, impressionist prints on the wall. There was even a picture of the Eiffel Tower beside the bar. Could a gypsy violinist be far away? Nick wouldn't have expected these people in this place; for them, the world-beaters, something new, something that flashed and hummed, a spectacle of mirrored walls and long lines, with fantastic concoctions at fantastic prices that no one really ate and no one reached into a pocket to pay for. This was the kind of place Nick would have gone to with Allison; he wondered if she'd picked it, thinking of him.

They'd begun to meet less often over time, and Nick noted that in recent months, she'd only called him to meet for events like tonight's, where they would be allied by their discomfort with the crowd. They wouldn't have to think about things too much; talk wouldn't go too deep. They were alike in so many ways, he knew: private people, who had invited each other in, knowing right away that they were right for each other. Nick scanned the bar again and saw that she was there.

Allison was rangy and lithe, in a cream-colored suit and pale blouse, brown hair that fell around her shoulders; she had a kind of anchorwoman balance between warm and cool, engaging but discouraging too close an approach. You wouldn't have guessed she was Cuban, a neighborhood girl. There was color on her cheeks. She must have gotten away somewhere, for a few days. Maybe she'd tell him. For a moment, Nick missed her, very much. He could almost smell her. And then he remembered the scent of Daysi amid her flowers, and felt a ridiculous twinge of guilt, as if Allison might catch a rival spoor. He laughed aloud. What a wild dog he could be, smelling two women in an hour! How long had it been since he'd felt for Allison what Daysi had done for him, to him? Years since he'd thought there was a future, back when they were all future, horizonless hope. Was she still the same woman he missed?

This was a favor. Allison would do the same for him, he knew, should any occasion arise. Not that many had—a few cop weddings, a few christenings, but Nick would not have thought twice about going alone. This was no favor to either of them, the way it was, letting go and pretending not to, neither of them willing to raise their voices and say, *No mas, no more. Let's be married or let's move on.* They didn't even have to raise their voices, but it had to be said. Something did. Both of them were too good at keeping their mouths shut, a good instinct that had become a bad habit.

Nick looked through the window for indications of welcome, warning signs. He saw a male of the species, suited expensively, leaning in hard to her. Late thirties, avid and potbellied, on his third drink, at least; Nick took him as a strong earner, likely to die before fifty, arguing at a golf course. Allison would have introduced Nick immediately to him, pointing the conversation, as if to let the guy know she had a dog in the apartment who didn't like strangers. When the golfer stumbled away, Nick imagined that their thoughts had met, the two of them, the three.

Allison seemed unperturbed. She talked to someone else, an older man, silver-haired. The conversation was easy, semi-confidential. He was the boss, she the protégée. A professional relationship, with fond, familial overtones. That was good for her. When the golfer came back—it was the bathroom, his zipper was open—the older man spoke sharply with him, raising a finger, and he left. Allison did not need Nick there. She wouldn't put on a brogue and call him a powerful help. Nick scanned the scene for more portents, but there were none. A crowd walked past him, chunky ladies in sweat suits, laughing, almost late for a play. Nick looked back inside.

The maître d' was tall and gangly, with a gleaming bald skull framed by tufts of white hair at the temples, so that his head looked like a kind of military decoration. He addressed the guests, bowing and making florid gestures with his hands, and then turned to the mestizo busboys, barking words that seemed harshly foreign even in Nick's imagined lip-reading from behind the glass. The older man took Allison by the hand, and then Nick called, to see if she would answer. She opened the phone and looked at the number. She closed it again, shaking her head. She didn't check the message. Nick had not left one. If only someone would say something, if one of them had the kindness, the coldness, to say what had to be said.

Nick walked away, west down the street, to get on the subway, uptown. He called Allison again before he went underground, this time offering apologies. He'd been caught up at work, he said, and hoped she would be all right. He knew she would be. She could have picked up, he thought. He had asked for a sign, from her, from the skies. When Nick walked down the stairs to the A train, he felt grief pull him down like the hand of a drowning man.

NINE

The next morning, Ivan Lopez went to the precinct three times. Two black eyes and a swollen nose did not make his face look any more honest, and the swaddled, splinted pinkie resembled a sports fan novelty prop, all the more so when he waved it, which was nearly constantly. When he marched up to the desk, fulminating about having been robbed and assaulted by detectives, he was kicked out for shouting at the sergeant. When he came back, in a calmer state but still flush with indignation, the sergeant called the squad. "Um, there's this guy, he's saying . . ." Nick felt a queasy confusion—robbed? And why did he want to see him? Did he want Nick to arrest himself? "Send him upstairs. I'll take care of it." Anger felt better than anxiety, at least at first, when the specifics of the accusation were made clear. Lopez's driver's license had been "stolen." The license was on Esposito's desk. Nick had checked Lopez's background as part of the suicide investigation and had found that he had a warrant for traffic tickets. At the squad, Nick preempted Lopez's tirade by informing him of the warrant and taking out his handcuffs. Lopez began to stammer an apology and collapsed into a seat, holding his sad head in his silly hand. Nick softened, and softened further when Lopez said his daughter was missing. He was sent away, one last time, for a picture of the girl. Nick had expected a lawsuit from Lopez, even respected its merits, and so this reversal in their relationship was welcome.

On his return, Lopez presented a photograph of a girl not more than thirteen, in a miniskirt and a halter top that said I BRAKE FOR MEN, taken in front of a hot-pink background with Playboy Bunny heads printed at regular intervals. She was as skinny as a broomstick, with uneven bangs, and she squinted in anticipation of the flash. Nick could not remember seeing anything quite so sleazy.

"She seems lovely. . . . What's her name?"

"Grace."

Nick was glad that he'd told the truth about that, at least, when they'd first met, but the pious simplicity of the name made the picture all the more garish.

"How long has she been missing?"

"Two days."

"How old is she?"

"Twelve."

"She's been gone two days?"

"No, thirteen."

"Thirteen days?"

"No, she's thirteen. She's gone two days."

"You're sure?"

"Yes. Thirteen years old. Two days gone."

"Two days, and you didn't report it until now?"

"I thought she would come back."

"Does she have a boyfriend?"

He became indignant. "She is twelve years old! Thirteen!"

Napolitano breezed in, coffee in his hand, case files tucked under an arm, talking on the cellphone—"Nah, nah, nah. Not tonight." He looked down at the picture as he marched past. "Who's the jailbait?"

A brief sob escaped from Lopez as Napolitano continued on to his desk, still talking on the phone.

"Has she done this before?"

"Yes."

"How many times?"

"Once, twice."

"Where was she then? How long was she away?"

"A day, maybe. She wouldn't say."

"Does she do well in school?"

"Yes, very good."

"Has she missed school?"

"No, she goes. She just don't come home after."

"Why don't you get her at school, then?"

Lopez shrugged, downcast. Half the parents of runaways were like him—clueless and listless, making the report only out of fear they would get in trouble themselves if they didn't. It was a receipt for pretending to give a shit. They never knew a single name of any of their kid's friends, where they went after school—if they went to school—or what they did. The chronic cases made reports every month or two, though they might have made four or five times as many, as the kids drifted in and out of the house. The police didn't look for the kids, either, unless there were exigent circumstances, a specific danger. The paperwork was a dance of the veils, the cases opening and closing and opening again, as if the cops cared, or the parent did. And yet missings were tricky. Every now and then, one of them went bad, and you had to explain why you hadn't hunted for the boy who'd cried wolf, as his mother wept over his bloody clothing.

"And the mother? Is she in the picture?"

Usually, the question was reversed—*Was there ever a father, or do you just have a nickname and the late-won wisdom that you shouldn't mix tequila and rum?*

"No. . . . She died, a while ago. We weren't really together, except in the end. She came back when she was sick. When Grace was eleven, we got married, and she died the next year, cancer. I can't be too strict. She is a little girl. And a stranger. She goes to Catholic school now, Mother Cabrini. She just started. I work, I try . . ."

"All right, Mr. Lopez. I'll look into it. Give me a call if she comes back."

As Nick walked him out, it struck the detective that he had reached a point in his career, his life, where decency surprised him more than the lack of it. Lopez had hit a few of the pressure points, Nick knew— mother, cancer, Catholic school—and Nick may have given Lopez more credit than he deserved. He'd been hiding something the other night, but everyone was a little odd, everyone had secrets. There were otherwise fine and functional people who walked beaches with metal detectors in the firm conviction that they would find Blackbeard's hoard, who scanned the skies for visitors in silver ships. In the past, Nick had come across the remnants of rituals in the park—burnt ends of candles, feathers and bones left by those seeking favors from the santos. Was that what he'd been doing? As Lopez walked down the stairs, Nick called after him.

"And by the way, why were you in the park the other night?"

Lopez smiled and waved as he left the stairwell, as if he hadn't heard. Nick hated the thought of having to change his mind again. Back at the desk, he slipped the picture of Grace under the blotter's clear plastic cover. Other detectives put pictures of their children thère, sometimes wives. Nick put Grace there so he'd remember to stop by the school later and nip this case in the bud. She would be his child for the day. No more than that, with any luck. In any case, it would take less time than a lawsuit.

Lieutenant Ortiz was hovering near the meal room, waiting for someone to make coffee, when Esposito walked in. The lieutenant looked at him, then up at the clock on the wall. His thought processes were fairly transparent.

"Two hours is late, even for you, Esposito."

"A well-rested detective is a productive detective, Lieutenant. Management 101."

"What have you got for me?"

"Good news, only good news. And milk, and coffee cake. I picked it up on the way. Whaddaya say I make a fresh pot and tell you about it?"

Lieutenant Ortiz was fully appeased; it took that little effort. His predictable habits and reactions couldn't really be described as a "leadership style," but it amounted to leadership, and in the style to which they'd grown accustomed. Most of the detectives knew what they were doing, and required no instruction. For Esposito, especially, in the days after a homicide, he didn't have to be ordered to work; he had to be ordered to go home. Nick followed them into the room as the coffee perked.

"So, whaddaya got?" the lieutenant asked.

"I got a line on the shooter—his name, where he is. I just got that an hour ago. I got a call from a little friend out there."

"Is it solid?"

"Yeah, I think we'll get ahold of him. We got nothing on him, though, not for the homicide. He's got a bullshit warrant—he skipped a court date on a weed case—and we can take him in. We got a long day of talking, a long night. You good to run with me, Nick?"

"Yeah, I got a stop to make. Then I'm good to go."

"Good."

The lieutenant cut a slice of coffee cake and poured himself a cup. He lit a cigarette and collected the cake and coffee before marching back to his office, content with his breakfast and the progress of his men.

"Let me know how it goes," he said over his shoulder.

Garelick joined them, calling out to Perez with cordial welcome, "You wanna cup? Fresh pot here."

Both Esposito and Nick noticed, and exchanged glances. Perez noticed, too, or at least he noticed the change in Garelick's tone. Perez didn't drink much coffee, but he came inside the meal room, drawn by the unexpected solicitude.

"How do you take it?"

"Regular."

They had worked together for months, and Garelick didn't know how he took his coffee. Most partners knew after the first hour. Garelick even poured the milk and sugar for him; Nick thought that was a little over the top.

"Here you go."

"Thanks!"

"So, how did it go with the girl from the diner? Marina, wasn't that her name? Did you ever call her?"

Perez took a deep drink of his coffee, and warmth flushed through his face. It was as if the attention were strong liquor for him, too strong. He had an odd smile; it looked like a stroke in reverse. Half of his face—mouth, cheek, and eyebrow—lifted up, while the other half remained still, as if it didn't get the joke.

"I called her, and we did a lot more than talk! She is one wild woman! Believe me, I can barely walk today, I'm so sore."

Garelick let loose a high cackle of glee. Nick rushed to leave the room, knowing he couldn't keep a straight face, tapping Esposito to follow. Nick snatched up the first file he saw on his desk, hoping it was the one he needed.

TEN

ven the idea of a woman, Nick thought—half-thought, since he could not finish. He was straining not to run, not to lose control. He was just beyond the door, with Esposito a step behind, before they broke down, laughing. They were in the car, several blocks south on Broadway, before they settled down.

"Poor Ralph!"

"Silly sons-a-bitches are made for each other. Hey, speaking of—never mind that. How'd it go with the missus last night? You get lucky?"

"Which was it, 'silly sons-a-bitches' or 'made for each other'? What reminded you?"

"Nice catch, but you still dodged the question. You get lucky?"

"With your wife, it isn't getting lucky."

"Call it what you want. Good for you."

The compliment hung in the air for a moment, and Nick wondered whether to correct his assumption. When it struck Nick, with some dismay, that Esposito was the only person he'd had a real conversation with in recent memory, he decided not to lie, or let the lie remain.

"I skipped it. It was some kind of business dinner."

Esposito nodded before venturing, with unaccustomed caution, "Things between you and her . . . they done?"

"I think so. When I think about it, I think so."

Esposito nodded again, and let it rest. Not the time to think about it, not now; work to do. Let the past pass. Nick began to shuffle through the cases, then put them down to look out the window, to take in the city, the brightness of day. Here on Broadway, there was braying novelty, a bazaar of small stores, sometimes two or three of the same on each block. Cellphone places, suddenly everywhere; five-and-dimes stuffed with

Chinese-factory plastics, Day-Glo bath mats, dust mops, flip-flops, nearly worthless and nearly eternal; flashy little jewelry stores, barricaded behind Plexiglas and buzzers, Arab and Korean and Spanish, offering gold teeth, nameplate rings the size of brass knuckles, and giant tortured crucifixes, Christ's eyes dotted with rubies, which made him look enraged, as if he'd come back to settle a score. The better ones only sold gold; the worse ones bought it, too, and were not judgmental if the rings came in with bits of finger in them. Hair salons and nail salons, bodegas and botanicas, full of candles decorated with half-breed saints. Corner diners for café con leche, rice and beans, pernil wallowing in steel trays of sweet grease, rows of spitted chickens in the window, toasting under lightbulbs. There were Dominican stores that looked more like garage sales, strange hybrid twofers and threefers, so you could buy video games where you got a haircut, batteries and cheap shoes where you picked up a money order. And then, a new one—

"Look!"

"What?"

"The Dominican store, over there, by where the bum's pissing."

"Where— No, I got it. Fresh Fruit and Financial Services. Never seen that before."

" 'I'm considering diversifying my portfolio. Plus, I want a coconut.' "

" 'Can I roll over these IRAs into . . . this mango?' "

" 'I would like to discuss estate planning, and a banana.' "

And yet, it made a kind of sense. *You want this? No? How about that?* Nick didn't know if the fruit was rotten or the advice was, but so much of everything else here was candy, candy and toys. Christmas morning, all year round. Twenty blocks up, twenty years back, it was less of an arcade. It was butcher, baker, newsstand, bar, bar, bar—Up the Republic! God, it brought out the scold in you, Nick thought, when you lived here long enough. Still, why was it that in the poorest neighborhoods, most stores might as well be called The Last Thing You Need? You didn't have to leave the block if you wanted fake fingernails or clip-on braids, bootleg DVDs of movies that opened yesterday; you didn't have to leave the neighborhood if you wanted your car windows tinted limousine-black, or a license plate frame with blinking lights, or spinning chrome tire rims that cost more than a car payment. But if you wanted to buy a book, that meant a trip on a train. There were libraries here, too, but once the after-school programs finished, they were so quiet Nick often picked them as places to meet informants. There was no risk of discovery. It brought out the scold in you, it did.

As they stopped at a light, Nick got an elbow in the ribs. Children played in a school yard, racing and throwing things, and a handful of boys huddled in a corner, in intense conversation. Two black ones, five or six tan ones, one pale child with red-gold hair.

"Guess which one's the cop's kid."

"If either of us left bastards around here, at least they'd blend in a little better."

The remark sounded harsh, even as Nick said it, and Esposito let it pass uncomfortably. But pass it did. On the next side street, he pulled over; another elbow, and when Esposito asked "Wouldja?" the question needed no further context.

"I can't really see her."

"I know. Me neither. Wouldja?"

A female figure approached from midblock, in a short skirt, ample up top. You couldn't quite make her out, but for Esposito, the point of the game was to commit before you could see her clearly. There was no fun picking an obvious beauty; it said nothing about your instincts.

"No."

"I would."

"I know."

Esposito grabbed a random mug shot from the glove compartment. A tree branch and then a van blocked a view of the woman.

"Excuse me! Excuse me, can I talk to you a minute?"

"Yes?"

Esposito had guessed right. She was a beauty, dark-skinned, with long curly hair pulled back, in a sexy-secretary outfit.

"Police. Can we talk to you a minute, show you a picture?"

"Okay."

"Have you seen this guy?"

He folded the paper in half, covering the name. She took it and stared for a moment, her smile fading. "I've seen him. Why?"

Espo caught the reaction, and hedged. "We're looking for him."

"Why?"

"You know him?"

"Yes."

"How?"

"He's my brother. Why do you want him?"

"We just want to talk to him. He might have seen something."

"Last time cops told him that, he did four years."

"Really? For what?"

"Like you don't know!"

She marched off, irate at being patronized, and they watched her form recede down the sidewalk. Esposito looked at the picture again— Anthony Gomez, arrested for assault—and tried to find the resemblance to the woman. He was pudgy, light-skinned, with a flat nose; she was none of these things. Nick had guessed that the comeuppance would one day come when the woman that Esposito picked turned out to be a hunchback, a nun, a man. This wasn't the expected lesson, but Esposito didn't seem to learn from it.

"That's why you gotta be careful with local girls."

"That was careful?"

Esposito ignored the question, posing his own. "Can you picture this guy with a hot sister?"

"No."

"Can you picture me, palling around with this guy, going for beer and ball games, to get close to his sister?"

"Yes."

"Me, too. Wonder what he's wanted for. Let's get out of here."

Even the idea of a woman, Nick began again, but he was no more able to finish the thought, and maybe less willing. Let the past pass. He took out his notebook and looked at his errands. When they went for Kiko, it would take the rest of the day, and maybe the next, so Nick wanted to get his cases done first. The jobs had the feel of a household to-do list— flower shop for Maria, pick up Grace after school. Esposito was anxious to get ahold of Kiko, but Kiko had no reason to run. He might lay low awhile, but the killing had been territorial, and you don't give up the territory you've just won. All they could hope to do was ensnare him in a conversation, trick and trap him into a statement after hours of interrogation. And what they did know was not promising. He was Dominican, which meant that his English might be bad; the interrogation might be like talking a cat out of a tree. Even if the cat came down, it was not because it had been persuaded by your rhetorical gifts. And because he was Dominican, he might be tied in with people who frightened him far more than the cops did, who knew where his family lived, back on the island.

They didn't know if Kiko had killed anyone before, but he had shot someone and walked away from the case. A crackhead customer had gotten mouthy with one of his dealers, and Kiko had put one in the guy's foot. The crackhead had limped away and learned to keep his mouth shut. Flower shop for Maria, school for Grace.

"Now what?"

"The flower shop, talk to Daysi."

"I'll always make time for Daysi. You wanna call first, make sure she's there?"

"No. What if she just gave me an address for Maria? We wouldn't have a reason to go."

"We wouldn't have a police reason."

"I like to have a couple."

"You only need one."

The store was a few blocks down, but they couldn't even find double-parking on the street. Esposito found a hydrant around the corner, muttering about cops who don't do their jobs. Nick noticed him running a hand through his hair, catching a glance in the mirror, only because he had done the same. The door of the flower store opened with a chime.

Daysi was on the phone in the back, writing on a pad, speaking in rapid Spanish. She smiled at them and nodded, holding up a finger. Esposito and Nick took in the garden in the aisles, the colors and shapes, the humid perfumes. On the far wall were memorials, crosses of tightly banked carnations, wreaths draped with ribbons that proclaimed condolences, and a floral clock, showing the time, seven-thirty. Nick studied it until Daysi's mother let loose a musical *"Hola!"* and vanished into the back for a moment. She returned with two boutonnieres, a red rose for Esposito, a white rose for Nick, and pinned them to their lapels. Daysi hung up the phone and laughed, then poured forth a torrent of insincere reproach at her mother's flirtation.

"Excuse me! Excuse my mother, I'm sorry. I told her men don't do that here. She said she doesn't care, it looks nice."

"That's all right," Nick said. "It does look nice. How are you?"

"Good, good, busy, thank God."

Esposito found a mirror to examine himself. He wore a dark suit and managed a dangerous expression to go with it. "I wish guys still wore fedoras. I'd look sharp."

"You look like a pallbearer," Nick said.

"No, he looks very elegant!" Daysi interjected.

"I feel like a pallbearer," Esposito said, turning from the mirror to the memorial displays. "Look at all this!"

"That's a big part of the flower business, Detective, weddings and funerals."

"Ours, too. Love and death."

"Really? Where does love fit in?"

"It doesn't," Esposito said, striding around the store to look at the arrangements. "Women send detectives after the guys who don't send flowers."

"That's not nice."

"No, it isn't."

"What's this clock for? What does it mean?"

"We don't get too many of those anymore. It's an old Southern thing. They say it's African. The clock gives the time the person died."

"I've been to a lot of funerals," Esposito said. "I've never asked that question, never been asked. 'Exactly when did he die? Not seven-thirty! I thought it was at least quarter of!' Who needs to know that? Is somebody putting in for overtime?"

"I don't know—maybe it's like an anniversary. It makes you reflect. Maybe the next day, or the next, you see the time, it's seven-thirty, it makes you look back at the person you lost, remember him. And remember that life is short, we shouldn't waste time."

There was no rebuke in her voice, but the words themselves were hard enough that they brought conversation to a stop. There was an uneasy moment before the phone rang.

"Excuse me, I have to get back, but before I forget, I have an address for you, from one of the girls. 'Maria' is all I have for her name. She was staying with a man."

Daysi handed Nick a slip of paper with an address, as she took the call—"Ortega Florist. Un momento, por favor."—and put it on hold. Nick noticed that there was no ring on her finger.

"She thinks it's 2B, on the second floor. But it's definitely the second floor, the second apartment to the right, when you take the stairs up. She lived with a man, just moved in, two or three months ago. The girl didn't know his name, but he wasn't Mexican. She saw them once together and said hello."

"Did she say what he looked like?"

"Short, thin, thirties. Nothing to look at. One minute—*Ortega Florist. Un momento, por favor—*"

"Dominican? Puerto Rican? South American?" Nick asked.

"I think Puerto Rican. They had a joke, 'Maria met a man, with the prettiest blue passport.' *Sí, diga, Ortega Florist . . .*"

Daysi beckoned her mother to cover the phone, so she could finish with the detectives. Nick tapped Esposito on the shoulder, to move on. Esposito stared at Daysi in dopey awe, turning to Nick a full five seconds after the tap—"Whuh?"—his reflexes preposterously slow, like a lummox in a sitcom. Nick felt a jealous twinge, then laughed, at his partner and himself, at how the most adult instincts bring out the most childish reactions. He'd seen her first.

"Let's get to it. Daysi has work to do. We do, too," Nick said.

"Yeah, right. Plus, I'm hungry. You don't got anything useful here, do you, Daysi? I mean, tomato plants, banana trees? I mean, it's all pretty to look at, but a man's gotta eat."

Daysi laughed, too, not least at the transparency of his suggestions, when his appetites were so plainly carnivorous.

"You'd be surprised," Daysi said. "Both of you, open your mouths, close your eyes."

They obeyed like trained seals. After a few seconds of blind surrender, Nick felt a moist petal on his tongue, silky to the touch and grassy sweet, almost melony to the taste. His reverie was broken by Esposito's moan. Nick opened his eyes and looked over, to make sure his partner's pants were on. Daysi laughed again, and Esposito opened his eyes, too, the spell broken.

"My God! That shit was great! What was it?"

Daysi twirled a pom-pom of a bloom, ruffled in tangerine and crimson layers. She twirled it like an umbrella.

"Marigold."

"Really? You can eat them?"

Daysi set that flower down and picked up a long-necked stem with a star-shaped flower, golden with pink edges. She smiled at Nick.

"And you had a daylily. I'm sorry but I forget the variety. Some people think the different colors have different tastes, the reds a little more like apple, the yellows a little lemony. Maybe they imagine it, but it's still nice. What did you think it tasted like, Nick?"

"Like lettuce in heaven."

This time, Daysi let loose a laugh that left her coughing and holding her mouth, and the involuntary suddenness, the abdication of soft-porn delicacy, made it all the more erotic. Nick stared at her, smiling, until Esposito, who had a better sense of the moment, touched Nick's shoulder, then hers.

"This was incredible, Daysi, but I gotta warn you, I've been a cop for a long time. When you start sampling the product, it's all downhill from there."

Daysi collected herself, and was gratefully distracted by her mother calling her over to take an order in English. She waved to them as she picked up the phone.

"I'll come back another time, if you don't mind," Nick said. "I'd like to talk to the girl who knew Maria."

Daysi nodded and waved again, and took out a pad for the phone order, to play her ceremonial part in whatever love or death had struck again uptown. When Nick walked out of the store, he felt sad, the way you feel when a favorite song is over. As they got into the car, Esposito looked over to him, shaking his head, and bit his knuckle—the Sicilian version of a cold shower.

"Sonofabitch, you're lucky you saw her first."

ELEVEN

The man with the pretty blue passport lived ten blocks down. Nick told Esposito the address, and there was a momentary thrill when Esposito said that Kiko lived there, too. Convenience became coincidence, and coincidence seemed like conspiracy, before Esposito checked his notebook and saw that Kiko in fact lived across the street. Detectives are superstitious people; they are trained to look for patterns, to connect the dots in the dark, where inspiration can veer into hallucination. What would it have mattered if they'd lived in the same building, shared the same birthday, if it had turned out you could scramble the letters in Kiko's name to get the other man's? Nothing, *nada*. You can always find meaning in things, Nick thought, that doesn't mean anything. He realized he was still a little giddy from seeing Daysi.

"Did you notice that I got the red rose?" Esposito interrupted, divining his own meanings. "Red, for passion, romance? In a word, ass? What does white stand for here, white boy? It stands for 'Why doncha get outta the way?'"

"Did you notice it was the mother who gave it to you? Do you think it might be that she has the hots for you? That she wants us to double-date, me and Daysi, you and Grandma?"

"You know, you just spoiled it for me."

"Good."

The building had once been grand, with a columned foyer and marble lobby, but the details that had once announced its quality now highlighted the decline. The white marble panels had turned a urinal yellow, with pocks and divots all over, showing the thinness of the veneer. Tattered posters announced the monthly schedule for the exterminator, bus junkets to the Atlantic City casinos, a reward for a lost cat. There was an alcove for the mailboxes, in the far corner, from which sharp Spanish words of abuse could be heard. *"Hijo de puta! Animal! Perro! Pinche mugroso!"* The detectives crossed the lobby to the alcove, where a man with his arms full of groceries barked at a crackhead pissing in the corner. The man with the groceries was young and strong, in a crisp white guayabera shirt, with ropes of gold around his neck and wrists. He would have put the bags down, but the crackhead had made that option less attractive. The crackhead was jittery and put-upon, and determined to finish. "Yo, yo . . . gotta go . . ."

"Hey! You, ya savage! Get the hell out of here!"

Both men turned in surprise at Esposito's voice, and neither seemed pleased to hear it. The crackhead zipped up hastily and walked out past the detectives, and the other man hesitated, then began to walk as well. Esposito stepped in front of him, intrigued by the reaction. The grocery bags were filled with rolls of plastic wrap, twenty at least.

Esposito asked, "Everything okay?"

The man gave a polite nod, and he got one in return, toward the grocery bags.

"There was a sale?"

"Qué?"

"Yeah, whatever."

Esposito let him pass, and he walked up the stairs. They followed him without comment up the first flight, and he seemed relieved to see they were no longer with him—*"Buenos días! Gracias!"*—as he continued up. As instructed, the detectives found the second door on the right, 2B. Nick knocked hard, and the door opened. He never liked that, an open door, especially when he wasn't in uniform. It gave people a reason to come after you, or an excuse. Nick knocked again and stepped inside. His case, his call. A long hallway led to a dim room with a couch.

"Hello? Anybody home? Police here. *Policía* . . ."

Nick heard Spanish television on in the back, and kept knocking on the walls, calling out again in nonthreatening tones as he went down the hall. When they reached the living room, he heard a dull growl, low and throaty, and they stopped short. Esposito bumped into him from behind. Nick had no love of being bitten, but Esposito's dread ran deeper, and he had already about-faced to scramble back out before Nick could turn to run. The growl turned to a screech, an awful noise that joined a war whoop with the sound of a kicked cat, and the creature who'd created it flung open the bedroom door with a bang. Nick was made speechless by the wild-eyed little man who leapt out, improbably costumed in a blue tank top with a silver star on the chest, tight red underpants, and black slippers. Nick started to laugh, thinking that all he lacked was a cape and mask to be a superhero. He kept laughing even as the man rushed him with a machete.

Esposito pushed Nick aside before the man reached him, holding the machete overhead with both hands. He led with his belly, back arched to deliver the maximum blow, and he ran with cartoonishly piston-quick steps on duck-splayed feet. His movement and his battle gargle stopped abruptly when Esposito dropped him with a kick to the crotch. He collapsed onto the floor, and the machete fell with a clank. Esposito picked it up and tossed it to the back of the living room, where it smashed a goldfish bowl. The fish flopped haplessly on the rug. Nick began to laugh so hard that tears filled his eyes, and he had to sit down. Esposito looked at him with concern, wondering if he'd been hurt. A moan rose from the man on the floor.

"No fair . . ."

It was the perfect thing for the man to say, balled up and bawling in kiddie clothes, a protest at cheating in a pillow fight. Esposito leaned down to place a knee in his back and cuffed him. He looked over to Nick, who shrugged; the situation was more ambiguous than it had at first appeared. Yes, he'd tried to chop their heads off, but they were intruders in his home. He could argue that he'd thought they were burglars, and he might even have believed it. The detectives had gone there for a brief exchange of information, news of a death for the name of the dead. They had other things to do, and had no interest in arresting him, in making another case out of this. They knew nothing about him; that, at least, should change. Nick found a wallet on the kitchen counter and took out the license. He called the squad and had them run the name—Raul Costa—and was told that his criminal history consisted of one arrest, for hopping a turnstile in 1993. He might not have been much of a superhero, but his villainy was barely more impressive. They let him catch his breath, waited for his nausea to pass. This could go either way, Nick thought.

Costa lifted his head from the floor to regard them with wary, watery eyes. He had smooth cheeks and curly black hair, a pouty mouth that formed, eventually, a question. "Well?" As Esposito lifted him to his feet,

Nick kicked the goldfish and as much broken glass as he could manage under the couch.

"What's the matter with you? What the hell's wrong with you? You could have killed somebody. We could have killed you, you shithead!"

Costa smiled weakly at Esposito, evidently flattered at being considered such a figure of danger.

"I didn't know. . . . Will you let me go now?"

"No. Turn around. Face the wall."

Esposito looked again at Nick, who raised his hands. The threat had passed, as had the phase of the ridiculous; he still had somber business to finish. He remembered the bruises on the Mexican woman—Maria. She had a name, Maria. Nick went over to Costa and led him to the couch. He was "thin, thirties, nothing much to look at," as Maria's friend had said. He wasn't especially short, but Nick could see how the women would think so; smallness was an impression he left you with. They sat him down, still cuffed.

"Do you know why we're here?"

"No, why?"

"Is anyone else here? Do you live alone?"

Though he was shackled, nearly naked, before strangers who had kicked him, Costa no longer seemed perturbed; instead, he seemed strangely content with the arrangements. Tufts of snaky hair escaped from his baby clothes at the armpit and crotch.

"Nobody here but me . . . and the dog! Ruff! You should see your faces!"

Esposito took out his pad and pen, trying to redirect Costa's attention back to the realm of angry officialdom. Esposito turned off the TV and scanned the dingy room, hoping to see a bag of marijuana, court paperwork, an illegal partition between rooms, anything to hang a threat on. Except for an old photo on the wall of a woman with a young boy, tinted in pastels, the place was as dull and impersonal as a motel room. Esposito was angrier than Nick, or at least he showed it more. Nick stepped in before it escalated too far, too fast. Nick didn't like Costa any more than Esposito did, but open hostilities would only prolong the conversation. After a few questions, they'd be done with him.

"Guy, listen, nobody's in trouble here, but we got work to do, so let's do it and move on. Do you know where Maria is? Your girlfriend?"

"I know a lot of Marias. Everybody Spanish does."

" 'I know a lot of Marias,' " said Esposito, going into sardonic-repeat mode. "Are you kidding me? Where's your girlfriend?"

"I got a couple of girlfriends."

Esposito whirled to face him. "The man says, 'I got a couple of girl-friends.' "

Nick wasn't pleased by the direction it was taking. Esposito stepped away, but what he said next was not entirely under his breath.

"That's where he gets his panties."

"What?"

"What—what?"

Nick cut in again. "Stop messing around. Your girlfriend Maria, somebody reported her missing. Where is she? When did you see her last?"

Esposito stepped in close. "When's the last time you saw her alive?"

"What?"

"You heard me."

"You said no one was in trouble."

"That was before. When was the last time you saw her?"

"Three or four days ago. We had an argument."

"Over what?"

"Stupid stuff, nothing."

"Over what?"

"She didn't live here. She only stayed sometimes."

"What was her full name? Date of birth? Did she get mail here?"

Nick broke in. "What happened to her?"

"She didn't get mail. She was Mexican."

"What the hell does that mean?"

The man was still off balance, but he was beginning to recover. Esposito and Nick both stepped in to him, close, looking down. Esposito tapped him on the chest.

"What's your name?"

"Costa. Raul Costa."

"Raul Costa, answer every question I ask you, when I ask it, or I will knock your teeth down your throat."

Costa's lip trembled, and then his lips pursed into a self-pitying, sulky frown. But there followed in short order the information they needed: Maria Fonseca, who'd turned twenty-one in August. She had lived there for six months, more or less, and he had a phone bill with a call to Mexico on it, from when he'd let her talk to her family as a birth-day present. The detectives uncuffed him and let him go to the bedroom to find it.

"Do you believe this guy?" Nick asked.

"I've met him five minutes, and I wanna hang myself, too."

"Did you notice, he hasn't asked much about her?"

"I think he's enjoying himself."

Esposito went over to the photograph of the woman and child.

"I bet it's him and his mother. She shoulda strangled him in his crib."

Nick went back into the room with Costa to check on him. The room was small and neat, and he fished through a stack of papers from a dresser drawer. He glanced back at Nick when he came in, then contin-ued to look. There were no feminine possessions in the room. Had he packed them up already, thrown them out? In the closet, there were two blouses, one with red and white checks, one flowered. In a paper bag in the corner, there were balls of yarn, patterns for making clothing, rolled into loose tubes. There was a white sweater, the top of a white sweater, that could have been for a child, a girl barely in her teens, the same white wool Maria had used in the park.

"What was the fight over?"

"Because . . . I have other girls!"

Costa had a smirk on his face that he didn't try to suppress. He re-turned to the old bills, then took one out and handed it to Nick. On August 10, there was a long number, an international call. Nick took the paper and put it into his pocket. When he leaned in to look at the other papers, Costa tried to block his view. Nick picked up a pile of snapshots and saw the topmost, Maria and Costa. At the beach, on separate towels. She smiled. He had a sullen glare. Before Costa could protest, Nick barked at him—"Evidence!"—and put it into his pocket. Costa said noth-ing, tensing up. Nick was alert to the tension and pushed him back a pace before checking the second photo. The image didn't register; it was out of focus, a haze of shapes. The next was appallingly clear, and Nick flung the stack of pictures away, disgusted. He had many curiosities about Costa, but whether he could put his ankles behind his ears, absent even his revolting underpants, was not one of them. Nick rubbed his hands on his jacket, shaking his head, and Costa seemed pleased as they returned to the living room. The sight of Esposito took some of the spring out of Costa's step, but the detectives were done with him, and he knew it.

"Did she kill herself? She said she would kill herself. Did she leave a note?"

"Yes," Nick lied.

"Can I see it?"

"No."

"What did she say?"

Nick took the DOA Polaroid from his pocket and held it out to him. Costa reached to take it, but Nick pushed his hand away. Nick wouldn't let him touch it.

"Is this her?"

Costa stared at the photo, without evident emotion. "Yes . . . but she didn't . . . I mean, can you at least tell me what the note said?"

All he wanted was gossip, Nick knew, to flatter himself as he laughed in his little underpants after they left. Nick couldn't stand to look at him. Esposito laid a hand on Nick's shoulder to calm him, and turned to Costa.

"Mr. Costa, I'm sorry for your loss. I'm sorry about how we were when we came in. It's a bad situation. We have to be going now."

All the anger was gone from Esposito's voice; instead, there was almost a sniveling civility, as if he were concerned that Costa might make a complaint. It wasn't like him, and Nick didn't like it. He had come to appreciate his partner's vigilante instincts, even as he hoped to restrain them; the idea of Esposito kissing ass—and this ass, of all asses—was more than Nick could stomach. But when Nick turned away, he took in the picture on the wall: Mother now featured a fine set of whiskers and a shiny black nose, six tits, and a tail. Nick turned again and began to hurry out of the apartment. Esposito took his time following, but he kept to the far side of the room, so Costa would not see the improvements to the portrait. Costa trailed behind, returning to his earlier cockiness, seeing that they had nothing on him, that his secrets had been taken to the grave.

"What did she say? Did she say anything about me? I have a right to know!"

Nick was at the door when Esposito responded. Again, he was regretful about the earlier misunderstandings.

"Mr. Costa, since you weren't married, it's confidential. It's a legal thing, about suicide notes. But man-to-man, it's a lot of hysterical female bullshit about syphilis, or one of those type diseases. The doctors, they can cure it with one shot. Most of 'em, at least the ones they know about. I think. Anyway, I thought you should know. Sorry, I don't shake hands—nothing personal."

This time, they heard the door lock behind them. As they descended the stairs for the next errand, Esposito looked back and grinned. He held up his pen, and gave it a little wave, like a conductor's baton.

"No dog? Now he's a son of a bitch. . . . Didn't I tell ya, Nicky? You gotta make 'em pay."

TWELVE

Outside the building, they paused for a moment, not from tiredness but to let the last place leave their minds a little. Nick bowed slightly to Esposito and tapped his forehead in salute. He had conjured plagues and abominations upon the enemy. Esposito returned the bow, graciously. They crossed the street to Kiko's building and went upstairs. Esposito took the lead spot at the door; this visit was for his case. Salsa music dunned inside, making the walls vibrate. No one would answer even if someone was home, because no one could hear, and they pounded the door and kicked it, more in frustration than in a belief that anyone would answer. Nick tried the knob, and the door opened. How was it that people felt safe on this block? Maybe the rest of the neighborhood kept their doors locked against Kiko and Costa. Nick and Esposito stepped inside, and Esposito moved past Nick, to take the lead. His case, his bullet.

"Yo! Anybody home here?"

Again, the long hallway, and the rest of the layout like Costa's, a small one-bedroom. Nick touched the wall and could feel the beat of the music in it. Again, they were uninvited, but at least they'd announced themselves.

"Hey! Police here! Hey!"

Again, an assailant. A little boy of two or three charged down the hall and grabbed hold of Esposito's legs, hugging him. The boy was naked except for a diaper, chubby and golden-skinned, with wild curly hair. The child was odd-looking, with popping eyes, a wide upturned nose, and a long lower lip. His face could have been made with bits of bat, bug, and monkey. Still, he was a sweet-natured beast.

"Hi!" the boy said.

Esposito holstered his gun and picked him up. "Wouldja look at you!" He carried him over to the stereo and turned off the music. There was a comfortable little couch with a single throw pillow, a vast new wide-screen TV, slim-bodied and freestanding on the floor beside a video game console. Nothing else in the room. The floors were bare, as were the walls. *Sesame Street* was on, a song about the letter *N*.

"Hey, little man, who's watching you?"

"Hi!"

"*Dove es su mama, su papa?*"

Esposito sometimes slipped bits of Italian into his subway Spanish, the loose change of foreign words from his own childhood. Nick's Spanish was pidgin, but when he heard Esposito's accent, the word stuck out—it was spoken with Italian leisure instead of Caribbean speed.

"*Dónde*, not *dove*. Don't confuse the kid any more than you have to."

"*Dónde es su mama, su papa?*"

"*No están.*"

"Beautiful."

Esposito set the child down, and quick peeks in the kitchen, the bathroom, and the bedroom proved him truthful. The child took hold of Esposito's hand while he looked. There was a mattress in the bedroom, and clothing in piles and plastic bags; the kitchen had no furniture at all.

"*Donde es su mama, su papa?*"

"*No están.*"

"No shit."

"Very nice," Nick said, fretful. He was disturbed by the child left alone, still angry from the Costa encounter. These people, he started to say to himself, not knowing what he meant, only that he didn't like it.

"What?"

"His memoir. I can see it: 'Chapter One, in which I am abandoned by my parents, and a policeman teaches me to curse.' "

"Oh, relax. He don't know a thing we say. *Habla inglés, bambino? Habla inglés?*"

The baby smiled, uncomprehending. He was no prettier for it, poor kid. Esposito crouched down and picked him up again.

"What's your name, little man?"

He pinched Esposito on the nose and laughed.

"We're in the clear. Look at the mug on this little bastard—ugly little thing, isn't he? The babysitter probably watched him for an hour and jumped out the window. *Cual es su nombre?"*

"Mi nombre es Jose."

"See?"

"Sí."

"No, not you, junior. Anyway, as long as I have you here, do you hereby give me permission and authority to search this apartment, for evidence relating to a homicide that occurred within the county of New York, including but not limited to weapons, papers, and communication devices that could have been used in the course of or the furtherance of this crime, and are evidence thereof? Well, do you, Jose?"

"Sí."

"Well, there you have it."

"He'll make an excellent witness. The jury's gonna love him."

"Only if they put him on closed-circuit TV, and put a dot on that face."

Jose pinched Esposito's nose again, and, squealing, kicked to be let free. Esposito set him down, and a pursuit ensued—"I'm gonna getcha! I'm gonna getcha!"—as the detectives considered their options.

"We could arrest the first person who walks through the door," Esposito said.

"Yeah, it's something. But it doesn't get us anywhere."

"No."

Nick went back down the hall and locked the door. Whoever came in wouldn't surprise them. There had been enough of that today. Nick didn't think they'd find the shotgun here, and they didn't. They were as likely to find golf clubs. There was nothing—nothing in the bedroom closets, some milk and leftover Chinese in the refrigerator, three cans of beans in the cabinets. But Nick saw a cable bill from February on the floor beside the bed; they had been here since the beginning of the year, at least. Kiko lived here. Had they surprised him, Kiko might have fought them, or he might have come quietly, for an hour of polite denials; Esposito was prepared for these possibilities and more, to make a civil impression, or a brutal bond. He was not prepared to babysit.

"Well?" Esposito asked.

"Yup."

"And?"

"Leaving is out. Beyond that, I don't know."

"We could call somebody."

"Who? The cops?"

If they locked up Kiko, or Mrs. Kiko, it would be for endangering the welfare of a minor, a misdemeanor, a wonderfully broad charge. Child Welfare might take Jose away, or they might not. What had happened today? Mrs. Kiko might have had a twelve-year-old girl from down the hall watch Jose, and her mother had called her home. There might not be a Mrs. Kiko, and it might not be Kiko's kid. Whatever it was, it wasn't bright, and it wasn't right, but nobody necessarily needed to get arrested for it. And they weren't here for the baby.

Child abuse was like art and obscenity—you knew it when you saw it, and what they had wasn't yet clear. People like Esposito and Nick tended to hedge when making the child abuse call, though threatening to do so was often useful. The detectives' parents would have been arrested any number of times, by today's rules. No one had worn seat belts, or helmets when they'd ridden a bike; they had felt that a smack in the ass often had done more good than harm. From the end of the school day until dinner, and for the whole glorious summer, Nick and his friends had wandered the streets like stray dogs. A hundred blocks down, childhood was conducted like a military campaign, the days mapped to the minute, the kids tested, counseled, tutored, drilled, and driven like future astronauts, and half of them were allergic to air. As it had become clear to Nick and Allison that they would not have children, other peoples' had become dangerously important to them; toward the end, their best conversations together had been exchanges of overheated opinions about mothers who were overbearing, fathers who had left.

Look, there was little Jose, eating a nickel from under the couch cushion.

"Espo, get him . . ."

"Spit it out, you little bastard."

"Would you—"

"He don't understand a thing."

Espo expertly scooped him up and dug the coin from his mouth. He carried him into the kitchen, took out a carton of the leftover Chinese—pork fried rice—sniffed it, and tipped a pile of it onto a paper plate. He set the child and the plate down on the living room floor.

"You have a three-year-old, right? Do kids this age eat real food?" Nick asked.

"Yeah. My little guy would eat hubcaps. You'd think they'd have stuff for this guy, though—cereal, fruit, a little pasta. There's none of that."

"No. No toys, either."

"And no pictures. Do you know a woman who doesn't have pictures of her kid up somewhere? Even this kid."

"How do we know there's just one kid? Another one could have wandered. Nobody's watching."

"What do you want to do, check the basement, the roof?"

"I don't know. We wait awhile, I guess."

"Well, I'm not paying for college."

Jose finished eating, and began to dance on his plate of fried rice. A mouse scurried across the far floor, along the wall molding, and the baby shrieked with delight. He gave chase as the mouse dodged back and forth with jittery little hops before disappearing under the radiator. Jose slapped the hollow steel sides and bayed in joy.

"I wouldn't worry about that," said Esposito.

Esposito picked up Jose and the plate again, and took them into the kitchen. He tossed the plate aside, and washed the child in the sink, hands and feet, tickling him as Jose struggled under the water. He offered Nick the squirming child, but Nick raised a hand to demur.

"Not big on kids, Nick?"

"If he'd caught the mouse, maybe. I don't want to reward him if he doesn't win. Sends the wrong message. You hungry?"

"I could do with a bite. What are you thinking?"

"There's a joint on the corner. It's not bad, they deliver."

"And if the Kikos come back?"

"And if the Kikos come back?"

The invasion had turned into an occupation; like it or not, they were obliged to remain. And to remain, they had to eat. Esposito looked out the window to get the name of the restaurant, and called in an order of Cuban sandwiches and *plátanos*. When he sat on the couch, Jose climbed on his lap and pulled at his cheek. Esposito fished for the remote control and flipped through channels as Jose nuzzled into him. Nick wasn't sure if he was envious. Esposito stopped channel surfing when he came across a Spanish music video with a nearly topless blonde.

Ten minutes later, there was a knock at the door. Nick and Esposito looked at each other for a moment, before realizing that the Kikos wouldn't knock. Still, Nick drew his gun and checked the peephole before uttering a guttural *"Qué?"*

"Comidas."

"Okay."

Nick opened the door and paid the man, who looked confused. Nick gave him twenty bucks and held up a hand as the man started to count out the change.

"Gracias."

"De nada. . . . Sabe que vive aquí? Habla inglés?"

"Sí. Man and lady, baby."

"Good people?"

"Good customer . . ."

"You know their names? Where they work? Phone numbers?"

"No, I sorry."

"No problem."

Nick locked the door and brought the bag of food back to the couch. They dug into the sandwiches, and Esposito fed bits of his to the baby, taking apart bread, pork, ham, pickle, and cheese, to see what he liked. He liked them all, except for the pickle, which he spat onto Esposito's collar.

"Thanks, buddy!"

Espo pulled out the pickles and tore off a corner of the sandwich. Jose took a bite, chewing greedily and swallowing it down. He opened his mouth for another. Esposito hadn't started his sandwich, and Nick had eaten half of his by then. Esposito looked at Nick with irritation. When they finished the sandwiches, they picked at the *plátanos.* Jose slid down from Esposito's shoulder and lay on the couch. He put his feet up on Esposito's leg, to maintain contact. The baby had taken to him. Nick settled back and took the remote. CNN had a story about a missing child in California, red-haired and freckle-faced. He reminded Nick of the fair-haired boy at the playground, the one they'd decided was the cop's kid.

No missing children here in the Heights, Nick thought. They had extra, more than they wanted. People left them like stray cats, feeding them on leftovers and mice. He had a missing child, too. At work. The Lopez girl. The girl wasn't even really missing. She was playing hooky in reverse, skipping home for school. Not a priority, not even a case. A favor. Nick considered the baby dozing by Esposito, how Jose needed to touch him, even with his feet, newly in love with his newest friend. If they did their jobs, Nick realized, the baby would grow up fatherless.

"That's enough of this," said Esposito, taking the remote. He flipped channels until it came to a local station, where the two detectives they'd met at the diner were being interviewed about their pattern rape case. A brunette reporter held a microphone in front of the younger one's face; the other held a sketch.

"And can you tell us that number again for our viewers to call, if they have any information?"

"You gotta be kidding me!" Esposito started to yell, curbing his volume as Jose almost stirred beside him. He flung the remote at the TV and missed. It clattered against the wall. Further frustrated, Esposito seized the throw pillow beside him and hurled it at the screen. It did not miss, and the TV tilted back and toppled with a kind of slow-motion majesty, an air of almost political significance, as if it were a section of the Berlin wall. It fell with a crunch and went silent. Jose did not wake, but Nick felt the need to whisper.

"You could have just changed the channel."

Esposito shrugged, unsure at first whether he should be ashamed of himself. He hadn't intended to break the TV, Nick figured, but as Nick watched the diffident twist of his mouth reshape itself into smile, Nick knew that Esposito had rendered a verdict in his own favor.

"Now what are we going to watch?" Nick asked.

But Esposito held a finger to his lips—"Shh!"—and then to an ear. *Listen.* Nick thought it was a diversion until he heard it, too—the sound of the key fiddling in the lock. Esposito held up a hand to warn him against jumping up; they were not the ones who should be worried about getting caught. At the same time, this was not the right kind of surprise for Kiko—two strange men in his home, with his child. The lock was sticky, and the door creaked as the key turned one way, another, trying to find the trick spot to unlock it. That's why it had been open, carelessness and confidence at once. Esposito stood, and Nick followed him down the hall. He opened the door to a shocked Kiko, who had a key in one hand, a bag of Chinese food in the other. No gun, and no time to get one.

"Good afternoon. We're from Child Welfare," was Esposito's stern greeting. "Can you tell me why this little boy was left alone, in an un-locked apartment? Are you his father? Where's his mother? Please, come inside."

"The lock, it's broken. I told the landlord, like, five times. . . ."

Esposito took him by the shoulder and guided him in, as Nick walked ahead.

"Is my baby . . ."

"Jose is fine. No thanks to you."

"Sorry."

Leaning down to the couch, Kiko lifted up Jose, who didn't wake; looking down, he saw the fried rice on the floor, the broken TV, but he was in no position to complain.

Kiko asked, "You want to sit?"

"You sit."

Kiko was slim and wiry, with fine alert features and a goatee. He was the same color as Jose, with the same curly hair, but the baby was strap-ping while the man was slight; there was a facial resemblance, in a kind of bestial parody, so the sight of man and monkey-boy together sug-gested that a great evolutionary change awaited, though in which direc-tion was not clear. Nick and Esposito stood above them, arms folded, and let the silence weigh down on Kiko. Holding the child both calmed and unnerved him.

"You really from Child Welfare?"

"You really his father?" Esposito had the advantage.

"Yeah."

"We're not from Child Welfare, but they're on speed dial—you feel me? We came to talk to you, but all we found was Jose, home alone, run-ning around trying to stick his fingers in electrical sockets. He knocked the TV over, almost got killed. How many cases we get like that, Nick? Kid-crushings, TV-related?"

"More than you'd think," said Nick, grim-faced.

"It's messed up, I-I know," said Kiko, disconcerted, stammering. "My wife, she went out. Then I just went to get something to eat."

Jose stirred from sleep and kissed his father. He turned to the detec-tives, smiling, then dug into the Chinese food bag, evidently familiar with the lunch special. He found the egg roll, tore open the wax paper, and mashed it in his mouth.

"Easy, papi."

Jose scrambled down from the couch and ran over to Esposito, dropping the egg roll on the floor, and then offering it to him, his damp little
hands the model of generosity. Kiko looked guilty as Esposito picked
Jose up and had a bite, a gesture that took some discipline, as he was fas-
tidious about food. But it was worth it. Kiko slumped in his seat, and
then Esposito set Jose down. They should have taught the kid their
names, Nick thought; it would have galled Kiko terribly.

"How long were you gone, Kiko?" Esposito began.

"Like, fifteen minutes."

"No."

"How long were you guys here?"

"Stop playing games."

They meant the opposite, of course. They meant, Keep playing and
keep losing. It was going so well that they almost forgot they had nothing on him. Esposito and Nick pummeled him with questions, asking another before the last one could be answered.

"Like, two hours, maybe three."

"Where's your wife?"

"What's her name?"

"Where'd she go?"

"Belkis. . . . She went shopping with her sister."

"And she left Jose with you?"

"Does she do that a lot?"

"When does she get back?"

The idea was to keep jabbing, to make him run, to make him think he
was failing the test, without overwhelming him entirely, which would
shut him up.

"She should be back soon."

"You know why we're here, right?" Esposito asked. Nick let Esposito
pursue this line alone.

"Yeah."

"And why's that?"

"The *moreno* who got killed."

"Yeah, that *moreno*. What was his name, Kiko?"

"I don't know."

"No shit, you don't know. He was the wrong *moreno*. He was his
brother."

"I heard that."

"Yeah, word gets around."

Kiko shook his head.

After every admission, you had to decide—push ahead or pause? Every question was a risk. So far, the admissions had been small but significant, legally worthless but psychologically promising. The way these conversations moved, it could be uphill on gravel or downhill on grease. Now the road ahead looked beautifully greasy.

"You knew the brother. Malcolm."

"Everybody did. He killed my cousin."

"Nobody would say Malcolm didn't deserve it. But that's not what happened, am I right?"

"That's what they say."

That was not good, the passive voice, as if he were a face in the crowd, a whisperer among the whispers. Push or pause? Esposito pushed.

"What do you mean, 'they,' Kiko?"

"You know, everybody."

"You're right, everybody says it. There were people who saw it, witnesses. Everybody knows what happened. There's no secrets with this one, no argument. You know his name, Kiko?"

"Nah."

"Can I tell you his name? Do you want to know it?"

"Nah."

"His name was Milton Cole, not Malcolm Cole," Esposito went on. "He didn't hustle. He was a straight kid. He wasn't in the game, Kiko. He didn't deserve this. You know he had a kid, same age as yours? You know what his kid's name is? The kid's name is Jose. I think the girl is Dominican. But same kid, same name, same age. You know that?"

"Nah."

That part, Esposito made up, Nick knew. Still, it seemed to work, and Esposito kept at it.

"And you know about Milton's mother, right? She has a heart attack, when she hears about it? She's dead, too, Kiko! You missed, my man! You can't miss with a shotgun, but you did! You killed a beautiful kid and a nice old lady, and you might as well have killed the baby, because little Jose, he's been screaming ever since."

"That's messed up."

Push.

"No shit, it's messed up. It's messed up, and you messed it up."

Push.

"Yeah," Kiko said.

"You know you gotta come with us, Kiko, and deal with this."

"Yeah. Who's gonna take care of Jose?"

"Now you care? Why not just leave him again?"

Kiko sagged deeper on the couch. "Can I call my wife?"

"Do that. Make it quick."

Kiko slipped a hand into his pants pocket, and pulled out a cellphone. Esposito stopped him. "Listen, Kiko, all you say to Belkis is, she gotta come home, because you gotta go. No scenes. Be a man about this."

That was a targeted appeal to the demographic, and it worked. The detectives couldn't follow all of the Spanish words, but there weren't many—"*Me tengo que ir . . . sí . . . diez minutos? Muy bien.*" Nick was not unimpressed with the brevity of spousal negotiation.

"Can I eat?"

"Yeah."

That was a risk, but the reward was due, and it was a needless confrontation to deny him. That he even asked meant he had defaulted to prisoner mode, but food changed the body, changed the mood. He could find courage, or need a nap. Still, it was better to indulge him; this was not the fight to pick. As he opened up the bag, little Jose, happy little prop, clambered back onto the couch with him. Kiko's eyes were teary as he smiled, opening up the spare ribs, and his breath was short and shallow. Nick thought Kiko might cry as he handed over a rib to Jose, and Nick wondered whether the crying would work in their favor. A little early, he thought. He was broken, but they couldn't let him disintegrate just yet. Jose took the rib and devoured it like a caveman, tearing the flesh off the tip with his lower teeth. Attaboy, kid, you've earned it.

And then Jose's smile faded from his face, and his breathing changed, much as his father's already had; but where Kiko seemed to inhale and exhale rapidly without any profit in air, Jose was stopped like a bottle. Both Kiko and Jose would have screamed if they could have managed it. Kiko leaned forward and held him up, giving him a shake, as if the boy were a vending machine with a stuck quarter. He set him down again, from lack of strength. Golden little Jose turned pale, then blue, and Kiko became pale and stayed that way.

"Do you believe this?" yelled Esposito, taking the measure of what was happening. He snatched up Jose and turned him upside down, with

Jose's back against his chest, and gave him a light thump—one—which brought a strangling sound, and then another thump, slightly harder—two—which caused a gargling spit, and a scream. Two it was, and he was turned around again, for Esposito to pluck out the chunk of pork from his mouth. Even as he began to shriek, Kiko's desperate attempts at breath became more pained and failing.

"You call an ambulance, Espo, I'll try and help this guy."

Nick patted Kiko on the chest for a moment, as if he might get the engine started again. Then he checked Kiko's pants pockets, front and back, without result.

"Asthma? You have asthma?" Nick asked.

There were weak nods, and Jose began to scream still louder when Esposito put him down. The detective picked up the radio. "Squad here, Central. I have a choking baby, severe asthma attack . . ."

Nick asked, "Do you have an inhaler?"

A nod, and fluttering eyelids.

"Ah, shit."

Nick checked the pants again, and then Kiko's shirt—Had he had a jacket when he'd come in? No?—before running to the bathroom. In the medicine cabinet—Hadn't they checked here?—there were tampons, a hairbrush, bobby pins. The baby screamed and screamed, and Nick hoped he would scream more, as inspiration. And then he thought he could hear the wail of the sirens, thank God. Esposito kept the radio mike keyed on, so the dispatcher could hear the pandemonium, so the fear would carry over the air. Four blocks away, there was a hospital, and tanks of oxygen, but they needed air here, they needed more. Even now, Nick saw, Esposito's instincts were that of an impresario. *We gotta make this work for us, we gotta keep Kiko alive. The baby's a sound effect.* "Central, we have an adult male having a severe asthma attack, and a baby. The baby is turning blue, still choking. We need this forthwith. Can you raise EMS direct, get an ETA?"

"They're rolling up, rolling up now—you're third floor?"

"Third floor, Central. Can't miss us."

Nick opened the door, so the tricky lock wouldn't be a problem for the medics, and Mrs. Kiko pushed past, screaming, slapping him fiercely and catching a nail in his eyelid, before racing down the hall. Nick put a hand to the eye that burned, and followed, taking in what she did, guessing at what her first impression might have been. Kiko was on the couch,

with the color and animation of week-old fish, and Jose had howled himself beet-red. Every breath he took in was expelled twice over, in volume
that threatened to shatter glass. Nick hadn't thought the baby could be
uglier, but there it was, clock-stopping, mirror-breaking, dog-barking
ugly. Esposito took hold of her shoulders, and she smacked him; he
smacked her back. She fell, but he kept hold of one shoulder, and with
the other hand he took hold of her face.

"Mama! Inhaler!"

Esposito mimicked the spray of medicine in the throat.

"Donde! Donde!"

The medicine in the throat, spray, spray. She paused for a moment,
shaken, then went to work. She opened her purse, took the inhaler out,
knelt down, and pressed it to Kiko's mouth. She was easeful and expert,
tucking the chin up, holding the nose, as she pumped the breath into
him.

"Tranquilo, papi. Estoy aquí. . . . Tranquilo . . . Sí."

It was the most beautiful thing Nick had ever seen with one eye, and
even the baby's screams softened into exhausted gasps as the paramedics burst in, four of them, with kits and carts and machines. Two
went for the baby, two for the man, gently separating Mrs. Kiko to put on
the oxygen mask, and though they talked and shouted to one another, it
seemed that calm filled the room, and everyone now could breathe. A
medic picked up little Jose. "Look at the poor little guy's face." He might
have been talking about how swollen it was from crying, but Esposito
and Nick looked at each other, and had to turn away, quickly, not to
laugh.

Two of the medics were the ones from the Cole apartment, the Spanish woman and the white guy, and they looked at the detectives for a
longer time than might have been considered polite. Esposito didn't care
for that. "We ask for you guys now in particular, whenever we try to kill
somebody. You shoulda given us another five minutes."

"I didn't say nothin'," the white guy said, smiling a little. Nick
couldn't decide whether the smile was accusatory, or it displayed con-
spiratorial glee in some darkly imagined act.

"You got a problem?" Nick asked.

"C'mon now," said his partner, the Spanish woman. "Let's get these
people out of here."

The other two medics went about their work in purposeful avoidance of the conversation, and Mrs. Kiko didn't acknowledge whatever she might have taken in. She turned away from Kiko as he was lifted onto the stretcher and took Jose from the medic's arms. His cries became soft and rhythmical. The crew began to pack up bodies and machines, and the detectives followed down the stairs. Kiko was strapped to the stretcher, and the caravan moved through the lobby, to the street, where two ambulances waited. Kiko was lifted into one, and wife and child followed. Before the door was closed, one medic peeked out the door.

"Anybody under arrest here?"

"No."

"Okay."

The door closed and they drove off. The medics they knew stayed behind, and the woman approached Nick. His partner and hers stood apart.

"How's that eye? Can I look at it?"

Nick took his hand away, and she took out alcohol and gauze from the back of her ambulance. She swiped it clean, and he flinched.

"Don't be a baby."

"I make no promises."

"It's not bad."

"Good."

"Do you want to go to the hospital?"

"What would they do?"

"Topical antibiotic maybe. Not much."

"I want a glass eye."

"You can get one. You just won't have any place to put it."

"What's up with your partner?"

"What's up with yours?"

"The last place we were? We were telling a family about their kid who got killed. That kid, he was killed by this kid."

"My God! And you can't lock him up?"

"We were trying. We were on our way until the asthma attack."

"My God! Well, my partner, he's nice, he's good—he'll be good, but he's young."

"We're not."

"I know, baby, but try to stay that way!"

She gave him a pat on the cheek and walked away with a little laugh, waving her partner into the ambulance. They drove off. Nick blinked a few times, and looked over at Esposito, who was standing alone, angry.

"Let's get out of here."

"Yeah."

Esposito fished in his pocket for the keys and looked down the street for the car; it seemed a long time since they'd come here. They looked up and down, like old men, believing it was not far, but remembering nothing. Had they taken the blue one, the green one? Nick followed Esposito when he crossed the street.

There it was, the blue one, right there, with Michael Cole sitting on the hood. As they walked over to him, he stared back, not smiling, not angry. He took in Nick's eyes for a moment, and then Esposito's, and then he waited—one, two, three—before he sucked his teeth and spat.

"You're late."

Esposito was almost thankful for the distraction, after the loss of Kiko. "Did we have an appointment?"

"Somebody did."

"Who's somebody?"

"You tell me."

"I'm asking."

"I guess you gotta ask, 'cause I got the answer."

What did that mean? Nick and Esposito surreptitiously checked each other, shaking their heads. *Do you follow this? No, me, neither.*

Esposito asked, "Anything we can help you with, Mike?"

"I don't need your help. You're the ones, all empty-handed."

Michael drummed his fingers on the hood of the car and forced a cool half-smile. Nick had the feeling he'd practiced this conversation in the mirror, working on his gangsta-glib repartee like a Berlitz course. The labor he put into it made it ridiculous, but the ridiculous aspect made it seem dangerous, almost. Michael spat again, and the drool caught on his lip. He wiped it quickly with his sleeve, but the tough-guy effect had been ruined, and Nick joined the conversation to avoid prolonging the humiliating moment.

"I know why you're here, Michael."

Michael rejoined the game, upper lip curling for a rancorous rejoinder. "Do you?"

"Yeah," said Nick.

"And why are you here? Is it the same reason why I'm here?"

The catechetical sophistication threw Nick for a second—to what end?—before he went for mood-stabilizing social worker cant.

"Yeah, you're here for your brother. Us, too. We do care—"

Michael erupted in an eerie screech of laughter. "You don't know my brother!"

Esposito had heard enough of the obscurities and distractions; this was a dance that wouldn't lead to a date. "Stop. Mike, I'm sorry for your loss, I really am. Your mother, your brother. Milton. And the other one, stabbed. I knew 'em all! You wanna kill Kiko? Man-to-man, I understand, and the reality is, I can't really stop you if you're gonna try. I wouldn't cry, neither, if you did, but I'd lock you up after. Guaranteed. Life in jail, maybe it's worth it. You'll find out! This is the world. Welcome aboard! If that's okay with you, it's okay with me—let's let everybody do their job here. In the meantime, get the fuck off my car."

The last words were a mistake, Nick knew. Michael tensed, and Esposito started to step to him, but Nick signaled him to stay, with a touch of his arm. Maybe not a mistake. Michael seemed disappointed that the confrontation had been denied him. He smiled at Esposito and fixed Nick with a hard glare. He sighed and slipped off the hood, dusting off his legs. Roll on, little nutball, roll on.

"I'm like the Unknown Soldier . . ."

"What?"

Nick was curious, because Michael was entirely unlike the Unknown Soldier, in that he was known and not dead.

"I pop out when you least expect it."

Nick refrained from laughing, though it almost hurt him not to; he couldn't keep his eyes from rolling at the ridiculous boast, and that was a mistake. Michael caught it, and there was heartfelt hatred in the look he gave in return. He waited a moment—one, two, three—to show that he chose the time of his own leaving, before turning to walk away.

When he had receded a sufficient distance, the detectives got into the car and drove off. Both of them were made uneasy by the way the incident had tipped between high lunacy and low comedy, how the moonbat conceit had fed the menace. Esposito concentrated on the line of cabs that seemed to appear suddenly in front of them. He leaned on the horn and stepped on the gas, pointing his Roman nose ahead.

"You know, Nick, I think he likes me better than you. I don't think he likes you at all."

THIRTEEN

Rikers Island always looked more like a college than a jail to Nick, with its blocky modern buildings spread out over wide lawns. Big institutions looked like other big institutions, built to handle the volume. Rikers was another of the lesser islands of the city, a heap of nowhere in the dirty churn of the Long Island Sound, but you couldn't call it one of the failed ones; it had found its function in the thirties, and its acreage had since doubled with landfill. In a city jail, the inmates were either awaiting trial or serving misdemeanor sentences, for up to a year. Each group had their own little bedside bottle of hope—*I could beat this!* Or maybe, *Only two months to go!* But you knew there was always the other bottle they could drink from, that made them think, *From here I go north, for years and years, until I die, or until everyone I love forgets me.* Maybe it was a kind of college; it was definitely an education.

Every time Nick crossed the bridge from Queens to Rikers, he never thought as a cop. He looked at the curlicues of razor wire atop the hurricane fences, the water, the checkpoints, and had a brief daydream of escape, scanning the grounds to see how many guards he'd have to take out, scanning the water to see where the currents might take him. They were near Hell Gate, where the tides collided from the East River and the Sound. Not a good place to swim. Fear of shipwreck, fear of drowning, were plaintive in the names of the waterways—Spuyten Duyvil, Kill Van Kull, Gravesend Bay. Death by water, with the shore lined with spectators. On the little islands, you had as little faith in the system as you did in nature. Even if you weren't a crook at heart, you knew how fast the world could turn against you.

Esposito had engineered a little lie to conceal their errand, not out of any particular mistrust of the Department of Corrections, but because it was no one's business. Inmates kept close watch for breaks in routine, to see who was called away; among the staff, carelessness could be as bad as outright corruption. A chance meeting might lead to a chance remark, to a girlfriend, a brother, a friend, and news of a conversation might find its way back to the neighborhood before the detectives did. It didn't even have to be true for people to die.

Malcolm Cole had a history of ulcers, and it was arranged that he would claim to have an attack on the days he wanted to speak to them. Esposito knew a nurse at the Rikers infirmary who would relay the message and reserve an out-of-the-way examining room were they could speak. Her name was Audrey, and she was tanned, short, and curvy. After leading them to the examining room, she winked and walked away. Nick wasn't introduced. She was pleased to play the part; all of them were. Conspiracy is a kind of religion, bringing solace to people in dark places, lending significance to their losses. Malcolm was in a hospital gown, waiting with a wry smile. There was an ease in his body, a poolside slouch as he reclined on the examining table.

"Hey, Malcolm, how you doin'?"

"Not bad, not bad."

"They treating you okay?"

"I been in worse places. Yo, Espo, you look sharp today!"

Esposito was in a black suit, with a red shirt and tie. Nick thought he looked like a racketeer in a school musical.

"Thanks, pal. So, what you wanna talk about?"

"I got shit for you."

"I'm here."

"You lock up Kiko?"

"No. I went to talk to him yesterday. I wound up saving his life, his kid's life. His wife called a lawyer from the hospital. He's not gonna talk to me now."

"Shit."

"Yeah."

"What do you do now?"

"I don't know, something. I'll figure it out. What else you wanna talk about?"

"I got guys who got bodies, uptown, Harlem, Bronx. I got guys who even got bodies in Brooklyn."

"You see any of this, or you just hear about it?"

"Both. What does this do for me?"

"It depends. I can't give you numbers. I can't say, 'This many murders, this many years.' Five don't get you ten, two don't get you five. I can say, you help me, I'll help you. Nobody ever got burnt working with me, unless they tried to burn me first. We get along, you come out ahead."

"We both come out ahead."

"That's it. Tell me about one you saw, the last one you saw."

"Kiko, last summer. Him and his cousin, the one . . . I shot, did the drive-by on Little T, in the projects by me. Little T was my man. I came up with him. He raised me in the trade."

"The one . . . I shot." The hesitation was brief, and inspired not by conscience but by tact, choosing simple words carefully, without pride or shame.

"Wasn't it Little T who killed Fafa, the month before?"

"They said it was, but it was Dirty Moe."

"Dirty Moe worked for Fafa?"

"Nah, Fafa worked for Dirty Moe."

"Little T shot Fat Hector?"

"Everybody know Little T shot Fat Hector. Back up, back up. With Dirty Moe and Fafa, it had nothin' to do with that. Fafa threw a bottle, scratched Moe's car. It had nothing to do with work. And we didn't have no problems with the Dominicans before Kiko. We was mad cool before then. Kiko come from wherever, decides he has to tighten shit up, playin' Scarface. Fat Hector was his man."

"And you saw 'em shoot Little T? What did you see?"

"I saw Kiko with the cousin—that cousin, the one I did. He leans out the window with a big silver burner, and it was—Pa! Pa! Pa! Three shots. He hits Little T twice, the neck and the leg. Little T, he just sits down and looks at me, like, 'Can you believe this?' "

"Who drove?"

"Kiko."

"Who shot?"

"The cousin."

"How do you know?"

"I saw 'em, I saw 'em both. Plus, it was Kiko's car, a white Escalade, Jersey plates, spiderweb rims. He never let anybody touch it. He shot a crackhead through the foot for sneezing on it."

"Crazy Joe? Rasta Joe?"

"Shit, you know Joe?"

"Yeah, I know him. Another guy had the case."

"What he tell you?"

"He told me that Joe said it was a hunting accident, he was wrestling with an alligator."

"Ha! What you do?"

"We didn't go looking for alligators."

"You know, Crazy Joe, he really had a alligator? That's why he said it. Kept it in his bathtub, fed it chickens. Live chickens, real chickens. You know they sell 'em on Tenth? What they call 'em, 'vivo—' "

"Vivero," Nick said.

"Whatever. That was when I was a kid."

A meditative look crossed Malcolm's face, as if he were viewing his life so far, and it wasn't half-bad. A sweet youth, which ended yesterday—crack and alligators, few regrets. From there, he detailed three more homicides, two of which he'd witnessed, and four more shootings, one of which might have been a homicide, but he hadn't waited to see how it had ended. Nick believed what he had heard. Malcolm didn't try to show off, and his memory of events was detailed without being suspiciously complete. An informant like Malcolm was money in the pocket, a skeleton key, a passport. These were spatter-pattern cases, a bloody mess at first look, and second, and third, until the fine tip of a red droplet pointed you in the right direction. Esposito knew some of the cases, to some degree, and Nick filled a notebook with specifics of who had stood where, and how many shots had been fired, and what time it was when it happened, and who drove what after, to test what Malcolm offered against what they'd find in the case files, to match the unstable brilliance of the been-there moment against the documents and diagrams.

There was a blitz of nicknames—Cagney-era gangster monikers, scumbag moderne, Spanish. Nick had offered the word "vivero." Otherwise, Nick stayed out of the conversation. These were all perp-on-perp hits, thug family fratricides. It was not his cup of shit. But it was Esposito's. He understood them, understood the contest, the battle for territory, meat, and mates. He liked these cases because they were like him. They were Espositos in parallel, in reverse. It was one of the reasons he was so good at this, Nick reflected—Esposito didn't hold it against them. Nick's partner leaned forward on the chair, hands on his knees, and Malcolm was in the same position until he let out a breath and listed back on his seat—enough for now. He lounged on his side, playing with a fold of his ludicrous hospital gown, and smiled.

"So. We good? 'Cause I got plans."

The remark struck both detectives; the tone was so politely peremptory, an executive brush-off. Esposito took pains not to appear snide. "You have a lunch meeting, Malcolm? Tennis lessons?"

Malcolm laughed. "No! I'd take 'em, though! You wanna get lunch, you wanna play tennis, I'm all in! My plans, they ain't for today. I got a lot positive goin' on, real positivity."

Esposito looked to Nick, who was unhelpful. Nick had gotten tired of the hoodlum almanac, but he couldn't stand the word "positivity," the jargon of parole board karaoke. *Umm, and I know now I gotta be a leader, not a follower. . . .*

Malcolm took no offense. "I got kids, a wife, business—legit. A couple of 'em, doing good. What you think I been up to since I been on the run? You think I'm just another raggedy-ass street hustler, every dollar I get I put into gold for my teeth?"

Nick thought it best not to answer. Esposito, in his shrewdness, answered with a kind of question of his own. "I heard you was down South, in Carolina somewhere."

"Close!"

Malcolm's teasing reply gave Esposito a chance to maneuver again. "It don't matter to me, Malcolm. For one, the sooner you get out, it means the better we done by each other, so I'll be waiting for you when you get out the door. We'll go out for a beer. Second, I ain't the drug police. Whatever cash you got, whatever you came out with, good for you! I ain't gonna try and game you for hints, where you got all those coffee cans full of twenties and fifties, where you got 'em buried."

Malcolm smiled again, shaking his head. "That's funny, that's good. But nah, I got two laundries, a barbershop, in a town down in Georgia. My sister, she's assistant principal at the high school. My wife, she sings at the church. Property taxes, business taxes, they are nothin' down there. It's beautiful, when you're on top. You think my kids are little hood rats, shit in their Pampers, brought up on food stamp formula, government cheese? I been out of this, awhile now. I was up, checkin' on my moms. Milton, he was my little man. Was gonna take both a them down with me, take 'em in and set 'em up. I ain't been on the run. I just moved. Hey, Espo, look at your partner! He thinks there's only one system where I fit in!"

Nick shifted in his seat, uncomfortable at having been caught in his assumptions. There was so much more to Malcolm than what Nick had first supposed, days ago, in the project apartment, grimy and poor, luck-less and mean. No, that hadn't even been the first mistake. The first had been believing him to be the blasted corpse. But the surprise of seeing Malcolm walk in the door had been no greater than now, with his reve-lations of substance and sense. Or on the jaunt from jail to the funeral home, from hell to hell, when he gave thanks. "Even a day like today . . ." These truths did not cancel one another out—ghetto predator, Mayberry shop owner, paterfamilias—but Nick could not quite reconcile the con-tradictions, could not see the whole man made of such outlandish parts. It was a relief when he remembered he would not have to. Malcolm was a killer, and he had been caught. The job was done. Everything else was positivity.

"Yup, family—that's what it's all about," said Esposito, casual in his segue. "So, you talk to your brother? You talk to Michael?"

Malcolm's eyes tensed a little. "Nah. He hasn't been to see me, I don't call. What he do?"

"It's not what he did. He didn't do anything. But I'm worried about what he might do. Do you worry about him?"

Malcolm eased and tensed again. "We never been close. Not since I was little. I got a big family, and we got different fathers. Lots of us, with half-brothers and sisters we're never gonna know. My father? Mine was never there. Michael—Michael and Milton—their daddy looked to be a real daddy, to me and them both. He worked. He was a doorman down-town, at a rich white people building. He took us to the beach once, in the Bronx. He had a car. I never seen that. I never seen sand. Can you believe that? Ten years old, I knew what street was, I knew was dirt was, but I never seen sand, never stepped on it. My feet didn't believe it. It was like a made-up thing, like snow for a Puerto Rican or something, you know? Big fat guy, his name was Jerry, Jeremiah. He was sweet as pie. He bought me a bike. Then, heart attack. Pop! Done. We had in-and-out dad-dies after that, some of the old ones, sometimes new. Back like it was be-fore. Me and Michael, we was close till then, but I didn't mind both ways.

I liked the 'Didja do your homework' daddy, but when he died, I didn't have to do homework.

"Milton always looked up to me, but Michael, after that? Michael looked away. Michael is the older one. He's in his twenties. Milton was . . . I don't know, but I guess he wasn't twenty-one, or else . . . or else he wouldn't need my ID."

Malcolm's aspect darkened, and Esposito pushed ahead, so Malcolm wouldn't dwell on what couldn't be changed.

"How many brothers and sisters do you have?"

"About six."

"About six?"

"There's half-ones and step ones I lose count of."

"Okay."

"Anyway. Michael, he wasn't the same after. Never was a happy-go-lucky kid, but after, he was as fun as a funeral. Worked hard, good at school—he went, even when it snowed! Hot, cold, wet—he went to school, whenever it was open. Couldn't play ball, couldn't hit a ball if you tied it to the bat. He woulda had the black beat off him at school, in the neighborhood, if it wasn't for the rest of us. He had glasses. You remember my brother Nelson? They called him N-Dog?"

"Yeah, I remember. Stabbed at a club? Downtown?"

"Three years ago, God bless. Him, me, our whole peoples, that was what let Michael be Michael. You know that my man took violin lessons for a while? Shorty walkin' around the projects with a violin case and glasses. That's not even like havin' a big 'Beat me!' sign on your back. That's like advertising on the radio. It was all us, respect for us. He played like crazy after Jerry died. First it sounded like he was frying cats, but nobody could say nothin'. He was special, he was sad, and then he got good. He got mad good, all this old-timey shit. I don't even know what it was—classical shit, I guess, I don't know. All these songs, it was like the movies, when the nicest white girl dies. Sad and special, just like Michael. Everybody wanted him to shut up, and he wouldn't, and then nobody wanted him to stop, and he did. He is one backward mother. . . . It was right before I went upstate—a two-year bit, for hustling, but you knew that, right?—that he quit. He joined the army. Something to do with 9/11 maybe, but I don't know, I don't think it had to do with that. I think he just wanted somebody to fight with.

"I gotta laugh at you guys—no disrespect. You guys figure, we're brothers, we're like . . . brothers. But it ain't like that. I went upstate, he went into the army. We both got back, the same time. My moms had a party for both of us, but Michael wouldn't come."

"Shit, Malcolm, there's a war. How'd he get out of the army? He fight somebody?"

"That's all he wanted to do. But no. He got sick. He didn't even get sick—they found out he had something, a disease. What they call, you don't got iron in the blood?"

"Anemia."

"Yeah, it was that, but the opposite. He got too much. I don't know what they call it, but I guess if you bleed there with it, they can't fill you back up. Every guy in the world gets dragged there, they don't want to go. He wants to, they won't let him. Drop that on somebody who was pissed off to begin with, and what you got is Michael."

"You think he's gonna kill Kiko?"

"You kiddin' me?"

"You think you can talk to him?"

"You been listenin' to me?"

"You want him to wind up with you?"

"I don't want me to wind up with me, you feel me? All I can do is talk, and I been talking! To you! My talking gets me to you. You guys are the ones gotta make things happen! And not happen! I ain't gonna lie. Kiko dies, I ain't gonna cry about it. He killed my brother. Milton. And I loved him. But I ain't about getting even. I'll take that, if it comes up, but I'm about getting out. You feel me? It's in God's hands. Yours too, maybe. Not mine."

"Okay, Malcolm, I got you."

"Michael ain't even gonna call me. But if he did, I wouldn't tell him you saved Kiko's life, saved his kid. You know? You come to our house, all these people die; you go to his house, you're all, like, *Baywatch*—lifeguards on the beach, pullin' everybody out whose drownin' and givin' 'em mouth-to-mouth. Not for nothin', Espo, but you can't be like Santa Claus with him and Freddy Krueger with us. I know you ain't wrong, what you did, but even if I talked to him, how could I tell him he ain't right?"

"We deal with what we get dealt, Malcolm."

"You ain't kidding. You know what that muthafucka Kiko and his crew do? These Dominicans, I don't know, Espo—these are some bad people. They're off, you know? Believe me, they are not like us."

Esposito nodded, and Nick pursed his lips—*Us?*—as Malcolm went on. "This is what pisses me off. Kiko ain't even in the business no more, he ain't a hustler. This corner don't mean shit for him. They kidnap other hustlers, their own kind, Dominicans. They wrap 'em up, with that plastic shit, like tinfoil? They wrap 'em up like mummies. They beat 'em and burn 'em with irons till they give up the work, kilos and kilos, like hundreds of thousands. Me, my people? We just makin' a living, just—"

"What they do?" Esposito asked.

"Burn 'em with irons—"

"Plastic wrap, like for leftovers?"

"Yeah. The other day, I heard they took some kind of priest. Dominican kid I know, Flacco—he ain't one of the bad ones, he still cool with me. He went to school with Milton. He felt bad—"

"Priest?"

"Yeah, minister, priest, whatever, one of them."

"Nick, we gotta get out of here. And, shit, Malcolm—why didn't you tell me this before?"

Malcolm stood up and stretched, aware the conversation was over. He smiled at Esposito and laid a hand on his shoulder.

" 'Cause I didn't know you. See how good things can be, now that we're friends?"

FOURTEEN

A random encounter, an offhand remark—the scraps of information were so slight by themselves, so persuasive together, that the detectives felt that destiny was in play in the discovery. Drug dealers had kidnapped a priest, were burning him alive. Nick and Esposito were as desperate to leave the island as any inmate, but the Department of Corrections bus, blue and orange, boxy and slow, rolled ahead of them at a lackadaisical pace. The guard at the gate avoided looking at them as he talked on his phone about how his backyard deck was refinished last year but the wood was already warping. When he finished, he didn't hurry as he checked the trunk for contraband and hidden prisoners. The delays felt spiteful, and their absurdity tested Nick's and Esposito's belief in the moment, that it was inevitably theirs. Once they were out, Esposito flew through the toll on the bridge without stopping, and he barely touched the brakes on the mercifully clear midmorning roads. Nick called the squad and found Napolitano, who rounded up whoever he could. They would be waiting for them by the building. All the forces felt like they were again falling into place.

"Do you think it's a real priest?" asked Nick.

"No."

"A reverend, a minister, something like that?"

"Maybe," said Esposito, thinking aloud as he worked through the probabilities, skimming through his mental scrapbook of atrocities. "They got somebody special. These home invasions they do, they go for drugs or drug money, gambling spots. Sometimes they hit cash business people, who sell jewelry or deliver cigarettes to bodegas. Dirty money, clean money, as long as it's cash. Dirty money is better. The victim's not gonna go to the cops. But sometimes they get the wrong door, the wrong guy. How long are they gonna burn the guy with the iron before they believe him?"

"Kiko makes more sense now," Esposito continued, talking to himself as much as to his partner. "He's a tough kid. I can't believe he looked like he was gonna go so easy. The guy who had him in on the Rasta Joe shooting, he told me that when he brought Kiko in, he laughed and spat, wouldn't give up the time of day. He's gonna roll over for us when we got him on bad babysitting?"

"Maybe he's not afraid of us. He's afraid of Mrs. Kiko—he's afraid he's gonna get it from her, if we take the baby."

"Maybe. But this is a guy who tortures people for money. He don't give a shit if he kills the wrong Cole brother. There is no wrong Cole brother to kill."

"We just surprised him?"

"We definitely surprised him. Milton Cole was old news already. He's already in the ground. Kiko's got a fresh one, and we almost walked into it. You know what he felt when we started talking about Milton? Relief! Can you believe this shit, Nick? He was happy to go back with us to the squad—it gets us off the block, away from the priest. We think we're gonna get a statement from him, but the only thing he's gonna tell us is, 'Thanks guys, for the perfect alibi!' "

The meeting point was around the corner from the apartment, out of sight from the windows, wherever they were. Napolitano and Perez were there, and Lieutenant Ortiz and Garelick rolled up as Nick and Esposito parked. The situation was explained—the news from Malcolm; the sight of the man with the shopping bags full of plastic wrap; the five-story building, five apartments per floor. All were different men from the ones who had fussed over breakfast—taut and pointed, alive to the purpose. All had questions for Esposito.

"The guy walked up past you when you went to the second floor?"

"Yeah, but he would have kept walking anyway."

"He didn't hesitate, he didn't look on two?"

"No."

"But were you really watching him?"

"Yeah, we watched him. He stood out, and he was a little freaked by us. But there was nothing more to it, right then, and we had shit to do."

"What do you think about the super? Any contact with him? Think he's dirty?"

"The building is dirty—him, I don't know."

The superintendent of a ghetto building was always in a difficult position. Most landlords wanted a clean and orderly place—unless they were looking to sell it, or tear it down, or turn it over, in which case the dirt and danger were assets to drive the old tenants out. The super worked for the landlord, but the super also lived there, usually in a basement apartment, and had to deal with the tenants, face-to-face, day to day. In the worst buildings, there was often some kind of understanding, a fearful truce. Sometimes, the terms were more forthright and direct, and the super was an ally and employee of the hustlers upstairs.

"If we talk to him, we gotta leave someone with him, so he doesn't raise the alarm."

Garelick nodded. "That's about my speed."

"Because it's a priest, Harry?" wondered Lieutenant Ortiz. "If it was a rabbi tied up in there, would you be the first through the door?"

"Not if it was a boxful of rabbis or a pope on a rope."

"All right. Let's hit it, then. Meehan, Espo, you work from the top down. Perez, Napolitano, from the bottom up. What did you say, five apartments per floor? Mark off the one you hit already. I'll cover the street, in case somebody goes out the window. Harry, see if you can work through the tenant roster with the super, knock off any place that doesn't fit. They could rent the apartment out from somebody, an old lady, whoever, or it could be vacant. Keep your phones on, and listen close at the doors. Any problem, we pull back, call in the cavalry. Remember, this is an investigation, not an invasion. Otherwise, somebody's gonna get hurt."

"What are we gonna go with—the 'missing kid' bit?"

"Yeah. Anybody got a picture?"

Napolitano pulled out his wallet, and took out two little photos, portraits of a boy, a girl, in First Communion costume, the boy in a dapper suit and bow tie, the girl in a white lace dress with a veil. Hands folded in prayer, the smiles goofy and beatific. He handed the little girl to Esposito. At other times, there might have been a wisecrack; not today.

"I want it back, Espo."

"I promise."

The answer was grand, Nick thought. Napolitano was not worried about the picture. It could be replaced. The detectives couldn't be, or at least they liked to think so. Esposito was making guarantees, more than he had a right to, but his confidence rang out like a trumpet, brassy and gladdening. They walked around the corner and filed in, according to assignment. Lieutenant Ortiz loosened his tie, sat on a car hood, and lit a cigarette. Garelick disappeared down the alley. Napolitano and Perez each took a door in the lobby, leaning in to eavesdrop. Esposito called softly to them as he and Nick mounted the stairs.

"There won't be kids there. There should be loud music, TV, to cover up the conversation, any screams."

Both nodded as Nick and Esposito went ahead. Though there was no need for silence, they stepped carefully up the chipped marble steps, stopping at each floor to listen, before ascending to five. Music throbbed from behind at least one door on each floor. At the top, Nick and Esposito each chose a door, to listen for the something, the nothing, that might tell. Nick remembered his patrol days, when he'd get a report of a gas leak. The firemen would press their faces into the doorframe, close enough to kiss, sniffing for the odor, however faint. You have more sense, more senses, than you know. You have to pay attention, pay and pay. The doorframe was tobacco-brown, the paint troweled on in rough annual layers, and he scanned it for roaches before wedging his head in, cupping an ear—muttery, dim news in Spanish, *noticias*. He looked over at Esposito, who was already knocking across the hall, briskly, not too loudly, attempting to be casual. Nick did, too, leaning back in again to hear if there were footsteps, scrambling to hide, or the lax padding, barefoot or in slippered feet, of an ordinary woman answering an ordinary door on an ordinary day. Good people wonder who it is at the door; bad people know. There was a slow, rhythmic swoosh, an off-beat two-step, of calluses on old floorboards, an innocent sound, an innocent rhythm.

"*Sí?*"

"*Policía, señora.*"

"*Sí? Por qué?*"

Nick looked over at Esposito, who had another woman at her door, younger, in her late forties, in a bathrobe. He had the picture of the Napolitano kid, and they were talking.

"Have you seen her? She's missing. Everybody's very worried. Do you have kids? Who do you live with? Is there anybody inside who might know something?"

"My God, what happened? Is she all right? Did somebody do something to her?"

"We don't know, miss. Your name is?"

"Colon. Awilda Colon."

Nick rapped again on his door. *"Abrir la puerta, señora. Esta la policía, quiero hablar . . ."* As if he could talk. The peephole darkened for a moment. The woman was looking to see if the face, the suit, matched the bad accent. When she opened the door, he saw a thin woman, wary but civil, nearing eighty, with a meringue of white hair and a black housedress.

"Sí?"

The detectives drew both women out into the hall, so the information could be pooled.

"Could you talk to this lady for us? Could you ask if she's seen this girl?"

Esposito handed the picture to Awilda, who walked over to the old woman and showed it to her. They chattered rapidly in Spanish, with dramatic interruptions and exclamations.

"Yes, she says she's seen her!"

"Here? In this building?"

"Hang on—"

The operatic volleys went on for a minute, with fluttering hands clutching hearts and heads in turn. They were caught up in the drama— too much, maybe—imagining things in their desire to help. Nick's heart stirred, too, drawn into the passion play of a child who was not there.

Awilda asked, "What's her name?"

Esposito hesitated, unprepared. "Her name?"

"What's the little girl's name?"

"Grace," said Nick, unsure what prompted him to speak.

"Ay, dios mío!"

Nick didn't see how it was more poignant than the abduction of a little Francine or Joanne, but there it was. Esposito pressed ahead. "Did she see her here? Your friend?"

"Un momento . . ."

The conference resumed with urgency. The old woman shook her head, briefly, so that it seemed as much a tremor as a denial.

"No. She hasn't seen her in the building, but she thinks she's seen her in the neighborhood. Do you think, do you think little Grace is here with us somewhere?"

"Yeah, we got a tip. Somebody called it in, said she was here in the building. Do you know people in the building? Have you lived here long?"

"Is she hurt? Who took her?"

"We don't know. . . . I can't get into it right now. We just gotta find her. How long have you lived here?"

"Me? Like, five years, but I don't talk to people here. It's a messed-up building. There's drug dealers here, bad people, and they don't do nothin' about it. Not the super, not the landlord, not the cops."

"Yeah, sorry. How about this lady? Has she been here, does she know anybody?"

"Rosa? She know everything, everybody. She been in the building for years. Like, fifty. Nobody spoke Spanish when she got here. Now she don't like anyone, but she won't leave. You can ask her anything."

"Okay. Who lives on this floor? What about the other three apartments? Has she seen anything strange here?"

The conference resumed with Rosa's watchful decades now put to use. She had waited a lifetime to be asked, and she answered at length. Awilda turned to them for the recap. "Okay. I'm in 5A. Rosa's in 5E. On this floor, we got six Africans in B, Islamics. They're quiet. Mexicans in C, six of them, too, sometimes ten on weekends—that's when they go off, but they only fight each other. And there's a crazy old black man with Social Security in D. He has whores come in the first of the month, when the check comes in. He cries about Vietnam for the next three weeks. He sometimes wants to help Rosa up the stairs with groceries, but she won't let him. . . ."

The census proceeded to the next floor, duly noting race, religion, income, and other relevant data, which the detectives absorbed with polite frustration until mention of the probably lesbian Colombian X-ray technician, who "don't talk to nobody, not even the gay guy, since she got into a fight with the super about the people in E. Because, you know what? There ain't suppose to be anybody in E! And the music is loud! Like the biggest party in the building for the last week, and nobody's invited! There's good people here, but it don't come to nothing—"

"This party, what's that? Is there a lot of people there? Do they come in and out?"

"Nope! A guy here and there, but it's just all noise. Rosa here, she's called the super, but he said she must be imagining things, she should go to a home. Can you believe that?"

"And that's in 4E?"

"Yeah. You don't think little Grace is there, at some wild party? My poor baby!"

"I don't know if she's there, but that's a good place to look. Who comes in and out of this party?"

"Nobody, just guys now and then. And the music goes on and off. I meet these guys walkin' up the stairs, they're like hittin' on me, hard, but on the fourth floor, it's like I got bad breath. Just like that! What's up with that? When's the last time a guy wants you but shuts the door, when maybe you might go in? I mean, you guys are still guys, you follow me? I ain't dead yet, and you know? I still got my body!"

Nick stepped in between them and smiled, placing a hand on her shoulder.

"Awilda, you are far from dead, and you are a big help here. How about the guy in 2B, Raul Costa? You know him?"

"Him, in 2B? I don't like to talk bad about people, he never done nothing to me, but he's a freak. Right, Rosa?"

The conference resumed in Spanish, and Awilda updated the detectives after some vigorous nodding.

"He gets his mail in his underpants. His little boy underpants, with his little thing half sticking out. Freak!"

Rosa remembered a last urgent detail about their downstairs neighbor, which Awilda translated uncertainly: "And she says he went crazy yesterday. He was screaming about something—cops, about cops did something to his mother? They put a dog face on her? I don't know. Rosa don't know what he was going off about, but he was mad. Him! I wouldn't put it past him to take a little girl!"

"We'll check. Thank you, ladies. We're going to have a look downstairs."

Nick's phone rang as he and Esposito walked down to the fourth floor. It was Garelick.

"Apartment 4E. It's vacant, but there's people."

"The super was cooperative?"

"I had to jog his memory. Napolitano and Perez are on their way up."

"Wait with the super."

The two other detectives joined Nick and Esposito, their breath heavy after the march up the stairs, the adrenaline percolating through middle-aged blood. Esposito started to lean into the door of 4E, listening for voices, but Spanish music thumped, the horns and the drums, the galloping rhythms. The detectives spoke in stage whispers, but they didn't need to; the noise that covered what happened inside the apartment covered them on the outside.

"We gonna knock?"

"We don't have to. The super says it's a vacant apartment. We're checking on a burglary. So we get to break in."

"Do we want to surprise them?"

"Do we want them to be ready for us?"

"Let's at least raise the lieutenant, let him know we're looking at—what is this, the southeast corner? We face the front, the alley. We got a fire escape. Do we want somebody on the roof? Perez?"

"Perez speaks Spanish. We want him here."

"We want to go in speaking English, even if they don't understand, so they know it's cops, not other dealers come to rip 'em. We want Ralph nearby, though, if there's more than a couple there, if they say anything to each other."

"Okay, Perez stays. Napolitano on the roof."

"Maybe you hang out on five, midway, that way you can go up or down, if they run."

"We can't do that and cover the roof."

"We need more guys."

"We need more guys."

"We need more guys."

"Right," said Esposito. "Ready? Let's do this."

Napolitano backed up the stairs as he called the lieutenant, directing him to the point on the sidewalk where he could watch the windows of 4E. He cradled the phone on his shoulder, muttering into the receiver, and gave the thumbs-up.

Esposito took a dozen steps back and rushed the door. His feet struck the floorboards in percussive beats, quick and quickening, like a drumroll, but instead of the tinny clash of the cymbal, it finished with a dull, momentous crunch. He bore down with his left shoulder, his momentum adding hundreds of pounds to his angry weight. The door caved in through the frame; above the knob, the lock pushed back through the splintery old wood, giving back three wheezing inches, four, when the chain caught. It was the only time in Nick's life when he wished Spanish music were louder. Esposito stepped back and freed the door with a kick. He charged in, gun drawn, and the rest followed.

"Police! Don't move! Police!"

"Get down! Hands up!"

"*Policía! Manos arriba! Quiero ver manos! Policía!*"

The room opened up before them, and it was as if they were in sudden, bright light. A predator needs movement to read a scene. In that first second, when all is still, a standing man is a lamp, a man lying down is a rolled-up rug, and only motion—in fear, to fight—tells the target, the threat. Even with the delay from the chain, the detectives were faster than the reaction to them; the men inside had made the mistake of stopping to think. There were three men sitting on folding chairs, on three sides of a square, as if playing cards, though there was no table between them. One of the men was small and heavy, cocooned in plastic wrap. His arms were cellophaned to his body, and his body was cellophaned to the chair. Atop his body, his bloody head seemed to emerge from the casing, as if being birthed. Closer was the man Nick had seen in the lobby with the bags of wrap, stunned, unmoving. He held an electric iron in his hand. At his feet were a bucket, a wet towel, and a gun. On the far side was Kiko, now up and running, into the back room. He had done his thinking. The door slammed behind him.

Esposito followed Kiko, out of instinct, out of injured pride, but this door held against him, at least against his first push. Perez and Nick pointed guns at the bag man, who weighed his options still, gripping his electric iron as the seconds stretched out. He stood and held the iron up, like a shield, and Nick kicked him in the balls. When the man doubled over, he pressed the iron against his own leg; he screamed and fell back. Napolitano appeared at the door, and Esposito yelled to him—"Roof!"—and gave the door another solid shoulder, which knocked it loose. Esposito and Napolitano vanished from the room as Nick kicked the gun on the floor over to Perez. Nick walked over to the screaming man on the floor.

"Watch!" Nick called over to Perez. "The room's not clear. I got this guy. Watch me!"

The man on the floor began to reach for something, the iron. Nick stepped over to him and gave him a kick in the ribs. The man clenched, pulling the iron over to his arm, searing himself afresh on the biceps. He screamed again. The music was still blaring, the antic brass in lively rounds, and Nick knocked over the TV. After it smashed, the silence was almost lunar for a moment. They could have been alone on a pale rock at the edge of the night sky. The bound man sighed and began to weep. "Gracias . . . Dios mio . . ."

Nick stood over the man on the floor. "Hands! Give me your hands! Manos! Tu manos!"

The man clutched and clenched and moaned. He didn't do what Nick told him. Nick kicked him again.

"Hands! Hands behind the back! Ralph, say it in Spanish!"

"Manos atrás!"

When Nick put his foot on the man's neck, he felt him tense again before he eased into obedience. The man flattened, facedown, and extended an arm back. Nick put a cuff around the wrist. They were in, he thought, this was done. This was a surrender. To quit this much was to quit altogether. Nobody gives up just one hand. A thug fakes it at first, doesn't fight—I can't move. It hurts. I can't hear you. I don't understand. It hurts—but if he's still faking it, he doesn't let a hand go in the cuff. The cuff connects him, to the radiator, to a rail, to the cop. And it's over. Nick could smell the burn on the man, the burnt polyester shirt, the burnt hair on the arm, the burnt skin. He was finished. Perez checked the kitchen, then the bedroom that Kiko had fled through. He looked under the bed, in the closet. He was still there as Esposito walked back through the front door, sweating, his collar loose, hair rising up in loose tussocks. He looked at Nick and shook his head. And then they heard the toilet flush. Esposito and Nick looked at each other again. Nick felt the arm tense in the cuff, and he yanked it back. He put a knee into the shoulder. There wasn't much give. There wasn't supposed to be. Nick spoke quietly.

"The other hand, now! La otra mano . . . El otro mano!"

From behind the bathroom door, they heard the toilet cover drop, and the sink turn on in sporadic gushes. Esposito adjusted his stance, blading his body sideways, and extended both arms, aiming the gun at the bathroom door. He had made a promise to the men that they would go home today, and the promise would be kept. As the plumbing groaned in the pipes, a voice could be heard, an off-key sing-along, growing louder.

"Mi amor . . . da, da, da . . . mi corazón . . ."

There was a fumbling at the knob, and they heard the old metal gears of the lock, the soft oof of the door that barely fit in the frame. He must have been shy, closing the door so tight. He walked out, and he looked like Kiko, but maybe seventeen, in a tight purple shirt. He was slim and lithe, unworn yet by life. He stepped with a teen bravado, singing, making his grand entrance, his finale, arms outstretched. He had clunky headphones on, and he sang whatever was sung to him, as a joke, but with feeling, eyes shut and smiling.

"*Y mi corazón . . .*"

And he bowed with a flourish, clicking his heels. When he looked up, he froze, and his knees buckled for a moment. Esposito yelled for him to put up his hands, but he dropped them both to his waist, digging for the gun, any gun, both guns, as if he might have had two, slung on either side, quick draw like in a cowboy movie. There were two shots, and he fell down. The man under Nick jerked his arm, and Nick pulled it back, hard. He felt the tear of gristle, a little pop. The man tightened, but there was no more fight in him. Nick got the other arm out, cuffed it to the first. Perez came running out of the bedroom, gun drawn. Esposito stood there a moment, staring down at the boy he had killed. Nick called over to his partner, who stood there, blankly contemplating, as if all of this were over. They'd been wrong about that before.

"Cuff him up, Espo! Go there, cuff him up, call for an ambulance, call the boss."

Perez stood also, staring. Nick patted down his cuffed perp for weapons and called again, "I'll call, Ralph. Just go cuff him, check for the gun."

Perez walked over to the body—it was a body already, no longer a boy—that sat slumped against the wall. Perez touched him around his waist, hesitant, repulsed, as if the body might jump up at him. There was nothing there. He wore a tight purple shirt, tight white pants; you would have seen the gun, Nick thought, if he'd carried it tucked in his belt. Perez looked back at Esposito, in wonder and fear. Esposito holstered his gun and stood there. He was in his own movie now, and it was a horror movie, about a man trapped in a small room with a dead kid, a kid the man had killed, and neither of them would ever leave it, and only one of them would always be young. Maybe that was Nick's movie. He looked again at Esposito, who stared down, shaking his head. His expression, Nick thought, was resentful. But his voice was calm.

"Check the bathroom, Ralph. That's where he was. Don't touch it, don't move it, just check for the gun."

The man on the floor strained to look around at the body, and Nick put his gun to the man's head.

"Don't look. Don't move."

The man turned back to the wall. Nick walked over to the body and touched his neck for a pulse. The flesh had a little give, a softness without response, like a pork chop in the supermarket. Nothing there; done. It reminded him to attend to the victim, who had fallen silent at the speed and violence of his deliverance. Nick walked over to him, and he looked at Nick, blinking. His head was bloodied all over, red in bright rivulets, brown in crusty smears.

"It's okay. You're safe. We're the police."

The man began to laugh, so weakly at first that Nick thought he was weeping, but when it grew more vigorous, there was an unmistakable bitter glee. He shook his shoulders, to tell Nick to unwrap him. Nick took hold of a piece of the cellophane by his neck and tried to tear it; the layers at the edge frayed, but the thicker midsection held. He would remain mummified until he was cut out. Nick wished he had a camera, wished he had a knife. He stepped back to look for something sharp, and the captive leaned over to spit on the man at his feet, who flinched but didn't move.

Perez called out from the bathroom. "Got it! I got the piece!"

Napolitano hustled through the door, flushed and sweat-soaked, and the lieutenant pushed breathlessly past him; he leaned down, hands on his knees, and coughed up phlegm. He looked at Nick, unable to ask what he needed to know. Nick made the report:

"We're good here. One perp down, one under, one on the run. Two guns. None of us hurt. The victim—this one—he's beat up, burnt, but he's still got some fight in him. This one here, he's past helping. He don't need an ambulance, but we need Crime Scene. The runner's Kiko. We got him for this even if he walks on the homicide."

The lieutenant nodded, and his breath seemed to grow more regular as he took in the information. The worst news was far better than what he'd imagined on the labored run upstairs, and you could almost picture his blood vessels relaxing, easing back into the ordinary flow.

"I already called the ambulance. There should be about a hundred cops here in a minute," the lieutenant said. "You guys are both okay? This is . . . all good?"

Perez stepped out from the bathroom, a new man, nearly swaggering. "The gun's right there, next to the body."

"All right, good. What do we got here?"

Nick spoke up before Perez got a chance; he didn't like how Perez improvised.

"Espo took the door, three guys sitting in chairs, the victim between two perps. Kiko ups and jets. The guy on the floor doesn't get to. Junior is in the bathroom, he's got headphones on. The music must be blasting, 'cause he walks out like he's stepping onto the dance floor. Clueless, not a clue. He goes for his waist—that's that."

Lieutenant Ortiz nodded, then fumbled in his pockets for a cigarette. When he lit the match, his hand shook, and he had to steady it with the other before taking a drag. When he exhaled, all of the detectives did, and Nick could feel his pulse drop. He had seen what had happened, but he hadn't begun to take it in until he'd said it aloud. It had been a good shoot, as they said, meaning that it was justified, that it would pass the test. Nick looked around the room, at the sweat, the fear, the dishevelment. They looked like an accounting firm who had been dropped into boot camp, their attaché cases lost somewhere on the obstacle course. Napolitano could have come from jogging through a car wash. Perez glistened with perspiration, but he was otherwise kempt. He began to pace back and forth.

"Muthafucka! That was close!"

While the lieutenant and Napolitano watched Perez move, walking in an odd circle—it looked something like a victory lap, something like a failed sobriety test—Esposito fixed his eyes on Nick. He was grateful for the simplicity of the recap, and was mindful that he hadn't been asked himself. He turned to Lieutenant Ortiz, and the wryness faded from his expression. When Esposito placed a hand on the lieutenant's shoulder, Nick wasn't sure if it was to ask for support or to offer it.

"Let's get going for this. Let's get everybody out for Crime Scene," Esposito said, taking it in. "What about this guy, the victim? We gotta get him out, I know, but I'd hate to lose the picture. With a picture of this guy, like this, we don't have a trial—we have a plea. Their lawyers will beg for one. Anybody?"

Nick wondered if Esposito wanted the picture to look at later, for when he thought about the dead boy and needed reassurance that he had done what was necessary, for when he needed proof. Then Nick wondered if it would be a kind of trophy, a head to hang on the wall. He stopped wondering after that. No one had a camera.

When Nick had been on patrol, he'd carried one for a while—a number of cops did—for souvenir purposes as much as evidentiary ones, but the habit had fallen away. Nick should have had a camera and a knife, he thought. For that matter, a radio and a vest. A lot of detectives discarded the old tools of patrol for defense and attack because their new tools worked so well, so often, and all that mattered was your mind, your mouth. You talked them in, when you could, and you never fought them, when it was possible, because you had to talk to them later on. Someone else was always the tough guy, the bad guy. Nick could hear the sirens gathering in the distance. The cops were coming.

What would have happened if they'd run this drill by the book? Had met dangerous opponents with body armor, paramilitary tactics, superior force? Would they have done better—one down, one gone, one under arrest, successful rescue, no cops hurt? Before they had taken the door, they'd been chasing a rumor.

Esposito ran a hand through his hair, thinking, then thinking aloud.

"The two ladies upstairs, in 5A and 5E, they were ready to help. One of them's probably got a camera."

Napolitano was closest to the door. He tucked his shirt in, smoothed his hair back.

"I got it."

The hostage moaned again—"*Ven aquí. Ayúdame.*"—and Nick went over to him, telling him to wait, it would be all right. The man shook his head, pointing his chin over to Esposito—*Look!*—and then chinned down to his own neck. He called over, hoarsely, and Perez translated his request.

"He has a necklace. Take it out. He wants to show you."

Nick pulled back sheets of bloody plastic, gingerly, and saw a string of beads, black and red, in alternating grouped bands. The man nodded again to Esposito, in his red and black clothing. Perez led them through the new significance.

"*Los colores, negro y rojo.*"

"The colors, black and red."

"*Son los colores de Elegua.*"

"*Elegua?*"

"*Elegua.*"

"He says they're the colors of Ellegua, whoever that is. You're a priest? *Es usted cura, sacerdote, clero?*"

"*Sí.*"

"*Qué tipo?*"

"*Santero.*"

"Shit, he's a voodoo guy. . . . Santeria. That shit creeps me out. . . . Basically he thinks Espo is his voodoo avenger, that he called Esposito here."

"Shut up. Don't even joke like that," Esposito said.

Lieutenant Ortiz raised his hand to cut the conversation off. There would be enough paperwork to do without the metaphysics.

"You think they knew and they still kidnapped him? Isn't that bad luck?"

"It looks like it was bad luck."

"What do you think, they took him for his pot of gold?"

"That's leprechauns, jackass."

Napolitano had returned, with a little disposable camera. The sound of sirens neared outside, as Napolitano stepped into the room and began to choose where he'd snap the pictures. The santero grinned, delighted that his service to Ellegua had borne such fruit. Napolitano told him to stop.

"Tell him not to smile, okay? It's just too weird. A good lawyer's gonna look at him all happy and say it's some kind of S&M thing."

Perez instructed him, and his facial expression varied between grim stoicism and silent-movie horror, as if he were a damsel tied to the railroad tracks. Napolitano took the last picture in the roll, and they wondered if the santero was a little loony, playing up for the camera, but when Esposito tried to tear some of the plastic from his arm, he shrieked. The plastic had melted into the skin, where they had burned him with the iron. Had he been tortured for a day or two? More? He was entitled to make all the faces he wanted, to laugh whenever he found it in himself, and to thank God, the New York City Police Department, and whatever imaginary friends who took the trouble to visit. Esposito touched him on the shoulder, kindly, and stepped back.

Cops began to arrive in numbers, and the lieutenant kept them calm, outside the apartment; Nick picked the man up from the floor, struggling in his cuffs, and sent him away with two of the cops. EMS arrived soon after, among them the same pair, their old friends. When they walked into the room, the white guy was visibly amazed, while the Spanish woman knew enough to conceal her amazement and get to work. She went to the santero, while the white guy went to the dead guy, touched his neck. He looked at his watch.

"Time is 11:32."

And then he looked to Nick, wondering. There was no accusation in his face. If anything, he looked admiring, cocking his head toward Esposito.

"Jeez. This guy—you guys, again? Which one did it?"

Esposito scowled. Napolitano stepped forward, as if to backhand him, and the EMT stumbled back. Napolitano was the union delegate. He knew that every shooting led to either a medal or an indictment. This one looked good, but he was unwilling to bet. And he certainly was not going to allow a statement to a stranger.

"What I do?" the EMT asked.

His partner cringed and went to him, for consolation and cover. Esposito shook his head as Napolitano walked up to them, shaking an angry finger.

"We have to read people their rights before we ask if they killed anybody. I guess you're a special kind of detective, get to do whatever you want."

"Sorry. I just—"

"Yeah."

"Easy now, everybody." The woman EMT put a placating hand on Napolitano's shoulder, then another on her partner's, and led him over to the priest.

"Come on. Help me here. Baby, get a razor. Let's get this guy out of this stuff. There's second-, third-degree burns here. I don't think the scalp and face lacerations are too bad. . . ."

Lieutenant Ortiz joined them around the man in the chair, in part to separate the teams.

"Easy with the plastic, okay? We're gonna have to save it, check it for prints, DNA, see if we're missing any of the players."

"You got it. I think there may be twenty, thirty yards of it, maybe more."

"Yeah."

As they cut through the plastic, a dark-skinned man emerged from beneath, nearly fifty years old, with a bare barrel chest and a substantial belly. His arms were thin, and his legs didn't quite reach the ground. There were a dozen burns on his arms and half as many on his legs where they had to cut around the plastic because it had been seared in; the doctors would have to remove it later on. His underwear was dingy and white, or once had been. It was now sallow yellow at the front, giving off a foul waft when his legs and lower body were finally cut free. Some covered their faces. Some made sounds, disgusted. Most stepped back. The Spanish EMT caressed his face.

"Todo está okay, papi. No te sientas avergonzado."

The priest began to cry now, maybe for the first time, as if the pain had been somehow bearable but the shame was not. Bound and brutalized, he'd been able to stand whatever his enemies had inflicted on him; sitting in dirty underpants in front of a compassionate woman was beyond his endurance. He began to sob and cough in erratic rhythm, and the EMTs ushered him to his unsteady feet before helping him up onto the gurney. They guided him out of the apartment, into the crowd of cops in the hallway, where a dozen blue arms reached around the stretcher to help carry him down the stairs. Nick wondered what the color blue meant for him, what devil or divinity he had called upon to bear him away, after the red god had shot his way to freedom.

FIFTEEN

There was work to be done in the apartment, but it wasn't theirs; Crime Scene would take photographs, measurements, specimens. All the documentation and cataloguing, the dull science of it, was theirs to slog through. There were interrogations to be conducted in the precinct, regarding the crimes to be proved and disproved. The detectives gave the lieutenant their guns, to establish which had been fired. Nick would have to give a statement, later on, but there was still business for him to do with his partner. They pushed through the crowd outside the apartment—cops and the curious—and forgot again, like the last time, where the car was; was it an hour ago when they'd met, hiding around the corner? Ages ago, that hour. Nick breathed more deeply and easily when they found the car, and again when they left the block, so that it felt like, with each stage of departure, he was finally getting real air. Esposito had wiped his forehead with his arm a few times, but his suit was a poor absorbent for the sweat that flowed from him.

"How you doin'?"

"Fine," said Nick, almost believing it. "You?"

"Yeah, me, too. I got an idea. Let's take a break."

Esposito made a sharp turn right, and then another one, so that they weren't heading south to the hospital anymore, but north, toward the precinct, and wherever else. He pulled over by a bodega and returned with a brown bag before heading west. At the far end of 181st Street, they left the car. There was a short walk over a pedestrian bridge that crossed the highway, the railroad, and then they went into parkland, lawn and trees, green and rolling, near the foot of the colossal steel supports of the George Washington Bridge. Down to the left were massive gray boulders, piled to the river's edge, where an old man in a black suit reached into his pocket and tossed handfuls of bread crumbs into the water. A few Canada geese paddled in close to him, bumping like tugboats, their snaky necks thrashing down at the crumbs.

The detectives scrambled down the embankment and sat down on the hillside. There was more air here, again, and Nick breathed it as if it had just been invented. The river flowed past, as dirty as an old nickel, but the breeze felt fresh. Esposito took a quart of beer out of the bag and handed another one to Nick. They raised the bottles and tapped them against each other. Esposito poured a few drops of beer onto the ground, a libation. The movement was quick, surreptitious, as if he did not mean for it to be observed. There was a gap in the air, as if there were something that needed to be said. Esposito spoke first, with a kind of cracked curiosity in his voice. "You know what's the most fucked up thing about all of this?"

Nick was startled; he had expected some expression of sorrow or regret over the death, but the tone was jarring, almost angry. He didn't respond, and after a few seconds, Esposito continued.

"The EMTs. This is the third time we get these two in, what, four days? Three times in four days, when there's dead people and almost-dead people that some people might say was our fault. My fault. Come on, Nick! What are the chances? What do you think, it's one of them or both? The girl or the guy?"

"What?"

Nick was relieved that the crisis was not what he had at first feared; beyond that, he was baffled. They had just lived through a moment of mythic intensity—door crashing, lifesaving, death dealing, with good witchcraft and bad music—and the last of Nick's preoccupations was the fluky cameo in the aftermath. Esposito looked at him, half-smiling, his black hair sticking up in sweaty clumps and weedy blades where he had rubbed his head in his penitential moment, now past. He was reanimated now, awake to a new challenge.

"Nicky, come on. You're supposed to be the smart one."

"I'm not."

"They're IAB, Nick. Gotta be. Twice is coincidence. Three times is a conspiracy. Can you believe these people? We're lucky to scrape up a handful of guys to bust up a kidnapping. How many of these fucks are working on us, on overtime, watching to see if we fuck it up?"

Nick took in the news like a snake swallowing a rat—yes, a

rat—slowly, in difficult stages, but with certain result. Esposito mistook the shame in his face for fear, and laid a hand on his shoulder. More than one thought went through Nick's mind; the last one was that he was not trusted himself, by the people who'd sent him.

"Interesting," Nick said.

Esposito gave him an easy shove. "Don't worry, pal. I got a knack for these people. I can spot 'em a mile away."

Now Nick knew. Love brought the gift of not-seeing. He laughed in turn, and Esposito was reassured that his partner had not lost confidence, either.

"Was it a good shoot? Tell me, Nick, whaddaya think? Me, I think it had to go that way. It was meant to be."

Nick nodded, eager to talk about something else. He hadn't tried to picture what was behind the apartment door, waiting to see it instead. In retrospect, the result had been predictable, the most likely end if not the inevitable one—three trained men surprised three distracted amateurs, and advantage prevailed. Seconds later, Nick realized that was not the case, not it at all. The result had been a blind bull's-eye at the end of a crazy chain of wanton whatiffery. A sturdier front door, a different break-fast for the boy in the bathroom—skipping that last cup of coffee, having cereal instead of bacon and eggs—or a lack of headphones might have led to an entirely different outcome. Esposito was beguiled by his own charisma, a kite that thought it ruled the wind. No, that wasn't quite right, either. Choice and chance, in a game of hide-and-seek. Ellegua was as good an explanation as any, and it would do for now.

"Yeah."

"And? What else?"

"Perez moved the gun, for what it's worth," Nick reflected. "The way I figure it, the Dominican kid forgot he left it in the bathroom, came out trying to shoot with an empty hand. Perez moved it, so it was next to the body, after. In the end, I don't think it matters much."

"Yeah. That's the way I figure it, too. He wanted to frame a guilty man for me, tighten it up so I come out all right. Guys like that, the help-ful ones . . . Last year, there was a rookie in the precinct, him and his partner make a great collar, take a machine gun off a guy wearing a rain-coat on the hottest day of the year. His partner says to him, 'Can you say you're the one who found it? I got a family cookout tomorrow. I can't spend the day in court.' 'Yeah, no problem.' There was somebody walking by with a camera in their phone, took a picture of what really happened. The guy with the machine gun, he walked away, scot-free. They let the rookie take a plea to a misdemeanor."

"He meant well."

"They always do. I can make enough of my own trouble. Jesus, Nick—look at Perez's new girlfriend. If she was a blow-up doll, at least she'd be real."

The first things had been said. That felt better than the beer. You could be sad about something that happened, even if you'd do it again. Esposito ran a hand through his hair, considering things.

"You okay, Nick?"

"Me? Yeah, sure. This isn't about me."

Esposito spat out his beer, laughing. Nick was discomfited when he realized that he'd just quoted the voice in the pipes in his apartment. Esposito slapped his knee, raised his bottle.

"I'm glad you were there, Nick. I'm glad you're my partner. You're a thinker, but it doesn't get you down. You get it, you get me, and I know you got my back."

Right then Nick thought about returning to the Bronx. He'd find the lieutenant, the mystery caller, and tell them they had the wrong man. Two wrong men. The calculations, the implications—Did two wrongs make a right, or did you need more?—all of it was too much. No, he'd stay here and keep the best of his promises. He watched the elderly gent at the shore as he turned and began to walk away, age in his hips, his step slow and careful. Esposito drank his beer and looked at the river.

"The old guy didn't bring much food for the ducks."

They weren't ducks, Nick knew. He didn't know what to say. He asked, "Do you feel bad about it?"

"No," Esposito said, after a moment of thought. "I love life. I love my life. I got kids. What kind of chances should I take?"

"None you don't have to."

"Do you think I shouldn't have shot him?"

"No."

"Do you think you should have shot, too?"

"No."

"Why not?"

"I was on the other guy, the plastic wrap guy. He wasn't cuffed up yet. It would have been a mistake for me to let go. I needed both hands."

"Do you wish it turned out different?"

"Wishing is a waste of time."

"Yeah."

With that, it was over for Esposito. Nick watched him hold his beer out to the side, tilting it for a moment, so the liquid ran up the neck, to the lip of the bottle. Then he drank it, without a drop spilling on the ground. Such tribute as would be paid had been paid. Let the dead bury the dead. He spat and shook his head.

Nick sought to reassure both of them. "Perez doesn't matter. We have what we have. We saw what we saw."

"What did you see?"

"What you did."

"Tell me."

"We took the door. The three guys were there—bag man, voodoo man, Kiko. Kiko goes running, you follow, I cuff up the bag man. You come back, bad guy walks out of the bathroom, makes to pull a gun, you shoot him."

Esposito didn't look at Nick as he spoke, but stared straight ahead. When the story was finished, he took a long drink. They were convincing themselves that all had gone as it should have, as it had needed to. It wasn't a lie, but it felt like it. Esposito took the part of the challenger, knowing the challenges would come. Theirs was an adversarial system, they were constantly reminded, an immense and unstable collection of rules—constitutional principles that the highest judges disagreed about, new administrative procedures that spewed out of headquarters like rolls of sheet music from a player piano. So many rules that you could barely count them, so many that it felt like you were breaking some of them even if you were sure you did everything right. Trials were a fact-finding process in which the most crucial facts were often withheld from the jury. You couldn't say a victim picked a perp out of a mug shot, when the whole case existed because a victim picked the perp out of a mug shot. A man could confess to murder, but if he began his confession by saying he wanted to talk to a lawyer first, he hadn't confessed to murder. If you locked up a crack dealer for the fifth time, you probably couldn't tell about the first four. And most of these exclusions and suppressions were premised on a belief that a jury's blind bias favored the state—the cops—when that was not the world Nick lived in and knew. It was astonishing that it worked as often as it did.

Esposito cleared his throat and rehearsed the cross-examination. "Did you see the gun in his waist, Detective?"

"No," Nick answered, playing Esposito's future part.

"Did you see the gun on the floor, after?"

"Yes. After-after."

"Just answer the question, Detective."

"Yes, I saw the gun on the floor, after, beside the body."

"Did you see Detective Perez place a gun there?"

"No, I did not."

"Can you testify, with positive certainty, that you observed the entire contents of the floor in the general vicinity of the deceased?"

"No, I cannot."

"Thank you, Detective. The witness is excused."

"That's it?"

"That's it."

The beers were half-gone. As the two men looked west over the river, the tension of the past hour began to subside. The geese didn't stray far from the shore, waiting to see if there were more crumbs for them. When there were none offered, they mustered up on the rocks.

"This kid," Esposito began, trailing off before he could decide on a description. "You think he's Kiko's brother?"

"He's the spitting image. He's gotta be."

"Malcolm Cole's gonna be happy to hear that."

"An eye for an eye."

Kiko's brother and Milton Cole, both with headphones, lost in the music until the end.

"A brother for a brother," Nick said.

"Do you have brothers?"

"No, solo, only child."

"Same here. Parents?"

"One, father."

"I think I knew that. Mother only here."

Nick knew Esposito didn't have a father, but he couldn't remember who had told him; he hadn't known that Esposito had no siblings. Everyone else did, it seemed, if they were their age. No father of that vintage said one is enough, no mother did, if they were born in the first half of the last century; from the slums, from the farms, it didn't matter, most of them didn't know how to say no, even if they wanted to. The two detectives had been working together for months, but it hadn't come up; a lot hadn't. Nick knew that Esposito had a wife and kids, but he didn't know their names. The two men spoke constantly when they were working, but seldom when they weren't. They'd call to tell each other if one was taking a day off, or working earlier, going to court. It was a friendship of necessity, which may not be real friendship; it was confined to work, but they were, too, it seemed. Nick loved work now, sometimes, which was more than he could say for most of his life; Esposito loved work, far more than Nick did, even though he had a family to whom he was devoted, in his way. When Esposito spoke to his wife on the phone, the conversations were jokey and teasing, or full of affectionate reassurance; Nick never heard an argument. As far as Nick knew, Esposito made his wife as happy as any faithful husband he knew.

Nick shook his head. "Should we go?"

"Yeah," said Esposito, his mind already moving on. "Let's talk to Papa Doc in the hospital, get his statement, start on the perp back at the station house. Plus, we're gonna have ... our friends from downtown waiting to talk to us."

They bagged the empty beers and stood up stiffly.

"And then we hunt Kiko again," said Nick, thinking as his partner did, a few moves ahead.

"Yeah. Is this a real kidnapping? I'm a little rusty on the law there. We don't really get too many of these. Does there have to be a ransom?"

"No. That's only one kind. The victim has to be held for at least twelve hours, for the purpose of 'terrorizing' him. With the plastic wrap and the iron, they got the terror part covered. We don't know about the clock. But I bet we're okay, time-wise. I bet they had him yesterday, when we ran into the guy in the lobby with all the plastic wrap. When we saw Kiko and his kid."

"That woulda been something, if we took him in for endangering the kid yesterday? It would have been a nice alibi. Last night he must have gone to sleep laughing, couldn't believe his luck. He walks away from us on the homicide, and we don't have a clue he's got a hostage across the street."

"He didn't even have to pay for a babysitter."

"He paid," said Esposito. "Come on. Let's do what we gotta do."

There was neither sorrow nor satisfaction in his voice. Nick felt both, and more, as his mind slipped between images of the young man dead, the older man saved, thoughts of his own faithlessness and new friendship. They took their time leaving, brushing bits of grass and leaves from their suits, stretching their legs. Spies in ambulances? He couldn't even pretend he'd ever understand or really wanted to know. Nick looked a last time at the river, where the geese had begun to drift downstream. He wished he could stay here, but wishing was a waste of time.

SIXTEEN

At the precinct, the crowds were already beginning to form, the workers and wonderers forming up into little camps outside, the first ripples of snap and reaction. It wasn't as bad as all that. They had gone by Kiko's building before the trip uptown and had seen the small combustible head-to-heads forming up between cops at the perimeter of the scene and the local trouble. Nick had glanced up at the roofline and had seen more cops stationed there. That would keep the bricks from raining down, at least for now. This would be a day of noise, because a cop had killed someone. Esposito had rolled through the block, to take the temperature of the street. They'd seen the crackhead who had pissed in the lobby the day before; he laughed when he saw them, and gave them the thumbs-up. You could only control the rumors so much, but when the santero had been rolled out in his fantastic plumage, Nick was later told, he had called out that the police had saved him. When the boy had been carried out in the bag, half an hour later, the onlookers had not been able to see his wasted teenage face.

Right now it was still the afternoon, so the night people, the merchants and the creatures, had not yet stirred to offer their commentary. No, this one wouldn't be bad. At the precinct, there were four or five news vans, and two or three cameras pointed at reporters who used the precinct as a backdrop, speaking into their microphones, in front of the cinder block. One reporter brought a garrulous old woman in front of a camera, but when she began to scream about Jews breaking her washing machine, the reporter made the cutoff sign. The detectives drove into the parking lot and walked in through the back entrance.

The media and the police machines were in simultaneous, sometimes rival motion. Neither was unfriendly, so they reminded the detectives, a

little too often. Everyone wanted to know, and even though there was no
bad odor to this one, both machines had to act as if there might be. More
union delegates arrived, with pizza, warning Nick and Esposito to be
careful what they said. The two detectives had serial interviews, official
and otherwise, some taped by Internal Affairs, and some conducted by
the other cops, when they stepped out for coffee, or into the men's room
for a piss. Lieutenant Ortiz remained in his office, at his desk, as men of
higher rank and lesser time surrounded him, testing his decisions. "If
you thought it was nothing, why did you go yourself?" "If you thought
it was something, why didn't you go with more people?" Nick could see
his hand gestures, cutting through clouds of smoke. It was as he'd said
before, the operation had been an investigation, not an invasion, a jail-
house rumor coupled with a chance meeting. Lieutenant Ortiz could
handle the chain of command. The suspect Nick had arrested was in one
of the rooms. When he was interviewed in English, he didn't understand. "No comprendo," he said. When he was interviewed in Spanish, he
didn't understand any better. "No comprendo," he said. It was a philosophical approach. You could say it was the inspiration for philosophy itself. It didn't help them. It didn't help him, either.

Once Internal Affairs interviewed Fernando at the hospital, the mood
in the office palpably changed. Word came in that after a detailed account of his abduction and day of torture, he told of the detectives' arrival like knights on horseback, their expertise and restraint; more to the
point, he had seen the boy, Miguelito, draw on them, had seen the glint
of steel, the barrel yanked from the waistband, and he'd seen that Esposito had done the minimum necessary, to his maximum gratitude. Fernando's story would play beautifully, uptown and down. He did not
expound on Ellegua and vengeance, the red and the black, and he had
agreed to speak to the media. The police did not discourage him, and the
doctors made only mild complaints. It would hit the five o'clock news,
and the six, and on news radio it would play every ten minutes, followed
by traffic and weather. It would hit the Spanish media even harder, but
after tomorrow's papers, it would be gone. The chiefs left, with firm
handshakes and clipped smiles.

When Nick and Esposito went to the hospital, the EMTs were still
with the victim. They were in a little bay, behind sheets of loose curtain
that were too short, like hospital gowns, depriving you of dignity
where they were supposed to preserve it. A cop waited just outside, and

Esposito reminded him to bag up the plastic wrap. Great swaths of it, cloudy, clear, or pink-streaked, were heaped around the bed. There were tufts of it melted into his thighs in three or four places, and as many again on his arms. One eye was swollen, and his lower lip was fat, but there was less damage than you would have guessed. When the blood was wiped away, he looked no worse than if he'd been in a bar fight. His body had been cleaned; there was only a faint odor, not much stronger than the disinfectant air of the emergency room. The victim held the woman EMT's hand. Nick reached out to take her other one.

"You know, I never got your name. I'm Nick."

"Odalys."

"Odalys, would you mind staying a minute here with us, with this guy? He seems comfortable with you here."

"No problem. If you need his information, I have it here, on the chart."

Odalys handed it over to Nick to copy down. Fernando Dotti, aged fifty-one, of San Francisco de Macoris, Dominican Republic. Local contact, a niece, a few blocks away. Odalys spoke softly to Fernando, and he smiled weakly back. Esposito stepped over to them, anxious to get a statement before the painkillers kicked in.

"He knows we're police, right? We're all police, right—Odalys?"

She nodded, oblivious to his little joke, and Esposito did not belabor it. Nick was proud of himself when he did not cringe.

"Just let him know again, he's safe now, we're all here to help him."

"I told him. He knows," Odalys said. "He says 'Thank you,' you were an answer to his prayers."

"That's okay. Let him take us through this, bit by bit, all right? Who did this to him?"

"The three, the three who were there, and another one."

"Did he know them?"

"No, not before this."

"Why did they do this? What did they want? Why him?"

"His brother. His brother Rodolpho died, last month. Heart attack. Fernando came up here just after, to help his brother's family. The brother had money. The men thought he had a lot of money. He had bodegas, taxis. They took Fernando to make his niece give it to them."

"How much did they want?"

"A hundred thousand."

"Did she have it? Did she agree? Does he know what happened?"

Until then, the conversation had been concise, to the point; Fernando's voice, though hoarsening, had been steady, expending no excess effort and no emotion. When Odalys brought up the next topic, however, he wheezed and growled, then gargled up a throatful of phlegm and spat it out in contempt. It caught the lower part of the curtain and hung there, dark and glistening, waiting to drop. They all watched it in reluctant fascination until Fernando began to hold forth, and Odalys tried to divine his relevant speech like a soothsayer amid his digressions and curses.

"Her husband, the niece's husband, he's—how can I call it, excuse my French—he's a miserable prick. . . . He offered five grand and a Honda Civic. Three years old, two doors. It had thirty thousand miles on it. . . . Excuse my French, but he calls him 'pudejo.' It's basically 'private hair.' "

Odalys winced as she went on, as if she were unsure which group was more sordid. "Fernando remembers the kidnappers arguing over it. The main guy, who ran away—he thinks they called him Kiko—he said it was a good car, the Japanese make the best ones now, they run forever, it could run for another two hundred, two hundred fifty thousand miles. But then the other one, who got arrested—they called him Miguel—he said he didn't do this for a bullshit used car. And then the little one, Miguelito—he was Kiko's brother—it turned out Kiko had bought him a Honda, not new. . . .

"So he got mad that Miguel called the car bullshit, and they had a fight over it for an hour. . . . And then Miguel gets the iron out, and he burns Fernando. . . . And Kiko says, 'Go easy with la plancha'—I mean the iron—'because it means they go to the hospital after, and the cops get involved.' But Fernando doesn't think Kiko meant it, meant to stop Miguel. They were gonna kill him. They talked about sending fingers to the niece, her cheapskate husband. And the little one, Miguelito, he was gonna go out and get a knife. He went to the bathroom before—he had to go. Then he was gonna go out for the knife."

"How long did they have him?" Esposito asked.

"He's not sure. Yesterday morning, he thinks. He went out for breakfast. Then it was dark and light again."

"How did they take him?"

"In front of the house, the niece's house, two guys with guns, Miguel and Miguelito, and they put him into a car, put a bag over his head. There was a driver, he doesn't know who. . . . They drove around in circles. His head was between his knees. The car stopped, and they sprayed him in the eyes with something that made his eyes cry. They took the bag off, put a baseball hat on his head, pulled it down low. They stopped, took him out of the car, walked him inside, upstairs. Miguel and Miguelito were on either side. They both had guns, and the spray that made his eyes cry. It was like he was drunk, they were helping him. Inside, upstairs, it was just them, then Kiko—maybe he drove—and they hit him on the head. And then they wrapped him up.

"'I tell them'—That's what he says. He says that he tells them, 'Miguel? Miguel and Little Miguel? You're both named after San Miguel, Saint Michael, the angel.' That is the other name of his . . . *orisha*, whatever. His Santeria devotion, Ellegua. But they don't listen. The little one steps back, but Miguel, that's when he first takes out the iron."

"Who burnt him with the iron?"

"Mostly Miguel, but Miguelito, too. After a while, he doesn't remember. It was a lot the same after that . . . hours about where was the money, where was it, and then the argument about the car."

"Did he hear them ask for the ransom? Did they talk on the phone about it, or did he just hear them talking to each other?"

"Both. They had a cellphone, Kiko did."

"Who was the fourth man? How long was he there? What did he do? Could Fernando recognize him?"

"He doesn't know. He knows there was another guy there. He didn't see him good. It was after they hit him in the face. He brought something—food, maybe—and they talked respectful to him. Not like Kiko to Miguel, or Miguel to Miguelito. Not like he was their boss, really . . . but you could tell he was older, or they treated him older. . . ."

"Could you—"

"He wants to thank you."

"That's all right. He's welcome."

Odalys paused, uneasy, hesitating to translate the next line, until Esposito reassured her that she had nothing to fear, there was nothing he wished concealed. Nick thought he was pushing it a little, but Odalys continued, "He wants to thank you for killing the . . . little boy. He was the worst one, because he was young. He could tell. . . ."

Esposito flinched at the praise. It was not how he would have put it, "little boy." Nick asked another question, so Esposito wouldn't dwell on it.

"What does Fernando do in Santo Domingo?"

"He's a santero, a Santeria priest."

"Anything else?"

"Yes. He's an accountant."

"Did he work for his brother?"

"No, for a tobacco farm, a group of farmers. A coalition? No, a cooperative of farmers."

"Okay . . . anything else?" Esposito asked. "Can you think of anything? Nick, Odalys, what do the doctors say? He's gonna pull through, right?"

"Yeah. There's the burns. He was in shock, probably, and we don't really know his medical history . . . but look at him, his belly. And with the brother dying of cardiovascular disease, this experience . . . They'll keep him awhile here, watch him."

"Does he have to go back soon? To the Dominican Republic? After his medical treatment, can he stick around a little? There are DAs who have to talk to him. We already have Miguel, and I promise you, we will catch Kiko. We just have to know how to get hold of him, to talk to him, down the line. What did he say, just now?"

"He says San Miguel is also the patron saint of policemen."

"Very nice."

"He has a son at home, also a policeman. His name is Miguel."

"Oh."

"He says he trusts you. He trusts you both."

"Good."

"And he says—he says—I don't know if I should say this—"

"Say it."

"He says he knows there won't be a trial."

Fernando released Odalys's hand, rubbing it gently. He looked at the detectives, extending his hands to them, and they took them. He spoke quietly to himself, so quietly that Odalys couldn't understand. The lips barely moved over his teeth, as soft breath crossed, in and out. His eyes rolled up for few seconds, exposing the dizzying whites of them, and then his gaze again became direct. His grip was firmer than expected, and he smiled and nodded, then released their hands, as a sign for them to go.

SEVENTEEN

In the boat basin at Seventy-ninth Street, the fleet of sailboats and cabin cruisers rocked on their moorings, as gentle as sleep, masts furled, and guano-spotted tarps covered the decks. A dog walker with a hydra-headed leash held a pack of proud exotics, Pomeranians and borzois, and was being drawn forward like a fantastic carriage. On the green hillside, an aged man in black pajamas guided a tai chi class, arms raised, then drooping like wilted lilies. Two women with crew cuts walked by, singing a cowboy song, holding hands. There was so much to see in this part of the city, but it was not what Nick was looking for. He had a feeling he was being followed; he'd felt it for a while, on and off, like a ten-second flu, since Esposito's observation about the EMTs. When his phone rang, with a blocked number, he answered without hesitation.

"Can you talk?" the voice asked.

Nick nodded, then laughed. Why was he making gestures to someone on the phone? Secrecy had become so ingrained in him, and the meeting was supposed to be face-to-face, with his heretofore faceless contact. "Contact." Nick didn't like the word, hated the whole self-important and self-conscious language of espionage, but he supposed it was better than "handler," with its connotation of the dog show, the pooch on the professional leash. He half-expected a mud-masked figure to pop out from a trash can, or a man in black to rappel down a nylon line from a passing helicopter.

"What's so funny?"

The shrewish response made Nick laugh again. "Nothing. Never mind. Where are you?"

"I can't make it. Sorry. At least you didn't have far to go. You only live a couple of blocks away. That's why I picked the spot. Anyway, what do you have?"

It wasn't far from where Allison lived, that was true. Nick supposed he should have been grateful for the consideration; he was certainly glad of their ignorance. Esposito was right. These guys couldn't catch a cold in a leper colony.

"Yeah. . . . What do you mean, what do I have?"

"Meehan, stop playing games. You're not the only—"

The speaker stopped abruptly, but Nick could finish the sentence. *Not the only one we have on this, watching your partner, watching you.* A sly riposte began to form in his mind, alluding to the EMTs; he didn't finish his thought, so he would be less tempted to say it aloud.

"We're invested in this case," the voice said. "We believe in it. And we're going to get him, one way or the other. There might be federal involvement. . . . I won't get into that. You can help, and we can help you, or . . . we can't guarantee what might happen."

The pitch wasn't bad, Nick thought—resolute and high-minded. And the invocation of the Feds, with their vast and not-quite-rational power, their loose rules and life sentences, was an effective interrogation ploy, though a fairly standard one. He had made the argument himself, many times, often with some success. Had this man ever made the argument when it counted, to a murderer, alone in a room? The responses were fully formed in Nick's mind, acid and accurate, but he said nothing, suspecting that the smart comeback was half the reason Internal Affairs was so durably focused on his partner. He had a courtroom speech at the ready, declaiming to the gallery that Esposito was innocent, innocent. Malcolm Cole was now working with them! And Kiko hadn't even recognized Esposito when they'd first met. Did that fit with the claim that Esposito was on the crew's payroll for a thousand dollars a week? But Nick knew they were not interested in his opinion. One way or the other, as the man said. IAB would have to get Esposito for petty violations, procedural hits. On patrol, they'd write you up for wearing white socks or signing out in blue ink. Or living where you worked. They could always get you on something. Nick said nothing.

"Guys like Esposito," the voice went on, after a breath, shifting tone to something more genial and philosophical, almost man-to-man. "The bad guys on our side, who give us a bad name, they're why I decided to become a cop."

The pompous fraud was too much for Nick, even though he knew what he said next was a mistake. "When do you plan to start?"

It's what Esposito would have said. Maybe they had started to rub off on each other, more than Nick knew, or maybe he needed to demonstrate to himself that his loyalty was not altogether lacking. He spoke again quickly. "I mean, what do you do next?"

There was no sign of offense, and Nick couldn't tell at first if the man was thick-skinned or thick-witted. The second, he decided, after hearing the aloof confidence of the reply.

"We plan to interview Mendoza."

"Who?"

"Miguel Mendoza. The, uh, survivor of last night's shooting."

"That's standard, isn't it?"

"Yes."

"Well, good luck. He seemed to be a man of few words."

"You are, too, Meehan. That might not be such a good thing for you."

Nick hung up and watched the tai chi class for a few minutes, until the languid control of the teacher's movements made his back ache. He walked back to the train, a little pleased with himself for his petty show of solidarity, a little sad that he had no one to share the joke with.

EIGHTEEN

T here was confusion at the school when Nick asked for Grace Lopez. She wasn't listed as Lopez but rather as Lopez Santana, the former name belonging to her father, Ivan, from whom she evidently wanted some distance. She answered only to Santana, her late mother's name, and students and staff tended to accommodate her. That was the report of Sister Agnes, the assistant principal, who was doughy and brown-skinned, with a single black brow on her forehead that stretched out like the silhouette of a gull. She was Indian, maybe by way of Trinidad, but her faded accent had the singsong of Hindi, rushing from one phrase to linger on another, dipping and rising in pitch. She could have been just past forty years old, or nearly sixty, changing as little as her circumstances, or as little as she would permit them to change her. She wore a long skirt, a blazer, a veil of rough brown wool, a white sweater, and a wooden cross around her neck. She led Nick down hallways as they spoke.

"Grace just started this year, her first in high school. We have one hundred and seventeen students in her class—all girls, of course. But I recall Grace, because of what her father told me about the mother."

"Which was . . ."

"That she drowned. Which touched me terribly, because my own brother drowned. He was with my father, a fisherman in Kerala."

"Sorry."

"Thank you. I cannot see how she is missing. She has not been absent one day. She has not been late one hour. She has joined volleyball, the yearbook. . . . Grace is a new student to us, Detective, but there is nothing to indicate she will not do well, or is experiencing any personal difficulties. Of course, you must tell us if there are any . . . household issues . . . that may come to bear. The formation of her character is as much our charge as the formation of her intellect. How many days has she been missing?"

"Just one."

Because Nick was taller than Sister Agnes, and because they were walking, she couldn't see his face. Nick was glad she couldn't. He had a feeling she would have hit him for lying so badly—hit him twice—first for lying, and second for doing it so badly. Nick didn't know if Grace belonged with her father, but he thought she belonged here.

"Even so, for a child her age, she must go home to her daddy. Does it not seem like a loving home?"

"I don't know, Sister. I'd met him before in the neighborhood, and he asked me to look into this. There's no official report, not yet, and as far as I see it, there won't be one. She's not missing, technically, if he knows where she is. Maybe she told him she was staying with a friend, and he forgot, or she left a note, and he didn't see it."

"I hope so. Her father is making a sacrifice to send her here. Quite frankly, we are making a sacrifice, too. She has a scholarship, and it is not merely because she is quite bright, which she is. As I said, we were touched by her personal circumstances. But most of the families struggle to send their girls here. Many are immigrants. Almost half didn't grow up speaking English. That is our mission. Our foundress, Mother Cabrini, is the patron saint of immigrants. Perhaps you would like to see . . ."

Sister Agnes had stopped, and indicated the entrance to a chapel with a wave. Nick stepped inside, and she waited, standing squarely in the doorway. The far wall was covered with a gold mosaic, with numerous figures of a woman in a sweeping brown habit, sometimes alone, sometimes with one or two others. The images were haphazardly patterned, like notes on a bulletin board. Below the altar, which was covered with white cloth, there was another image of the woman, lying down.

"I will take the young lady out of class and bring her to talk to you here. I have parents in my office; another teacher is speaking with them. Here is better, anyway. Mother Cabrini was born a poor Italian peasant. She came to America and founded hospitals, convents, schools, orphanages. She was an immigrant, like I am. She was a saint, the first American saint, which I will not be. Today, one of the girls told me it was important to save the whales because if there were none left, the ocean would be too low to sail across. I did not strike her, but I was terribly tempted. It isn't done anymore."

"Cops are in the same predicament, Sister."

"Perhaps so. In any case, the shrine is a place to reflect on our better nature, which will be suitable for all concerned. Excuse me."

When Sister Agnes left, Nick looked around the room, to make sure no one else was there. She hadn't locked him in, but the interview tricks were the same—place yourself between the subject and the door; arrange the physical circumstances to emphasize the authority of one, the dependence of the other. In the interview room, you try to put the subject in a little rickety chair, while yours is large and comfortable. Tricky, tricky nun! Here, there was no suitable place for him and Grace to sit together, and after he scanned the room, he decided they wouldn't share a pew. They would stand, in the corner, he supposed; if Nick were a braver man, or a far worse one, he could have seized the high ground and stood behind the altar. He had to remind himself that this was not adversarial, there was no confession to be had, there was no crime here. This was a non-missing missing child, who had to be spoken with, who had to be told to go home. This was not detective business, not even police business, except in the broadest sense of service.

To serve Ivan Lopez, or to protect from him? How had his wife died, and why did his daughter run? "Cancer" had worked on Nick, he realized, "drowning" on Sister Agnes. Each story had struck them, had made them willing to travel with him, even carry him awhile, when they would have otherwise dropped him, moved on. Lopez must have been looking at the river, thinking about it, when he told that story to the nun; it was more troubling for Nick to wonder what had reminded Lopez of cancer when they'd spoken. Still, Lopez was likely no worse than a lost, lonely man who had scammed an excellent education for his daughter, and conned an experienced detective into becoming a private bloodhound to look after her when she was safe but not in eyesight. What was wrong with Lopez? Somebody should drain it from him and bottle it, and drop it into the water supply, let it flood through every sink in the city.

A few months before, Nick had called a woman to tell her that her son had been shot in the head.

"Grazed. Somebody called, from the block. I heard it was only a graze wound."

It was true, the wound had been slight. And Nick had locked up the son not long after, for shooting someone else. And the son had been shot before, and had lived, obviously. But she had said "Thank you" and had hung up, with casual civility, like Nick was a telemarketer and she was presently satisfied with her service. He had been so struck by her response, that he'd looked up her background, expecting to find a crack whore, a parolee, but instead he'd found that she was not just not a criminal, but a corrections officer, a city worker. Why hadn't she hustled detective friends, acquaintances, strangers, into being bloodhounds for her son? Nick wished he hadn't thought of the dog again. Lucky, Brownie, whoever you are—tell the truth, bitch.

Nick sat down in a pew, in the front. His head hurt. He looked at the altar, draped in white, with tall white candles and bouquets of yellow roses above, the woman in brown below. Not a picture—a glass-fronted casket, the body in repose, head on a pillow, hands clasped. The garments were a deep brown, the color of coffee or soil, and seemed to flow around her, the veil, the cowl, the robe, utterly still, of course, but fresh-seeming, as if a wind had arranged them to drift and drop, just so. The face was a white mask, wax perhaps, as were the hands. They would have to keep that cool, wouldn't they, or the sight of a saint melted to jelly would send the girls screaming to Buddha. Maybe it was ceramic. That made more sense. But it was the body that drew his eye, something in the contours, how the cloth tented the frame, gapping oddly on either side of a slight peak in the middle. That was it, the hip. The cloth followed the bone closely, dropping off from the ribs and picking up again at the pelvis, falling again below. The robes obscured the fact of death, at first, and then they magnified it. It made Nick somewhat uneasy, which he didn't understand, because this was not even the first body he'd seen in the last twenty-four hours.

The women came into the chapel without his hearing them. Tricky, tricky sister. The first voice Nick heard was faintly nasal, prickly and poised, almost sure of itself.

"It's just the body. It isn't the head. The head's in Italy. Right, Sister?"

"That is correct, Grace."

Nick stood and turned. Grace was a pointy little thing, all straight lines and sharp angles, with thick black glasses, choppy bangs, and a tight ponytail. The modesty of her uniform, with its plaid skirt and light-blue blouse, was discordant, dissonant with the picture he'd seen, as if she wore not merely a costume but a disguise. Almost like Allison, Nick thought with a shudder, muddling the transition of one geek-girl who became his wife, with the other geek-girl, who became the thing in the picture, third world junior hoochie, to be had for a pair of nylons and a Hershey's bar.

"Hello, Grace. I'm Detective Meehan."

Nick extended a hand and she took it, limply, with a kind of demure uncertainty. He turned to the nun.

"Would you mind if we spoke alone, Sister?"

This was always an awkward moment, separating a parent from a child for an interview. You had the boy in the hospital with the gunshot wound in the calf—a strict vertical path, through the muscle—who insisted that a stranger shot him, from across the street. You had the girl who insisted that the man in the elevator only punched her when he robbed her, but she jumped when the nurse touched her leg. You are telling them, in a roundabout way, that their child is lying; you trust that they will understand—or won't understand—until it's too late.

"Yes."

"Thank you. It will just take a minute."

Sister Agnes did not move.

"Sister?"

"Yes? I said I would mind. I will stay."

"Ah."

Grace took note of the adversarial tap dance and seemed pleased by it, but took care not to let it show too much. Nick was going to do the authority bit, the stern voice, the rote words of warning, but he didn't know what he had in Grace—wild child, grieving orphan? But possibly an abuse victim, too, with her disappearances and sexual posing. If this had been just a runaway to return, Nick might have done it; but if this had been ordinary, he wouldn't have bothered to take it this far. He would have told Ivan Lopez, *If you know where she is, go get her yourself.* But Ivan's fear that there would be problems at the school if the sisters knew that Grace was not what Ivan had told them, what he had sold them, had become Nick's concern as well. Whatever his frustrations with Sister Agnes—she had outmaneuvered him, she outclassed him at what was ostensibly his profession—he could address by scribbling that she smelled funny, in a cartoon with vigorous stink lines, in a bathroom stall before he left.

"Grace, your father told me that you didn't come home last night. He was very worried about you. If you stayed with a friend, to do homework or whatever, you should have told him."

The two easy outs he'd provided—that it was one night instead of three, and that there was an academic pretext—inspired a rich gratitude and some confusion. She looked down for a moment, then to the side. A classic liar face, touchingly amateur—a little ashamed, buying time to figure out the next part of the story. Which was to say, not a liar, not much of one before now. Nick wondered if it was too much for her to read the situation. Did she think of him as an ally of her father, whom she probably disdained, or had he provoked her to reappraise him, as competent, complex even? She fidgeted, and Nick could see the wave of indecision travel from her shoulders down to her feet. She held one foot behind the knee of the other leg, as if about to begin a jig. No, she was new to the lying game.

"I guess I forgot."

The lazy, juvenile deception was enough to provoke Sister Agnes.

"Grace! You are many things, but not forgetful! A girl of your age does not forget to go home, or to tell her father! This was terribly, terribly naughty of you! Who was this young friend, with whom you had a sleepover on a school night? Was it another girl from this school?"

In her reaction, far more innocent than that of Grace or Nick, Sister Agnes had also built in options for Grace's response, likely better than the ones that she was mulling over at the moment.

"No, Sister. Somebody from the block. I'm sorry."

"I should hope you are, Grace, and I should hope that we shall not be hearing about this kind of 'forgetfulness' again."

"I'm sure we won't, Sister," Nick said. "I can drive her home to her father, if you want."

"Thank you, Detective, but it is not school policy to release our girls into the custody of strange men. Excuse me. Perhaps I could have put that better. I think it best to call Grace's father, Mr. Santana . . . Santana Lopez . . . Which is it, Grace?"

"His name is Lopez."

"Yes. I will call Mr. Lopez and have him pick up his daughter. There is no great harm in this foolishness, Grace, but the three of us—you, your father, and I—will discuss the fact that events such as this are not to happen again. Do we understand each other?"

"Yes, Sister."

"Yes, Sister."

When Nick echoed Grace's response, it was not intended to be mocking, and it was not taken that way.

"Thank you, Detective. Is there anything else I can help you with? You can find your way out?"

"I'm fine, Sister. I can. Actually, would you be able to direct me to the men's room?"

NINETEEN

At the squad, Nick listlessly pushed papers around his desk. Esposito had gone downtown, to court, on the santero case. Nick had a few hours to play catch-up, on matters that had not grown more attractive with age. Grace's picture disappeared beneath complaint reports and notes; he didn't need to see her face anymore. Just below her was the confiscated snapshot of Maria Fonseca, happy at the beach. There were no bruises on her legs. How long before had it been taken, earlier that summer? Nick had folded the picture in half, so he didn't have to see Costa. He was unwelcome in the family gallery. There was a phone call that had to be made. Nick would get to it, but at the moment he didn't have the stomach for it. The phone rang, and Perez picked it up.

"Nick, for you."

"Who is it?"

"I dunno, some foreign guy, sounds Hindu or something."

Intrigued, Nick signaled to Perez to transfer the call. He had no Indians, no Pakistanis in his cases. Did Sister Agnes have a brother, some lethal fighting monk, who had found the cartoon in the bathroom?

"Squad. Meehan."

"Good God, Nicky, you sound fierce! Even the rough ones, they must sit up when they hear that out of you!"

Indian! It was his father.

"Da! Hey, hi."

Perez looked over, unsure what language was being spoken, wondering what talents Nick might have kept hidden. Nick shook his head, waved him away. This was the first time his father had ever called him at the office. His father mistrusted cellphones, didn't understand them.

Before, he'd call Nick at his place with Allison, every week if Nick had not called first; now there was no need for the phone. Nick had come home late the last few nights and had left without seeing his father in the morning. The call worried him.

"I was thinking."

The remark had been made many times across the kitchen table, but this new context was unsettling.

"You always are, Da."

"I suppose I am, like everyone. But this is the thought, the one that stuck—we should go home."

"How do you mean?"

"We should make a visit, take a trip. See everyone, catch up."

"All right," said Nick, agreeing without either consideration or re- serve. "When?"

"Soon."

"Good. Where?"

"My people and your mother's. The grand tour. Ask Allison if you want, if you don't mind me mentioning. If you don't mind me being the third rail!"

"Wheel."

"What?"

The correction was made without resentment. Nick was touched by the effort, the near-diplomacy of the phrasing. Nick was decorous but ex- plicit in his response, as if he were explaining traffic rules to a tourist.

"Da, you were in Transit. 'Third rail' is where the power comes from on the subway, the electricity. If you step on it, you get fried. 'Third wheel' is a couple with a friend. They take him along, to be nice. Or her, so she won't be lonely."

The noise on the other end of the line was one that Nick had never heard before from his father, a giddy giggle.

"Third rail, third wheel, I can manage both!"

"I don't doubt it, Da."

"Will you be home for dinner tonight? I've made a pot of stew. It's a winner, better than ever, if I don't say so myself."

The dish was his father's favorite, and Nick liked it, too, but he hoped the question didn't become a habit. As Nick had grown accustomed to the deprivations of bachelor life, he was determined to maintain its poor benefits, and the first of them was the lack of such obligations. He also didn't know what the day would bring.

"I can't say, Da. Leave some for me, though."

"All right, Detective Meehan. 'Squad. Meehan!' Over and out!"

"Over and out."

Nick laughed as he hung up the phone. He looked at Perez, who was now playing solitaire on his computer. The brief irritation Nick felt toward him passed, glad as Nick was with his father's delight, knowing he needed Perez as a translator for his next task. All of these foreigners. Nick picked through the papers on his desk. There it was, the phone bill from Raul Costa's house, the long line of grouped digits for the international call.

"Hey, Ralph, you busy?"

Perez hesitated a moment, wondering what kind of favor would be asked, before he realized that Nick had seen his computer screen.

"No, Nick. What do you need?"

"Notification. Bad news. My suicide the other day, the girl who hung herself. I got a number for the family in Mexico."

"Jeez."

"Yeah."

"What's the story?"

"There isn't one. Maria Fonseca, twenty-one years old, unlucky in love."

"Shit. She leave a note?"

"No."

"All right. You know any names, the family names?"

"Maria Fonseca is all I got."

Perez shook his head and picked up the phone. He dialed the numbers with deliberation, two at a time, and waited.

"What time is it there?" Perez asked.

"I don't know."

"*Sí. Buenos días. Hablo del departamento de la policía de la cindad de Nueva York. Soy Detectivo Perez. Busco a la familia de Maria Fonseca. . . . Sí . . . Tengo noticias, son muy malas. . . . Sí . . .* It's not the family house. It's a pay phone at some kind of factory. They make clothing, I think. Maria Fonseca's mother works there. Whoever picked up is going to get her. . . ."

Less than a minute passed before Perez resumed his speech.

"Señora Fonseca? Es usted la madre de Maria Fonseca? Sí, habla el departamento de policía en Nueva York. Soy el Detective Perez. . . ."

Nick pulled his chair in closer to Perez, as if it might help him somehow. As Perez broke the news, he held the phone out from his ear, and Nick could hear the wails on the other end. The details were supplied in small, controlled doses—days ago, hanging, boyfriend, morgue. Perez ran his fingers along his bald scalp, as if he had hair.

"She wants to know what will happen to the body. She can't afford to fly her down there for burial."

"The city will bury her."

"In Potter's Field?"

"Yeah."

"Sí, señora . . ."

Looks of curiosity and concern passed over Perez's face as he murmured various forms of condolence and assent, until something stopped him short.

"Shit . . . *Lo siento, señora.* . . . The lady says her other daughter, Mercedes, left to meet her, to come here and live with her. The kid's fifteen years old."

"How is she traveling? When will she get here?"

Perez found out that the sister was walking, trying to cross with a friend and a paid guide. If they made the border in Arizona, they would take a bus to New York. It could be weeks before they arrived, if ever.

"She wants to know what we're going to do about her. What should I say?"

"Does she know anyone else in New York?"

"No. I already asked."

"Take the girl's information. We can report her as missing. It goes into a national database. If she's stopped by cops anywhere, her name will pop up. That's if she uses her real name."

Perez took down the information for Mercedes and provided in turn the numbers for the squad and the morgue. He told Mrs. Fonseca that the police didn't work with Immigration, that Mercedes would not be in trouble. She should call the squad. He said that the city was no place for a young girl like her. She should go back home. When Perez hung up the phone, he looked spent.

"Do you think she believed you? About Immigration?"

"I don't know . . . probably not. She's afraid of cops."

"Yeah. Well, thanks, Ralph. I appreciate it, all your help with this. It was a tough call to make."

"No problem. She sounded like a nice lady. . . . It's too bad. I hope it works out for the kid. That kind of shit bothers me. . . . You know, what's been so nice, hooking up with Marina—I mean, the sex is great, don't get me wrong—but sometimes we just talk. I can tell her about anything, the Job, all the bullshit, all the bad stuff, like this. I can go on and on, you know? And she doesn't say a word, she just takes it all in. She gets it. Know what I mean? It's lucky. I'm lucky to have her. You got anybody in your life like that, Nick?"

"I can't say that I do, Ralph."

"One day you will, Nick."

"It wouldn't surprise me."

"You got a lot going for you, Nick. I didn't know you spoke Indian!"

Perez gave him a gentle tap on the shoulder as he walked back to his desk. It occurred to Nick that there was more emotion—not to mention actual contact—in that touch than anything that had transpired between Perez and Marina; it felt unkind to think it. He wondered if he should worry about Perez, now that his playboy exaggerations had taken on a more clinical aspect, and then he thought about the problems with his own marriage to a woman who actually existed. Next time, he thought, he might try something different. No one would be able to say he hadn't given reality a fighting chance.

TWENTY

When Esposito returned from court, it was afternoon. For a moment, Nick studied him, as if to see whether yesterday's killing had changed him, had left a sign in his eyes, making them hard or haggard. There was nothing; he was the same. He swept into the room and tossed his coat over the back of his chair, dropping a case file onto the desk. He looked rested, fresh, ready for more. No ghosts for Esposito, thank you very much. There had been a contest, and he had prevailed. His indifferent vigor made Nick feel old.

"So, what do we got going on today?" asked Esposito, with an oddly satisfied air.

"The usual," said Nick warily, unsure if he meant it, or even what it meant.

"Maybe you think so right now, but we got plans."

"Plans?"

"Yeah, but I'll get into that later—don't worry, it's all good! I stopped by the hospital. My buddy Fernando's doing all right. He'll be out in a couple of days. He loves us, he loves me. If there's any voodoo favors you need done, let me know—love potions, backache, striking down your enemies. Sky's the limit! His niece and her husband came to visit. He got so mad, they had to sedate him. He threw them out. But we gotta get ahold of them, get their statements, whatever workup needs to be done on the phone records, for the ransom demands. Not to mention getting hold of Kiko, this time for good. You ready?"

Nick picked up his coat. "We gotta put the funeral under surveillance, too."

"Yeah. We got people for that, Fugitive Apprehension, warrants, whoever. We don't have to be there. Better for me not to be. At least not up close."

"All right. Let's do it."

"Attaboy."

They drove through Kiko's old haunts, without expecting to see him. Esposito wanted to check if his people were around, to see if the operation had collapsed or the work was still getting done. There should be noise, if not news. Maybe Esposito would recognize a face on a corner; better yet, someone would recognize him and spread the word. Mostly he wanted to keep Kiko in the front of his mind, to show that there would be no rest until it was done. No grace period, no cease-fire, no time-out to bury the dead. Esposito saw someone and pulled over.

"This guy, what's his name—Tino, that's it. He was with Kiko when he shot the crackhead, Crazy Joe."

Tino was short and big-bellied, nearly thirty, leaning against a broken pay phone beside a bodega. He stiffened when he saw them approach, but he was old enough to know not to run. He was old enough, too, to refrain from displays of overt hostility, to put on a show for the street, the three or four younger guys who waited beside him. He greeted the detectives with a curt nod, and raised his shirt to show there was no gun in his waist. Esposito stepped close to him, and Nick flanked him, to cover the little ones. The young guys were the danger, in their hunger for reputation. They were Kiko's brother's age. What was his name? Miguelito.

"What's up, Tino?"

"What's up."

"You tell me."

"You know."

"Tell me anyway."

"People say you people, one a you cops, killed Miguelito."

"Which cop?"

"People say it was you."

"That's right. See? You know plenty. Where's Kiko?"

"I dunno."

"You seen him? When?"

"A while back."

"Okay, Tino. Excuse me a minute, wouldja? I gotta make a call."

Tino stepped back, thinking that Esposito was going to use the pay phone, but Esposito put a hand on his shoulder. He reached into Tino's shirt pocket and took out the cellphone. The younger ones stirred—"Yo! He can't do that!"—but Tino raised a hand to quiet them. Esposito flipped the phone open and scrolled through the directory, to *K*.

"Here we go. 'Kiko.' Gotta be him, right?"

Esposito dialed the number and held the receiver out a few inches from his mouth, so it would sound like a bad connection, and offered a low, indistinct "Yo" when it was picked up. The little Miguelitos tensed up again, and Nick took hold of his gun, wondering if Esposito would take it to the next stage—*Where you at?*—in front of them, in their faces. Tino tensed, too; the affront was so purposeful and public that he wouldn't be able to contain the corner if the Miguelitos made a move, and maybe he wouldn't try to stop them. All were relieved at the next words.

"Kiko, this is Detective Esposito. . . . Yeah, that one. . . ."

Esposito spoke quickly, and there was an edge to his voice, but he never yelled. The aura of control was compelling, to Nick and everyone else who heard it on the corner.

"No, you don't know what happened. You ran. You left your little brother there. You left your baby brother to try and shoot it out with a bunch of New York City detectives. You ran away. I chased you. He didn't run. He was still a baby, right? He didn't know. How could he? And you pulled him in, to kidnap a priest, to burn him with irons, *las planchas.* A priest whose son is a cop, a cop in the DR. I wouldn't think about going back there, Kiko. The cops there, they don't mess around. You know that. There is no place for you now, Kiko, not in New York City or the Dominican Republic, not on heaven or earth. . . ."

"Yeah, sure, no problem."

Esposito nodded to Tino, and handed him back the phone.

"Kiko wants to talk to you. We gotta go."

As they walked away, Tino began to chatter in speed-Spanish, a blur of words. The Miguelitos clustered around him, focused on the newest emergency, amazed beyond their immediate capacity for teenage rage. The detectives got into the car and drove away, without conspicuous speed. Esposito glanced out the window, but didn't stare. The point had been made. Nick considered whether Esposito had planned the encounter, if he had withheld the plan from him. No, he thought, probably not, but they didn't talk for a while as they drove off. He was bothered by the freelancing, by such an impulsive confrontation. In his mind, Nick had pledged allegiance to his partner, had cut off rival ties to the finger-pointers downtown. Of course, he couldn't explain that, but that wrong didn't offset the rightness of Nick's complaint. What had happened to Esposito's old partner, with his suicide? He'd meant to ask, but the moment was never apt. It was a curiosity, no more than that, but curiosity was an underestimated force in human history. Apples and whatnot. Nick shook his head, trying to convince himself that his allegiance was well placed. It was, he thought, but he was still not happy. Esposito noticed.

"Want coffee?"

"Yeah, sure."

"Here's good. Lemme pull over."

"I got it."

"No, I got it, pal."

When Esposito was back in the car, Nick ventured a comment. "You might have told me you were going to do that."

"I would have, if I knew myself. Where do you think it gets us?"

Nick had to think about that. "One, it was very personal. . . . I guess there's no way around that part of it. Two, you discouraged him from becoming an international fugitive, at least to the Dominican Republic, which is the only other place he knows. That part's good. The bad part is, if he doesn't become an international fugitive, he stays here. Options? Two—kill himself, kill you. Or somebody on your side, our side."

"You, for example."

"That would work, but I'm not worried. It would be random, whatever he could manage. Retaliation-wise. Whatever guys Kiko had before, he has less now. And I don't think any of 'em is in a rush to die as a favor for anybody. They're not in Gaza or Iraq. They're not jihadis. Kiko doesn't offer forty virgins in paradise."

Esposito paused and considered. His qualification was not what Nick expected.

"Isn't it seventy?"

"What?"

"Seventy virgins. Yeah, definitely, seventy."

"What, you saw a brochure?"

"No, I just remember."

They drove around for a while, having exhausted their immediate store of conversation. Esposito drove more slowly than usual, his ordinary impatience in abeyance, as if to spare his partner any more nervous strain. Nick noticed, and the implication of frailty got on his nerves. He'd been troubled by the stunt with Tino, irked—at the correction of trivia—more than he'd like to admit. And his mind had been fidgety since the morning's non-meeting with IAB. Esposito noticed his mood, but he didn't push it. Nick remembered something from earlier on and broke the silence, hoping to show he wasn't annoyed.

"What are these plans you mentioned? For tonight?"

"I won't tell you now. You're mad at me."

"You're an asshole."

"See?"

"You are an asshole. Now, what's with the plans?"

"You got something lined up?"

"My father made a pot of stew. It's not regular stew. It's a stew for the ages, I'm told. What do you know about stew?"

"I work with him."

Esposito was immensely pleased with his joke, and it did cut the tension. Nick smiled, in spite of himself. "Fuck you. What do you got for tonight?"

"Wait. Watch. It'll all work out. Trust me!"

"I wish you wouldn't put it that way."

"Yeah, well— Whoa! Would you look at that!"

Nick never got to see whatever unique beauty had transfixed Esposito, because as the car stopped short, Nick's coffee spilled over his shirt and tie.

"Shit!"

"Shit, sorry! Shit!"

"Shit."

Nick spent some time examining his shirt. It had been white. The tie would also have to be cleaned. Esposito looked over, laughing and apologizing. Nick found himself peculiarly relieved, now that his previously free-floating irritation was now grounded in fact. His mood could be changed as easily as a shirt, he thought, the idea warming him like the liquid soaking through to his chest. And now he could force Esposito to drop his coyness about the evening's plans.

"Nice work. So, is dinner on you, or just the dry cleaning?"

"It is a night out."

"What? Who? Where?"

"Why? You got a date with Daysi?"

"No."

"Yes, you do."

"You're full of shit."

"You gotta pick out a restaurant. On the classy side. You're a downtown guy. You can handle that."

"I used to be. Not classy—I mean—Are you kidding me? C'mon!"

Nick couldn't quite believe the idea, and he was almost afraid of how happy it made him.

"Why do you like her?" asked Esposito in a teasing tone, as if he were hosting a talent show. "What do you know about her?"

"Not much."

"I do. She's divorced, one child. Her birthday is in November. She loves museums. Her favorite painter is a guy named van Goo, something about sunflowers. She's tired of assholes looking to hit on her just because she's sexy and because she has money. She doesn't meet the guys she wants to meet, where she is. She just wants someone, she says, someone she can talk to. I think she's full of shit, in a cute way. But so am I."

Nick had to think for a while. He still hadn't taken it in. He didn't feel as old anymore, or maybe he just didn't mind. Van Goo? That didn't matter. Nick needed to be clear. " 'Ortega Florist. Daysi Ortega, proprietor.' "

"*Sí, amigo.*"

"You called her. For me, not for yourself?"

"Of course. I'm a happily married man. You? You need to get laid. You're lucky you saw her first."

"You called her, for tonight, for me. And she said yes?"

Nick was touched, deeply, by the first thing, then the second, so much so that the trespass did not bother him as it otherwise would have.

"So, where do you want to take her? She's in midtown now. You just have to tell her where. Seven o'clock." .

"That's an hour and change. . . . Where my wife was the other night looked good."

"There's an endorsement. I wouldn't bring it up at dinner. What kind of food?"

"French, I think."

"Perfect. Continental, you might call it. What's the name of the restaurant again? Where is it?"

Nick told him, and Esposito flipped open his cellphone, to call Daysi.

"Hey, Daysi, day's eye, this is your detective friend. One of them, you're right. Nick's picked a place. . . . No, I never been there. If you don't like it, call me and we'll ditch him, find a joint, just you and me. . . . Well, you never know, do you? See you."

The click of his phone when he hung up had a decisive sound, of clean closure. That should have been his call, Nick thought, but then again, he should have made it yesterday.

"Hey, Espo? Thanks."

"You need a little push sometimes, Nicky boy."

"What I need is a clean shirt."

"Whaddaya wanna do?"

"Let's swing by the apartment."

"Must be nice, having everything here, all in one place."

When they pulled up outside the building, Nick stepped out of the car and told Esposito he'd be back in a minute. It brought unexpected protests. "You're kidding me! You won't invite me into your house? For an Italian, this is like spitting in my face!"

"Yeah? For a non-Italian, it's a little weird, like you're trying to hustle your way inside at the end of a first date."

"Yeah, but it isn't our first date! How long have we been working together? You don't want me to meet your family?"

"My family is my father. You never saw an old Irishman before? Rent *The Quiet Man*. You'll get the idea."

"What, are you ashamed of him? I'm not the one being a little weird here, Nick."

And he was right. Esposito had a way of getting close to him with sudden gestures, straightening his collar, brushing a crumb from his chin, that bothered Nick at each first instance, struck him as intrusive. Sometimes it was that kind of primate intimacy, picking nits from a pal; at others, the interference was different, like with Daysi, because Esposito knew better, and wanted to know more. And he was right about this, Nick knew. It was not as if Nick were ashamed of his father, as such; it was more the general circumstances of how Nick found himself, at this moment. He had to think, were there still Little League trophies in his room? No, they were in boxes, in the closet, along with the other tokens of meager and remote accomplishment. Or tucked safely beneath the bunk bed. Had he made the bed? His father would have. He did that; he had time. To bring a friend over had a nightmare quality, as if he'd slipped back into an iteration, a film loop of childhood. Would his father offer cookies? Would Esposito expect them? And yet a visitor would give his father something to talk about, to mull over; it would open up a brand-new conversational line. Nick couldn't deny him that.

"Relax. Come on in, if it means that much to you."

"See? That wasn't so hard. This is why Irish hospitality is famous, the world over."

As they walked through the lobby, Nick noticed how much it was like the places they went to at work. It was better than many, in that it was clean, but its worn linoleum and chipped plaster columns placed it square in that category, that class. At least Jamie Barry wasn't nodding off in the corner. A lot of cops came from places like this, but most didn't stay. There was a great pride in poverty, or at least in lack of privilege, as long as it was in the past. More cops came from stolid brick two-families in Queens, or little ranches and colonials out on Long Island, or in the upstate counties, reaching increasingly north. The cops from upstate and the Island descended from blue-collar refugees who set out in the sixties and seventies, prompted by a fear of crime and a fetish for mowing lawns, as if the possession of that patch of grass were a truer proof of American arrival than any paper handed out at Ellis Island. On one of the lobby walls, Nick noticed for the first time a Magic Marker scrawl: "Nagle Ave is pussys and fags." Tell that to the Cole brothers, kid! Tell it to their faces! Ah, to be home.

Nick knocked first before unlocking the door—"Daa, it's me!" The same bare hall, the bare table in the kitchen, the threadbare couch in the living room, across from the television Nick had given him, the first color set, ten years ago. He was in his beloved black vinyl recliner in the corner, and the footrest receded as he pulled a lever on the side. He stood and approached, intensely curious.

"Hello, Nick! Hello?"

"Da, this is Espo, my partner."

"Hello."

"A pleasure to meet you, Mr. Meehan."

"Likewise . . . Espo?"

"It's short for 'Esposito.' "

"Ah! Italian, is it?"

He pronounced it "Eye-talian," as if he had grown up with that pronunciation, though Nick couldn't conceive of any occasion when he would have had to say the word at all, on the little Meehan farm in Roscommon. The particularity of Nick's father's interest couldn't have anything to do with novelty—there were Italians in New York, they were not new and not few—and yet it seemed to intrigue him, as if Esposito had claimed to be a Navajo chief. Nick realized how few people his father spoke to, and he delayed his trip to the bedroom to change his shirt.

"Yeah, Mr. Meehan. I'm Italian, both sides."

"Both sides, are you? Is that how many sides people have, two?"

The younger men could not decide if the question required an answer. The old man settled the issue with a bit of nothing. "Well, how about that . . ."

Esposito smiled, and pointedly avoided Nick's anxious glance. Whether Nick's father would impress Nick next with some insight, or embarrass him with some off-kilter retrograde remark, Esposito stood to enjoy it. As the next conversational blank awaited filling, Nick shifted his stance, and a floorboard groaned beneath him. Here it comes.

"Quite a few Italian plumbers, I understand. You're not a plumber, are you?"

"No, I'm not, Mr. Meehan."

"Please, call me Sean. Not a master plumber, I mean. You wouldn't be a policeman had you a money trade like that. But even a few years of apprenticeship? No?"

"No. I mean, I know the basics. I have a house. You need to be handy with things. What's the problem?"

"Ah, yer the man! It's the toilet, the water flow or some such. It's become fierce lately. You haven't noticed, Nick?"

"No. Da, he's not a plumber. If we need one, we can call the super—"

"Not at all, Nick. I'd be happy to have a look at it."

Nick had seen the toilet before, and felt no need to join them in the bathroom. He went back to his room and found a clean shirt. The toilet flushed, and a respectful silence followed. Nick could picture his father's gaze, moving from the bowl to Esposito, awaiting his diagnosis. His face must have registered some disappointment when it came.

"Well, it looks fine to me. What's the problem?"

Nick joined them by the bathroom, to have a look in the mirror as he tied a new tie.

"It doesn't seem unusually high to you, the water?"

"No, not so you'd notice."

"What is it, Da?"

"Nick, there you are. Does the water hit your balls, too? It hits mine when I flush. It's been happening for a while, but I only think about it at the time. I'd just gone in, when you came, and with Espo here—good man, he is—it seemed lucky. Tell me, Nick, does the water rise up on you like that when it flushes?"

"Sweet Jesus."

Nick walked down the hall, and Esposito followed.

"We don't need a plumber, Da. Espo, let's get out of here."

"What? Why not?"

"Think about it. God help me, you made me think about it, too. . . ."

Nick couldn't bear to turn as he headed down the hall.

"How do you mean?"

"Balls and water, Da. We've ruled out the water."

"Pleased to meet you, Sean."

"Likewise, Detective. . . . Good God, am I that old?"

TWENTY-ONE

As they crossed the lobby, Nick looked over to Esposito, who shrugged haplessly, raising both hands. It was as if he knew what Nick was thinking, and he did not want the picture in his own mind. The old man naked; the thought of his physical decay, his nearing death. And Nick could not swear as to which thought he found more horrible. Or rather, he was glad not to be asked, under oath. It was not what he should be dwelling on, en route to meeting Daysi. First dates, last rites. Why had he picked that restaurant? He hadn't eaten there, hadn't even gone in. The only time he'd been near, he'd lingered outside, praying for a sign about Allison. Was this the sign? Not likely, unless there were patron saints the Church didn't talk about, go-to guys for no-fault divorce or getting a piece on the side. Live a little, Nick thought, before realizing that's what he'd been doing—barely living, just getting by. He had to live more. It was time to get on with things, to get moving again, before the balls hit the water.

They were on the highway before they spoke. Esposito had insisted on driving him, in his own car, mentioning offhandedly that he was going to meet Audrey, the nurse from Rikers, for a drink farther downtown. Nick chafed a little, feeling like he was being dropped off for his first day of school.

"I can pick you up after dinner, if you want."

"That's all right."

"I know a guy, does security at the Marriott. He can get you a room, cheap."

"I'll let you know."

Nick strained not to be sharp with him, to not overreact even when his partner was meddlesome. None of this would have happened without him, Nick reminded himself. Without Esposito, tonight would have been stew night. Still, he was nervous, and he wasn't sure whether it was because of what tonight meant for him with Allison, or what it could mean with Daysi. What time was it? Were they late?

They were half a block from the restaurant when Esposito called out—"Hey! *Hola!* Baby!" That brought a wave from a woman approaching from the opposite side. He pulled over, and Nick stepped out of the car. Yes, they were late, he'd kept her waiting. Daysi waved, then put her hand back into her pocket. A long leather jacket, tawny-colored. She was cold. It didn't seem cold to Nick. Indian summer still, barely cool, though there was a wind from the river, lifting the golden tangle of hair from her face, the green eyes, the violet dusk behind her. The Manhattan solstice, when the sunset aligned with the street grid—when was it? It would have seemed fake-fateful if had been today, like a horoscope, something to laugh at but still half-believe. He could have told her about it. As it was, this was only beautiful. Would that be enough? She kissed him on the cheek. Yes, it would be enough. She lightly clasped Nick's arm, and leaned over to say hello to Esposito.

"Hey, you! And what are you up to tonight?"

"Gotta meet a friend from prison," he said, driving away. Nick had not expected such a speedy exit, but he was glad for it. Esposito had done enough for him, and it was his to take from here.

"He's funny," said Daysi.

"He's not boring," Nick agreed. "Hungry?"

"Starving."

Nick liked the way she said that, but he liked the way she said everything. He led them to the restaurant, and held the door for her.

Inside, Nick was immediately disappointed, let down. When he'd been watching through the window, it had looked snug and unassuming, a little hokey but with real warmth, a vagabond charm. Was that just because there had been a crowd there, and Allison, with Nick outside, pressed against the glass? Now it seemed old and shoddy; the vibe was brittle, chilly. Nick thought of a funeral parlor in the provinces, a wake for the town miser. An elderly couple got up from their table, and the owner, with his egg head and weird hat brim of hair, pulled back the lady's chair, speaking clots of consonants—Hungarian?—in quiet speed, as if he feared being overheard. The restaurant was otherwise empty. Nick thought about turning around and making a run for it, but the owner seemed overjoyed to see them, and it would have been a slap in the face to leave. With a flourish of the hand, he directed them to a banquette. That was that, Nick thought. This is it.

Later on, looking back at that night, Nick realized how hard it was to tell a good story about a good time. What happened? The two of them surprised each other with their easy candor. They ate and talked, and it felt like there was music in the restaurant, though there wasn't. They told funny little stories of childhood, places they'd been, that stopped and started and flowed from one to the other, one picking up from the next. The food kept coming, on little plates that made them want more. With the wine and candlelight, the emptiness of the restaurant shifted to intimacy; the shabbiness seemed like character, good-natured and enduring. What mattered to Nick was Daysi, listening to her, feeling how close she was, taking her in. For most of the night, Nick wouldn't have noticed if they'd been on a park bench eating potato chips, but every once in a while he did notice where they were, and he was glad.

Everything Daysi said was fresh to Nick, of moment and interest. She had come over when she was eight, and, at first, she'd had nightmares that the island of Manhattan would sink, because there were too many people on it. Her father died when she was twelve, when a machine at a factory exploded, and for years after, they were very poor. When the family got an apartment in the projects, they felt like they'd won the lottery. She had three sisters, all older, all of whom had since moved to Florida. Daysi studied art in college, planned to go back when she had more time, just for herself. Esposito had been right, she loved museums. She had a son, she said, fourteen years old. Nick didn't ask about him or the father. Dessert had arrived when she asked, in an uncharacteristically coy way, "Do you like being a cop?"

Nick had sought neither to avoid the subject nor to introduce it. It was the largest part of his life now, not to mention the reason they'd met. But the way she said it made him think for a moment that she liked him despite it.

"Yeah."

"Getting the bad guys?"

The same note again. Not antipathy, but maybe a vague disbelief, as if there were something boyish about it, like paintball or drag racing. The attitude was one he'd seen before, in people whose lives had been untouched by certain kinds of trouble. Nick liked that, too.

"Yeah. But not just that. I like being out there, as opposed to—what, inside? Finding things out, sometimes fixing them. 'Helping people' is something I have a hard time saying with a straight face—you come off like a contestant in a Miss America pageant—but it's true, I think. Sometimes it's true. You try, at least. How we met, you and me—the woman, Maria in the park—I wasn't much help to her. But at least her mother knows now. She doesn't wonder. . . . Well, I guess she does wonder. I guess she stares at the sky instead of at the phone, waiting for it to ring. It's not good, but it's better. You know for sure that one of them is a waste of time."

That was grim, Nick thought. Didn't he have any autopsy stories he could regale her with? Not the one about the dog and the DOA? Child abuse, animal cruelty? Who had told him that the way to a woman's heart was through the abyss? At least Daysi hadn't asked him if he was married. He wasn't sure how he'd answer, and whether the answer would be any more cheerful. He laughed nervously, afraid he'd broken the mood. "Sorry. That was bleak."

"That's all right. We're both grown-ups here."

"Speak for yourself."

Daysi laughed, and reached out to take his hand. Nick wished they were just starting dinner, instead of finishing. What next? Where to? Nick had no idea how this was done anymore. He supposed there would be an awkward pause before they kissed, but he believed they would kiss. He didn't know where—her place, at the door? Which door, in the lobby or the apartment? He wished he'd taken the number for Esposito's friend, at the Marriott, but he couldn't imagine how he could suggest that they go there. He was almost tempted to call Esposito for advice. They'd had coffee and dessert, even brandy, and there was nothing more to have unless they were staying for breakfast. The owner appeared at the edge of the table.

"Will there be anything else?"

That's a hell of a question, Nick thought. He looked at Daysi in the candlelight, at her wine-moistened mouth. His heart ached as her lips narrowed, and she barely shook her head. She smiled again. No, not "no" to everything—just no more, not here. Still, Nick hated to leave. He loved this place. Another brandy, maybe? He wanted to call Allison to thank her. No, not another brandy.

"Just the check, thanks."

As Nick paid the bill, he became slightly anxious again, ashamed of his schoolboy eagerness as much as his schoolboy naïveté. When his phone rang, he was thankful and resentful at once, hesitant to answer—*How dare you! Bless you! Please don't be Allison or IAB!* It was Esposito, and the conversation was brief. Nick's eyes nearly welled up with gratitude. The next decision had been delayed by the new opportunity.

"I know it's getting late, Daysi, but would you mind making a stop on the way? Trust me, you won't mind."

"I trust you."

As Nick helped her on with her coat, he felt a little dizzy. He took her arm and led her outside to the still-summery night, raising a hand for a cab that seemed to be waiting for them. In the backseat, they sat close and kissed. There was no awkward moment. Ten blocks passed in ten seconds, and when they stopped and got out, Nick was thrilled to see in her face the almost fearful joy he'd felt throughout the evening. At Esposito's most towering moments of vanity, his admiration for himself would have been dwarfed by Nick's regard for him right then. They were at the Museum of Modern Art. Esposito knew a guy there.

"Really? No! How?"

Nick just smiled and tapped on the glass doors, and the security director approached, silver-haired and trim in his blue blazer. Daysi clung to Nick's arm as the man let them in. He was a retired detective, and Nick didn't even catch his name as they shook hands. He knew Esposito from wherever, whatever, how about that. He led them past the souvenir counters and ticket booths of the lobby—those were for ordinary people, not for them, not tonight—to the elevators, the top floor. Wide spaces, white walls, blond wood floors. Glass walls showed sheer drops, a backyard garden.

Daysi wanted an unguided tour, Nick knew, and he waved her on, seeing that his host, like many retired cops, was still hungry for shoptalk. Nick chatted with him about this captain, that case, mindful of the hospitality. The man was charming and affable, a natural storyteller, and Nick wanted to punch him in the head. Would he ever shut up? Nick wanted to be with Daysi, undistracted. He had mostly avoided thinking about Allison, and Esposito had kept his distance, however reluctantly. He owed them both vast and very different debts, and would settle in due course. Even if Nick had never really been alone with Daysi tonight, he was determined not to let things get any more crowded, with a third wheel or a fifth. *Buddy, whatever your name is, please—I'm not getting any younger. My balls are gonna hit the water. . . .* The old detective may have sensed that Nick remained with him out of patience rather than interest, and he was tactful enough to bring the conversation to a close.

"Anyway. So you're the great Espo's new partner, huh? You're in for a ride. I don't think he gets a fair shake from people. Just don't get between him and a collar. Or a broad."

The man laughed, and Nick did, too, without much enthusiasm, uneasy with the casual zigzag between compliment and backbite. They shook hands again, and Nick thanked him again, and as soon as he returned to Daysi, he forgot what had been said. She slipped an arm around his waist.

For long moments, they were church-quiet, humble trespassers, savoring the freedom of the empty space. There were pictures you saw on postcards, or dimly remembered from textbooks, worn out by too many dutiful viewings—now here, themselves, not just images but things. Bigger than you thought, or smaller, but always with another dimension—roiling surfaces, the paint shoveled on, scraped, shaped, made rough and real and deep. Names that were a daunting blur to Nick—Monet, Picasso—and the things that made their names: Water Lilies, *Les Demoiselles d'Avignon. Starry Night,* by the great van Goo.

"I can't believe this, I can't," she said. "The last time I was here, it was mobbed. It was still wonderful, but next to this, now—it was like watching TV on a crowded train. Somebody's always moving too fast, or taking too long. They mush up on you and you smell what they ate for lunch. Oh, look! Nick, come here, quick. . . ."

Small ecstatic noises escaped from Daysi, but Nick was hardly less touched by it, the sense of privilege and discovery. There might have been some stellar alignment at work here, after all, he thought, beyond what his partner had finagled. And so they walked through the galleries, Nick just behind Daysi, so he could watch the beauty contemplating beauty, until the time came for them to go, home or not home, as luck would have it.

TWENTY-TWO

The sheets were thick and soft, with a velvety nap, and when Nick stretched out his arms, they didn't reach the side of the bed. That was his first disorientation. Light in the room, sunlight pouring through lacy curtains. Not his place, definitely not. He hadn't moved much, his eyes had just opened, but now he held still, motionless for concealment, until sense came back to him. A bowl of fresh flowers on the nightstand—what, in the business, was called a clue. Pale gold roses in a glass bowl. Yes, he knew where he was. What else? Nick was still happy, almost completely, but he was on guard against something, wary. His bad habit was still a good instinct, now and then.

It seemed they had talked about everything last night, but Nick had only really taken in what he'd wanted to hear. When they'd come home, come here, she'd urged Nick to be quiet, and he'd asked why. She had said something about her mother, her son. In the dark, she hadn't been able to see his face, which was good. Yes, Nick knew about the family, he'd been told at least twice, but it had clearly failed to register. And it clearly failed to matter. Now he listened for voices, for the sound of footsteps, and did not move. He was happy not to, almost completely.

Nick slept again, a little longer, but so lightly that voices or footsteps would have woken him. Now it was time to go. Gun? He slipped a hand beneath the mattress, slid it around till he touched metal. Good. The gun was the worry, even though the shield could be more dangerous, in the wrong hands. If the gun was there, the shield would be. Clothes were over a chair. Watch? Nightstand. It was eleven o'clock. What had he slept, nine hours? That was more than he could remember sleeping in a long time. Maybe he should come here more often, wherever it was.

His cellphone announced itself, vibrating with a low hum, somewhere below. Nick picked it up from the floor and checked the caller: Esposito. Nick answered in a low voice, as the coast was not yet clear.

"Yeah?"

"Hey there, sunshine. Awake yet?"

"Yeah, I already did my yoga. What's up?"

"Why are you talking like that? Are you hurt? Did the bad lady touch you?"

"You're a pisser in the morning. Don't let anybody tell you different."

"Relax, Nick. It's after eleven. Mom's at work, kid's at school. You need a ride?"

Nick breathed deeply, and he was tempted to fall back to sleep. Now he was completely happy. He could get used to this, he thought.

"Yeah, cool. Twenty minutes? An hour, make it an hour."

"You got twenty. Why I called? Remember Miguel, from the Kiko kidnapping?"

"Yeah?"

"Dead."

"In jail? On Rikers?"

"Yeah."

Nick wasn't sleepy anymore, and he wasn't happy. How long had that lasted, eight seconds? There would be phone calls about this from downtown, and the thought of blocked numbers reminded Nick of Allison. He needed coffee.

"How?"

"They say he tripped."

Gun, shield, handcuffs. Watch, phone, wallet, keys. Naked still, Nick had all he needed. Sunglasses even. All the better, ready to go. Nick put them on, so he wouldn't forget them. He jumped from the bed and then stopped, turning around to look at it. The sweet sheets, still mussed. Nick didn't even want to try to straighten them. Time to go, to love this and leave, at least for now. What should he call the mother? Señora? Mama? Mami? The son's name was Esteban, Spanish for Steven. He remembered that he'd been told. Too much, too sudden; don't get too far ahead. Enough to think about, the last night, the next. Still, it felt limitless, with Daysi. Nick went to the window and looked out—the river, the bridge, the Palisades, the country and beyond. Hadn't he seen all that, the other day? Different eyes. Nick made the bed and went back to the window. It was so beautiful here. Would Allison— Stop. He wasn't a cheater in his heart, but he'd manage.

Nick had started to scowl, when he caught himself in the mirror, over the vanity, on the far side of the room. Bare-assed except for sunglasses, scratching himself, admiring the real estate. He laughed so hard he spat, and had to wipe up a wet fleck on the wall. Nick took off the glasses. Look for something, a note, a reality check, a note. The vanity is where the note would be. And yes, it was there, as short and sweet as he'd hoped for. "Hey, Sleepy! So much fun last night, thank you. I have to go to work, Mama, too, and Esteban is at school. XXOO, D." Yes, perfect. He couldn't believe she had dashed that off, the tone so breezy and fond. Nick had a pinball machine in his brain, and she got that right the first time? He picked up his clothes and went to shower. It calmed him, and he concentrated only on the beauty of the past night. He had to live a little, he told himself. He began to believe that he might.

Outside, Nick could have whistled at the day. The sun was warm, the wind mild, the trees red and gold, the river a stately gray. Gulls circled in the middle distance, a hawk in the farther sky. The line of buildings northward gave way to wild spaces, and south it led to the city, the sea. He had a moment to take it all in before Esposito pulled up, handing over coffee and a bottle of cologne.

"Thanks. Do I stink?"

"We all do, don't we?"

"Tell you what—let's swing by the apartment. I could use fresh socks and underwear."

"Look at you, fancy restaurants and clean drawers. Ain't you the society type!"

"I like to look my best when we go to Rikers. We're going there, right?"

"We'll stop by, have a look. They say he took a header down a flight of stairs. I set it up so we could have a word with Malcolm Cole, see if he's got any news for us today."

"What's the story?"

"What I got, I told you. Maybe they'll have something more when we get there."

"Like your voodoo buddy said, there won't be a trial."

"That he did. But Kiko's still out there. Fernando Dotti has to stick around to talk to the DA, unless Kiko turns out to be another exceptional clearance. Don't get me wrong, I'm all for it. If Kiko gets zapped by a lightning bolt, I close two cases, the kidnapping and the Milton Cole homicide. He's lawyered up on the homicide. I won't get a statement. And without a statement, I got shit."

They took the West Side Highway up to Dyckman Street, and Nick watched the river again, as if it might have changed. It had to; it always does. He rolled down the window for the breeze to catch his face. The coffee was good, and he could feel the sun on his arm as it dangled outside. Moments from last night came back to him and blended with the new glory of the day. Was this what it was like to have a good life? Nick was excited and content at the same time, charged up and at deep ease; was that all it took, to share a meal and a bed?

Esposito looked over, bemused, as they moved up Broadway.

"I'm glad to see you happy, Nick, I am, but if you start singing show tunes, I'm dropping you off right here. Unless it's *Grease*. I liked that one."

"Don't worry, I'll keep the song in my heart."

"Jeez, Nick, that was cute! I gotta get you laid more often."

"Hang on. Look over there—"

There was a scuffle on the sidewalk in front of the apartment building. A scrawny white man flailed away at a smaller black man, who parried stiffly. The white man—Jamie Barry, yes, it was—threw loose, useless punches, his arms slapping around like windblown sheets, while his opponent held himself with awkward intensity, hitting back with jerky, almost rusty-jointed jabs. The Scarecrow versus the Tin Man, Nick thought, unfearful for either's safety. It had the squared-off look of a bar fight, but it was the wrong place, the wrong time of day. They were on the far side of the street, and there was traffic; no opportunity to rush over, and no need.

"You know these characters?" Esposito asked.

"The white junkie. Lives in the building. The black kid, I don't know."

"No? He looks like Michael Cole."

"Let's go."

Livery cab after livery cab dodged in and out, the fares few and the competition savage. Esposito didn't want to hit the siren, but as he cut in, then cut over to make a U-turn, the tires screeched and the horns began to blare. Jamie dropped his hands to watch, poor dope, and the black kid landed one on the temple, dropping him. The kid looked back quickly—half-profile, half a second, Nick couldn't make him—before he jetted, sprinted back into traffic, now filled with stopped cabs, honking and angry, some of the drivers stepping out to shout and curse.

Esposito parked the car and waved on the cabbies. He leaned over Jamie and tapped him on his face. The eyes blinked, rapidly then slowly, before opening altogether. He took in the sight of Esposito, the burly white guy in the suit; he could smell cop.

"Hey, thanks, Officer. . . . That black bastard tried to rob me!"

"Come off it, Jamie."

"What? Come on, I mean— Hey, Nick! Nicky, how you doin'?"

"Just fine, Jamie. How you doin'?"

"Not so good, nah. I mean, not too bad, I guess. He got a cheap shot in. I got distracted for a second, and it was like, Pow! I think he pistol-whipped me."

"Come on. Let's get you up."

Each of them took an arm and helped Jamie to his feet. He was happy with the attention, and he stamped a little on each leg, trying them out, as if they were new. Nick wanted to talk to him before he could think. Sweat flowed from Jamie in ominous profusion, like the first leaks before the dam broke. Skinny and pale, slackness in his skin; the hippie-Jesus look, lank locks of hair curling over the shoulder, pubic beard. Nick tapped Esposito on the arm, to let him know to stay back. Jamie's eye had begun to swell.

"What happened, Jamie? What happened with this guy?"

"I think . . . What I think he was gonna do, was—"

"Hang on. Start from the start. Where were you coming from?"

"Home. My dad, he always asks about you, Nick—"

"Your father's a good guy, Jamie, but let's start from the start. Today, this morning. You woke up—when?"

"Like, an hour ago. My father made breakfast, but I wasn't hungry."

"Why? You have your wake-up shot today, Jamie? You get well yet?"

"What? I don't know what— Hey, Nick, you know me—"

Jamie wasn't really offended by Nick's question, but he had a junkie's obligation to deny everything. Esposito grabbed him by the back of the neck, and they walked into the lobby. The front door opened, without resistance, without a key. So much for security. Nick checked the lock as Esposito walked Jamie in. The bolt was in the mechanism, flush, hidden like a turtle's head. It could have been Jamie who had jammed it, to get back in late at night, to spare himself an hour of lost-key weeping on the stoop. Or it could have been Michael Cole, if it even was Michael who'd been there. Or it could have been one of the ordinary things that happen to old places. But the lock had worked the day before. Esposito put Jamie against the wall, and Nick made a show of trying to calm him down.

"Easy, Espo, I know this guy. It's all good here—Jamie, let's cut the bullshit, though. You need help, and I can help you. You need?"

"Yeah! No! Shit, Nick, I don't—"

"Take it easy. You walked outside when?"

"I dunno . . . twenty minutes ago?"

"Where was the black kid?"

"I started to walk out, he walked in, but not like he was goin' anywhere, you know? He was lookin' around, snoopin' at the mailboxes. I stepped to him, you know. I live here. . . ."

Esposito grabbed Jamie by a handful of shirt, and Nick didn't stop him.

"So, you work security here, do ya? So why were you fighting outside?"

"Hey! Nick!"

"What did you say to him, Jamie? He wasn't inside, was he? Was he outside?"

"Yeah, he was outside . . . but he was gonna come in. . . . Lemme go!"

"Easy there. Sorry, Jamie. Tempers are hot here. Espo knows my father. He's concerned about anything in the building—I am, too. Jamie, how about this? Ten bucks for the truth. Price of freedom, here and now, as long as I don't smell a bit of bullshit in it, okay?"

Jamie and Nick looked at each other, both of them trying to put on a mask of sympathy, to cover the cutthroat need. Nick put a hand on Jamie's shoulder and squeezed, gently, as if they were old friends, the agreed-upon conceit. Neither of them had ever met the other in their present roles. Nick always quickened his step when he saw Jamie, offering a curt hello and an occasional dollar. Jamie had noticed Nick's new act as well, and gave him his due credit.

"Ahhhh . . . Okay, Nicky. I come out to clear my head, to sit on the stoop, and the kid's standing there. Just standing. So I stand, too, to see what's up—what's his hustle, is he a junkie, a freak? He don't belong, you know? And he looks nervous, not nervous but pissed off, but he acts like he's just there, and if there's a problem, it's my problem. So I wait, standing there, knowing I can stand on the stoop with the best of 'em. It's all I done, half my life! And it's like he's trying to outdo doing nothing, going head-to-head against me. Doin' more nothin'! Doin' less! Now he has challenged the black belt!"

Jamie crouched down into a martial arts pose, and Esposito covered his mouth with his hand, to hide his smile. Jamie's eye had started to darken and close, but he began to play to the audience. He had a connection to something now, other than a needle in his arm. When he was on the mooch, at least with Nick, he always traded on secondhand sentiment instead of second-rate comedy. Still, Nick was impressed by the workmanlike performance, even with the hackneyed lines, pitched to the middle of the crowd.

"Easy, Jamie. Ten bucks, bullshit-free, you understand?"

Esposito scratched his belly, then rubbed the gun on his hip, and scowled, growling low. "What set it off?"

"You ask him for a buck?" Nick asked. "Jamie, we're friends here, till we're not."

"No! Yeah, but not really . . ."

"What you offer? What he ask?"

"He didn't ask for anything. . . . I said it was my building. If he wanted to hang, he had to pay, it was my spot."

"And what did you ask him for, playing like you're Pablo Escobar?"

"Who?"

"Like you're a big shot. How much?"

"Five bucks."

"You play kingpin, and ask him for five bucks?"

"He thought about it! I had him for a minute! He ain't tough. He ain't a street kid!"

"Neither are you," said Esposito. "All you're gonna be on the street is a skid mark. Cut it out. What happened? You wanna hook him up, or hook up with him? What about the door? When did the lock break? Did the kid break it?"

Jamie began to mumble and deny, and Esposito's hand went up to Jamie's throat. Nick let it stay there for a minute. Jamie could tell the truth about as well as he spoke Swahili. He needed quick lessons.

"Nick," Jamie said, "you know my game. . . ."

"No, Jamie, tell me. Tell me about the lock. Did he break it, or did you?"

"The lock? I don't know. He was waiting to come in, so I guess he didn't know it was broke. I didn't know it was broke."

The spirit of buffoonish bravado had left him, and Nick was sorry it had. A funny junkie wasn't worth much, but it was better than the other kinds.

"C'mon, Nick. I'm a bum, next to a bum, but I don't hurt nobody. . . . I couldn't figure this kid. I didn't know why he was here, so I pushed it a little. I asked him for dope, and then I said I could get him some—and he went off. But you know, this is our building, you know? Guys like me and you, the old neighborhood—"

"All right, Jamie, I believe you. Take it easy."

"Yeah, cool. And . . . I mean . . . Nick, you said ten bucks, right?"

"Yeah, Jamie, ten bucks. I said it and I mean it. Now take a walk around the block for twenty minutes, and then come back here. I'll have it for you. I still need you."

"What's up, Nick? Is everything okay?"

"Hit the road. Take a walk now. Wait." Esposito was severe in his voice, and Jamie obeyed each instruction, taking two paces before going rigid on command. "C'mere. Empty your pockets."

"What? C'mon . . ."

When Jamie hesitated, Esposito took him by the shoulders and put him against the wall, patting him down. "You don't got nothing sharp, right? Nothing that's gonna cut me? You do, you forget, and I'll put you in the hospital. . . ."

"Yeah, jacket."

"Hand it over."

Jamie removed the syringe and handed it to Nick; he handled it gingerly, pinching it in the middle, as if the tip might whirl around and try to bite. Esposito pulled Jamie's pockets out from the inside—snot rags, empty books of matches, three buttons and six pennies, a dollar bill and a ten. Esposito pocketed the money and gave him two dollars. It was the standard drill for untested informants, to make sure they didn't do a side business with their own cash.

"Here. Get coffee. I'll hold the rest. I don't want you getting distracted."

"Hey! C'mon! That's my—"

"That's your situation, Jamie." Esposito's voice was a feral purr. Nick handed him back the syringe. Jamie looked at Nick, nodded, and walked outside. Esposito kicked the garbage from Jamie's pockets to the side of the lobby.

"Whaddaya wanna do?"

"Change my clothes. Don't tell my father about it. Michael Cole's never been collared, right? We don't have any pictures of him. Can you go back to the precinct, get a picture of Malcolm? They do look alike, right? We can't really rule him in, rule him out. What do you suppose is going on here?"

"Listen, Nick, I don't mean to spoil your day, but are you kidding me, kidding yourself? It's Michael. He was waiting here, and there's nobody to wait for here but you. This kid, he's changed the game. They're supposed to be afraid of us, looking over their shoulder when they walk home, not the other way around. You know? You know I'm right. I'm heading back for the picture, meet you in a few. I'm glad I set it up to see Malcolm today."

"Yeah."

Esposito walked out, and Nick waited for him to leave before going into his apartment, as if Michael might still be lurking outside. Michael couldn't know which apartment they lived in. There was nothing on the door, and the name had peeled off the mailbox years ago. Nick knocked on the door to give warning before he went in.

His father was at the kitchen table, tuna fish on toast, cup of tea. Noon exactly, by the clock on the wall. Nick could have used more coffee. His father got up to fill the pot, as if reading his mind.

"Late night, Nicky? At work all night? I looked in on you, and you weren't there. You look fine, though, refreshed and relaxed."

So much for mind reading; or maybe he had only read until the last page. But his father was right, Nick thought; Nick wasn't as concerned as he might have been. If it had been Michael Cole outside, it was more of a challenge than a threat. Barely that, despite everything. Nick had to fight himself not to make light of it. Lightness was the problem, the lack of gravity in the feel of the situation. If fear were a gas, it would be heavier than air; Nick had breathed it before, knew the pressure, the weight. But Malcolm had been so persuasive in his portrait of Michael's futilities, traipsing from failure to failure, quitting the violin and then disinvited from the war, where all manner of convicts and mouth-breathers had been made welcome. And then there was a knock at the door. That felt heavy, a burden on his back and a choked quiet in his throat. The old man looked up from filling the pot at the sink. "Who could that be?"

Nick stepped quickly from the kitchen before pulling the gun and walking along the edges of the hall, where the floorboards creaked less. The peephole had a brass lid like a little sewer cap—What genius thought of that?—that you had to lift to see through. Nick stayed on the side and jiggled it without looking, pulling his hand away quickly, so the shooter would go for the sound, center mass.

"Nick? Sean? It's me, Espo."

Nick reholstered just before his father stuck his head out from the kitchen—"Lots of company today!"—and opened the door for Esposito, who held up his hands like a surgeon.

"I just wanna wash my hands quick. Sorry. Hey, Sean, how you doin'? I'd shake your hand, but . . . a pigeon just shit on me!"

The improvisation was less than inspired, but it appeared to be satisfactory.

"How about that! A pigeon! Dirty things. Will you have coffee?"

"Maybe after. I gotta run to the precinct. I'll be back in fifteen minutes."

Esposito walked to the bathroom, which he had examined so closely yesterday. There was no pigeon, there was Jamie; Esposito had remembered he'd touched him, and he wanted to wash him off. Nick went into his room to take off his jacket, and Esposito was gone again before Nick came out. The coffee was waiting, and he sat with his father. He had finished his sandwich, and had put on another cup of tea. Twelve ten, another milestone in the day done. Six hours until dinner.

"So! A pigeon! Of all things . . ."

"Yeah."

"Did you ever see a baby one?"

"No. Why?"

"Me neither. Nor anyone I know. Odd, isn't it?"

"Yes."

"And yet, it only holds that there have to be."

When his father's eyes narrowed, heralding the arrival of another thought, Nick began to drift toward the door, preparing to dodge the next daft digression. But his father surprised him, even more than Jamie had, and Nick worried he might have read his mind after all, and seen how much of it was still on Daysi.

"Ah, well. I know you and Allison struggled, Nick. You can put up with more than you think you can. Still . . . Hard, I know, for both of you. Harder on her. It's always worse for the woman. Your mother and I had almost given up, when we had you. Not given up, but resigned . . . Well, you know—God's hands . . .

"D'ye think we should go to Galway first? Her sister Mary, I always liked. She was the best of the bunch. Second best! A widow. No children, either. She'd be touched to see you. Take Allison, if you want—my treat. I have money now, and I don't know what to do with it. If not—I don't mean to pry, you understand—why not Esposito? He seems like a good man, good fun. Does he eat normal food? I don't suppose we'd have to pack for him, the . . . spaghetti and such? We'll make do. Ireland's a very modern country now, Nick, it can't be helped. Ah! That reminds me, would you have some stew?"

"Sure, Da."

The last question was the easiest, and Nick had no trouble with the answer. He found that he was already sitting at the kitchen table, drawn back, drawn in. He enjoyed his stew, and didn't speak until it was finished. Digestion would come in time.

"Da, how long has the front door been broken?"

"Is it? I didn't know it was. I used the key only this morning, when I went for the newspapers. But then, I always put the key in the door, without thinking."

"Any strange phone calls lately? Or anybody call and hang up?"

"No, not so I noticed. Wait, last week, a woman called. She yelled at me in Spanish. Very angry about something, she was. She didn't listen when I tried to interrupt, to say I wasn't . . . Well, in truth I never caught the name."

"I see . . . but no hang-ups?"

"No, not that I recall. Why?"

"Well . . . burglars . . . the door. Sometimes they break a door, make phone calls in a building to see if anybody's home."

"Aren't they devious, then! The criminal mind!"

Another knock on the door, and then footsteps inside the apartment, in the hall, but before Nick could react, Esposito called out to announce his return—"Hey, Seanee, it's me!"—as if he lived there. He shouldn't barge in like that, Nick thought, given the circumstances. That Esposito called his father by his first name was slightly jarring, notwithstanding that it was by request, but "Seanee" struck Nick as extravagant. Mr. Meehan responded in kind, greeting him like an old fraternity brother. "Espo! Hello, lad!" Nick was bemused by the enthusiasm, mostly, and also felt a twinge of something between envy and chagrin that his relations with his father rarely showed such camaraderie and cheer. That was foolish, he knew. He was his father's son, and neither of them were much inclined toward emotional display. And it was worse than foolish to begrudge any exuberance in the house, as if his father were a museum piece around which his partner was throwing a football. The thought of museums reminded Nick of Daysi, and it warmed him, relaxed him. He left the two of them in the kitchen and went to change clothes.

When he returned, he found Esposito finishing a plate of stew, and a story about how he once caught a fugitive perp from a triple shooting by spreading a rumor that he was seeing the man's girlfriend. It was one of the standards from his repertoire, and Nick knew it well. Esposito made repeated, purely professional visits to see her, and upon leaving the apartment, he'd always make a fuss of buttoning up his shirt, fixing his tie, checking to see if his zipper was zipped. Word traveled, and the perp was arrested trying to knock down her door.

"The best part? Later on, I did hook up with her. She was a little . . . cutie. Ecuadorian, I think. Sandra? Something like that. She came down to see me testify at his trial. The guy took a plea right then and there. Fifteen years."

Nick was apprehensive about how graphic Esposito would get in his telling, and he was relieved at the effortful delicacy of "cutie." His father listened avidly, offering back lively "Ah"s and "No!"s as if he were in a revival tent. It heartened Nick to see him like that.

"A ladies' man, I knew you were, Espo. Me and Nick, well . . . How would you put it, Nick? The Meehans haven't that gift, or maybe we're inclined to wait our turn. Is that right? No—"

"Are you kidding, Sean? You should see the broad Nick went home with last night! Awesome, really unbelievable. You gotta see this woman. You wouldn't believe—"

You gotta shut up, Nick thought. He thought it with some violence, so much so that Esposito knew it at once, and there was a Mexican standoff of distressed expressions—Esposito at Nick, seeing the gaffe, the breach of privacy; Nick at his father, knowing that he had not followed the same path of rugged, lonely duty; his father away from both of them, simply sad again, and deciding it was none of his business. Nick's anger at Esposito dimmed when he saw his woebegone grimace, the genuinely stricken contrition. He had never seen that before; he had almost assumed that Esposito was immune to guilt or shame. Nick's idea of Esposito changed, and it was the dueling imbalances, the sea-sickening shifts in the ground with the two men who amounted to his family, that inclined him to hold steady.

"Well. All right, Da. We got . . . things to do. Espo?"

Esposito stood slowly, extending a hand across the table.

"Mr. Meehan, thanks for lunch. It was great."

"Anytime, lad."

His father sounded vague to Nick, which troubled him, as did Esposito's chastened return to formality. Too much and too little were equally poor choices. They were escorted down the hall, and when the door closed behind them, Nick heard the lock click.

"Nick, I am so sorry. The last thing I wanted was—"

"I know. Don't beat yourself up over it. You meant well."

Nick strained for a dismissive, affectionate tone, and the words came out of him more credibly than he'd expected. Esposito had done far more for him than he'd done for Esposito, and there were other accounts he never wanted to settle. Beyond that, Jamie Barry would be waiting.

Nick saw Jamie leaning against the lobby door and waved him in, giving Esposito an elbow. Jamie walked over, slurping a coffee that Nick guessed was half-sugar, casting surreptitious glances behind him like a confidential agent. Esposito took out another set of pictures, looking at them first, to make sure they were the right ones. Black-and-white mug shots printed on letter paper, six of them, six young black men, the pages folded in half, lengthwise, so that the name and the rest of the information was hidden on the back. Jamie would only see faces, one at a time. He studied each for a minute, then moved on to the next.

"Nah, none of these guys."

"None?"

"Listen. To me, they all look alike, but none of them was him."

"You sure?"

"Yeah, pretty sure."

"Who does he look most like?"

"I mean, a little like this one, a little like that."

Jamie shrugged, and Nick was impressed by how he had adjusted in twenty minutes, from hophead punching bag to portrait connoisseur. He picked Malcolm, and another, with diffidence. They bore a closer resemblance to Michael than the others, for what it was worth, which was little. Esposito pushed on.

"What is it about either of these guys that rings a bell?"

"What rings a bell? A punch in the face. Whaddaya think?"

Esposito grabbed Jamie by the shirtfront, and Nick signaled him to lay off as Jamie protested.

"Take it easy! Nick, c'mon, you know me! You want me to say something different, I'll say what you want, but these guys ain't the guy. The two I picked are close, but that's it!"

"All right, Jamie. Here's your money, the ten I promised. Espo, you got what he had before—eleven bucks? Good looking out, Jamie, but don't be hustling in front of the building. It kills your father to see it. You gotta quit this."

"Yeah . . . I know," he said, with a wistful and downcast pause. And then he looked up at Nick, offering a twitchy wink and smile, his last gag, his send-off. "I quit every day. . . ."

The three of them walked outside, but only Jamie had a spring in his step as he headed downtown, at a brisk pace, without looking back.

TWENTY-THREE

After crossing the bridge, they checked in with the guards at the front and then headed for the infirmary. The wind was chillier here, coming off the Long Island Sound, but the day was still balmy. Speedboats left rapier-like white traces behind them and leapt up to cross the greater wakes of freighters; planes took off from LaGuardia and cast racing shadows on the shimmering water. To the east, the span of the Whitestone Bridge connected Queens and the Bronx with a gracious symmetry, three pairs of cables draped between two piers; to the west, the island-hopping centipede tangle of the Triborough knotted Manhattan to them as well. It must have been a cruel view for the prisoners, all the transit and travel, the pleasure and the progress, the symbols of things and the things themselves.

Esposito's nurse—Audrey from Astoria—led them again to an examining room in the back, betraying no recent intimacy. Though Malcolm was friendly, the visit didn't begin as the first had, with the sense of clandestine fun. Nick hadn't considered how much Malcolm had done for them already. He had instigated the santero rescue, sparing a life and claiming one in revenge. Nick wondered which meant more to him, gave him greater solace. He wore an orange jumpsuit with a kind of light and knowing irony, as if it were a Halloween costume. He shook the detectives' hands, and they sat down, facing one another. Esposito waited a few seconds for Malcolm to fill in the pause. It was an interrogator's technique, and Nick wondered why he bothered; was there any need for a contest of wills? The moment passed, and the corner of Malcolm's mouth lifted into a grin.

"That was fast! I mean, not Kiko, but his brother. Even better! Now he know what it is to bury his people. . . . It was you, right? It was you, Espo, what done him?"

Esposito nodded, and Malcolm's smile covered the whole of his face.

"I heard about it. Then I read it in the paper, somebody had it. I had to check myself a minute, calm down, you know? In here, you ain't supposed to be all 'Yippee! Yahoo!' when a cop shoots one of us. 'Specially when it's the cop that locked you up."

"I could see how that might come off wrong," agreed Esposito. "Did you hear about the guy here? He fell, split his head? Just today?"

"Yeah, why?"

"What did you hear?"

"I heard he fell, split his head. Spanish dude . . . Why, he roll with Kiko?"

"Yeah. He was in Kiko's crew. Nothing funny about it?"

"Yeah, it was funny. It was like he slipped on a banana peel! There's all kinds of rumors—there's gonna be—but all guys got to do here is talk. . . . I know a guy, he was there on the tier when it happened. The lights go out a second, dude goes down the stairs. But he was alone, nobody was next to him. It wasn't like he was sliced, or birthday-caked, or nothin'."

Nick had to ask. "Birthday-caked?"

"They do that when you sleep. They put tissue between your toes, hold you down, light it up like candles. Sometimes they splash a little lighter fluid, whatever, to help it go."

Nick withdrew his feet slightly below his chair, and Malcolm was kind enough to pretend not to notice.

"Nice," said Esposito, pulling the conversation back. "With the guy, though—there was a power failure?"

"I dunno, I guess. The lights went out in the building."

"Did they go out here?"

"I dunno. I was in the yard."

"Act of God, I guess."

"No shit! If I knew he was with Kiko, maybe it woulda been different. . . . Nah, I'm cool. I'm workin' with you, I am. I appreciate it. I appreciate what you done for me, for my family."

That was one way to see it, Nick supposed. A view that was both harsher and kinder than Michael's, the inside and the upside. Closer to the truth, Nick thought, and yet selective to a degree that was either brilliant or batty. The detectives had still scared his mother to death and put him in jail, for life or close to it. Hard to get around that; Nick doubted he could have himself. But this was the broader perspective—past was past, and they had to move on, didn't they? Malcolm was an American, an optimist, a can-do man. Another likeness between Malcolm and Esposito, the hope so potent it seemed heartless, in certain lights. And that was not the only resemblance, Nick realized. If Malcolm took after Esposito, Nick had a bit of Michael in him, in his reluctance to let go. It didn't flatter either of them.

"Speaking of family," Nick remarked. "How about your brother? Does he come by, or call?"

"Nah, he wouldn't, like I said."

"Who does call? Who visits?"

"My sister, a couple of friends."

"What do they say about him?"

"That he's mad crazy about shit. He's hot to pop somebody. He was pissed off when you got Kiko's brother before he did. Now he has to find somebody else."

"How about us? He talk about goin' after cops?" Esposito was quick to ask it, and Nick was glad he did.

"C'mon, man. That's my blood you're talkin' about."

"No, Malcolm. It's my blood," Nick said, and he wasn't angry, but he wanted to know. "Not my relatives—I love 'em, don't get me wrong, I do—but I'm talking about real, actual blood, the stuff inside my body. I like to keep it there. Esposito, too. Has your brother talked about killing us? Killing cops?"

The silence now belonged to the detectives. It was theirs to work, to put into play. Malcolm thought for a while, and Nick could see him deciding whether what he'd say next was a betrayal. He looked down and rubbed his cheek. He had decided. He looked up at both detectives, from one to the other, eye to eye. There was no need for the words. It would be easier this way, at least at first.

"Does he got a gun?" Esposito took the same measured tone Nick had. There was no cause for accusation, no benefit to it.

Malcolm shook his head. "But he can get one, anybody can." Asked and answered.

"Who does he want?" Nick asked. "Me? Esposito? What has he said? Who did you hear it from?"

Malcolm took a breath, then grabbed hold of his chin, pulling down a few times, as if he had a beard. Nick didn't know whether this was hard for him or he wanted to make it look like it was. He would say it, they knew, and they waited. Malcolm tilted forward, elbows on the knees.

Esposito leaned toward him, in the same posture. "All right. You understand, this is not just whether we get hurt. It's whether he does. He goes nuts, tries to hurt a cop, odds are he loses, Malcolm. Maybe he gets the jump on some random rookie, walking down the street, but what is he gonna do? Tell me, what is he gonna do? Punch him? Shoot him?"

"He don't got a gun—that I know about."

"So you said."

"I don't know how he's gonna get it out of his system, whatever it is. All I know, somethin's gotta get out of it, and I don't know on who. You guys ain't first. Kiko is. That much I can bet. Like I said, I wasn't told direct by him. My sister told me, people I know. And I know Michael. Somethin's gonna go. Michael don't mouth off like that, he don't talk shit. I'm surprised he talked, said anything at all. But he walked my sister from one coffin to the other, Milton and Mama. He squeezed her hand in front of each one. Said he'd make this right."

"What else did he say?"

"Nothing. Like I say, he ain't much of a talker. But she knew what he meant."

"Could you talk to him?"

"If I got out, maybe . . ."

"That's out of my hands, Malcolm, for the here and now," Esposito said. "So, what do we do to calm him down? Find him a job? Buy him a puppy?"

Malcolm returned his head to his hands, leaning down to think. "Nah, he hates dogs. He's scared of 'em." He had given more thought to the pet than the job offer. "Kiko, he still on the run?"

"Yeah."

"The funeral today?"

"The wake is."

"All I know, ain't no way Kiko gonna walk away without sayin' goodbye, without showin' his face, somehow. I said my goodbyes. You let me. You helped me do it. That's why I'm talkin' to you, workin' with y'all. Michael knows it, too—he knows Kiko's gotta be there."

"That's gonna be bad, Malcolm."

"I know."

All of them leaned down, elbows on knees, chins in hands. It was Malcolm who sat up first. "So who's gonna change his mind?"

That was the question he left them with, as they headed out of the building. They still had to meet a supervisor from the Department of Corrections, and they were late. They walked awhile, then returned to the car to drive. Acres of landfill and dozens of boxy buildings, parking lots, and fields, all fenced in, the fences topped with razor wire. More than twenty thousand people once lived here. Now it was less. Still, this was its own city. They drove around slowly, making one wrong turn, then another, guided from one point to the next by random guards, leaving work, or going to it from their cars in the lots. All of them stopped at the sight of a slow-moving car. There weren't many visitors here in private vehicles. The reaction was always wary, the directions offered with a note of relief. "Yeah, okay, here's where you go. . . ." The building was found. Esposito had a name to ask for, a Captain Terence Smolev. They had spoken on the phone.

Captain Smolev came out to meet them, with a grip-testing handshake and a uniform that was as crisp as a marine's. Esposito managed a more cheerful greeting than Nick did, but both of them were anxious to leave. The appointment had been made, and it had to be kept. City agencies can be like society ladies, thin-skinned and grudge-holding about matters of etiquette. If the detectives skipped this meeting, the next time they went to see an inmate, he might suddenly be sent to court for the day.

"Good to meet you, detectives. Is there anything I should know about this?"

"No, not that I know of," Esposito said. "It's a big case, so there's always gonna be questions. At least we'll be able to say we came out here, we talked to you. It is what it is."

"I get it. No problem. What do you want to look at? We have video. It's not great. We lost power for a couple of seconds. Or if you want, we can go to the scene."

"Let's do the scene first."

Smolev led them to a secure room, to check their guns, before heading out to the unit where Miguel had been housed. They were examined from behind a camera, then a Plexiglas screen, before they were buzzed in; in hallways, barred gates swung closed behind them before the next gate opened. The inmates had been put into their cells while the detectives were there, and a few had begun to complain—hoots and curses, the look-at-me! noises. There were three levels on the tier, two flights of steel stairs leading up on each side from a concrete platform on the floor. Smolev took them to the platform on the far side.

"This is it, where he landed. All mopped up already. In fact, it was mopped just before he fell. One of the officers noticed that. It'll be in the report when it's done. There was a little puddle on the top. Maybe soap in the water? Who knows?"

Esposito walked up to the top of the stairs, counting them. Twelve. Not much height there, but in a contest of skull versus concrete, you needed very little momentum when you had the right angle. The one-punch homicides, they happened now and then—the uppercut that connects, the head on the curb, the horrified seconds that pass as the winner sees how thoroughly he has won. Jamie could have been that, earlier today. Esposito laid a hand on the banister, then yanked it back, as if stung.

"Sharp there," he muttered, giving his hand a shake before looking down. "Loose screw . . . Well, I guess we've seen what there is to see. Captain?"

From there, Smolev led them to the video monitors, back in the administrative building. As they walked, Nick tapped on his watch, and Esposito nodded. Nick couldn't think what they needed to do next, exactly, but it wasn't here. The video was not much more revealing. A bank of monitors, each split into multiple screens; a digital system, decent quality, but several price points below what you'd find in the average shopping mall.

"Fortunately for us, the guy fell in this unit. The video is good there. We had a mini-blackout, an outage for a couple of seconds, but the surveillance system runs on a separate power source. There isn't much light, but the screen just gets kinda dark, not black, and you can pretty much make him out."

A technician had the footage cued up and waiting. The second tier by the stair was empty before Miguel walked up to it, then stopped, as if called to. He put his hand down, then pulled it up, as Esposito had; then it went dark.

"No sound?"

"No."

"Can we see it again?"

Miguel stopped, looked, and put his hand up and down, as before, and you could see the figure pitch forward, a second of denser darkness. It was what it was.

"You have a camera on the floor?"

"Coming up."

Two groups of inmates, both talking, one an animated storyteller, arms swinging, the rest laughing at his joke. A corrections officer walked across the floor. The screen went dark for three, four, five, six . . . six seconds, and then the lights went on again. All had frozen, and then the officer did a little crab-step backward, three or four paces, lifting up his radio, ready to be jumped. Three or four of the inmates fell into combat stances, with balled-up fists, held up to throat level. A few more seconds passed, and then one of the inmates ran over to where Miguel lay. No one had been near the stairs, not within twenty feet. The officer rushed to follow and pushed the inmate back.

"That's about all we got."

"That's about all you could ask for," said Esposito. "Law of gravity is not in my jurisdiction. Any reaction from the inmates?"

"A petition for carpeting on the stairs."

"Any contact info? Next of kin?"

"No, not a name, not a number, not a thing. I bet 'Miguel Mendoza' isn't even a real name. He'll wind up in Potter's Field."

Captain Smolev left them at gun storage with two more punishing handshakes. They'd spent an hour on this, which was more than Nick had wanted, but it had needed to be done. An hour on a fatality wasn't at all bad. They knew what had happened here, or at least they knew what hadn't. Law of gravity, and too many variables for anyone to plan—a puddle of soapy water, a distracting shout, a spur of metal on the rail, a few seconds with the lights out. A false step, literally, with none of that three-card monte of impossible conjecture—Did he jump? Did he slip? Was he pushed? There was proof he'd been alone, for anyone susceptible to rational belief. And those who clung to faith in deeper forces, hidden causes, would not be swayed by any picture, hours old, always fresh, fixed somewhere in digital heaven, of a man bleeding in the dark, the colors of Ellegua, the black and the red.

TWENTY-FOUR

There was much to plan, but Nick's mind was scattered. Esposito had resolved to go to the wake, at least to watch it from a rooftop, and Nick knew that once they got there, he'd have a hard time getting Esposito to leave. It had the feel of a long night. A camera had been set up outside the funeral home, and someone would watch the monitor with Kiko's mug shot taped up beside it. But it wouldn't be the same; no one knew Kiko like Esposito did, how he walked and gestured, which way he was likely to run. Detectives always complained about not getting enough help on their cases, and then they complained about the help. Still, it was better to do it themselves. And worse—no one should get too close to the funeral, least of all the cops who'd caused it. If Nick and Esposito spotted Kiko, they'd call it in, have him collared a few blocks away. Esposito talked even as he turned up the radio in the car. Noise within, noise without.

On the drive back, Nick only half-listened as Esposito told about how when he was a new cop in the precinct, someone called in to say that a baby had been left in a sack in the park. A young couple stood beside it, watching something inside kick weakly, afraid to touch. Turns out it was a Santeria thing, a chicken in a pillow case. . . . It was a good enough story, but Nick was trying to think about his father, whether he should worry about him, whether he should worry more. Memories of Daysi from last night kept popping up—the restaurant, the museum, bed, how they'd shushed each other like teenagers, the fear of getting caught adding to the thrill. He was about to tell Esposito about the Galway vacation, when they were diverted by the sight of two blue-and-white harbor patrol launches in the Harlem River, cops from each raking the turbid water between them with long-poled gaffs. A body, maybe, but

since the boats were on the Bronx side of the river, it looked to be someone else's problem. Esposito began to tell about a floater he once had, but
Nick's eye was caught by a pigeon flying beside the car, at eye level, at
the exact same speed, for nearly a mile. "Synchronous," was that the
word? No, it wasn't.

At the precinct, Esposito went behind the desk to let the sergeant
know about the funeral, so he could make an announcement at the four-
to-twelve roll call to be aware of its hot-spot potential. Nick steered clear
of a delegation of Africans in the front hall, five or six men in lacy skull-
caps, a few women in bundled head scarves, all of them in florid flowing
robes, with determined looks. One of the men was negotiating unsuc-
cessfully with a gaunt older black cop for the release of a female prisoner.
If the cop had been assigned to handle them out of a presumed affinity, it
was misguided. He might have been intrigued by the dilemma—the
African spoke on behalf of a friend whose two wives had had a slugfest,
and the winner was in a holding cell—but he was resistant to the proposed remedy. "If you please, you will let her go home to eat, and one of
us will wait in her place? Her return will be guaranteed."

The cop began to wave them out, his arms a little stiff, saying "These
people . . ." without caring who heard. When Garelick walked past them,
coming in the front door, one of the African women tapped his shoulder.

"Excuse me, do you work here?"

"Depends on who you ask," he said, without stopping. The burnout
Zen of the comment would have provided Nick a few minutes of keen
contemplation, but he was distracted by an outburst from the dozen prisoners a Narcotics team had brought in, lined up against the opposite
wall. They would be strip-searched in the bathroom, one by one, before
being put into the cells. One of the cops called out for a female cop to
search the one female prisoner, and a woman walking in for her meal
break obliged. She took a pair of latex gloves and led the prisoner into
the ladies' room. The perp was kind of cute; the cop, less so. Both of them
popped back out of the bathroom in seconds, the cop shoving the prisoner ahead.

"You gotta be kidding me!" barked the female cop angrily.

"You didn't ask! Besides, I don't gotta say!" whined the perp, though
she didn't seem entirely displeased, even as one of the Narcotics cops
grabbed her arm.

"What is it? She have something on her? What did she have, a needle?"

"Outdoor plumbing."

"What?"

"She don't play on my team, guy. She's yours," said the female cop, tossing off her gloves as she walked away. The Narcotics cop looked the prisoner up and down, the full breasts and the slim hips.

"You're shitting me!"

"That's extra," said the prisoner, demurely, to a murmur of surprise on the prisoner line. It built in seconds to mixed shouts, of laughter and disgust. "Yo!" "No!" "No shit!" "No way!" "I knew it! The faggot! Yo, the cop's a faggot, too!"

When Esposito finished with his instructions to the sergeant, he and Nick headed upstairs as another cop shoved the last commentator against the wall, saying, "You talk shit now, bro, but I saw you ask for her number when you was in the back of the van. You get more than her number back there? I wasn't watchin' the whole time . . ."

Nick was glad to have the closing door muffle the chorus behind them as they headed upstairs. The catch of the day—fractious polygamists, a transvestite amid a miscellany of buyers and sellers of crack, dope, weed. What would people say in ten years, a hundred, about how all of this was handled? *Those people really got it about sex and drugs. They had it figured out perfectly.* Nick doubted it, couldn't even guess what the cops would make of it after the shift ended. The trannie would be the take-out anecdote for the Narcotics cops, later on, in the kitchen or in bed, but he didn't know if it would be cast as a comic throwaway or as a fable of the sinful city, whether the "That's extra" line would make the home version. Nick wouldn't tell his father, of course, but he would have told Allison, in their better days, if the mood had been right. It would be a long night, for all of them. Noise within, noise without.

As they walked into the squad, there were more cold calls, hustles and stumbles, miscues and hurried comebacks, missed signals and meaningful static.

"Ms. Santiago? I need to talk to your son, Enrique. . . . Do me a favor, Ms. Santiago, turn down the music. . . . Good, thank you. Okay. Now do me another favor. Finish chewing your food. . . . I know, I'm sure it's good, but finish, please. . . ."

"I don't care if Detective McCann told you just not to do it again. It's my case, and you have to come in and talk to me about it. . . ."

"What's your name, ma'am? I'm looking for Mr. Cooper. Is he your husband? Is he around? . . . You're Mr. Cooper? Sorry, I'm real sorry. We get some electrical interference on the phone lines here, makes the voices come in a little high sometimes. . . ."

Nick was about to sit down at his desk when he got a call on his cell, saw the blocked number on his phone. He abruptly turned around and went back downstairs, to step outside the precinct for privacy. He wouldn't dodge IAB calls anymore, he'd resolved. He was steeling himself to this new course and conflict when his wife greeted him. What had they come to, he thought, when he was disappointed it was not the mystery prick?

"Hey."

"Hey."

The same worn fondness was in both their voices, but Nick thought he caught something else in hers, a sense of impending accusation or confession, news painfully withheld. Whatever else had gone, they still retained their intimate surveillance systems, all the receptors alert to micro-fine shifts in texture and temperature. Allison misinterpreted the pause.

"Can you talk?"

"Yeah."

"Missed you the other night. Shame you couldn't make it."

There it was again, the cue of ambush in the landscape, as if the birds in the forest had all fallen silent. New for him, this brand of fear, not of being hurt but of getting caught. He liked it even less than the old one. But he could not think of a better night than last night, with Daysi. At least not in a long time.

"Yeah, I missed you, too. How was it? Same-old, same-old?"

"Yeah. No, it was nice, better than usual. I picked the restaurant. I go now and then. I like it. I thought it would be your kind of place, old-fashioned, and we could go there together sometime."

"Yeah, maybe . . ."

Come on, Nick thought, come out with it.

"You're not gonna believe who I saw the other night."

"All right. Who?"

"You."

"Really."

"Really. At the restaurant. Outside."

Though she had been clear in saying she had seen him the other night—not last night—outside the restaurant—not inside—the plain words did not immediately register in his jangled mind. He'd been caught, and at first he thought she'd caught him with Daysi. No, it was when he'd been alone, shamefully alone. That was better, but still not good. Nick really wished it had been the mystery prick who had called. He wouldn't have had an answer for him, but he might have had an attitude.

"I don't know what to say."

"I don't, either. I thought I saw you out there, and when I went out, you were walking back to the subway. I almost cried."

That was the end of the noise, and Nick was finally able to concentrate.

"I'm sorry."

"Yeah. Anyway, we have to get together, Nick, sometime soon. I'm not going to play games. I can't. . . . What we're doing, it isn't right. It isn't fair to either of us."

TWENTY-FIVE

There was an hour to kill before heading to the funeral home, but Nick wanted to get out of the precinct, to do something, to leave the last thought behind. He didn't know whether it was cowardice or courage that Daysi had inspired in him, but the break with Allison was now imminent, and not awful to contemplate. He was living a little more. Look, look at all of it—his wife and his lover, his father and his partner, his would-be IAB keeper and his maybe wannabe killer. A full house. How long ago had he woken up alone in his dank bunk bed, dithering and cranky, half-craving attention from voices in the water pipes? He'd been an old overcoat in a secondhand shop, waiting for someone to pick him up and try him on. Now all of the customers were pulling at his sleeves. Silly bastard. Enjoy it while you can. It's all about you. Whose voice was that, and did he really need to know?

"Hey, Espo, let's take a ride."

"Hang on. Can you give me a minute?"

"Yeah."

Esposito caught the note of urgency, and looked up. "It's important?"

"What is?"

Nick smiled—What is important? Deep question, that Esposito thought that he was caught up in some grim philosophy, and got up to leave with Nick, to nip the mood in the bud. He tapped his pocket, making sure the keys were there, and collected binoculars, a flashlight, and a radio from the desk drawer. The one thing, then the other. They drove uptown along Broadway, but Esposito turned on Dyckman Street to avoid the Irish neighborhood, the apartment, recollections of balls in the water, junkies in the lobby, looming threats on the stoop. No associations. He didn't know what had set Nick to thinking wrong. Then east, up the hill toward Yeshiva University, which would bring no allusion to the recent past. Another world here—a Moorish-Gothic castle with cop-per minarets; on the street, young men with black suits, new beards, young men without either, finding their way by the old wisdom, stop-ping at crosswalks, waiting for the lights. A few blocks south, and they had left old Vilnius for Santo Domingo, shtetl for barrio—two teenagers in a chin-up contest, hanging on fire escape ladders on opposite ends of an alley; an old man buffing his ancient black Buick to a resplendent gleam with a machine plugged into the jimmied base of a streetlamp. Nobody leaves it all behind, Nick thought. There are no clean breaks. And then the landscape answered—on Broadway and 175th, the Palace Cathedral, one of the last great movie theaters from the end of the silent-film age; lavish and slightly ludicrous, it belonged in the pictures, in a cockeyed epic of Nineveh, old Cathay. It was rescued from dereliction by Reverend Ike, who preached the prosperity gospel, his own foremost: *The best thing you can do for the poor is not be one of them.* He lectured on Thinkonomics and sold prayer cloth to rub on lottery tickets, betting slips; he had weekly Blessings of the Cadillacs. The marquee said, COME ON IN, OR SMILE AS YOU PASS.

When Nick smiled, Esposito did, too, relieved. Nick told him about the talk he'd had with Allison, and how he was sad about it but he fig-ured it was right, it was time. The night with Daysi had reminded him what life was like, what it could be like, and he wanted it. Esposito's re-action surprised him. "Nick, not for nothing, but you've known her, what—three days? Four? One dinner and one night in bed? It was a great night out, I believe you, but are you gonna bet everything on it, forever? Half the world is women. Look around! And not for nothing, but you're married. I know you don't got kids to worry about, and obviously, you and her got problems. But you hear how half the guys in the office talk to their wives, talk about their wives, the bitching and bullshit. You don't say much about your wife, but you don't run her down. I'm not telling you what to do, but I'd hate to see you throw it all away just because you got laid. I'm not against getting laid—you might have noticed—but I know what's what, who's who, and where I go at the end of the day."

This was not what Nick had expected to hear. Safety tips from one who danced on the high wire, laughing at the idea of a net; a defense of marriage from a playboy who played like he'd just broken out of prison. It was hard to take at face value. Esposito hardly spoke from bitter experience; in fact, he could only testify to the upside of risky lust, lusty risk. But when Nick looked over at his face, it was the image of compassion and concern, and he felt the wisecrack nearly die in his throat.

"I'm not gonna propose. At least not for a week."

Esposito looked sick; Nick laughed. Esposito did, too, then, but less heartily.

"I had you, Espo. . . . C'mon, relax! Don't be so serious!"

Esposito shook his head, more at ease, though his worried aspect had not entirely left him. "This is a switch—you telling me to lighten up."

"And you telling me to be careful."

"All right, all right. You're a little happy now, enjoy it. What I'm gonna do, since we got work to do, is drop you off to see Daysi for a minute. See how she looks the day after, worse or better. Maybe she's in a bathrobe and curlers, fartin' up a storm, all the flowers are dead. Maybe not. These are the things you gotta look into, the next day. She left before you woke up, right? You never know, until you know."

Nick did want to see Daysi, to see if she looked at him the way he wanted to look at her. Just a few blocks to 181st, and then they made the turn. Just past the shop, Esposito pulled over. Nick was starting to leave the car, when Esposito took hold of his shoulder. Nick was mildly annoyed, until he saw Esposito's fretful and affectionate expression. Was he going to offer a twenty-dollar bill, a condom, a breath mint?

"Hang on," he said. "Check yourself. Take a minute."

Esposito pointed to the mirror, and when Nick looked, he did seem wild-eyed, unkempt, a collar point sticking up. Esposito handed him a water bottle from the backseat like a valet, and inclined Nick forward, so he wouldn't spill on himself when he dampened and dried his face, flattened his hair. Nick was grateful for the attention, and he turned to see if he required any more correction. Esposito raised his hands, breathing slowly to inspire Nick to follow.

"Just this, brother. Maybe you two got a life together. God bless and good luck if you do. But you haven't had the same day. She left her bed this morning happy, maybe as happy as you were, maybe more. Maybe she don't got a problem in the world. But you, look what you did today, what you had—a lunatic outside your house, fighting your old junkie buddy from next door. After, you go to jail for an hour, and then you decide to get divorced. Nick, I got a more exciting life than most people, but today I slept in. And Daysi? Pretty flowers, that's what she is! That's what she does! Do I make sense? Am I right? Put it this way: Does she got a good life you want to be a part of? Or do you got a shit life you want to drag her into? And do you want to talk about all of this now, or do you just wanna say 'Hi!'?"

"Hi!"

"Attaboy! Let's hear it again, like you walked off the tennis court!"

"Hi! Hey, baby!"

"Hey, baby! That's it!"

Twice in twenty minutes, his partner had stunned him with his perspective—with his conservatism first, and then with his astute plan for progress. Nick didn't know Daysi, not enough, but he liked what he saw. All right, then, keep it casual, but move ahead. Nick looked in the mirror again, a last check, to make sure he wasn't visibly askew. He raised his hands—*Okay? Now?*—and Esposito waved him on.

At the store, Mama looked up from pink orchids she was arranging into a corsage—"Oh! Hallo!"—and ran to the back, offering a flirty smile before the door closed. Did she know he'd spent the night at her house? Focus. Don't plan, don't reminisce, just roll with it. Daysi came out and ran to him, for a kiss. Not a long kiss, but long enough, and then she pressed her face into the crook of his neck, held him. He smelled her hair, felt her side, tracing a hand along her flank, where it thickened and thinned. Nick liked all of it. It was just what he needed, had hoped to feel. But she pulled away a moment later, with a nod to the back. He thought he knew what she was talking about.

"Mama didn't see me this morning?"

"No, I set the alarm half an hour early, to get up before she did. It didn't wake you up."

"I'm glad. I was happy there."

"Me, too. You just getting up? You look great today . . . and I could use a nap!"

"No, you look great."

"You're sweet."

Nick wanted to kiss her again, and he did. She looked at him, then pulled away, brushing his cheek. A mixed message, sweetly mixed, but not as simple and singular as what he felt for her. Mama came out from the back with two boutonnieres, both red roses this time.

"You friend? Where is he?"

"He's outside in the car. I just stopped by for a minute. We're working. I can't stay."

Mama pinned one to his lapel, and Daysi laughed at the fuss she made, the way Nick's cheeks flushed. Daysi straightened it and put a hand on his shoulder after her mother left.

"Nick?"

"Yeah?"

"I don't want this to sound funny, but there's a big order we have to get out, right away."

"Yeah, sure, I understand. I gotta go, too."

"No, I don't think you understand. We've been getting walk-ins on it all afternoon."

Nick didn't get what she meant; it had been less than a minute from that kiss, from that sweet kiss to the bum's rush. "No problem. I'll let you get back to it. Talk to you later?"

"Definitely. But don't stop by the store for two or three days, okay?"

"All right . . ."

Daysi cocked her head back to the wall, trying to make her point before his feelings were further bruised. There was a cross made of pink carnations, nearly six feet tall, with the name Miguelito draped across on a silk banner. Nick walked over to look at the card. "From your brother Kiko. I will never forget." The back of the store was filled with flowers for the wake, one arrangement shaped to look like a Cadillac medallion. Classy, Nick thought.

"They said he was killed by police."

Nick nodded, but added no further information. "All cash? No credit cards?"

"All cash," said Daysi, still smiling, but her eyes were starting to look worried. She glanced to the front of the store. Nick took her hand and kissed her. "I'll call you later."

"You better."

The worry had almost left her eyes, and Nick got the smile again, the real smile, when the door closed behind him. When he was on the street, he looked around to see if anyone had watched, or if anyone followed him. Tricky business, flowers. Nick was glad that Esposito had parked down the street. When he got into the car, Nick handed over Esposito's boutonniere. Esposito pinned it on, then tried to mush the mirror around, to see himself.

"Let's go," Nick said.

Esposito abandoned the mirror with reluctance, and they drove off. "Well, you look half-happy, which is pretty good for you. What's up? She had to be glad to see you. You got roses for both of us. Or that was Mama?"

"It was Mama, but Daysi was happy to see me. I had to clear out of there. . . . You wanna know why? Guess what's the big account of the day."

"What, a wedding? Shotgun wedding? Yours? I don't know, what?"

"Opposite of wedding."

"Funeral . . . Holy shit! For this thing?"

"More flowers than they got at the Botanical Garden. A big pink cross, taller than you, that says 'Miguelito' on the front. From Kiko."

"God damn! Isn't that kinda sacrilegious?"

"I don't know."

"Did he pay with a credit card? It might give us another address, something else. Sorry, Nick, but maybe you shoulda asked . . ."

"I did. He didn't."

"Didja! Good for you. . . . Maybe we could put a camera in the flowers, right in the middle, get some good shots, everybody up close looking at it. Nah, a little late for that. Plus, we don't wanna get Daysi involved."

"No."

"I guess not. Anyway, let's get set up. We'll get to see all the pretty flowers delivered."

All of this, it was so close to home. They drove past the funeral parlor, checking out the nearby buildings, to see which might offer the best view. They were all quaintly the same, a set of old six-story brick apartments, with ornamental stonework topping the cornices and running down the structural lines, like slices of a wedding cake, the sturdy stuff piled in layers, the pretty stuff running through, gracing the top. How many good families, bad parties, had they seen in the past century, and good parties, too, even when the family wasn't at its best? All of it new once, in the new part of the city. A block uptown there were the same buildings, probably the same builder, which was good for the detectives.

The roofs should run together, front to back. Alleys and airshafts would not separate them from the southern view. Esposito found a legal parking spot, so they wouldn't have to leave any police markings on the dashboard. The first building they tried had a roof alarm. If it worked, it probably would have stopped in a minute or two, but it was better not to risk the attention. The next building had no alarm, and they walked out onto the tar paper roof, spongy from the warmth of the sun.

Esposito found a milk crate, and Nick found a bucket. They brought them over to the far edge of the roof and sat down on them. The top of their heads might have been visible, barely. There was a little parapet at the edge, gapped like the top of a castle, so they could peek through. The alleys between their building and those to the east and west, a divide of six or eight feet, had fire escapes leading down; the buildings across the street were twins of theirs. Esposito took the binoculars out of his pocket and looked down at the front of the funeral parlor, playing with the focus. They would be here for a while. Nick looked at his watch—four-thirty. The sun was warm, and he was tempted to take off his jacket. But the shirt was white, as was the face, and Nick didn't want to heighten the contrast. Two white guys in suits on a rooftop, it was clear who they were. That was a good thing, sometimes. Not here, though, not now. Esposito scanned the block with the binoculars.

"How stupid is Michael Cole?" Nick asked.

"Not stupid, Nick. Stupid has nothing to do with it," Esposito said, still scanning.

"Fine. He's not stupid, but what's his play? Walk in and start blasting?"

"If he'd made it to Baghdad, in the army, like he'd wanted, he'd know how to fill up a truck with explosives, pull up front. Boom!"

"And why won't he?"

"I checked. He doesn't have a license. Poor sonofabitch can't drive a car, but he's gonna hit a Dominican funeral. A drug dealer funeral. A kid funeral. He's gonna take it on, as a one-man show."

"All right. So whaddaya think?"

"I think it doesn't pay to try to be a step ahead of crazy people. You can't picture it. You can't plan. Me? You? We're here, looking down, thinking, 'Where's the exits? Is there a back door? How's traffic? Is this a one-way street?' And he's thinking, 'If I wear a Viking helmet and whistle, my magic horse will come and take me away.' "

"I don't know if he's that kind of crazy."

"I don't know, either. Look, he's coming here to kill Kiko, right? Do we know if he knows him? Has he ever laid eyes on him? Does he even know what the guy looks like?"

Nick had to think about that. "He knew where Kiko lived. He was waiting outside when we went there."

"He knew the area. Maybe not the building or the apartment. We don't know anything else."

Esposito had not put the binoculars down through his analysis. He hadn't stopped looking, searching the street for faces. The thoughts were offhand, but they cut to the bone. Nick was glad he worked with him. Esposito was good at this. Nick shifted on his bucket, finding a better position, knowing they would have a wait. He looked downtown, at the Empire State Building, the Chrysler, the other nameless towers that shaped the skyline, the narrow horizon. Appointments were being made for drinks and dinner. Cars were being called, women. Billions of dollars were moving through electronic signals, contracts were being signed, glasses were clinking after toasts. Deals were sealed, with kisses and signatures, for the new million-dollar face for a perfume campaign, a hydroelectric dam in Peru, a mob hit in Jersey. On Forty-seventh Street, five hundred people bought engagement rings, learning about clarity, carat, cut; a few blocks west, men cuddled with transvestite hookers in hourly motels. Just south, editorials were being written that would be read in every capital, and would draw angry calls from the White House. This city was the world. Even the post offices were poetry, poems in the names of them: Ansonia, Audubon, Cathedral, and Cherokee; Gracie, Hell Gate, Knickerbocker, and Morningside; Planetarium and Prince. The bucket was not uncomfortable, and the view—well, there it was. The view was free.

Probabilities and singularities, patterns and randomness, coincidence. Why had he picked that restaurant? He'd followed one woman there, and had gone home with another, three days later. Nick thought it sentimental to believe there was only one woman in the world who was right for him, whom he was meant to be with. Impossible, even. The odds were in the billions. Not that a person could be happy with *anyone*, but as long as you started right and worked to stay there, the chances were better than even. People might be as unique as their fingerprints, but when a couple held hands, it was just like any other couple, holding hands. Nick doubted he could marry again, any more than he could equal his best high school half-mile time; the heart didn't pump as it had, the legs would never be so light. Still, with Daysi, he could made a run for it, make a fresh start. He was not yet pushing his luck.

"Shit. Nick, this one walking down the street is unbelievable—a stripper, definitely. Not a bad idea, sending a broad like that to a wake, make sure the guy's really dead."

"Lemme have the binoculars."

"Nope, no way. I saw her first."

Masculine friendships often began at the lowest of thresholds—he likes beer, he likes football, he lives next door—*Hey, buddy!* But police pairings were more like marriages. Tests had to be passed, as well as time. Fraternity depended on function, how challenges were met. Over the years, every cop worked with lots of others, had opinions of who was better, who was worse. But at the end of a career, few would hesitate to name their real partner, the one they wanted at their side for a rooftop chase, in an interrogation room, or when the building was on fire. Great cases—events of consequence and difficulty, in which you made the tip-over difference—were almost as rare as great loves. You shouldn't expect one a year, or one in ten. Would this be one? Esposito elbowed him. Here they were.

A beat-up blue van parked in front, and the driver got out to ring the bell of the funeral parlor. Two men in black suits came to unload the fields of flowers, making trip after trip, the Cadillac medallion and the garish pink cross last.

"Would you look at that! It looks like a pool toy. You could float around on it. I thought Italians were bad. . . . You send one of those to my funeral, Nick, I swear I'll come back and haunt you. Think about all the money your girl is making from this! Next time we go out, Daysi pays."

On the roof directly across the street, the door jerked open from the stairs, stiff on its hinges. Nick touched Esposito, and he looked over. A pit bull wandered out, followed by an older woman in a red housedress. The dog scampered about, stretching its legs, before nosing around to pick a spot. The woman spoke on a cellphone. She stayed near the door, making sure it wouldn't shut. The dog sprinted for a few yards at a time, stopped, sniffed, and shat, then did it again, then a third time. It looked like he was compressing the whole of a fine dog day into a minute on the roof. The woman waved the dog over, and he jogged back inside. She shut the door behind them, still talking on the phone.

"No alarm," noted Esposito. "I bet half the building uses the roof as a dog run. There's shit all over it."

At five o'clock, visitors began to drift into the funeral parlor. Family first—older women in black, older men, some in suits, some in guayabera shirts, leather jackets. They would be there for the duration. Three or four of them had a last cigarette on the sidewalk, before beginning the vigil. A few other women soon followed, in ones and twos, older, more conservatively dressed, neighborhood women who wanted to pay respects before the rough crowd came. The detectives would soon start to lose the light.

"Where do you suppose our camera is?" wondered Esposito. "Maybe we should have sent in an undercover. Narcotics has an informant. He's gonna stop by, let us know if Kiko shows."

"Who in Narcotics?"

"Martone."

"Jimmy Martone? Who worked with Sean O'Sullivan, from Housing?"

"No, Kim Martone."

"Kim Martone! She's amazing. Good cop, too. Don't tell me she's another one of your special friends?"

"Nah, I wish. Somehow, she has found me . . . resistible. But we're gonna meet later. She'll let me talk to her snitch if this doesn't work out."

Another dog person on the roof across the street, a man this time, with a German shepherd. You didn't see as many of them as you used to, the shepherds and Dobermans, the old guard breeds. This neighborhood was all pit bull now, a different breed, a different statement, shifting from defense to attack. Plus, you saw a lot of Chihuahuas, for what it was worth. Maybe, Nick thought, he shouldn't read too much into it. Different dogs for different days. This was an old dog, treading out unsteadily to finish his business, on a patch of roof he chose without much concern. The man stroked his back with affection, and they went back inside.

Esposito tensed up and elbowed Nick. A livery cab had arrived, and when the door opened, three men walked over from the front of the funeral home to greet the passenger. A dignitary, worth watching, but the figure was obscured by hugs as soon as he stepped out of the vehicle. Respects were being paid. When the huggers stepped back from the passenger, Nick saw he was a fat guy in a white sweat suit, made of material so shiny it nearly glowed. The best sweat suit, worn only for formal occasions. Fat guy. Not their man.

"Who is it?"

"Tino," said Espo without hesitation. "I guess he steps up now. I didn't think he was under Kiko. Maybe he wasn't, but now there's vacancies—Miguelito, Miguel, Kiko. He's gonna fill all the spots, the fat jackass. Watch. After he goes in and sees all the stuff there, he's gonna send a bigger cross tomorrow, even pinker, to show how much he cares. Daysi's gonna make even more money. That business would make a decent cover. If you were in the game like these guys, you could move a lot of cash through it."

"Stop."

"Sorry. You oughta run a few checks before you marry her, though. The ex, maybe—"

"Stop."

Nick didn't like it when Esposito mentioned Daysi, when he talked about the dealers. Nick didn't like it the first time, and he liked it less, hearing it again. But he wasn't going to bring it up now. They had to concentrate. Nick put it out of his mind for half an hour, more. The sun began to decline over the river. There were no other arrivals of street-readable significance, but the clothing started to change to flashier stuff, people dressed for nightclubs, guys in groups, some with dates. It was getting cool on the roof, hotter down below. Esposito was starting to get frustrated.

"Kiko's looking to make an appearance, probably not a big show. Probably not, but who knows? All these people, does he want them to see his face, show he's still got balls? Or maybe he slipped in before visiting hours, like we took Malcolm in."

"What's the hours for this? Is there a dinner break?"

Esposito raised an eyebrow, as if he suspected Nick was asking for himself. "An hour for dinner, but I'm not leaving. I'm hungry, too."

"Easy. Just asking. I ain't going anywhere. You know that."

"Sorry, pal. I just know this is gonna happen. I don't know how. . . ."

The light was going. Not a lot of people left the funeral home; a few did, but others came back, with bags of food. Another dog on the roof across, a terrier mutt with a teenager. Nick went back on the roof to piss. Another dog, and then Esposito went back too. At seven, the streetlights were lit. Behind them on the roof, a solitary lightbulb was mounted above the stairwell enclosure, barely glowing in the dusk. There was one on each nearby rooftop, beside them and across the street. They seemed more ornamental than useful, like holiday decorations. Nick went back to unscrew the bulb. When he returned, he said, "The food last night, it was unbelievable. One thing, then another."

Esposito put the binoculars down. "You're killing me, Nick."

"For me, the best was the soup—no, the soup was second. First was—"

"Nick?"

"Yeah, all right. . . . I wonder, maybe we shoulda done something with Tino's phone."

"Nice change of topic. Believe me, I appreciate it. But Tino's phone was point-to-point, the walkie-talkie thing. Can't triangulate on it the regular way. Subpoenas, and it's still weeks before we get the cell sites. And all they'd tell us is he's in the neighborhood. Which I know. I wish Kim Martone gave me her snitch. . . ."

"You wouldn't give up yours. You wouldn't let anybody talk to Malcolm."

"No. But it don't matter. . . . This is a pissing contest here, and I'm gonna win."

Esposito rubbed his face, and picked up the binoculars again. Nick wondered what he could see. Not much, but Esposito could read in the dark, the patterns in the traffic, who curtsied in the dance. More and more people came in, in bigger packs. Nick watched the dog roof when someone else came out, a middle-aged man, a young dog—another mutt, too shaggy for a pit bull. The faint light above the stairwell enclosure cast the figures in silhouette. The dog started to bark at the building next door, leaping up to the wall on the west side, over the alley gap.

There was a man there . . . a dark figure, in dark clothes. The binoculars got you closer, but there was no light. No eye could reach. The dog began to yelp, to leap into the air. That was what it knew, territory, who belonged, who didn't. The dog made a show. The dark figure on the roof fired a gun at the dog. Three shots, four, five. The dog's owner ran to the door and closed it behind him, quitting outright. The dog ran to the door, then ran back to the wall, yelping and leaping; his post would not be abandoned, even after his master had abandoned him. Another shot, but the dog wasn't hit. Kiko? No, not Kiko, Michael Cole.

There were a few people on the sidewalk, and then a few more, looking up, stupidly. The man on the roof lifted his hands up, both of them, and threw them down. A car window smashed on the street. Michael Cole, yes. Nick couldn't see him, his face or much of anything else, but there was no question, no doubt. Six shots, a revolver, and Michael had emptied his gun even before he'd begun what he'd come for. Another brick, another stone, down to the street, buckling the hood of a car. The people below began to scatter, even as more ran out from the funeral home. And then there were three shots from Nick and Esposito's right, from the roof next to them, shooting across the street.

They hadn't seen anyone there, either, but it had to be Kiko. It had to be. Michael Cole threw another missile down; another window smashed. The funeral home emptied out. "What? What? What?" Two more shots, and Michael Cole looked around—"What? What?" *Somebody's shooting at you, stupid. That's what.* Kiko shot again, near the detectives. No. Nick saw the muzzle flash, pointed away; this was from below, armed mourners. A window beneath them popped, shattered. Nick crouched in, close to the parapet. Esposito put a hand on his shoulder. *Quiet. Let it play. . . .* No need to say so. Nick knew they were invisible still. The magical thinking of a child still in bed, closing his eyes, making the bad ones go away. No, it was true. They were on the sidelines, not yet part of the game.

The alley between the buildings was six feet, maybe eight. The same layout, identical buildings facing each other. The dog made his own calculations, running back, rushing across to leap. A gap between the walls, for the fire escapes, the alley between. Good dog, good jump. Falling stones, breaking glass, so many guns that Kiko had to duck down before he shot back. The dog scrambled up, then leapt across the alley, clearing the next roof. Michael ran inside the door, yanking it shut behind him. He would face a mob, enraged and battle-ready, but not a dog? Michael had escaped, for now, from the dog. The crowd? Well, Nick hoped he had his helmet on.

Kiko yelled down to the gathering mob on the street, a swirling pattern of men looking up, dodging, taking cover and letting off rounds.

"*El otro lado! Al cruzar la calle!* The other side of the street!"

Kiko dropped down again to avoid friendly fire, then ran back across the roof. He yanked at the door, but it wouldn't open. Maybe he wasn't strong, maybe it was badly rusted, maybe an upstairs neighbor had locked it behind him, just to be safe. He yelled curses, but the door didn't open. Nick and Esposito crouched, still quiet, watching Kiko look around for a way out. Shouts and shots were coming up from the street. Kiko picked up his phone and screamed, then shut it. Not a good place for reception, not a good time. He walked to the far side of the roof, then walked back; the near side was better. Six feet, maybe eight. They do it in movies, all the time. Across the street, the dog barked on the other rooftop, circling the door, on the hunt. Not the hunt; his territory had already been won. Kiko still hadn't seen the detectives; he reckoned the distance, the way out, the way across. Six feet, maybe eight. He stepped back to make a run for it. One jump. He would cross over, he would run downstairs, he would be back in the thick of it, be the hero of the funeral games. From fifty feet, in the dark, Nick could see the picture in his head. But after Kiko started to run, Esposito stood up and turned on his flashlight.

"You coming to me, Kiko?"

These five words were spoken with bold slowness, and there was a solemn and martial music to them, familiar and arresting, like taps or reveille. Esposito put the flashlight down, then rolled it across the rooftop, so it wouldn't give Kiko a target. But Kiko had already jumped, and the five words stopped him in the air. Reveille, then taps. He did not cross over. Could Nick hear it, the fall? Yes, he could. A soft call going down—"Ohh!"—no screaming, no protest, two bumps along the fire escape, garbage cans spilled when he hit. Nick walked past Esposito and looked down, as if he might have been able to see the bottom, as if he needed to know how it had ended.

"We oughta work on getting outta here," Nick said.

Esposito nodded, and took out his radio. "There's no way to put a good face on this.... Central? Ten-thirteen, ten-thirteen, ten-thirteen. Multiple shots fired, man down, large crowd, lots of 'em shooting. Be advised, you got two detectives on the roof. Advise responding units.... Yes, Central, I will stand by. The address is ..."

Bedlam. That was the word for it, the only one. They tried to barricade the door with the bucket and crate. Footsteps coming up the stairs, yelling. Nick didn't think the yellers were cops. Esposito grabbed Nick's arm and led them over to the fire escape before the door broke. They started creeping downstairs, slowly, from the sixth floor to the fifth. The fire escape shivered with each step, lurched when their weight gathered at weak points. Angry men on the roof now, shouting, shooting guns anywhere, nowhere, into the night. Down from the fifth floor to the fourth. Better, but Nick knew that when they got to the ground, there would be a bigger crowd, madder still, when Kiko's body was found. More guns, but Nick heard the sirens, too, the cavalry, the skull-crackers, hats and bats. Bring 'em on. They kept going down, but on the third floor, a woman opened her window and screamed. And then her man started yelling inside, and he started shooting, too. The detectives scrambled down the creaky metal stairs, the fire escape groaning against the building with the weight, rounds dinking off the metal bars as they moved down, flight by flight. There were missing slats and loose rails. The whole structure gave and groaned like a pained spine, the rusty bolts easing from the softening brick. Kiko had been found in the alley below by one man, two, who called out for witness, aid, revenge. One of them ran when the shots came from the third floor, but others came into the alley; more shots, more than you could place where they came from. A few of them in the alley, one of them shooting in the air. Nick and Esposito hugged the wall, and felt the platform sag.

There were flowerpots on the lowest ledge of the fire escape, a little garden, carefully tended and growing golden, green. Esposito started to hurl them down, the first with a warning—"Police! Get out! Get away, or I will kill you!" When shots came up past them, he grabbed handfuls of the pots, smashing them down below. Someone fell, groaning: bedlam. Nick shot two rounds into the back of the alley. Did that clear them? No, it did not. Nick took the radio and gave their position, keeping the line open when he let another round go, so Central could hear. The dispatcher began to scream, "Are you okay? Ten-thirteen! Ten-thirteen! Ten-thirteen!" The fire escape slipped and whined; it would not wait. Nick helped Esposito heave the last of the flowerpots over the side, aiming for heads. Another one down, with a brief, huffing sound, like a couch shoved on a carpet. Eight feet to the ground, maybe ten. They jumped.

Even as Nick landed on the garbage can, and even as he felt the ankle twist, the pain shooting up the leg—even then, he knew the landing could have been worse. The leg buckled under Nick, and when he fell over, the gun slid out of his holster, in the dark. Kiko lay beside him, arms bent back, head twisted, his face a few inches away. He still looked surprised. Esposito was oddly catlike in his drop, falling into a crouch, then alighting on agile feet. Nick felt for his gun and found it, wedged by Kiko's dead leg. Not a bad landing, not as bad as it might have been. Esposito stepped over. "You okay?"

"The ankle."

"Can you walk?"

"Gimme a hand."

Esposito turned to the front of the alley. It looked clear. He looked up. The fire escape made no more noises, no more threats to collapse. It would be good for another day, another week, until somebody else stepped onto it. It was time to go. There were sirens, the screech of cars in the street; their people were here. Esposito took hold of an elbow and armpit and lifted Nick up, as if he were light. "Easy, easy," Nick said. "Okay, I'm up now."

The right leg was solid; the left, not much.

"Can you walk?"

"Almost . . ."

"C'mere," he said, putting Nick's arm around his shoulder, grabbing hold of Nick's belt from the back. "Anybody comes in, you gotta shoot. I got my right hand holding your ass up. . . . Does Daysi sell pots?"

"What?"

"Flowerpots. If she does, I gotta get some nice ones for the first floor fire escape. They saved us. Looks like I brained a couple of guys. You can shoot?"

"I can shoot. But let me go if you gotta fight. I can hop."

"Okay, Hopalong. Let's get outta here."

What movie was that? Nick would remember later. It took a few steps to coordinate their tripod paces, but then they moved easily, toward the bright vertical bar of the exit, where the crowd surged, the nightsticks swung, and the threats and wails filled the air. It looked so much better than where they were, the fire escape ready to collapse, the dead man, the other two down, the shots going off; the alley made the street look nearly wholesome. Nick had his gun out, pointed down, as they marched, three-legged, to some better place. This fight was over for them, even if no one else knew. Bedlam still, for the rest of them.

A child ran up to them, bawling, then stopped. The ugly baby of the other day, Kiko's kid. Little Jose! Now in a blue velvet suit, with a bow tie. Jose stared at them for a moment, maybe remembering. With a tin cup and a fez, the kid could have worked with an organ-grinder, Nick thought, ashamed of himself that it even occurred to him. Fatherless, now that the job was done, not that the child knew. His mother screamed, too, but she did not notice the detectives as she caught up with Jose, snatching him in her arms to bear him away. She wouldn't have known about Kiko yet, either.

Bedlam. They had room to move on the sidewalk. They cut east, where the fighting was thinner, less out of fear than a desire not to take fighting cops from the people who needed fighting. They stayed close to the wall, to keep from getting hit from the roof. Nick felt the edge of the blow—a bat, a board—when Esposito's head bounced against his own. Nick was close to the wall and spun off it, still standing, as Esposito collapsed. The board came down again, on Esposito, on his leg, as he hit the ground. Bad noise, a pop, a thud, by the knee, maybe from the fall. Tino in the white suit, as round and white as the moon, taking another swing. Nick shot him, shot him again, leaning against the wall, then pushing off. Hard to stand. Not much kick to the gun. He held it firm. Nick stood on his one foot as Tino staggered, and it looked like Tino would have held himself in his arms, one arm, the other, but Nick had shot them both. Nick hadn't aimed at Tino's arms when he'd been pivoting on the foot, twisting like a scarecrow. The cops came. Finally, even though they'd been here the whole time.

Tino screamed as he was cuffed, despite his two shot arms. Good. Let him cry, let him bleed. Nick went down to Esposito on the sidewalk, pestering him to say something, gripping his shoulder. The top of Esposito's head was sticky, his breath shallow. Nick was ready to open Esposito's eyes, if they didn't open themselves. More cops came. An ambulance, another. A stretcher was laid out on the street beside Esposito, and he was lifted onto it. Cops lifted Nick up as well. He said he was all right. Esposito went into the ambulance, carried by cops. Nick was borne in later, to the berth across from him. There was a bed on either side, a space in the middle. A woman took his shoulders, gently, and told him to lie down.

"No."

"Yes. It's the rules."

"All right."

She fastened the belt loosely around his waist. Hey, Nick knew her.

"Hey . . . Odalys?"

"Hey, Nick. Where are you hurt?"

"Not bad. Espo . . ."

"We got him. He's good."

"Lemme see."

Odalys stepped to the front of the ambulance and sat down, so she wouldn't block the view to the other bed. Nick could see Esposito, almost, but another EMT was leaning over Nick's partner, someone else. Shit. If it was her, it was the other one, too. The other EMT, her partner, leaned over Esposito, tapping his chest, trying to rouse him.

"C'mon, Detective, wake up! Come on, guy! Wake up! Work with me! Whaddaya got in ya? Are you with me? Are you a fighter? You gonna fight? Are you a fighter?"

What movie was that now? Nick didn't like it. Esposito shifted and muttered. He raised a hand, let it fall down again. Muttered again. Nick called over to him, "Hey." Esposito looked at Nick with one eye, his annoyance plain despite the concussion. He didn't need a pep talk. The EMT tapped his cheek.

"C'mon! Are you a fighter?"

Esposito punched him in the face, which was an answer to the question, after all.

TWENTY-SIX

The room was not as Nick had expected. Not his, not Daysi's, not the hospital. Where, then? Too much of this, changing beds daily like a fugitive. The shades were drawn, but he could make out a dresser, a mirror, blue and white striped sheets on a queen-size bed, shared with the teddy bear beside him; not right. What did he have, a sprained ankle? Esposito had a concussion, a broken leg. Nothing that he wouldn't come back from. He hadn't even been admitted to the hospital. Hitting the EMT must have had great therapeutic value. Esposito became the most cheerful patient after, pretending he didn't remember. When Odalys checked him into the emergency room, he acted the amnesiac, asking why she wasn't working with the other one. She didn't push the issue. When her partner came over, keeping his distance, Esposito put on such a show of innocent apology that they shook hands when he left. Nick didn't believe it.

"You really don't remember? Espo, you are full of shit."

"Are you kidding? My children being born, punching that rat—if those memories cross my mind when I go, they'll bury me with a smile on my face."

"I'm glad you're okay."

"Yeah. How are you doin', Hopalong?"

"Still hopping."

Hours in the hospital, a hubbub of well-wishers, cops and bosses, others who didn't wish, well or otherwise, as far as Nick could guess. Lieutenant Ortiz told Nick that if he wasn't up to it, he didn't have to make a statement. Nick said it wasn't a problem. When Esposito was taken in for X-rays, Nick was interviewed by Internal Affairs, someone from the district attorney. The questioning was gentle, the answers brief.

Much easier than he'd thought it would be. Why? Nick learned later where the cameras had been placed—everywhere. The tops of buildings, streetlights, the door of the funeral home. The firefight between rooftops had been captured, showing that cops had not been involved. Kiko had not been pushed, despite the rumors that would later travel. Tino had made statements, angry ones, saying that he'd barely hit anyone, he didn't deserve this, but yeah, he'd had a baseball bat. He had been brought to another hospital, so visitors would not mix. The bat was recovered at the scene. A few bones had been broken in the chaos, but the stories were remarkably coherent.

Who came to visit? So many people, all the guys in the squad. When Nick left for X-rays, he was glad for some time alone. Esposito was adamant that no one call his wife, utterly clear and coherent about it despite all his painkillers. He didn't want to call her himself, with the hurt, groggy voice, but he didn't want a stranger on the phone—*Mrs. Esposito? This is Detective X. I have some bad news.*—to make her collapse on the other end of the line. And no one was allowed to go to his house. No state troopers at the door, waiting to tell a ghost story. Esposito had been late before, so often that he wasn't expected at any time, but the expectation had always been to hear his voice, see his face, whenever the day ended. Nick got that, he understood; he was saddened that he had never felt the need to develop any such protocol in the event of his own misadventure. His father might wonder about him if he didn't see him for a week; with Allison, longer. He wasn't expected anywhere. That bothered him. Should he have called his father, to tell him he was hurt? For whose benefit? To what end? He didn't know, and it bothered him. It bothered him more that he didn't know where he was. The teddy bear had a bow tie. He pushed it away. What else had there been last night?

"Kim Martone! How ya doin', babe?"

It had been good of her to show, and it had been good to look at her. Nick had met her, once or twice. Kim had short brown hair and wore jeans and a leather jacket; every sloppy cop dressed liked her, but she looked coiffed, put together, as if she were going on a date or coming from church. He wondered if she'd been working, or if she'd come in when she'd heard the news. She looked at Nick, briefly, before sitting on the side of Esposito's bed. She leaned over to Esposito and fixed his hair, shaking her head, with a fond look. She didn't look at Nick, even though she spoke to him.

"This idiot, this guy? He pushed me out of the way of a car. It was some skell we tried to stop after a buy, downtown. He broke his foot."

"Only a toe, baby, but I woulda given up a foot for ya."

"I know you would, babe. How you feeling?"

"Not bad. Were you around for the fun?"

"Yeah, we were doing a buy. You messed it up pretty good."

"Right there? At the wake?"

"Right there at the wake."

"You're kidding me—who? No, lemme guess—Tino!"

"That's a good guess."

"Beautiful. But you didn't make the exchange? How much was it for?"

"A kilo. And no, we didn't make it. Thanks, pal!" she said. She wasn't angry, as she leaned in and touched his cheek. It was strange to think, but there were cops who would have blamed Nick and Esposito for messing up the buy; it could take a lot of work to get there. So many agencies and agendas; the squad didn't know what Narcotics had going on, and who knew what the Feds had percolating in the Heights—FBI, DEA, and ATF—maybe talking to one another, maybe not. When one partner didn't know what the other was doing, there could be complications, Nick knew.

"Nick's the one who shot Tino. You can thank him," said Esposito cheerfully. "How was the package getting in? Did you know?"

"We're not sure, but we're gonna take a hard look at that flower van."

Esposito betrayed surprise, but covered it with a grimace, as if he'd had a spasm of pain. Kim huddled in close, concerned.

"Are you okay? Should I get a nurse?"

Esposito's face relaxed, tentatively, slowly, as if trying out each muscle to make sure it didn't hurt. He exhaled deeply, then put on his hustler face again.

"The nurse, she's cute. But who I wanna talk to is your informant."

"Espo, you are unbelievable! Would you just rest, tonight at least?"

"Does that mean you won't let me talk to him?"

"I told you I wouldn't. My guy is my guy."

"I thought I was your guy."

"You don't quit! But come on, what do you need to know? You got your guy. Your shit is wrapped up. Anything I hear, I will tell you. I told you that."

"I don't know what I need to know, until after I know it, and then it's too late."

"That's deep, baby."

"Isn't it? But, Kim, in case I do go—I don't think I will, but hey, you never know, right?—would you at least give me his name? I really do think I'll make it—what do these doctors know, anyway? I'll probably be okay. . . ."

"Now I know you'll be okay. You're back on the make."

"This could be our last kiss, Kim."

"It would be our first."

"I'll take it."

Kim leaned down and kissed him, briefly but tenderly. Esposito batted his eyes, as if ready to faint. Kim got up and laughed, looking at Nick again. There was nothing in her face that showed she knew anything about him and Daysi, or even anything about Daysi's van. Her smile was satisfied, and she looked at Nick with affection and trust; cops were the straight lines in a crooked world, with no thoughts of bending.

"See? He's gonna be just fine," Kim said as she left. "I love this guy, but my informant is my informant."

Because Nick never said much, no one noticed that he said almost nothing that night. He had just shot someone, but he didn't care. He felt no more anxiety or regret than Malcolm or Kiko had shown, or Esposito, for that matter. Tino wasn't dead, but if a cop had burst into the room with news that he'd flatlined, Nick would have been untroubled to hear it. He thought about Daysi, what it might mean, about the old blue van.

In a few hours, the sense of crisis had passed; the visitors dwindled, and Nick and Esposito were cleared for release. Lieutenant Ortiz wanted to have Napolitano drive Esposito home, but he was insistent again. "No. Only Nick comes, only Nick drives. Besides, he needs the practice. Somebody can bring my car up later. I don't need it. My wife has her own car. Besides, in a couple of days, a week, I'll be going stir-crazy. I'm gonna be desperate to have people come up and visit."

The lieutenant was reluctant at first, as they rolled out his detectives on wheelchairs, but he saw that Esposito was past persuasion. Nick was not eager to take the drive—What was the trip, an hour? An hour and a half?—but Esposito had just carried him out of a combat zone, and Nick wasn't going to deny him. Why did he want Nick to drive? Nick didn't understand, and then it came to him. Esposito wanted to talk. He didn't want the day to end. It had worked for him. He had closed a homicide. And Nick was fine, a little banged up but with a good foot for the gas and brake, good arms to turn the wheel. Esposito could reassure him about Daysi: *I don't buy it, but we'll find out.* That's what he would say; Nick had started to say it himself. He was fine, fine. Wasn't he?

"All right, Espo," the lieutenant acceded. "Your partner can drive you, if he's up for it—"

"Yeah, it's no problem."

"But I'm gonna have a car follow, just for my peace of mind. And that's not negotiable. Who wants to go?"

"I can. It's only half an hour from me anyway," said Napolitano.

"Fine. But listen for your phones. Nick, if you don't feel good, pull over and call Napolitano. I don't know why I'm even listening to you guys, when you got cracked heads. . . . Safe home. All of you, get home safe."

They helped Esposito into the backseat of the car, and Nick drove over to the highway. Esposito was right, Nick needed the practice. He stopped hard at a light, and Esposito slid on the seat, grunting at the sudden shift. "Sorry . . ." Nick wasn't phobic about driving; he just didn't do it often, or like it much. Up past Inwood, the park to the east, the river to the west, and then the Henry Hudson Bridge. The night-lit city—the sodium-vapor streetlights, the dirty gold haze of them; the cool fluorescence in offices, the light icy and thin; the warm, incandescent glow from homes; and then the stars, dim and flickering, kept more for sentiment than use. Into the Bronx, the mainland, past Yonkers, and then the countrified north, all of it country to Nick, city boy that he was. What vast differences in such small distances, he thought, thinking also of how his own geography had shrunk. Less light here, and no talk at all, though it was a while before Nick noticed the last.

"You okay? Don't fall asleep on me, Espo. I don't know how to get there."

"I'm okay."

Nick knew that without having met Daysi, he would have drifted on longer with Allison. And he knew that, for all her own promise and allure, Daysi was also a crutch for him, a shot of Dutch courage, in his choice to go forward or back. He didn't know where things would lead with her, but if the blue van delivered more than flowers, it was a dead end, full stop. Nick didn't believe it, honestly. She wouldn't have had dinner with him, taken him home. Still, the idea became a flea, lots of them, and they itched. He wished he weren't going home with Esposito. He'd trade a kidney for some privacy now. It felt like he was running away to join a merry band of outlaws in the forest. For Nick, upstate was associated with prison. Perps talked about going upstate, or "up north," for their sentences in the bastions of maximum security—Coxsackie, Dannemora, and Green Haven, Attica and Sing Sing. Nick felt the chill in the air, and he suspected they had already arrived in the penitentiary latitudes.

After another half hour on the highway, Esposito directed him to a county road, the six lanes going down to four, then two, before they hit a winding rustic route. It was lit only in patches, and gravel skittered up against the undercarriage. The leaves had already turned here, started to fall, and the advance in the season gave Nick the feeling they had slipped forward in time. All the pollution of the city, all the body heat, it kept the leaves green for a few more days, a week. As the detectives traveled from asphalt to roads with more and more gravel, the houses got fewer and newer. Some were big enough, and some were not big enough, with two cars in a garage as large as the house. The garage doors were always open, like display cases. Ranches and colonials, none of them older than the owners. This world had literally been built for them and their children. Even the woods seemed new in places, the trees young and thin, scraggly. Acres of the city had been created from landfill, reclaimed from the water, but here, how could they extend the edge of the earth? On the old globes, this was the white space, inscribed in a spidery italic, *Terra incognita*. "Unknown country." *Hic sunt dracones*. This is where the dragons are.

"You asked about my father?" Esposito said.

Nick never had. The car was as intimate and anonymous as a confessional, and Nick could almost picture the grille sliding open with a click, then closing the space between them when the talk was over. The impending disclosure made him uneasy, not least by the fact that he was the wrong man to sit in the absolution seat. He hadn't expected this gift of confidence, and he was unwilling to offer anything nearly commensurate in return. He felt a pressure in his neck, like a bully's knuckle. Esposito didn't wait for a reply.

"He was a bum. A knock-around guy. Not a real wise guy, not real bad, but no good. He had a messed-up arm. When I was a kid, he told me he got shot during the war. Which war, I never thought about. He was around when I was little. Then he runs away with some broad to Vegas, works in the casinos. He comes back when I'm fifteen for a year. He was sick. When he dies, I look to get the veteran's benefit, to help out with the funeral. Turns out, he was never in the service. And when I go on the Job—you know how they ask if anybody in your family has a criminal record? I say no, and the guy from Applicant Investigations tells me my father took a couple of burglary collars. He even broke his arm in one, falling off a fire escape. War hero! My mother still loves him, won't hear a bad word about him, never would.

"With your father, this morning? I'm sorry, again. Your father was more upset by problems in your marriage than my father ever was when he kicked his family to the curb. I don't know if that's crazy, or great. I hope it's great. I think it is. I hate to think that life's a lot better when you're a scumbag. You're lucky, Nick."

Nick nodded, knowing Esposito could see him, understanding that nothing more needed to be said. Esposito settled into the back, resting, content; Nick could hear it in his breathing. They had to be close to home. Nick found himself checking the mirror every few minutes, to see if Napolitano was still behind them. The headlights flashed from behind as his phone rang.

"It's Napolitano. It's his turnoff," Nick told Esposito. "Are we all right from here?"

Esposito started to laugh. "Yeah. Tell him we're good, we're five minutes out. Nick, we just came from a gunfight. Two of 'em. And a riot. You didn't shake, you didn't hesitate, you didn't even blink. But a quiet drive through cricket country, and you act like you're in a horror movie, like a lunatic is gonna jump out of the woods when the car breaks down."

"I saw that one."

"Which?"

"All of 'em. They taught me that people should live in apartment buildings, near Chinese restaurants that deliver, bars you can walk to. Civilization is lots of people, even when they're assholes. When's the last time we had the oil changed? We're okay on gas, I think . . ."

"You gotta relax, Nick."

Nick was relieved that Esposito had seen the least of his fears, just that one color in the spectrum. He'd stick to that, the city-mouse, country-mouse line, work it to the end.

"I will, when I get you home."

"You're staying over, too. I got room. Don't be stupid."

"Wouldn't it just be easier to have your wife drive your house closer? Meet us halfway? Or is it up on blocks?"

"Redneck jokes! Shit, Nick!"

"Do all the kids play banjo, or do the little ones make that hooting sound on the jugs?"

"Almost home, Nick. I'm gonna have my kids beat you up, then my wife. She's Puerto Rican, you know."

Nick had never needled Espo that way before, had never taken that dog-to-dog tone with him. A little aggression in it, in the smack-around play. It was fun to stir it up a little, to bust balls in a new key. Nick wanted to talk. He'd talk about anything. He'd even pick an argument to avoid talking about Daysi. Or Internal Affairs. Or Allison. Or—

"Look at you, Nick! Now we got you all feisty! Is it because I got a broken leg and can't get up to hit you? I could give you bad directions here, get you lost in the country. Then I whistle and have all the Apaches jump out on ya."

"You can't whistle."

"You never heard me. It doesn't mean I can't."

"Go ahead, I dare you."

"You dare me? What grade are you in? You wanna bet, I'll bet. That's what men do, not schoolgirls. How much you wanna bet?"

That's what Nick remembered, that's what brought him up to the moment. The drive in the woods, the back-and-forth, talking again, but not about what he was thinking. It was a surprise to hear him whistle. The shriek of it was piercing. Cabs must have stopped in Manhattan. A surprise that Esposito could whistle like that. More of a surprise than the deer, Nick thought later, because at the time he didn't have time to think. The deer, an antlered buck, a stag that could have stepped from a coat of arms, leapt from the bare trees at the side of the road, just before Nick hit the brake, skidding and swerving, the car coming to rest in the reverse direction.

The car clipped the deer on its haunch and knocked it flat. It lowered its head as if to charge, tossing its antlers back and forth. It made a chuffing sound, and plumes of steam left its nostrils in the chill air, rising up through the headlights. The deer rose on two skittish forelegs and attempted an unsteady stride forward before it buckled to the ground, falling out of sight in front of the car. Nick started to get out, stepping on his sprain, but Esposito took hold of his shoulder. There was a clatter of hooves as the deer recovered its lame footing, denting the front panel with a futile sweep of its regal head, before it hobbled off into the dark to die. Nick's eyes were red, from the pain in his ankle, for now. He felt on his hip for his gun; he had to find the poor thing, to end its suffering. Gone, the gun was gone. It had been taken at the hospital, by IAB, to count the rounds, to test his story. They didn't believe him like his partner did. Esposito laid a gentle hand on his other shoulder, urging him wordlessly to move on. They didn't speak again when they reached the house—less than a quarter-mile away—even after, when Esposito showed him to the room, the one he was in now. His eyes were still red, though not from the pain. This was where he was, here. He felt for the night table and found a pill bottle, forced a painkiller down his dry throat. His eyes started to well again before they closed. He would sleep on it, he would sleep for now.

TWENTY-SEVEN

Three of them, Nick counted. Why always three? A little one that zipped in and out of the half-light of the room, as if on a dare; a medium one that crept to the threshold, peering owlishly at the edge of the door; the largest—maybe ten years old, but stockier—who woke him more thoroughly when he dropped a shopping bag onto the dresser. When he left the room, Nick gingerly left the bed and checked out the bag: deodorant, toothpaste, hair gel, antacid, aspirin, nail clippers, a comb, toothbrush. Everything he needed, even underwear. Also, hemorrhoid cream and denture cleanser. That made Nick laugh, thinking of the story Esposito must have told his wife. No polish for a glass eye? And then Nick remembered that Esposito had done the same thing for Malcolm Cole, taking him up from Central Booking to the wake. That wasn't this—not tactics, only hospitality. Still, there was a resemblance between the gestures, even the words, "hostage" and "host." Nick went into the bathroom—his own, for the first time in his life—and cleaned himself up. The ankle was tender, and he was sore all over. A pair of Esposito's jeans and a sweatshirt had been laid out. They were baggy on him, but better than yesterday's suit. When he left the room, all three boys were waiting at the foot of the stairs beside their father, who was propped up on his crutches, wearing a sweatshirt and shorts that looked like donations from aid workers. Nick had only seen Esposito in a suit and tie before.

"Welcome to guinea heaven."

When Nick descended the stairs, he suffered the ferocious affection of their greeting—RJ, Johnny Boy, and Little Al, in reverse order of apparition. Nick thought RJ was big for his age, then remembered he had no idea how old he was—ten, maybe, strapping but still baby-fat, with a peculiar haircut, high and tight, the fluffy curls on top gelled. The same mob-kid Mohawk on the other two, the slim and pale middle one, and the youngest—chubby, olive-skinned, and energetic. It was with some effort that Nick dissuaded them from calling him "Uncle Nick," which was too much for him, not least because "uncle" was cop slang for "undercover." Once the greeting was complete, the children fled for better diversions.

Esposito had seemed more juvenile amid his offspring, a playmate among playmates as much as a father with his sons, and as they began the house tour, Nick felt like they were in a fort built with pillows and blankets on a bed. *Look what I did!* It was a kind of prefab palazzo, white and wide, a lofty two stories, with columns and vinyl siding. The lawn was yellowing, littered with toys, and there was a concrete statue of the Virgin Mary in a healthy row of hedge. You could see by what was cared for, and what was not, that the grounds were not kept to impress neighbors; there were none. All around was woodland. Nick had a flash of prisoner reverie, ungracious though it was, that the guards and hounds would find him before he made the river.

Back inside, Little Al whizzed by again, barking out in transit, "Can't catch me!" *Agreed.* Nick took in the white marble floors, red-and-gold brocade on the walls, many mirrors. There seemed to be a lot of everything. When Esposito tugged at Nick's sleeve, he thought at first it was one of the children.

"C'mon, let me show you."

From room to room Esposito led him, not quickly. There were a lot of rooms, some fancy, some wrecked with kid stuff—a den with soft, wide armchairs and a big-screen TV, insistently referred to as "the entertainment center." As they labored back up to the second floor, Nick wanted to tell him not to bother, but he saw how proud Esposito was, and let him continue. When Esposito mentioned that the shade of the wall paint was called Desert Dawn, Nick felt faint but held his tongue. Nick didn't need to know this, either as enemy or friend.

"This is my room. Our room, me and my wife's. Yours is across the hall."

"Am I putting anybody out?"

"No, it's a guest room."

"How many bedrooms does this place have?"

"Five. Six, really."

"How did you get the money for this? Did you rob a bank?"

Though Nick intended only casual flattery, the question reminded him of lines the mystery prick would have urged him to pursue as the infiltration proceeded. The thought made him choke. He was in the man's house, in the man's clothes. Uncle Nick knew his limits, the lines he would not cross.

"You okay?"

"Fly in the throat."

"Anyway, I'd have to, today. Not today, but a year or two ago, and prices haven't collapsed up here the way you'd think. In fact, it was my wife. She came across it in a divorce case, ten years ago. Guy who built it went under, needed the cash fast. Italian guy, like me—"

"I'd never guess."

"Ah, shut up. Anyway, when he built it, it really was the sticks up here—shut up again, you don't even need to say it, I saw you think it— but it drove his wife crazy. She split, and his business went under. I even felt bad for the guy, how little we gave him for it. Lena's a tough lady. I wouldn't want to get on her bad side."

Lena, Nick noted—that would be the wife.

"I'll try to stay off it. Where is she?"

"She went out food shopping. She'll be home soon."

"I'd hate to miss her, but I got to be getting back."

"That would put you on her bad side. Besides, the car's gone. Napolitano came by this morning to check on us. I told him about the deer. He took the car to his brother-in-law, a mechanic, to bang out the dents. It'll be back tomorrow. Next day, latest."

How long would he be here? There was a crash downstairs, and then two kinds of screaming, accusatory and agonized. Esposito shook his head and bellowed a warning before hobbling down to dispense justice. Was it like this every day? Family life must be like farm life, with all the bloody calvings and cullings, not for the squeamish. Nick waited awhile before following.

Nick had occasionally wondered about Lena. Most facts he knew were few and recent, such as her law degree. She was the mother of three children, and she and her husband did not hate each other, as far as Nick had reluctantly overheard. Once, on the phone, there had been something about school, the kids, and Esposito had said, "Well, the world needs laborers, too." He'd held the phone away from his ear for the response, but he'd baited the reaction. Nick assumed Lena was beautiful, maybe foolishly, and that she was patient, which was a theory with a better foundation. The first would have to be true for the marriage to begin; the second would have to be true for it to go on. Nick was glad he could think this well, with a head full of country air.

When Lena arrived, arms full of grocery bags, she was not what Nick had expected. In his mind, she'd had ample stripper hips and pert C-cups, dancing the cha-cha in her miniskirt as she'd fried the calamar'. She wore a winter coat, so it was hard to take in her full shape, but his first thought was that she looked plain. Mouse-brown hair escaping from a loose ponytail, a heart-shaped face, glasses. She put the bags down on the floor, and took off the glasses and coat to reveal a blue T-shirt and sweatpants underneath.

"Nick! Welcome. I've heard so much about you! God, I'm a mess. Oh, well! Boys! Groceries in the car!"

She walked over to Nick and stopped short, a few feet ahead of him, then leaned in to peck his cheek.

"So good to finally meet you! I don't want to touch you. I don't know where you're hurt. Two more broken toys in the house. Well, we'll have to fix them. . . ."

Up close, with the warmth of the greeting, Lena became instantly prettier. Her wide brown eyes and slightly crooked smile took him in with bemused pity and ready allegiance. She was as glad to see him, genuinely, as the children had been. The series of battlefield promotions that had deepened his bond with Esposito had been earned, he felt. They were part of the meritocracy of friendship. This kind of love, family love, ardent and unexamined, was pure windfall. He felt like an impostor, a counterfeit relation, a beggar at the door who'd concocted a story of shipwreck and separation from the name on the mailbox. It was thrilling. Nick noted, too, that one part of his fantasy was fact. Lena did have C-cups. He blushed, and she walked away, shouting orders to the children to unload the car. "Yes, you, too, John. I told you before, your foot's not broken. . . ."

It was overwhelming, all of it. So much of this was new to Nick. The appliances seemed to run constantly, beeping alerts; the food arrived in hurricane-prep quantities that made Nick fear the supply routes were at risk—brightly colored brand-name family-size boxes and bottles, lo-cal and high-fiber, junk for special treats. Nick was the solitary offspring of another solitary, who lived in a city packed with strangers; he had learned the etiquette of not making eye contact on the subway, of saying only what needed to be said at the table. Here, festival moved to riot and back. Nothing was unsaid—hungers, grudges, victories, states of mind, bowel updates—it was a town of town criers. Nick thought of Allison, how they had run out of things to talk about. This was the life that had been denied them. Pangs of envy and relief struck Nick in sudden, arrhythmic intervals, and he did not know what to make of it, embedded as he was, for the indefinite course. Still, his prison terrors began to fade.

Lena was the center of it all, and the apex. Her approval was sought most; her authority was final. With the children, Lena viewed Esposito as middle management or double agent, nominally adult but essentially male, and hence untrustworthy in his judgment about interesting dangers—sharp things, hot things, throwables, heights. She had bought all of Esposito's clothes for him, which surprised Nick, given how his high goombah style fit him like skin. Did she know his taste, or had she shaped it? The implications preoccupied Nick for an hour. Lena was the only one in the house who had firm impulse control, a fully developed sense of irony. On any given occasion of conflict or chaos, she looked to Nick to appreciate her position, and he did. Often, he just shrugged; mostly, that was all she wanted. She was so much prettier, he thought, than when he'd first seen her. Before dinner, Nick made a feeble attempt at helping her set the table, but she ordered him to take a seat.

"And you ought to call your father, Nick. He might be worried."

"Yes, ma'am."

"God, I'm sorry. Did I just say that? Did it sound the way—"

"Yeah, but you're right."

But he didn't. He didn't want to worry his father, but also he didn't want to think about the straitened life he'd return to, soon enough, let alone the disclosure of his overnight with Daysi. The table seemed crowded, with the six of them, everyone talking at once. Little Al erupted when he saw that his brother John had a plastic cup with Bugs Bunny on it, which he preferred to his own Woody Woodpecker; John obligingly switched, and peace was restored. Nick detected subtle favoritisms, in how Esposito treated John, how Lena dealt with RJ and Al; it intrigued him, because each favorite took after the opposite parent, one's dynamism, the other's discernment. All three had proclaimed their intention to be cops, which had drawn a pointed lack of comment from Lena.

There was salad, then spaghetti and meatballs. Lena watched Nick, to see how much he ate. Nick ate two helpings, not just out of courtesy. At the end of the meal, the kids had ice cream, and Lena led them out without argument, after they lined up, in age order, to give Nick a kiss. It was bedtime. John stopped at the door.

"When we say prayers, we'll ask for you to get better. Should we ask God for anything else?"

"Just tell him I said hi."

"Okay, I will."

Lena led them upstairs, and Esposito refilled the wineglasses. She would follow the children to bed, not long after. When the children were asleep, Esposito led Nick up to watch them. From the door, Nick could see the moisture and heat leave the bodies in a shimmer, the catlike languor of limbs draped off bunks, sudden twitches of fleeting dreams. Superhero pajamas—Batman, Spider-Man, Superman, ready for slumber battle. Esposito looked over, to see if Nick saw what he saw, if he got it. Nick had been amazed by how they loved him without knowing him, and was touched that they continued to, after they did. Esposito smiled and put an arm on Nick's shoulder, indicating they should go downstairs.

Esposito wanted a cigar and he wanted company. He was less direct than usual, suggesting that it was Nick who wanted to sit in the cold night, and he would oblige him, as a good host. Nick helped him with his coat, and got his own. They hobbled to the front stoop and sat. Nick suspected that there was a talk of some consequence about to happen. Would there be accusations, a revolver, a shot to the head? No, the kids were too young to help drag his body into the woods, and Esposito couldn't manage alone. Besides, Lena liked him. Esposito drew on the cigar, then blew smoke rings. How long had it been since Nick had seen a smoke ring? It seemed childish at first, like skipping stones, the kind of game you're determined to learn when time is all you have. The smoke rings were bright shadows, as bewitching as skipped stones, the first ones rolling into broad and loose circles, the later ones tight little O's, so that for a moment the whole of them made the shape of a horn. The announcement, it was time: *Ta-daaa!*

"So . . . whaddaya think?" Esposito asked.

Nick waited to answer, uncertain of the question. He was tactical in his reply.

"It is what it is. This is it, isn't it?"

Esposito smiled again, and patted Nick on the back. He had understood perfectly.

"Yeah. You said it."

Nick wished Lena were there, so they could exchange shrugs. A strange currency, sympathy, meaning as much as you wanted, and nothing, like a poker chip. Nick allowed a moment to pass, betting Esposito would elaborate. He puffed on the cigar, but did not bother with any more rings. No more signals in the smoke.

"These guys, my little guys, they're everything to me. I love how they are with each other. Even when they fight, they forget a minute later. One grabs the other, 'Look, that cloud looks like a big fat butt. C'mere, look!' They could each have their own room, but they like sharing that one. This is life to them, the way the world works. When my old partner offed himself—you knew that, right?—anyway, we weren't close, work was work. First he thought he was a hotshot, that he was better than me, and then he wasn't much of a worker. He went to hell. Never wanted to leave the office, and when he did, he wanted to drive by places where he thought his ex was hooking up, pretending it was for cases. He annoyed the shit out of me. Don't get me wrong—I'm sad about it, sorry about it, wish it didn't happen. A tragedy, I guess. But not mine. Some of the guys, they kinda gave me the hairy eyeball for a while after that. You know how people are. It's better now, but I don't forget.

"Anyway, I told Lena about it, on the sly, I thought. At least, I told her the basics. But Johnny Boy, the middle one—isn't he just like me, don't you think? Roman nose and all. Anyway, he comes up to me, crying, he hugs me, he tells me, 'Daddy, you must be so sad.' Because he figures it must be like losing RJ or Al. It wasn't. I almost laughed, at first. I gotta tell ya, somebody's always got me under surveillance—IAB at work, my kids at home—and they get it wrong half the time. More than that, thank God. Remember how Malcolm Cole said brothers aren't always brothers? That surprised me, because—well, what did I know about it? And my kid, Johnny— Anyway, it made me think."

Esposito ground out the last of his cigar and slapped Nick on the knee.

"Anyway, I'm glad you're here."

They stumbled getting up, lurching for crutches, grabbing hands, one to lift the other, laughing about how well the pills worked for the pain. Nick went to sleep, giving thanks for everything, to everyone, knowing that they would never have a conversation like that again, knowing there would be no need.

The next day, Nick resolved to go home after breakfast, then lunch, but the hours drifted, easy with leisure, rife with little diversions, balmy with mild opiates. Time seemed treasured and wasted at once, lounging in the bosomy armchairs in "the entertainment center." Nick allowed Al to sit on his lap, carefully. Johnny Boy sat on the arm of Esposito's chair, and RJ lay on the floor between them. These became their fixed places, and everyone went to them without question whenever they entered the room. Sports and cartoons, sometimes, mostly the history and nature channels. Both were nonstop pageants of atrocity: Panzer divisions in blitzkrieg, tearing through Poland and France; herds of wildebeests falling to crocodiles in their mad passage of the flood-swollen Zambezi. Cities besieged and sacked, some rising again, like Rome, or lost to legend: Carthage, Machu Picchu, Roanoke. It was odd how reassuring it all was, from the distance, from the comfort of upholstery, in the knowledge that the channel could be changed. The television shows were like campfire stories, told to conjure and banish dread. Nature was scarier, with the shaking-camera reenactments of shark attacks, or sadder, all the little sea turtles that never made it out of the egg. Natural death was rare in nature, Nick observed. The five of them never watched the news.

When Esposito staggered up for a bathroom break, Johnny slipped off the chair and approached Nick, his face earnest, his hand touching Nick's twice in a brushing, tapping gesture, like a dog that needs to go out. "Is it true you saved Daddy's life?"

"No, not really."

"Did you save him in 9/11?"

As Nick smiled at the muddled fantasy, RJ rolled over on the rug and tugged at Nick's pants leg. Though Nick expected a certain archness from him, an older brother's privileged irony, his question was far more blunt.

"Did you shoot the guy who hurt him?"

The forthrightness disarmed Nick, and the form seemed so much like cross-examination that he thought a DA should bark out "Objection!" It would not have been sustained.

"Yes."

"Did you kill him?"

"No."

"Why not?"

"I missed."

The possibility had not occurred to the boys; when they played war, no shots went astray. RJ continued to hold the cuff of Nick's trousers. Not his, but Esposito's, borrowed, as all he wore. Another week here, and Nick would have the same funny haircut as the rest of the kids.

"Mom and Dad said not to ask you about it," offered Johnny gently, as if to allow a moment for all of them to collect themselves.

"You should listen to them," said Nick, grateful for the respite, the opportunity to pretend to the obscurities of adulthood again. But Johnny was not finished, and his hand taps, needy and trusting, made his next question all the more painful and penetrating.

"Did Daddy ever kill anybody?"

Nick waited a second, so the answer seemed neither too rushed nor too considered. The boys must have had some advantage, some prior knowledge, when they'd asked about him. This question sounded like a guess, and Nick guessed his response, solemnly shaking his head. *No.* He didn't know if they believed him, but they knew they would get no more. This is how you learn to truly lie, Nick thought, with family, out of love. When Esposito hobbled back, they were watching a show about the hidden treasures of the Templars, and none of them betrayed any confidences.

Late in the afternoon, Nick got up and went to the kitchen for a drink of water. His ankle didn't hurt much anymore; the sprain must have been slight. Lena didn't look up from chopping onions as she greeted him. She must have recognized his tread, he thought. When she asked him if he wanted some water, he nodded, and she filled a glass for him. She filled another for herself and led him to the table, where they sat. Nick realized what a terrible spy he was, obtrusive but transparent, needy and biddable. Still, the water was just what he wanted, and he drained his glass. Lena brushed her hair back and smiled.

"You know, you're great with kids, Nick. You and—Allison—you never . . . ? Sorry, it's none of my business."

Nick felt both light-headed and unusually grounded. It was like breathing a different atmosphere here, with too little oxygen or too much. Lena knew his wife's name, even though Esposito had never met her. It didn't trouble Nick, either subject, Allison or kids, as much as he'd expected it would have.

"No, it's all right. We tried. Came close. Three miscarriages, the last one at six months. All girls, daughters. Wasn't meant to be."

"My God, poor Allison. And Nick, you, too—God bless you both."

Nick had never expected to say as much as he had, so briefly, never thought such consolation would come with still fewer words. It was sad, genuinely sad, and someone was genuinely sorry.

"Yeah. It threw us. Finished us, pretty much, I think. My father was sick. I went home to look after him, but it wasn't just that. When I go back home, Allison and I are going to have 'that talk.'"

Lena stood and almost hugged him, carefully negotiating whatever bruises she thought he might have. She tousled his hair, as if he were a child with a skinned knee. The phone rang, and both of them stared at it, resentful of the interruption. Lena scowled, then bellowed toward the entertainment center—"Get that! Do I have to do everything around here?"—and it rang a second time, but not a third. Nick was somewhat startled by the outburst, and Lena smiled, a little sheepish at her show of temper, a little proud of the result.

"I don't know what to say, Nick. I'm just happy to have you here."

Nick didn't know what to say, either. He was happy to be here, too. He was glad he'd told her about his losses, glad he didn't have to go on talking. Not that he ever had talked about it, even with Allison, summing it up as he'd just done with a quick litany of frank facts. *That talk* . . . Would it have helped, to talk more? What would they have been like, their daughters?

"I think I'm gonna take a walk."

Lena looked concerned. "Did I say . . . Was it . . . ?"

"No, Lena, you've been a pal. All of you have."

But as Nick rose from the table, ready to step outside for some air, to dwell on whether he should head back to the city or maybe relax for another day, Johnny raced in and grabbed his waist, weeping. Nick was about to tell him not to worry, that he wasn't leaving, before it occurred to Nick what vanity it was to think that he meant that much to Johnny. There was a crash of knocked-over furniture in a far room as Esposito stumbled behind, barking at his son angrily for a moment before he looked at Nick, his eyes also watery.

"John! I told you to wait! You never—Ah, Nick. I'm so sorry. There was a call, Nick, from work. Not about work. They said they tried to get you. . . ."

TWENTY-EIGHT

There were the saints, always, but Nick had no interest in them. People, that's all they were. Better of course, but people still. Not straight to the top, either; Nick was held back by the presumption, put off by the abstraction—Holy Agony, Holy Cross, Holy Name of Jesus, Holy Rosary, Holy Trinity. Forget about the further superlatives, Most Holy Crucifix, Most Holy Redeemer, Most Precious Blood. Something in between, high and low, a woman you could talk to—Mary, Help of Christians; Our Lady, Queen of Angels; Our Lady, Queen of Martyrs; the city was full of outlets. There were the old-world hometown angles, in the ward-boss put-in-a-word-for-you way—*Don't I know your uncle?* Our Lady of Guadalupe, Our Lady of Lourdes, of Loreto, Mount Carmel, Pompeii, and Vilnius. Plus there were the theme channels, available to anyone with the need, in the mood—Our Lady of Good Counsel, Our Lady of Peace, Our Lady of the Rosary, Our Lady of Sorrows, Our Lady of Victory. And these were only the parishes on the island of Manhattan. In the Bronx, there was Our Lady of Grace, of Mercy, of Refuge, and of Solace. In Brooklyn and Queens, Our Lady of the Cenacle, of China, of Consolation, of Miracles, of Perpetual Help, of the Angelus, of the Blessed Sacrament, the Miraculous Medal, the Presentation. What more could you ask for? In the worst weather, you had Our Lady of the Snows. It was not yet winter, but warmth had gone from the world. All the same Lady, all different ways of making conversation. Staten Island was a ferry ride away, for Our Lady of Pity; Our Lady, Star of the Sea. Nick closed the phone book. There was no point in calling any of them. He was from Good Shepherd; they were. That's where it would be.

When his father died, Nick thought mainly of his mother. He didn't feel bad about that. His father had been such a light traveler that his going from being there to not being there seemed a less radical transition than most. Nick's sense of his father was still fresh. Whereas his mother's absence was so long-standing that she was becoming obscured, covered over in hazy layers of memory like coats of varnish, the deepening amber beautiful but not true. Nick wanted to strip the image down, wipe it clean, to see her again as he had known her. Scraps of story and song came back—a cabbagy smell in the kitchen, falling asleep on warm skin. Never angry, not once. For days after, Nick could hear the sound of her voice, and images of her played in his mind—her soaping a mustard stain from a white blouse on the side of the tub; giving him a penny, saying it was lucky; the time she chased a fly with a swatter until it flew out the window, into the alley. She told him after that she might try out for "your Yankees," which made him sick with laughter. A powerful help, she had called him. He had never forgotten, even when he'd failed to believe it. He saw her again, more clearly than he had in years. She and his father were together now in heaven, the priest said. Nick had trouble seeing that, but there was no point in arguing.

His father had gone to sleep and not woken up. He had asked the super, Mr. Barry, to come by to fix the hall light, which had started to flicker. Mr. Barry had said he'd drop by later, around two. He found the door open. When he went in, he found Mr. Meehan in his lounge chair. It looked like he was napping, but he couldn't be wakened. The cops were called, and then the precinct called Nick, but his cellphone wasn't on. Six messages from Lieutenant Ortiz, two from Napolitano. Lena was profusely apologetic about having told Nick to call home the day before. He knew that she wasn't the one who should be sorry, the one who would be. That he had left Allison in order to care for his father was a half-truth that both he and Allison had been able to live with, at least for a while. But Nick's last thirty-odd hours as a make-believe uncle should have been spent as an actual son.

The building seemed dirtier when he walked in, more graffiti scribbled on the walls, the plaster cracked. When Nick closed the apartment door behind him, he wanted to go back out. The lounge chair was in recline mode, the footrest extended, as it had been only when occupied. The TV was on, tuned to a cooking show, with a sexy brunette tossing pasta in a pan. His father wouldn't have watched that, not even if it had been a special on stew. It must have been the cops assigned, waiting for the ME, the morgue truck. The ME could take a while, he knew. Another job, another DOA. You had to pass the time somehow. He pictured a bored rookie on the couch, flipping channels, his father dead in the chair beside him. Before he could become indignant, Nick remembered how often he had done the same. If there was no family there, what was the cop supposed to do—genuflect, tear his shirt, ululate? Nick should have been there, here, himself. Nick put the TV on mute. He did not turn it off for days.

Nick felt tired, and thought about lying down but decided against it, afraid he'd hear the voices in the pipes, afraid he'd be too glad to hear them. He went to the bathroom, to wash his face. Certain small objects became heartbreaking: a toothbrush in a glass, a threaded needle on the table, beside a little black button. He choked up when he saw them, reflecting that they had been deprived of their purpose, orphaned, and he nearly sobbed at the word. He threw them out so he wouldn't have to see them. Beside his father's bed, a stiff plastic suitcase had been laid out, hard navy-blue half shells on hinges, empty. The trip home, sooner than he'd thought. It was a comfort to imagine that his father had died making plans, reengaged with life, ready for something new; it was not a comfort to think that even the prospect of a holiday had been too much for him, too wild a ride. The Meehans did not thrive on change, had little talent for adaptation.

Nick went out to find Mr. Barry, who was in the alley, setting aside the paper and glass for recycling. He was a dim, sweet-natured man, long-faced, with a tight, thin-lipped mouth made for bad news. He pulled off a work glove and shook Nick's hand.

"A fine man. He will be missed."

Nick nodded. He hesitated before asking him anything, as if there might be some overlooked detail, some clue. His father must have died sometime after ten in the morning and before two in the afternoon, the day before. Had Nick felt anything then, some rend in the psychic fabric? No, he'd been napping, watching TV. Mr. Barry saw how he struggled with the question, and ventured a response. "He didn't suffer."

Nick smiled at the preposterous claim, mindless and kind. And yet he was decent to say so, and probably right.

"He was lucky to have a son like you."

Mr. Barry's upper lip trembled as if he might be stifling a sneeze, and Nick clasped his hand again. The remark was delivered with far greater authority than the medical opinion, nearly *ex cathedra*. How many late-night calls had Jamie made to his father from hospitals and jails, shrieking and pleading? How golden the Meehans' luck must have seemed to the Barry family. Nick went back inside to make coffee, a whole pot.

The phone calls to the funeral home, his father's union. He found the address book and called overseas, to Ireland, speaking to cousins he hadn't seen in decades. Three calls to Allison before he had the courage to leave a message. The neighborhood would tell itself. He picked a suit, a tie. The wake was one night, the funeral the next day. A lot of cops, more people from Nick's generation than his father's, showing their faces. "Yes, it was sudden. No pain." "For the best, yes." "God's hands." Jamie Barry came to the funeral parlor, with a new haircut and clean clothes, looking surprisingly sober. Nick tried to muster a compliment, but it escaped him; Jamie offered condolences and left quickly. Daysi came to the wake, Allison to the funeral. Nick hadn't arranged that— Allison had been out of town, the planes delayed by weather—but he was relieved by their separate attendance. Esposito and Lena urged him to come back home with them afterward. The boys were too young to come for this, it was felt, but they had made cards, with crayon and construction paper, hearts and angels. Nick was still on sick leave, had a week of bereavement leave after that. He wanted to go back upstate—it had been a sweet refuge—but the time had passed.

On the morning of the funeral, Nick was about to get into the shower when there was a knock at the apartment door. He couldn't think who was supposed to come—no one ever visited, except possibly Michael Cole—and he grabbed a towel and his gun before padding down the hall. The floor creaks gave him away, even as he stood to the side and listened.

"Nick? Is that you? Are you there?"

Allison. They'd agreed to meet here, and though she was fifteen minutes early, Nick had forgotten altogether. He didn't want to open the door as he was; he knew he wasn't supposed to look his best today, of all days, but this was too much.

"Allison! Hang on. I'm sorry—let me just get—"

"Nick, I have to use the bathroom."

"Hang on. Sorry—"

When he unbolted the door for her, both of them were struck by the sight of each other. Allison wore a black suit, and her chestnut hair was held back in a tortoiseshell clip. With her sunglasses on, she had a foreign-movie chic, the sexy assassin, cyanide in a secret compartment in a stiletto heel. Her poise, her composure, were so beautiful, nearly as beautiful as when she would lose both, snorting with laughter like a truck driver, then covering her mouth with her hand, like a schoolgirl in church. She looked at him again, laughed again, shook her head in apology.

"My God, Nick. You look like—I can't even say. You look like you spend time in a *really* dangerous steam room."

She giggled again, despite herself, and then brushed past him toward the bathroom—"Sorry. I really do have to go."—rushing unsteadily on her heels, punishing the old floorboards with them. At least it hadn't been awkward to see each other, Nick thought. He went to the kitchen and put the gun on the table. He rinsed out two cups, had begun to clean the coffeepot when Allison came in. She looked at him, smiled, and then embraced him. It was so warm and easy, the way they held each other, and though Nick had anticipated some kind of best-behavior, dignity-in-sorrow cast to their interaction, he hadn't expected to be reminded of how it felt to have her hands on the bare skin of his back.

"I'm so sorry for you," she said, and it was a moment before Nick realized what she meant. She had taken off her glasses, and Nick studied her eyes, whether they looked weary or worn. No. Maybe, a little, even though her face was unlined. Allison examined Nick's face, too, although she could not tell the grief of the day from the older vintage.

"Thanks. Let me make coffee."

"No, I can. You have to get ready."

She touched his cheek, stepped aside for him to walk to the bathroom. In the shower, Nick tried to think when she'd been here last. A long time ago; beyond that was too much effort to fix a date. The apartment might as well have been a safe-deposit box where his father had been kept. His father would come to see them, or they would all go out. Would she know how to use the coffeepot? In their apartment, they had an espresso machine, which Nick had thought affected, aspirational, like the leather couch, until Allison had mentioned that she'd grown up on Cuban coffee. Fancy-pants things, like the pasta maker, still in the box in a cabinet, or windows that actually let in sunlight, that showed more than the other side of the alley. Nick turned off the shower before he could think too much about the kind of place where he belonged. He dried off and walked to his room, where he'd hung his suit, shirt, and tie from the edge of the top bunk. Allison was there, too, holding up the tie, turning to him as he entered.

"This? Really?"

It was blue and gold, diamond-patterned. Nick had thought it conservative, sufficient. It was a tie.

"What's wrong with it?"

"It's wrinkled, and it has a stain. The rest of it, too. You're not an assistant principal, Nick, and you do have some nice stuff."

Nick smiled, because there was neither dry self-consciousness nor damp sympathy in her voice; she was being useful, doing what needed to be done, helping when he needed help. She looked at him, and he nodded. The closet door was already open, and she stripped the dry-cleaning plastic from several garments before selecting a suit, a shirt. Had she bought them for him? Probably. Nick didn't care. He was glad to see her, to watch her, and be taken care of, at least like this, for now. She held up a handful of ties in the weak light, examining them for blemishes before plucking one out.

"I can't really see. Can you? Come here. . . ."

So natural how she slipped her arm around his waist, led him to the window. Allison raised the yellowing shade a few inches, yanking at the string. Nick blinked at the alley, the secondhand daylight too strong for his eyes this early. They inspected the tie together, which seemed again to Nick to be sufficient.

"Isn't that better?" she asked.

"Yeah."

"See, was that so complicated?"

"No."

"Nick, I'm so sorry. . . ."

They looked at each other and kissed. Allison lowered the shade. Nick was careful taking off her jacket, laying it on the bunk with his own suit, but neither was careful after that. As they tumbled onto the bunk bed, they looked at each other and almost laughed, then didn't look again. It was so good to be with her, even with pity, though it was not that. Yes, it was pity. They were sad to see it go, knew that it was gone, even amid the assaultive joys on the old mattress, the kicked-aside pile of dingy sheets. The giddy double cheat of it, nearly strangers and still husband and wife; this was a ride. This was a ride, and that was the pity. After, they dressed quickly, without speaking.

Church was a blur—*qui tolis peccata mundi*—then bagpipes and bells, a hundred handshakes, firm or frail. Incense inside, cigarettes out. All had gone as it should have, the incidental touches of beauty, ancient forms for grieving, praise, acceptance of mystery at the heart of things. Roman ritual and Irish weather—tumbling dark clouds, gentle rain, sudden sunlight, clouds again. The white cloth taken from the dark casket loaded into the back of the hearse. There he was; there he goes. Nick was not unwounded, not unmoved, but he guarded against the emotions that might sweep him away. He understood his father better now, as a kind of chieftain of mourning, an old hand at it, knowing he hadn't enough tears for today, and he might need more, later on.

On the ride to the cemetery, Allison took his hand and squeezed it in the back of the limousine. Nick squeezed Allison's hand, then let go. He wondered which kind of silence this one was, the old and trusting kind, where there was no need for words, or the newer one, where they were just bankrupt of anything to say. It seemed silly to rent a limousine, but he was not going to drive, let alone hail a livery cab outside the church, haggling in broken Spanish over the price. Would his father have been delighted by the lack of fakery and fanciness, or would he have been insulted by the thrift? A city bus, like the ones he used to drive, that would have been the thing. Allison took his hand again, gripping more firmly than expected.

"Why'd you smile?" she asked.

"Nothing."

The hand left his again, touched his shoulder, then trailed away. It would be the second kind of silence, it seemed.

"Didn't Mike Quill live around here?" Allison asked.

Quill had been the leader of the transit workers in the fifties and sixties. He'd been an Irish immigrant who'd led a strike that had nearly crippled the city. The old man had loved him. It was the perfect remark for Nick, a gift she could have shopped for, apt and casual, personal but passing. A reference to city history, with intimate connections. This is what Nick gave back:

"Yeah."

The hand came back and rested on Nick's, gently. They moved onto the highway by Van Cortlandt Park, following the hearse. A police car from the precinct led the cortège, and a half-dozen cars followed the limo. Nick had discouraged most people from making the trip, but Esposito and Lena, old Irish ladies from the block, a few others, were not to be deterred. A post-cemetery lunch was traditional, but Nick had no appetite. He hated this, all of it. Could it have been worse? Yes, of course, always. Nick thought of Malcolm, not just orphaned but handcuffed; and then he remembered how, despite it all, Malcolm had lifted his eyes to admire, "Even a day like today . . ." Yes, it could have been worse; Nick realized that a felon with jail breath had faced the same moment with far more courage, more soul than he could muster.

His phone rang, from the blocked number. Nick looked to Allison, almost smiling, knowing who it was not. Any distraction was welcome, even this.

"Can you talk?" the voice said.

"Depends on who you ask."

There was a pause on the end of the line, uncertain whether it was a joke, and who it was on. When conclusions were drawn, offense was taken.

"You're playing games, Meehan. You're playing them with the wrong people, on the wrong side. This is dead serious, and you're out somewhere, off playing games. You have no idea what we know."

Nick smiled for the first time in days.

"Hello? Are you there?"

Nick didn't answer, knowing he didn't need to, not caring if he did.

"Meehan, I think you should know, this will get done, with you or without you. You have an opportunity. You are not necessary."

"That's always been my philosophy," said Nick without emotion, though he took less pleasure in the ironies with each exchange. When he heard what he took to be an argumentative noise stirring from the other end, he cut it off.

"The EMTs were a nice touch, I give you that. Beautiful, as an idea. Was it yours? You should be proud. The problem wasn't the idea. What was it—four times, they popped up? In how many days? Whoever was running that show for you, you should get rid of him. Get somebody who gets out more, who knows you can't have the same dog bite twice, and then again, and then another time, each one in a different part of town. I mean, a blind man would have noticed something's up."

No noise followed for a while, argumentative or otherwise, which Nick took as confirmation of his guess.

"I take that to mean you're not interested in helping us anymore, Meehan. That's a shame. I'd be very careful, if I were you. I think advice is wasted on you, but I'm gonna give you some, anyway. Watch your back."

"Wash my back?"

"What?"

"Wash what?"

Nick held the phone away at arm's length as he spoke. It was childish, he knew, but childhood was on his mind. He'd just had a glorious adventure in a bunk bed, and now the whole world was his orphanage. Allison smiled wanly at his labored irony. Nick had to assume the mystery prick did not.

" 'Watch,' not—Go fuck yourself, Meehan, if that's the way it's gonna be. I gave you fair warning, tried to help you however I could."

"Listen, this connection is bad, you're breaking up, and I gotta go. Anyway, I appreciate all you've done."

The other man hung up the phone, and Nick put his back into his pocket. Allison looked over uncertainly and stroked his arm.

"Some idiot from work," he said, before looking out the window again.

"Nick."

He grasped her hand, and she held on. They drove on in silence, and then Allison slipped closer to him on the seat. It was an interrogation technique, and Nick admired her for it.

"Nick, you have to talk to me. For anyone else, I'd think this was the wrong time. Not you. I don't worry about you. I do, but I don't. What do you want to do?"

"I don't know."

"Yes, you do."

"You're talking about big decisions?"

"Yes."

The sights out the window were no distraction. Bare trees and then Yonkers. It was rude to look away, and Nick stopped, but he couldn't yet look at Allison. They still held hands.

"It was bad, what we went through," he ventured.

"I'm sorry."

"Don't say that, Allison. I never blamed you."

"Yes, you did."

"No. I was sad about it," he said.

"There was more to it than that."

"What?"

"There was more," she said.

"Tell me."

She held his hand in both of hers now, and there was something gentle but relentless in her touch. Nick didn't know whether he wanted her to let go.

"There was a meeting you went to, a business trip, overnight, two days," Nick said. "You spent an hour packing, repacking. You had always spent ten minutes before, throwing a suit into a suitcase. You never fussed about it. This time—makeup, hair stuff, looking in the mirror. You saw me notice, then covered for it, asking if it was worth bringing a bathing suit—you went to Miami. When you got there, you told me the cellphone service was bad, I should call you at the hotel."

"Nothing happened there," she said, emphatic in her words but some turmoil in her face.

"The next week, you went to Detroit. Same fuss."

"I'm sorry. . . ."

"I don't want to know."

"But you do know, Nick, right? You did, you do. I'm sorry. But it was over between you and me then. That much was clear. You wouldn't talk. To me. Maybe to anyone, I don't know, but all that mattered was you didn't talk to me. We went back to work, both of us. We never left. I didn't. You went home to look after your father. I respected that, respected it enough."

Allison smiled, rueful. They squeezed hands again, both looking out different windows.

"This is it, then? Nick? I'm not saying I want this, but let's not get old, not deciding."

"All right."

"Say it."

"Yes."

"Say what you want."

"We should move on."

They hadn't stopped holding hands, but now it was tender again, like old times, now that they had let the old times go. They sidled into the middle of the seat, closer, and she laid her head on his shoulder. He could smell her hair. The ease of it, the fondness, the regret. They were not young anymore, like they were when they were first together; not together anymore, not young. She twined her arm around his, looking down, then intently at him. Allison drew the curtain to block the driver's view, but this was not the same kind of privacy they'd needed three hours before. This time, Nick did not husband all his tears, and they held each other until they reached the cemetery in Westchester. Gate of Heaven, where he came three or four times a year to see his mother. When the car slowed and halted, the driver waited for them to draw back the curtain before he came to open the door. They fixed up their black suits, and Allison dabbed her makeup with a tissue, looking for forgiving reflections in her compact mirror.

Allison stayed for the prayers, which were not long. Nick's and Allison's disarray was mistaken for grief. Not mistaken. The wind was cold, and they were on a·hillside. There was cause to shiver. Had they let the pipers go? Yes, but Nick still heard them. On the far side of the hill, near the wooded edge, a deer grazed, head rising watchfully every few moments before dropping down again to feed on the memorial green. Nick stiffened at the apparition, and Allison kissed his shoulder, mistaking his grief. Not mistaking. No apparition, only a sight. This was the country, another one. The deer lingered through the blessing—"May the perpetual light shine upon him. . . ."—remained even as the mourners began to move on. Allison would walk down to the cemetery office, where she would call for another car to take her back to the city. She and Nick kissed, quickly, before she turned away. Nick kissed Esposito and Lena goodbye, and Lena again asked him to come back with them. *Moving on, then.* Nick kissed the old Irish ladies. Did he know them? Did it matter? *Moving on!* The priest shook Nick's hand. The last mourners departed, some likely disappointed that there would be no lunch. Nick dropped down to kiss the ground by the grave and looked at the name on the stone, the space where another name would join it, before he walked back down to the waiting limousine. He looked out the window as the country became the city again—good old Babylon, Byzantium, Troy—saying goodbye to his father, his mother, his wife, goodbye to his anonymous and traitorous watcher, goodbye, goodbye, goodbye.

TWENTY-NINE

At work, there was something wrong with the phone. Not on every call, but every third or fourth time Nick picked it up, the cord slipped out of the receiver at some point in the conversation. Usually when he was asking a difficult question. There would be a lack of response on the other end when he challenged, "So, you never threatened the girl your boyfriend left you for? She has your guy, but she calls you all the time? When I pull the phone records, is that what it's gonna say?" Or, "What do you mean, he says he's coming after you? And you don't owe him money? How is he threatening you, with a lawsuit or to break your legs?

"Hello?"

Nick would take the lack of response as the person being evasive. It would make him angry. And then he'd realize it was the connection, and sometimes he could fix it, plugging the cord back in, and sometimes he had to call back. And sometimes when he asked the questions again, he got evasive silences that had nothing to do with the phone. Was it still October? Yes, for a few more days.

"Hello?"

The interpretation of silences, this was his new pastime. No answer— not happy, or not there? Nick wanted to quit, to go home. And then he remembered he'd come back to work early. He could have stayed home for another few weeks, at least, but he couldn't stand to stay there. Even the voices in the pipes had been quiet lately. He was deskbound, which meant he was confined to the minor complaints. Double-checking stories, poking for holes. "You can't say who stole your wallet if you passed out with twelve people in the apartment." At least half of the cases could be closed on the phone, after a kind word or a pointed challenge. Nick was an abstraction to them, and he felt abstracted himself; he was a handful of stock phrases repeated from a cubicle. "Sorry for the inconvenience." "Is there anything else I can help you with?" He could have been a customer service rep in Bangalore.

"Hello? *Hola, Señora.* Does anybody speak English? Hello?"

Day after day, there were litanies of petty grudges and grievances, eating time like tapeworms. Not that Nick lacked for time, but he resented its waste, at least when strangers were wasting it. He'd call the number on the report and find that it was disconnected, or he'd call and call, leaving messages, and when he sent someone to knock on the door, they'd say, "Why you coming to my house? I don't want people to see cops at my house!" Other people wouldn't stop calling; they wanted to talk every day.

Even when nothing could be fixed, everything had to be typed. Paperwork, then more paperwork. Handwritten, computer-entered, typed on triplicate forms. Pointless reports, stapled together and filed, like scraps of prayer stuck in the cracks of the Wailing Wall. Identity theft, credit card fraud, almost always a blind alley, a cold trail, and collective hours spent waiting on automatic switchboards, routed to more automated messages, his colleagues in India. Fifteen thousand dollars' worth of merchandise at a Home Depot in Texas, fifty dollars of gas in Vermont. One victim was an earnest man, a Senegalese immigrant, English his third language, almost. He believed in the system. Twice a week, he called to report more purchases, or new fraudulent cards in his name. Groceries in Nevada, furniture in New Jersey, all the buys weeks old before the bills made their way to him.

"There is . . . *development* in my case?"

He said it like a French word. Maybe it was.

"No."

"No progress?"

"No."

"Ah. Why not?"

"I haven't tried. I told you that I wouldn't. We don't travel for these cases. Can't go all over the country because these companies give out credit cards to anybody and his dog."

"*Un chien? Pardon, parlez-vous français?*"

"No."

"This man, he is not me."

"I understand. I understand completely."

"Thank you, Officer. I call you tomorrow!"

More paperwork, in the form of divorce papers from Allison. Nick knew it was coming, but he hadn't expected it to arrive in a stack of junk mail, between supermarket circulars and a preapproval for a credit card. The same day, at the office, more legal papers, a notice of claim for a wrongful death suit. The estate of Millicent Cole sought ten million dollars from him, Esposito, and the City of New York, in no particular order. Michael Cole had been taken in after the assault at the wake, but he wouldn't make a statement, and no witness would come forward to make a positive identification. Nick wished he'd been there; he couldn't have broken Michael, he knew, but he might have tempted him to brag. As it stood now, Michael was a free man, and the law was there to serve him. Maybe litigation was a better outlet. He could throw subpoenas instead of rocks from roofs. Nick skimmed through the reams of pig-in-a-wig indignation. The legal precedents were many, the claim harrumphed, but in the annals of human depravity, there were few precedents. Nick threw the papers against the wall before he'd finished reading.

When he left work that evening, he walked up Broadway, toward home. He glanced at his lobby and kept on walking; there was nothing for him there. Over the bridge, into the Bronx. Kingsbridge Road, then Fordham, pushing through crowded sidewalks, then Pelham Parkway, more houses and fewer apartments, the crowds thinning, a wide aisle of trees breaking the halves of the road. Night fell, and he sat on a bench for a while. Fewer walkers, more cars, moving faster as the distance between stoplights grew longer. The wind picked up, shivering the bare branches, and Nick found a yellow-gray grassy strip of highway shoulder to walk on before the bridge to City Island. Another world. He'd take it. An old village of fishing and boatbuilding, the main street now passed by wide asphalt lots, blinking neon testimonials to deep-fried clams. His feet were blistered in his shoes, and he'd sweated through his suit, even though he hadn't walked fast. Ten miles, at least, from the precinct. What warmth you could make, alone even, even in this icy air. PT boats had been built here, yachts that won races, and the oldest men remembered the winter when the Sound froze, and you could skate across to Queens.

Closer was Hart Island, where no one lived. Potter's Field, where the dead ones go when they have no money, no family, no friends, or no names. Corrections sent out a work detail for the burials. One ferry left from City Island with the bodies, another from Rikers with the workers. Inmates in orange jumpsuits were glad to be outside. They didn't have to dig. There was a machine for that now. The work wasn't hard when you did it together. A favor to get the detail, from one island to the other; Nick thought that maybe he'd have Esposito call to get Malcolm assigned there. Maria Fonseca should have already arrived. Maybe Miguel Mendoza, too, by now. It occurred to Nick that he'd have to take Allison's name off all the department forms as his next of kin, but he had no substitute. His own eligibility for Potter's Field was improving.

Nick walked to the end of the street, past it, down the gravel chute to the thin beach. "Shingle" and "strand," those were the Irish words for it. They weren't much for swimming over there. He wanted to see the water, and wished he'd been around that winter when you could walk across. Looking out to the east, there was no horizon, no break between sea and sky in the chill and listless dark, no difference between up and down. South, to Kings Point, a green light in the distance, minute and far away, intermittent. That was what Nick was trying to see when he stepped into the Sound, with both feet—up to one ankle, one shin, before he brought the more heedless foot back to the nearer depth. Could he stand this, could he wait, or walk farther? It hadn't frozen in ages. Nick would have liked to see that. He stood his ground, but in seconds, the cold hurt so much it felt like his bones would split. He yelled and jumped out, pulled his ruined shoes off and rubbed his feet, flailing on the beach. After a few minutes, he found himself no less wet, not much warmer, now gritty all over with sand. Nick brushed himself off and marched down the street, catching the first gypsy cab home.

In the lobby, Nick waited again, reluctant to go inside the apartment. He considered the floor for a while, the scuffed squares of checkerboard tile, and after he'd counted their numbers, reckoned their proportions, he turned to the walls. Most of the graffiti was hard to read, ghetto hieroglyphs and arabesques, stylized and semiliterate, proclamations of who was a killer, who was a whore. For all the bragging, the messages had the dull modesty of classified ads, the implicit plea that any offer would be entertained. Mr. Barry wiped away what he could, but he was getting older, slower. The chandelier in the center, a dusky spray of half-there bulbs clutched in a woozy spider of brass, with drifts of real cobweb. And more graffiti, even there. Bless 'em for the effort, if nothing else. It was hard for Nick to read—red paint, the script loose, the aerosol spray losing focus with the distance, and he struggled to make out the letters, the word, like the stars of a constellation. But it was there. He didn't have to project it, to start with the picture in his head of the dipper, the hunter, the dog, and rig their shapes to ragged points. The word was there: "G-Had." "Jihad." Death to the infidel, uptown style. How long had it been there? Nick didn't know—who looks at their own lobby ceiling? Jamie Barry had lain down here, but when he did, his gaze went no farther than his hand. Nick leapt up to try to touch it, to feel if the paint was still wet, but he couldn't reach. He felt like a jackass, jumping up like a kid being teased, the bigger boys playing keep-away with his hat. Was this Michael's handiwork? Was he tall enough to reach? Nick didn't remember him that way, but he might have grown some in the meantime.

Nick felt dizzy from staring at the ceiling. He reeled like a drunk before half-squatting, taking hold of his knees while his vision steadied. Such was his position as Jamie Barry strode out through the lobby, crisply attired in a charcoal suit, briefcase tucked under an arm as he talked on the cellphone. Nick gawked at him from his derelict crouch. The timing of his arrival, appearing as if conjured, and the executive metamorphosis were hallucinatory twice over. Jamie stopped and stared, equally unnerved by the sight of a decline equal to his rise. Nick was dirty, bedraggled, and wet; his eyes squinty and unfocused, as red as a rash; hair that could have been combed with a brick. Their roles were not completely reversed. There was an absence of avoidance and of ill-concealed disdain in Jamie's greeting as Nick wobbled to his feet.

"Nick! Hello! How are you?"

"Jamie! Shit, you look great!"

"Thanks, Nick," he said, nearly blushing. The smile faded as he searched for a compliment to return. "You . . . Are you okay?"

"Yeah, well . . . you know how it is."

Jamie knew how many things were, but he had the tact not to ask Nick which ones he meant. Nick was so impressed by Jamie's transformation that he had no sense of his own.

"Anyway, how long you been clean? I mean, you looked good at the funeral. How long ago is that? Did you do a program? Has it been thirty days since then?"

"Nah, I didn't go away. Methadone and meetings. 'Hi, my name is

Jamie. . . .' So far, so good. I went into the hospital for detox, right after I saw you, just twenty-four hours. Got out the day before the wake—I'm sorry, Nick, I am. It makes me appreciate my old man, what he's put up with. I got some lost time to make up for. . . . I will, though. I have. I've started."

The subject made Nick uncomfortable, and he jumped back into the direct questions, as if he were handling an informant.

"Yeah . . . and look at you! You look like a CEO! All Wall Street, with your briefcase and cellphone . . . and whatnot. The haircut! What are you doing now? What time is it?"

The addled list of inquiries and compliments did not fit the condescending posture, but Nick didn't notice the wince that preceded Jamie's reply. The goodwill that went with the patronizing blather was enough for Jamie to indulge it in return.

"Computer stuff, like I did before. Just temping now, but they like me, and something permanent might open up. It's not bad at all."

"Money in your pocket, people to talk to, a steady routine."

"All that."

As Nick spoke, some measure of his concentration returned, and he saw that Jamie's reversal of fortune wasn't quite as dramatic as it had at first appeared. The suit was shiny at the elbows and knees, and hung from a still-gaunt frame; the shirt and tie looked borrowed, probably Mr. Barry's Sunday best. The reappraisal cheered Nick, even though he knew that it was ugly of him, small, to be so mindful of the comparison between them.

"Even the midnight shift, it's not so bad," Nick said. "You might get used to it. Or, like you say, if they like you, they'll put you on days, a regular gig."

"What do you mean?"

"What?"

"Nick, it's almost six in the morning."

"Nah . . ."

Jamie swept his hand out to the front door, where the gray dawn proved his point without the need for further argument. Even such poor light as this was enough to show Nick how foolish he was, falling down in life, failing in hope. If one of the old Irish ladies had passed by then, glancing at the two lost boys from the first floor, whom she had watched grow up and come home, she might have mistaken them, but she would have known which to worry over, who would have been first in her prayers. Jamie laid a hand on his shoulder, gripping him gently.

"I gotta go. Get some rest, Nick. And if you want to talk, anytime, you know where I live."

Nick had never been very kind to Jamie, had never cared much for his troubles and excuses as he'd rounded his hamster wheel of addiction. It wouldn't have changed anything, had Nick offered his hand now and then, but it wouldn't have cost him much, either. As Nick watched Jamie walk out into the pitiless light, he was pained beyond understanding to see himself pitied, knowing it was more than he deserved.

THIRTY

When Daysi called, she left tender, tactful messages. "Thinking about you. Call me when you feel like it. . . ." A few days after the funeral, Nick called back, left a message for her. He stopped by the shop not long after. Her mother kissed him, and gave him another boutonniere, a white one. Daysi had stepped out for a moment— "*Momento!*"—and so he waited, breathing the green air. He hadn't returned to work yet, and so he wasn't wearing a suit. There was no lapel to pin it on, and he tucked it behind his ear. Mrs. Ortega was laughing when Daysi came back, stopping short, just in the door. Nick thought she looked pleased to see him, but more surprised than she should have been. She hugged him, and kissed him chastely on the cheek. Seconds later, Nick understood, when a boy followed her into the shop. Nick took the flower from behind his ear, a moment too late.

"Nick, this is my son, Esteban. . . . Esteban, this is a friend, Nick Meehan."

"Nick Meehan. Pleased to meet you, Esteban Ortega."

Nick offered a hand, and Esteban hesitated before extending his, pulling it back quickly after a loose grip, never looking at Nick. Esteban was tall and gangly, with a beaky nose and curly black hair that went to his shoulders and covered one eye.

"It's Otegui."

"What?"

Daysi interjected worriedly, "Esteban Otegui, same as his father."

"Basque?"

"Very good, Nick!" said Daysi, too pleased with the observation, as if her enthusiasm might compensate for her son's willful indifference, restoring neutrality to the room. Nick hadn't thought about Esteban much, and he had been in no hurry to make his acquaintance. Like Esteban, Nick wasn't eager to share Daysi with a stranger. Despite her brief remarks about him—his school, his interests—Nick had somehow pictured Esteban as a neighborhood kid, in a wannabe way, with low-slung pants and gangsta rap on his headphones. Instead, his tattered backpack and his slouch, his cup of Starbucks, gave him an air of hippie privilege. He went to a private school downtown. Nick hadn't been glad to hear that.

Though Esposito had since spoken with Kim Martone, obtaining assurances that the Ortega Florist van had not been involved in the kilo deal, the thought remained with Nick, a grain of irritant. Suspicion had entered his mind, and he couldn't be sure if it worked in his eyes like love or hate, seeing or not-seeing. Private school in Manhattan could cost twenty or thirty thousand dollars a year; that was a lot of flowers. Was there a scholarship, financial aid? Nick's wariness reminded him how serious he was about Daysi, how she stirred things in him, hope not least among them.

Esteban kissed his grandmother, and they exchanged pleasantries in Spanish. When he turned to his mother, he spoke faster, more singsong; he wasn't hiding what he said just in the language, but in the dialect. He couldn't have been more ostentatiously private if he'd clicked his tongue in Morse code. Daysi had a look of mild dismay before she turned hurriedly to Nick, offering abridged translation and chipper editorial.

"Esteban has a project for school. I'm going with him. It sounds like fun. What is it, Esteban? Tell Nick."

Esteban fixed him with his uncovered eye and uttered two dry syllables: "Goya."

"The bean people? I mean, the food company?"

"The painter," Esteban said, unsure whether to emote boredom or ethnic offense.

Daysi spoke up before he could decide. "There's a show at the Hispanic Society, on 155th Street. Do you know it?"

"I do. The museum of museums . . ."

"What? Anyway, we're going there. Do you want to come along?"

Esteban's shoulders rose, tense. This was not the time. In the twenty-five blocks between where they stood and the museum, there were ten thousand bags of rice and cans of beans that said "Goya" on them; it was not the worst mistake anyone could have made, Nick considered, and yet it was the perfect one, for him at the moment.

"No, I have something to do. I'll walk you to the subway, though."

"Oh, good. Honey, you want to leave your backpack? I don't know why they make these kids carry all this stuff. It's like a library on their backs."

Daysi reached to help him take it off, and he flinched. Nick knew that bad instinct, the need for attention and the allergy to it. Esteban didn't lift the backpack as much as he wriggled out of it. Nick wanted to kick him and take his lunch money; he also wanted a do-over, another chance at making an impression. This should have been easy for Nick. Not the situation—that was not easy—but the question. *Daysi plus museums; "Goya" means what?* Nick felt like he'd blown the word "cat" at a spelling bee. Lunch money or do-over?

As the three of them left the shop, Esteban started speaking Spanish again, until Daysi cut him off. Lunch money.

"Stop it. Be polite."

"Spanish isn't polite? *Pero, Mama, yo—*"

"Stop it."

In the street, amid the sidewalk crowds, it was almost better. Nick heard the strain in Daysi's voice, but he was spared the sight of the kid's expressions. No winners in this, better to dampen things down, delay. She walked between them. Nick touched Daysi's arm, once he was sure that Esteban could not see.

"Thank you, thank you for what you sent. They were beautiful."

Daysi had sent a vast stand of lilies and roses to the funeral home. The old ladies from the neighborhood had wondered at it adoringly, then had clucked at the card, Ortega Florist. Daysi laughed, forgetting Esteban for a second.

"My mother wanted to send a big shamrock, green carnations . . ."

"I'm glad you stepped in."

Esteban's near shoulder rose up, as if to defend against the dirty spray of affectionate talk. Daysi swept her hair back with one hand, nervously deciding whether to touch Esteban with the other. For a second, the hand didn't really wave, but the fingers flickered; Nick thought she was calling a tiny invisible cab. The hand lowered, caressing Esteban's arm.

"Nick's Irish. That's why your *abuela* wanted to send the shamrock. His father died."

The plea for sympathy was naked, obvious, and for a moment Nick was glad she'd made it. Esteban didn't jerk away this time, he'd become cooler and harder than that, but he veered to the farther edge of the sidewalk, as if to dodge an oncoming pedestrian. Lunch money, and dinner money, and breakfast. And then Nick felt for Daysi, knowing she'd made a worse mistake than he could have, talking about fathers who had gone. It was not a good subject, worse than cans of beans. This was the fight, and Nick decided to take a dive. You couldn't even call the fight fixed. The fight was never winnable—he was already dead. El Cid on his last ride, strapped lifeless to his horse; an inspiration maybe, but not for himself.

"You know, Esteban, the Hispanic Society is the only real museum still left there. The Museum of the American Indian, they moved it. Not enough people went there. It's too far uptown, and the neighborhood— I don't know if you remember, but it used to be really bad around here. All the names of the tribes are carved on the front of the building— Iroquois, Eskimo, Arapaho. It's weird to see the tribes are lost, and the museum is gone, too. The tribes who used to live in Manhattan, they were part of the Algonquin people. A lot of places in New York have Indian names—Canarsie, Rockaway, Hoboken in Jersey. Mannahatta, that's Indian, too. The museum was good, they had all kinds of artifacts, but I wished it had more about the neighborhood, because the history is here."

Daysi looked at Nick appreciatively, viewing the overwrought and overlong speech as proof of his genuine effort. They were at the subway entrance. Nick extended his hand to Esteban, as if they were both gentlemen, as if to offer assurances at least that the next round would be fair. Esteban stared down, casting his eyes around. Nick continued to hold his hand out until Daysi poked her son. Esteban's hand went slowly to Nick's, and then he jerked it away—hey, that old gag, not bad!—but then he slapped Nick's shoulder, and pointed down. Nick looked where he was directed, but he only saw one thing, on the top step of the subway stairs. It was a quart of beer, in a paper bag. Esteban tapped Nick again on the shoulder and pointed, so that everything was clear.

"Look, there's an artifact from your tribe."

THIRTY-ONE

Nick took to working afternoons, then evenings, later and later. After midnight, the phones usually stopped ringing, and unless there was an incident of some consequence, the office emptied out shortly after. When he went downstairs, the vacancy was more pronounced, given the ordinary chaotic traffic of precinct visitors, voluntary and otherwise. The cop behind the desk had the look of a fire-watcher in a remote forest tower, settling in for the rainy season. Once, when Nick went out for coffee, he saw a stray dog sleeping in front of the desk, unobserved. No notice was paid when the dog followed him back outside, a few hours later, wandering off on its own rounds.

Nick often walked around the block once or twice, to clear his head. Sometimes it worked too well. In the stillness, he noticed how the office machines made odd and spontaneous sounds, metrical ticks and buzzy whirs, conversational noises that accompanied no evident function from the printer or copier. It was as if the toys played with one another when the children slept. One night the phone rang, and when Nick picked it up, he was greeted with the serial beeps of a fax machine. A few minutes later, it beeped at him again when he asked how he might be of service. After a third robotic exchange, Nick caught on that it was set to automatic redial, but rather than ignore it, he was provoked by the idea that he could speak to it, persuade it to reveal the meaning in its digital code. What would it be, a Chinese menu, love note or death threat, instructions to fire an underperforming sales division in Akron? In his asylum privacy, Nick made several attempts at talking back, and hours passed in high bemusement. A pad for messages headed "While You Were Out" was dutifully and exclusively filled with the word "beep." In time, his interest dwindled and his patience thinned. His tone became bitter, and his voice took on an unexpected force that grew fiercer with each call.

Beep, beep, beep . . .

"That's a lie."

Beep, beep, beep . . .

"Just shut the fuck up already."

"What?"

"You heard me."

Someone had, it seemed. Had the code been broken?

"This is Captain Carver, from the Chief of D's. Who the hell is this?"

Chief of Detectives. Nick knew who they were. Not good. No code had been broken, but Nick might be. Still, he found it hard to care. What would Esposito do?

"Sorry, Captain, there's been a string of crank calls. How can I help you?"

"Who is this?"

Nick didn't have to think about the answer. "This is McCann. Detective McCann, sir. What do you need?"

"What I need, McMahon, is for you to get your ass down here to tell me why you answer the phone like you did. Plus, you will bring down the overtime figures, the arrest breakdowns of felonies and misdemeanors for the last month, and Sergeant Hanratty's report on why Pipcinski's sign-out time in the movement log doesn't match his DD-5 about canvassing for video cameras in case number 558. Got that?"

Who was Hanratty? Who was Pipcinski? No one Nick knew. The man might as well have been talking in beeps. This was another wrong number, another precinct, another squad. This was a gift.

"I don't think so, Captain. Not today."

Nick hung up and didn't answer the phone again. When Napolitano came in, not long after daylight, he threw his cellphone across the room. "These people!" It broke, and he cursed himself on top of everything else. Apparently there was some crisis in which union intervention was desperately needed.

"This prick captain from downtown wants to transfer half the Two-Eight Squad to Brooklyn. And this poor bastard McMahon, he's suspended. Can you believe these people, Nick? Can you believe them?"

"I don't know what to believe anymore."

"I hear you, Nick."

"You want coffee, Nap? I'm gonna step out and grab some."

"Yeah, thanks. You look tired, Nick. How are you feeling? It's early—you just get in?"

"Five minutes before you did."

"Coffee would be great, Nick."

Nick took his time on his errand, returning half an hour later with bagels and cream cheese, a dozen coffees and a gallon of milk. He felt a little better as he laid out the food in the meal room. Daylight calmed him, as did the sight of his colleagues, their normalcy and purpose. After taking food and coffee, the detectives returned to their desks to hustle the phones, their conversations no less strange than Nick's had been, when he'd tried to talk to a machine.

"I'm sorry to hear that, ma'am. I don't want the Lord to smite me. But your son, he's still gotta come in. . . . Yeah, people might be makin' up stories on him, just like the last time, but he's still gotta come in. . . ."

"I'm looking to talk to . . . the report says the name is 'A-Queen.' Is that right? Is that you? . . . No, it's your sister. What's your name? . . . B-Queen, naturally . . ."

"And what can you tell me about the man who robbed you? . . . He was a Gemini? How do you know that? Do you know him, know his birthday? . . . You just have a sense of these things. I see. . . ."

Nick sat in the meal room with the newspaper. No crime stories, or none but a few forty-word wrap-ups, nearly adjective-free, buried in the middle. At a block party in Edenwald, in the Bronx, four men were shot; in Corona, Queens, a man succumbed to his stab wounds after a dispute outside the El Caribe social club; on Mother Gaston Boulevard, in Brownsville, Brooklyn, an eighteen-year-old man died after being shot three times. Police sources say the victim had a lengthy arrest record, and the dispute appeared to be drug-related, name withheld pending notification of next of kin. Casualties were duly noted, like the lesser technical people in movie credits. All the big stories were of different kinds of breakdown—the financial crisis, mostly, but also crane collapses, steam pipe explosions, the electrocution of a beagle as it was walked by its owner near Gramercy Park. Pulses of crazed energy fled the subterranean city like the wrong souls loosed from purgatory, still half-fire, not yet pure light. Nick pictured the whole system, all of the systems—water, data, subways, electric, steam—leaking and sparking and wearing down to nubs. Red lights should have been blinking; maybe they were.

Thoughts of decline were not dispelled by Garelick, who walked stiffly into the meal room. He held up the gallon of milk to his own nose, then Nick's, sourness in his mouth, pointing the question.

"How does this smell to you?"

"I just bought it twenty minutes ago. It's good."

Garelick sniffed again. "Yeah, I thought so."

He topped off his coffee, and sat down beside Nick, exhaling tragic wisdom.

"This Perez situation is really getting out of hand. I'm concerned about him, I am. Sometimes I regret starting the whole thing in the diner."

"No, you don't."

Garelick blew across the top of his coffee, cooling the surface in little ripples. His true quandary was that in feigning friendship with Perez, he had warmed to him, in spite of himself.

"You're right. I don't. I am equal parts curious and worried. How crazy do you have to be before you're crazy? I mean, percentage-wise. Offhand, I'd say the high thirties. Where would you put it?"

"I have no idea."

"I'm surprised at you, Nick. I've discussed this before, with wiser men than you. Or me—don't take offense! Detectives in the old days, before your time. A lot of them posted pretty good percentages themselves. Men with problems, gifts. Bad gamblers but good detectives, great drinkers and horrible drinkers that were great detectives—most of them put it over the halfway point. Picture an iceberg—most of what you don't see, you don't want to. Now, the question is, what we're seeing of Perez, is this just a bad view, or is he really crazy as a shit-house rat?"

Nick considered what Garelick, or anyone, would have made of him talking back to the fax machine last night. It inspired defensive feelings.

"Perez works his ass off. He'd do anything you ask him."

"The idea of the trade-off is an attractive one. Isn't true, necessarily. Does being ugly make you smart, for example? In women, I mean—not us."

"No."

"Exactly. But if nature doesn't always compensate, people usually try to. They learn to play the piano, to cook. Something's happening here with Perez, and we might as well see this through to the end. I have an

idea in mind, what you might call the next phase of the trial. He'll be
back from the bathroom any minute. Watch!"

When Perez returned, Garelick beckoned him to join them in the meal
room.

"There you are! You just missed Marina. She just called. She seemed a
little upset. Is there anything going on? Is there anything I can do?"

"What?"

"Marina, she just called you."

Perez was noncommittal; there was a certain elegance to his forbear-
ance. "She called here?"

"You bet, asked for her old Ralphie. You got a hot date tonight?"

Perez made an uncomfortable shoulder-shifting motion, as if preparing for a contortionist's trick, yanking his arms from his shirtsleeves.
What a terrifying man he might seem, Nick thought, with his lumped
muscles and gleaming head, if you didn't know him. Maybe even if
you did.

"Did she leave a number? How did she sound? What did she say?"

Garelick was caught unprepared, but he was happy to improvise.

"The connection wasn't so good. She said something about . . . being
late."

Perez looked alarmed. "Late? Late for dinner, or late for . . . Late-late?
Woman-late?"

Garelick knew he had stumbled upon a rich prospect, but he knew he
had to handle it with delicacy. Nick doubted Garelick sought the utter
destruction of Perez's reputation. At first, all Garelick had wanted was
for Perez to sit at a farther desk in the office, and not to have to go out to
breakfast with him, and to be proved right down to the decimal point
about his crazy-percentage, as if he were guessing the number of jelly
beans in a jar. Still, to see his matchmaking bear such fruit must have
been difficult to resist. If Ralph were to announce that Marina was expecting, it would make Garelick the fairy godfather.

"I dunno, Ralph. You know me; I wouldn't pry like that. Why do you
suppose she'd call the office, instead of you direct?"

Perez shook his head, pensive and worried.

"I don't get international calls on my phone. She went back to Greece.
I don't really know for how long. We had our issues, everybody does, but
I didn't think . . . The little things, it's always the little things, isn't it? She

wants to go out, you want to stay in. Money. She thinks I'm made of it! You're right, I guess. She wouldn't call here to say anything important like that. Probably the plane was late, it was a tough trip, something along those lines. Shit, you're scaring me, though. She did put on a little weight!"

"Yeah, I'm sure you're right. Every relationship has its ups and downs, but what you got, it's special, Ralph."

"Yeah, thanks. Whatever. Women! You know? What are you gonna do?"

And with that, he waved a world-weary hand and returned to his desk. Nick was disappointed in him, and obscurely offended. Playacting, fun and games, varying between fetish and frolic, no harm done. But what sick bastard would fabricate a woman to bicker with over whether the chicken was dry, whose turn it was to do the laundry?

Garelick finished his coffee and raised his eyebrows. Nick refused to watch him savor this new twist in the strange saga. Nick shook his head and took the newspaper with him. He walked out of the office and went home for a while. He slept an hour and showered, then put on the same clothes. He didn't want the other guys to think he'd been there the whole night. Was that crazy, too? How much? When he came back, Perez wasn't there. He'd told Lieutenant Ortiz he had to leave early. The next day, Perez called the office to say that Marina had died in a ferry accident in the Aegean. She'd fallen overboard and drowned. The lieutenant gave him a week off to attend to his business. He didn't intend to travel, Perez said, but he needed time alone. Garelick went around the office telling people he'd read about it, seen something on the news, and took up a collection for flowers. Napolitano and Nick kept their silence. Garelick became more tolerant of Perez after that, even friendly. When Perez came back to work, he had a mustache, with unexpected streaks of gray. Nick took to avoiding both of them. He made sure the flower order went to Daysi, who made a special arrangement of myrtle and chrysanthemums, flowers that signified love and grief in the old myths.

THIRTY-TWO

On Thanksgiving, Nick covered the office. Perez was working with him, but Nick urged him to leave. Perez had cousins in the Bronx, and he could spend a few hours with them for the holiday dinner. Nick promised he'd call if anything happened. The phones didn't ring often, and Nick didn't answer often. If it rang more than eight or nine times, he picked it up. "Detective McCann. How can I help you?"

"Nick?"

"McCann here. Can I help you?"

"Cut it out, Nick—it's me, Espo."

"Hey."

"Happy Thanksgiving."

"Happy Thanksgiving."

"So you got stuck today, huh? A shame. The boys were asking about you. . . ."

"Give 'em my best."

"Listen, Nick," said Esposito, a wary, teasing tone in his voice. "I get a refrigerator magnet from the car dealer every year, says the same thing, but it's a little more heartfelt. Are you all right? Why don't you take a ride up here? Give your number to the desk. If anything happens, you can be back in a couple of hours. Nothing's gonna. You know how it is. Thanksgivings are pretty quiet."

"I appreciate it, pal, but I'm just gonna lay low here."

"How's Daysi?"

"Fine."

"That's it? 'Fine'? When's the last time you saw her?"

"We had dinner last week," Nick said, recalling how Daysi had been called home before dessert.

"You make it sound like you fixed a boiler together. Are things going okay with her? Didn't she ask you over for Thanksgiving?"

"Yeah, but I said I had to cover the office."

"Come on, it's around the corner."

"Nah . . . Her kid, he's a real piece of work. I don't want to deal with it."

"Do you think he hates cops, or just you? You want me to look into the ex? What's his name again?"

"No, don't. I don't know where it gets me. I don't know if I want to know."

"How about I find out, but I don't tell you unless you ask?"

"You must be getting pretty bored up there."

"You have no idea. If I have to play another game of Go Fish, I don't know what I'm gonna do. Listen, Nick, there's two ways to handle this. I could sleep with Daysi, and we could see if the kid hated me as much as he hates you. That way, we'd know for sure—scientifically—whether it was cops in general or you in particular."

Nick didn't laugh, but he checked his temper. It wasn't much of a joke, but he knew the joke wasn't really the problem.

"What's the other way?"

"I don't know, but there usually is. C'mon, Nick, wake up!"

Esposito knew the pitch had enough topspin for it to bounce around in Nick's brain, hitting jealous notes, warning him against complacency. And he was right. If Nick was to make a go of it, if he and Daysi were, he would have to come to terms with Esteban. Either Nick would be a private part of Daysi's life, separate from her son—not a secret, but not subject to his veto—or some other accommodation would be found. He thought of her shoulders, the three unexpected freckles on the smooth olive skin. He bleated out his question to Esposito.

"What the hell am I supposed to bring? It's the holiday. Everything's closed."

"Attaboy, I'm glad to hear you're in. Now, let's think. . . ."

"I show up empty-handed, I look like a bum. What is there—a bag of apples from a bodega? Cake from the supermarket? The liquor stores are closed. . . ."

"The lieutenant has a nice bottle of Scotch in his desk."

"Yeah? It hasn't been opened? How do you know?"

"I needed a pen once, a while back. In the bottom drawer, there was a box marked 'Private.' Why do they do that? It might as well have said, 'I dare you to look.' "

Esposito was right. There always was another way. Nick called Daysi to wish her a happy holiday, and, as expected, she repeated her invitation to come over. They were in the middle of the meal, she said, but he shouldn't mind—there was plenty of food, more than enough. Nick said he had a few things to do around the office, but he'd stop by within the hour.

"Perfect! Just in time for dessert! Flan. It's very good."

"Just like the Pilgrims had. See you in a bit."

For the next twenty minutes, Nick fussed and prepped. He washed his face and checked the mirror; found the Scotch and dug off the price tag with a thumbnail. It was a good bottle, or at least an expensive one. He dusted it clean. He wrote down the brand in his notebook, so he could replace it the next day. He tried to pronounce the Celtic gargle of the name: *Auch-na*-nevermind, a traffic jam of consonants. His father had known Gaelic, had spoken it as a child. Would he have known what it meant, or was it the private language of another island? In the old days, a squad commander always had a bottle in his desk, but Nick had never known Lieutenant Ortiz to drink anything but light beer. It was a tradition that had fallen away, like the fedora. The lieutenant talked about the old days, how much better it had been then, but in the old days, a Puerto Rican would never have had his office. What did Dominicans eat for Thanksgiving? Where did they weigh in on Columbus? What was the Spanish word for "turkey"? Nick realized how rattled he was and thought about having a slug from the bottle. *Shut up and go.*

Along 181st Street, most of the stores were closed. The house lights were mostly dark in the apartments above the shops, as people gathered for their meals, out of duty and pleasure. The night was cold and cloudy, and the streets were empty. The apartment building was a grand old Italianate relic on Riverside Drive, which he had barely noticed on his previous visit. This was the place, yes, but which apartment? His eyes had not been on the real estate at the time. Nick searched the tenant list and saw the name Otegui and rang the bell. Basque, you know. What else was Daysi's ex? Nick wouldn't have guessed the spelling, and made a note of it. He looked into the security camera, unsure whether to smile. The door buzzed open.

Daysi greeted him with an intense kiss at the door. She was nervous, too, he thought, as she looked at the bottle of Scotch.

"Nick! That was so sweet—my mother drinks Scotch. How did you know?"

"I'm a detective."

"Don't be, today. I mean, try not to pay too much attention, especially to Esteban. He's in a mood. And pretend you've never been here before. . . ."

The firmness with which Daysi took his arm disinclined him from making light of her precautions. She released him before they reached the dining room, where a fourth place was set at the table, as if he belonged there. A lace tablecloth, silver candlesticks; on a platter, a small turkey—less than half of it eaten—that gave off a spicy, non-Puritan aroma. Esteban extended a hand when Nick walked around to him, but his eyes remained fixed on his plate. Mama Ortega rose and hugged him, accepting the bottle with a knowing "Aha!" She opened it and filled highball glasses for the three adults. Daysi took hers gratefully and raised it. Nick toasted her and Mama Ortega. *Mama Ortega.* He called her that when he saw her in the store, and she was pleased by it, but he would be wise not to say it at this table.

"Happy Thanksgiving. *Feliz Gracias*—forget it. How do you say it?"

The reactions were as expected—a delighted smile from Mama, a scowl from Esteban, a wink from Daysi, before she downed the glass in its entirety.

"*Feliz Día de Acción de Gracias.*"

"You're kidding. All that?"

"*Por favor, Mama, es que yo—*"

"Stop it, Esteban."

"May I be excused?"

The question was sufficiently polite to offset the overt hostility of its timing, and Daysi cut her losses, nodding. All of the vectors and valences worked against Nick: age, culture, class—the hapless flatfoot could be derided from above or below, and Esteban could sneer at him like a hood rat, smirk like a rich kid. In the old stories, when the son of an absent father defends his mother against a new suitor, everyone knows who to root for. No one cares that the interloper was able to come up with a bottle of Scotch when the liquor stores were closed.

"I'll call you when it's time for dessert."

As Esteban walked off to another room, Daysi rolled her eyes and reached for the bottle to refill her glass. Mama took a plate and filled it with turkey and side dishes, despite Nick's protest. He was grateful that Esteban had gone. Daysi went through the show-and-tell of cultural difference. "Turkey" was *"pavo,"* and they roasted it like a pig, with garlic and oregano, stuffed with plantains and bacon. Pigeon peas and rice, salad. It was not what Nick was used to, but he and his father had eaten Thanksgiving at diners. With Allison's family, the holiday had been stridently American despite their Cuban roots, with red, white, and blue dishes and cranberry sauce from a can. Nick ate quickly, like an inmate. Mama cleared the table as he finished, and left for the kitchen.

"Does he get to spend much time with the father?"

"Six weeks, every summer. And he'll fly down for the weekend a few times during the year."

"The father doesn't come up here?"

Daysi shook her head, clearly uncomfortable with the subject. Nick had thought it adult to address it, though he regretted the tone and tack he had taken. "The father," was the phrase, he had said it twice. What was he, a social worker? And what good did talking do? Daysi clumsily changed the subject.

"He doesn't like flying. . . . How was dinner?"

How did the father get here the first time, did he swim? *Stop*. Hadn't she asked him not to be a detective? Yes, but he couldn't help—*stop*. He knew that this first family dinner was bound to be uncomfortable, but he didn't feel like they were moving beyond it, making progress toward détente. He wished he hadn't come here. Nick wiped his mouth with his napkin, slapped his belly somewhat flamboyantly, as Esposito might have.

"Great. Who's the chef, you or your mother?"

"Mostly her," said Daysi, trying to smile again. "Do you want more? There's plenty."

This wasn't working. Nick needed a distraction. Should he shoot his gun, let a round go out the window? Not just yet: Mama Ortega came out of the kitchen with some sort of pie. After setting it down, she called out for Esteban to come back to the table, *la mesa*, Nick followed that much. The smiles faded as the minutes passed without response.

When Esteban appeared, he held out a telephone to Daysi. "It's Papi. He wants to wish you Happy Thanksgiving."

Nick noticed both that it was the first time Esteban chose to speak English, and that the phone hadn't rung. A detective again. He couldn't help it.

"Tell him I'll call him back later."

Her tone was icy. Mama Ortega got up to clear more plates, and Nick decided to help her. As he left the room, he could hear the voices raised behind them.

In the sanctuary of the kitchen, Mama and Nick exchanged embarrassed glances. She nodded to the leftover food on the counter—"You friends. They like?"—and when Nick assented, she began to put together a plate. She took out plastic wrap from a drawer and unpeeled a sheet the size of her wingspan, and tore it loose. Crackle-crackle, rip. The sound was like a record skipping, not just an ugly noise but a mark of ruined music. Another sheet. Crackle-crackle, rip. Nick looked away, so she wouldn't see him flinching. Had he not seen the stuff, heard it, since the santero kidnapping? He gripped the edge of the counter, and had to force himself to let go. Mama put the plates and containers in a shopping bag for him. She gave him a kiss, letting him know that she was on his side, but the tightness in her mouth showed she knew it didn't matter. At least that was what he read into it. When Nick made an excuse to Daysi about having to go back to the office, she didn't protest. Esteban had left the room, and she escorted Nick out, clutching his arm, indifferent to witnesses. At the door, she had tears in her eyes.

THIRTY-THREE

Nick worked Christmas and New Year's. He talked to Daysi every day or so, and they met at least once a week. One evening, Nick brought Daysi back to his apartment, and though he'd warned her not to expect much, he was ashamed of how she looked at it, noticing that it wasn't just as bare and worn as a hostel, but not particularly clean, either, with tumbleweeds of dust that scattered down the hall as he opened the door. A few minutes later, Esteban called her on her cellphone, complaining he was sick. He always called when they were out, at least once. This time, Nick didn't mind as much; she hadn't even seen the bunk bed. Daysi apologized, and took a cab home. It would remain a house without women. Their talks became even more frequent as their real time alone with each other—Were they still dates?—required increasing negotiations. Esposito called Nick daily, too, eager to hear about what was going on. Nick wished he had more to say. Work was sometimes a bitch, sometimes a bore. He didn't want just a phone partner of either kind, but it was the best he could manage.

Nick found that stopping by the shop worked best, not just because it was where he'd first seen her, with all its fragrant reminders. Mama Ortega was always delighted to see him. If Daysi was busy, he could leave; if not, they could see each other for a moment, chat and catch up, maybe kiss. Often enough, it was still a nearly religious revival to see her, hold her, to hear her laugh at something he said, or something he hadn't realized he meant. But he dreaded the idea they were sliding toward a match of problems rather than possibilities, something middle-aged and sympathetic. With Allison, at least—well, there was no point in dwelling on the past. It was essential for Nick to resist what he'd been taught, in school as doctrine and at home by example: that you only get one shot at this, in life and in love.

Daysi called in tears once, saying she thought Esteban might be experimenting with drugs. He was moody, sleeping late, and he was rude to her, wouldn't talk. Nick hated the term "experimenting" because it was a lie. Was he using the scientific method, with a control and placebo? Was he publishing his findings in medical journals? Nick didn't say that to her. He lied, too, offering vaporous sympathy. He didn't ask, *What kind of drugs? The same kind his father sold?*

Nick had broken down and asked Esposito about the father. Esposito had been desperate to tell, but for Nick it was knowledge without profit. Esteban Otegui had been a midlevel boss, had been gone from the scene for almost a decade. One of his workers, a nephew, had killed three people. Otegui's name had also come up as a suspect in the shooting of a cop, who had been wounded in the arm during a foot pursuit. The cop never got a good look at his face. Otegui left town around that time, headed back to the Dominican Republic, just before he was indicted for narcotics conspiracy. He had a sense of the moment, it appeared, an instinct for the opportune move. A federal fugitive warrant had been issued, but the reality was that Otegui had successfully faded from view. Little effort had been made to find him, since at the time the Dominican Republic didn't extradite, and when the treaty was later signed, the list of higher priorities grew longer by the week. Whoever had coined the phrase "You can run, but you can't hide" had possessed little practical experience in law enforcement. Esposito said he could keep on digging, but Nick told him not to bother. Daysi had other relationships that threatened Nick more.

In the past, they had avoided talk about her ex for the usual reasons—Nick scarcely spoke of Allison—and when Nick asked Daysi once, over dinner, what her ex did for a living, she said that he had "an interest" in this, "advised" and "consulted" in that. Nick found it hard not to laugh. What a man did was a noun—cowboy, astronaut, ditchdigger, dentist, cop. If you needed more than two words, it was a euphemism, a half-truth with a bad toupee. In a sense, he preferred the idea of the ex as a criminal. If Daysi had dumped him because she hadn't wanted to help him disable land mines, save the rain forest, counsel gay dolphins, whatever, Nick could hardly see himself as a worthy substitute, let alone an improvement. But mostly, he didn't think about her ex, didn't really care.

Nick had only ventured the casual, cruel question about employment because they'd had to leave the restaurant halfway through the meal, after another crisis call from Esteban. What had it been that night? Had there been a thorn in his paw, or had a troll kept him from crossing the bridge?

When Daysi called the next time, she was cheerful, relieved. She'd had a heart-to-heart with Esteban, and was convinced he knew the danger of drugs, that he would never touch them. The moodiness was over a girl he liked, who didn't like him. "Isn't that sweet? My poor baby . . ."

"Well, thank God for that."

Still, the moodiness was contagious. Hour by hour, Nick resolved to break it off, and then he resolved to work through it, to have a talk with Esteban, spend time with him, or avoid him altogether. Every night with Daysi was a one-off, an opportunity seized when Esteban was staying at a friend's, or was on a class trip. At hotels, they joked about whether they should register under their own names, but neither could laugh at their need for aliases and alibis, ridiculous but real, and the nearly professional level of deception required of them.

Nick stopped by the store late one winter afternoon, an unseasonably mild but still bleak day that made the lushness and color of the place seem all the more like an oasis. He was glad to see the store empty, at first, with no customers, no other claims on her attention. He called out "Hello?" as his phone rang. Esposito. He'd talk later.

When Esteban walked out from the back of the store, the gaze was more forthrightly hostile than usual. Nick nodded to him—*Hey*—a greeting that was not returned, and the boy strode toward him with increasing speed. The face tightened, and he emitted an eerie rage-choked wail that would have frightened Nick had he heard it in the woods at night. Nick thought Esteban might cry before he got to him, but then he broke into a run. When Esteban took a swing at him, Nick dropped his phone. Esteban stepped on it, maybe on purpose. It was the only damage done, almost.

Nick punched Esteban in the stomach, dropping him. It was squalidly joyous to slip loose from months of constraint, his rival at his feet with little more effort than it took to turn a doorknob. The incoherent curses that poured from Esteban were music to him. Nick had been careful in choosing the gut, even as he pinned the boy's arms behind his back, resting a knee on his side. He couldn't leave a mark. It was not a fair fight, never could be, and even as Nick savored the moment of victory, he began to doubt he had won. Mama Ortega rushed out from the back office. She looked angry, and she shouted at both of them.

Nick felt an instinct of adolescent protest, a temptation to blurt out *He started it!* Instead, he rose from his knee, stood, and stepped back. Esteban scrambled up and ran back into the office, yelling, shoving past his grandmother, without even looking at Nick. Mama Ortega started to scowl at Nick, then stopped, smiling sadly. Nick raised his hands—*What?*—and she shook her head, lifted her hands as he did, answering his question with a question: *Who knows?* She knew more, Nick thought, but it wasn't her place to tell him, even if she were able, if she'd had the words for it. When she followed Esteban into the office, she didn't say goodbye, which Nick tried to hope was a good sign.

Nick picked up his broken phone and left, taking a roundabout walk back to the office. He wished the little bastard had at least managed to get out an accusation, so Nick would have an idea if there was a new kettle of shit on the stove, or just the old one boiling over. He didn't know the cause, couldn't guess its effect. Would Daysi be furious at him for hitting her son, or desperately apologetic for the outburst, grateful for his restraint? It felt good, but it wasn't good, of that much he was certain; what he didn't want to consider was whether that same phrase described the rest of the relationship, what he and Daysi had together. And now, he couldn't even call to ask. He didn't remember her number, since it was programmed into his phone.

At the squad, he shifted papers on his desk, distractedly played with his computer. He didn't want to work, didn't want to talk to anyone who wasn't Daysi. Whenever the phone on his desk rang, he hesitated before answering, hoping someone else in the office would pick up to screen the call. The delaying tactic bought anxious intervals of twenty minutes or half an hour at a time, until he began to catch annoyed looks from his colleagues. He took the next call on the first ring.

"Detective McCann. Can I help you?"

"Detective McCann, I'm glad I caught you. You've been hard to find!"

"Which McCann? We have several in this office. . . . Would you hold on, please?"

Nick transferred the call over to Garelick, who was not pleased to receive it. Nick stuck with the tactic, the name, when the phone rang again.

"Nick? Is that you?"

It was Daysi. She didn't sound like herself, either.

"Sorry, I've had some crazy person calling me all day."

"I didn't mean to call you here, but your cellphone was off."

Nick thought of what he might say, but it had the same whining sent-to-the-principal's-office tone as "He started it."

"Huh."

"Can we meet? We have to talk."

"Yeah, I know—is everything all right?"

"No . . ."

"Should I come to the shop?"

"No, that's not the best place."

"Where?"

"Come downstairs. I'm here outside. I need to talk to you. Let's take a walk."

Despite his resolution not to speculate, Nick had nonetheless assumed she would be angry at either him or her son, the only two reactions he could conceive at the crossroad. But she sounded frightened and resigned at once, and he didn't understand how she could be both.

"I'll be right down."

It had been an odd winter, with balmy stretches broken by cold snaps, but there had not been any snow. It was still mild, even as the weak sun was setting, but Daysi shivered in her long leather coat, a red silk scarf around her neck. Her lips were cold when they kissed. How long had she waited outside? She took Nick's arm and led him down a few blocks, to 180th Street, before they walked west. She wanted to avoid passing the shop. They were at the river before she clenched his hand again and found the courage to speak. The speech was planned, maybe the scenery, too. The night fell faster this time of year. You could not see beyond the black water; you could not see the black water. You just knew it was there.

"I can't take this, Nick."

God, no, he thought. This was what was coming? Done, was it? Every childish impulse he'd fought for the past hours flooded back, and this time, he did not fight them. He would not go down with dignity.

"It isn't that cold."

"Don't. You're not like that."

"Maybe."

"No, you're not. I've been with you because you're not."

Nick didn't know if she expected him to say something, but he didn't. The news was for her to break, for him to bear.

"The sneaking around, the hotels, it seems so sleazy to me—not sleazy, really, but tired. It was fun, at first. But I'm not a kid. I don't want to be. My mother, she thinks it's beautiful, but Esteban . . . I don't know what he knows about his father, what he thinks, what he thinks he knows. That's the past, you know? And, Nick, I'm glad you never asked. Esteban and his father, I get shit from both of them now. Neither of them has any right. Esteban does. I love him, and I understand why he has a tough time with this. Not his father. It isn't right."

"What does he say?"

"He says, 'My son tells me you're sleeping with the police.' "

Nick wasn't asking about the father.

"Maybe I should talk to him."

He didn't mean that. There was nothing to be said between the Oteguis and the Meehans—the Meehan, the last of them—no bargain to be struck, no middle where they could meet. Daysi paused in uneasy thought before asking for clarification, "Which one would you talk to?"

"Either."

Daysi looked down and shook her head. "Nothing good would come from it."

Nick studied her face. "Are you afraid of him?"

When she smiled, Nick felt a chill; it crossed his mind that this would be the last time he saw it. She shook her head again and looked at him; the smile was gone.

"Why would you think that?"

"Just asking."

She laid her head against his shoulder, clasping his arm. Nick could feel the subject drift away, and he was grateful. But in the silence that followed, Nick knew the subject had passed like the smile, the good with the bad, all of it gone. There was no need for them to go into it, because there was no "them"; she held Nick and began to cry.

"He was arrested at the airport this morning. My husband, my ex-husband. He called from jail, federal jail. It's . . . bad. You can imagine how Esteban's taking it. He thinks you're behind it."

Some blame might reasonably be apportioned to Otegui himself, Nick thought. He had a horrified intuition that she was about to ask him for help, for legal advice, to call someone downtown to see if they might go easy on him. He was wrong. When he heard her, he wished she had.

"I can't do this anymore, Nick. I can't fight all the time. I'm right—we're right—but I can't win."

They held each other, and Nick felt her sobbing, gentle and in diminishing rhythm, like a child who soothes herself to sleep with the sound of her cries. She looked up at him, and in the dark he could see her face glistening. In the dark, he knew she asked for approval, more, as much as release, and if he could not deny the one, he didn't have the strength for the other, his blessing. *Yes, yes, I understand. May the saints of God go with you, and the peace of God be upon you, your rotten kid, and his rotten father and all the rotten money he gives you.* Otegui had gotten rich poisoning his neighbors—Nick's, too—but it would be rude to bring that up. What with the busy funeral trade and all. Awkward, awkward. Mustn't hurt the feelings of the Opium Papi. Nick choked a little at the joke.

Daysi thought he was crying, too, and she stroked his face tenderly. In any light, it would have been hard to tell the grimace from the grin, but here there was nearly none. She felt the choked spasms, two or three before he breathed a little easier, and she pressed her head against his chest. She kissed him again and looked at him. *And in conclusion, I would like to thank everyone for coming here tonight . . .*

"I should go."

Had she said that?

"Will you walk with me?"

Nick shook his head. A last kiss, a long one, and she walked away. Nick did not watch her leave. He walked off the path to sit on the rocks and watch the river, whatever he could see of the river, and the bridge, with the steady chug of after-work traffic, heading west to the missus, home to the kids. In a few minutes, it began to rain, and Nick walked away, too.

THIRTY-FOUR

Nick had no family life, no love life, little social life beyond phone chats with Esposito. It had been some time since he'd gotten any blocked calls. He had been back to full duty for a while, but he had never felt less able or engaged, and the daily satisfactions he'd once taken from work grew increasingly scant and elusive. At least Michael Cole still seemed to want something from him; even so, Nick skipped several appointments with the city lawyer on the Cole lawsuit. There was a dull abundance of little cases, and Nick was abrupt on the phone with complainants, hostile in reaction to the slightest sign of duplicity or evasion, impatient with delay. One of them asked for his case to be reassigned to another detective, and Nick snapped that things don't work that way. Nick was thinking about that, wondering how things did work, when a cop walked into the squad.

"There's a guy downstairs. He says he knows you."

The cop was cautious, young, Spanish.

"He came in to see me, or you locked him up?"

"He's under arrest."

"For what?"

"He beat up three kids. Not kids, teenagers. He says they raped his daughter."

"Did they?"

"She says they didn't. More of a gang-bang type thing. He walked in on it. He beat up the kids, pretty bad. The parents—two out of three, one mother, one father—they're downstairs."

"The kids? Where are they?"

"Hospital."

"The girl?"

"A different hospital, in the Bronx."

"Ah . . . What's the guy's name? I mean the perp?"

"Ivan Lopez. Do you know him? He had your card."

"Bring him up here. I'll talk to him. How bad are the boys hurt?"

"Two are just kinda lumped up. The third, though, he was bare-assed when he tried to jump out the window, onto the fire escape. He broke the window, and I don't know how he managed it, but he cut open his ballsack."

"Ouch. Is it . . . Are they . . ."

"I don't know. I didn't check."

"No, you wouldn't, would you."

Both of them crossed their legs.

"For Lopez, it's assault, right?" the cop asked. "But what about the kids, do I charge them, too? What with?"

"I gotta figure that out. . . . Did you call Special Victims?"

"Yeah. They're all out on something in Harlem, the serial rape. The guy hit again."

That was in the papers again the other day, the case with Esposito's old friends. Almost two dozen victims now, aged twelve to sixty; the perp pretended to be the super's helper, or a plumber there to fix a leak. Nick hated sex cases. They were painfully simple—*My mother's boyfriend, he touched me*—or painfully simple, once removed—*A black man, a stranger, he came through the window when I was sleeping.* These were the worst, because there usually wasn't any strange black man who came through the window. After hours of interview, of reassurance and challenge, the story often went back to the mother's boyfriend. Lieutenant Ortiz fought constantly with the lieutenant at Special Victims—was the chain-snatch with the tit-grab a property crime or a sex crime? Both squads tried to steal the promising, interesting cases and kick the losing propositions back to the other side; there were rules about who was supposed to get what, but they didn't always matter.

Grace was thirteen, below the age of consent, but Nick had to get out the law books to see how the lines were drawn for nonconsenting consenters. A test question from the Police Academy, and he didn't know if he had gotten it right, all those years ago. He rummaged around the office for a copy of the penal law. Here it was, the wisdom of the legislature: If the boys were fifteen, it was an experiment; if they were sixteen, it was a felony.

"How old are they?"

The cop began to flip through his memo book, then nervously closed it.

"I'll have to check with my partner. He's at the hospital. I think the kid who got cut, he was the oldest, seventeen maybe. His mother's downstairs. Should I bring her up?"

"Yeah. No, wait. Bring up Lopez. Mrs. Ballsack can sit tight. We're gonna have to go to the hospital, talk to these kids, get a story. Why is the lady here instead of with her kid?"

"I dunno."

When the cop left, Nick read over the statutes, to see who would end up where, if the story stayed where it was. It made him feel like an amateur, a rookie. Misdemeanor assaults for Lopez on the two kids, but what about the third? Reckless endangerment, probably, another catchall. Rape in the first degree, second degree, third. Look at this—sexual misconduct, which covered dead bodies and animals. Lovely, lovely. The cop brought up Ivan Lopez, who had smears of blood on his shirt.

"Officer! You must help me! They tried to rape my daughter!"

"I understand, Mr. Lopez. Have a seat and we'll figure this out."

Nick hated this, the pinball logic and volcanic emotions, the sticky fluids. He wasn't up on the law, wasn't into the subject. There was a recent case in Texas, where a woman was in bed with another man when her husband walked in. She started to yell that the man was raping her, and the husband shot him. The woman was convicted of manslaughter, recklessly causing the death of another. A fair decision, in an unfair life. Did Grace say anything when her father walked in, or did her look say something to him; did he understand that look in his daughter's eyes, or did he understand it wrong? So many stories to hear, three boys and a girl, a father, and how many mothers, whoever else? The numbers. Ivan Lopez put one and three together, and the math drove him crazy, past caring about consequence. One was too many; three was infinite. Nick thought about all the stories he would hear, and wondered how many of them would be lies.

The cop closed the door of the interview room and locked Lopez inside. He looked at Nick, awaiting instructions. Napolitano and Perez walked over; Garelick waited at his desk, watching to see if there would be a general summons for assistance. Napolitano laughed. "Nick, you want the fuckers or the fuckee?"

Nick was thankful for the offer of help. Would it be enough? It was the kind of thing Esposito sorted out quickly, and Nick missed him.

" 'Want' is not the word."

"I know. Which bit you gonna take?"

"I've dealt with the girl before. I'll talk with her."

"Fine, we'll get the boys. They're all together?"

"Yeah, they are. Nap, would you mind bringing Mrs. Ballsack down there to the hospital with you? And the father of the other one? What's his name, Officer? And what's your name? Never mind. I'll go down and see them. You come with me, to the Bronx. We'll talk to the girl. You drive. I'll tell you where to go. Garelick can stay— Sorry, Garelick. Would you mind watching this guy in the room, while we're out?"

"No problem."

Nick was talking to himself, but no one disagreed. The cop followed him downstairs, and it wasn't hard to spot Mrs. Ballsack hovering at the waiting area, gripping her plastic seat at the edges, letting go and gripping again. There was a row of these seats, red, blue, and yellow, fixed to a steel rail, like in a bus station. Decency, dignity, comfort were to be avoided; people might feel encouraged to stay. Mrs. Ballsack was a heavy woman, in an ankle-length down jacket and slippers, hair in curlers. Night shift or nonworker? When Nick walked into the room, she stood up and walked over, quivering with indignation. He had an idea she'd prepared her opener.

"Do you have children, Detective?"

"Yes, three."

"Boys or girls?"

"One of each."

"How old are they?"

That was enough. Nick had thought he was past caring, but apparently he wasn't, raising a hand to stop the conversation. He almost called her Mrs. Ballsack, which wouldn't have set the right tone. Still, it had to stop.

"Ma'am, this is not about me."

A truer lie was never spoken. She started to cry, turning away, then toward him again, wondering whether to be angry, guessing it would not work.

"Detective, I just, I just . . . He's my only son, and that crazy, that crazy mutha—! That crazy *cabron*, what he did to my baby, he—"

That was a nice word, *"cabron,"* as if Grace had been cheating on her father with the boys.

"Were you there when it happened?"

"Are you crazy? Are you stupid?"

"Ma'am, watch your mouth. How old is your son?"

"How old? What kind of question is—"

"How old is your son?"

"Eighteen, but he's a baby. . . . He's just a baby, and that *animal,* who cut him . . ."

"That animal saw his daughter with three young men. She's thirteen. She is a baby. Eighteen isn't. I know your son was assaulted. I don't know if he committed a rape. How old are the others?"

That was the wrong thing to say, for so many reasons. If it wasn't a rape, it was a terrible accusation. If it was, he shouldn't have warned her. So wrong, all of it, but it shut her up for a second, and that was all he wanted. She shouldn't have asked about his children. Couldn't she count?

Mrs. Ballsack shuddered, then yelled, "My son is not bright! My son is slow! And he went with his friend, this man's son!"

She pointed to a little man in the corner on one of the bus seats, who was with her, up to a point. Nick surmised he did not understand what she said.

"This idiot's son, Enrique, he is fifteen years old! And my son, he knows him from the building, and it's idiot Enrique's idiot friend, Flacco—what's the little shithead's name?—this little prick, he's only fourteen, but he's the one who brings 'em both into it! Some little *puta* from down the block, he says, she'll do 'em all! My son is in a special school. He is a baby. . . ."

She broke down in tears. The little man went over to her and patted her shoulder. Ballsack sobbed to herself, bending over, holding her knees. And then she pushed his tender hands away, and rose up and bellowed, "I want to talk to another detective! This one has no feelin's, no feelin's at all! I wanna 'nother detective to talk to!"

Ballsack spoke for public benefit, playing a part, but her anguish was genuine. Funny how people started to say that, that they wanted someone else to talk to, a more sympathetic ear. This time, Nick would accommodate her.

"Another detective will be down to talk to you."

Nick turned and walked away. When he was outside the precinct, he turned to see if the young cop was still with him. He wasn't sure if he wanted him to pay attention, wasn't sure what he wanted him to take away from all of this. Ugly, all of it ugly. The cop nodded uncertainly and got the car, and Nick sat in the back. He was tired and lay down. Cops don't ride in the back of cop cars; the backseat was for non-equals, prisoners and dignitaries. The young cop seemed confused, unsure whether to take offense. Nick remembered the last time he'd been chauffeured, couldn't guess when the next would be. No point in dwelling on that, at the moment. The cop knew how to get to the hospital in the Bronx, didn't need directions. Nick closed his eyes. They were here.

The doctor had finished her exam, was packaging her samples in a box to give to the cop. The doctor was a slender woman with a brown ponytail, young, probably closer to Grace's age than Nick's. She had a no-nonsense air, brusque but not unkind. Grace was on a bed behind a curtain, five feet away, and Nick and the doctor went to the far side of the emergency room to talk. Filipino nurses and Nigerian doctors shuffled between cardiacs, diabetics, asthmatics.

"How is she, Doctor?"

"Basically, she's fine."

"Really? No trauma?"

"Nothing physical. And emotionally—well, she's pretty matter-of-fact about it. I don't know her social history, her personal situation, aside from a few basics. But she's only really sorry the party was over so soon."

"Not her first time, then?"

"No. She said she slept with one of the boys once before, and there was another boy she slept with three times. There's no symptom of disease, either—she said she always used a condom—but we have to wait for blood work. If she was twenty-three, or thirty-three, I'd say, 'Just be careful,' and walk away. Even though she's only thirteen, I can't think of any other advice. If she was my daughter, I'd chain her up in the basement. I know I'm not supposed to say that. I couldn't say she seems maladjusted, but we'll make a referral for counseling. She's bright. She answers questions directly. She asked me about medical school, how long it would take, how much it would cost. Very self-possessed. She brought her homework with her, so she could keep busy while she waited. She doesn't seem to think much of her father, but that's not really unusual for the age. Do you have something to tell me, something I should know?"

"Not that I can think of, right now."

"How old were the boys?"

"A little older, not much."

"Well, unless there's anything else, I have other patients. Go ahead, talk to her, and please let me know if anything changes."

"Is she decent?"

The doctor laughed as she walked away. "She has her clothes on, if that's what you're asking."

The cop did not follow when Nick went back to Grace, behind her curtain. Nick called out "Hello!" before he pushed the heavy blue polyester drape aside. Grace wore her school uniform, and she sat on the side of her bed, digging through her backpack. Her books were spread out. She straightened her glasses before she looked up, smiling.

"Hi! I remember you!"

"I remember you, too, Grace. How are you?"

"Fine."

She closed the books on the bed, and began to put them into the backpack. Nick waited for her to finish. She sat up properly, as if in class, and waited for him to begin.

"Grace?"

"Yes?"

"What happened today?"

She rolled her eyes and exhaled, brushing her bangs back from her forehead. It seemed like she was being a good sport about things.

"I liked Enrique, and Flacco was his friend. I slept with Enrique once. He dared me to, and I figured, why not? Flacco said Enrique would only come over if I did him too. And the other one, the fat one, I felt sorry for him. He couldn't really get it up. And that's when he came home, my father. . . . I feel bad, how they got beat up . . ."

"None of them made you do anything? Did any of them hit you, or hold you down? Did they threaten you?"

"No."

"Did you ever tell them to stop, or want them to stop?"

"I got tired of the fat one after a while, but he was tryin'. Flacco laughed at him. That was mean."

"That's not what I meant. Were you ever afraid?"

Grace looked down and said, "Yeah . . ."

"When?"

"When my father came home."

"I didn't mean that, Grace. Did your father ever do anything to you, anything that ever made you uncomfortable?"

"All the time!"

"Like what?"

"Any time I see him!" She rolled her eyes, and let out a harsh laugh.

"I don't mean that, Grace, and I think you know that. You're very grown-up, and so I know I can talk to you like a grown-up. I'm asking if your father ever touched you, or ever did anything sexual to you."

"That's disgusting!"

All of a sudden, she was a child again. She stuck her tongue out, then pretended to throw up. She packed up the rest of her books, shaking her head.

"How about your mother, Grace?"

That stopped her, but only for a moment. She looked ahead, at no one, gathering her thoughts. She zipped her book bag shut and faced Nick.

"She's dead."

"I'm sorry. My mother died, too. I was young. I was your age. It was bad."

Grace looked at him, intrigued by the confidence. For a moment, Nick felt like he was lying, as he had about his babies half an hour before, saying what was useful. Grace's rueful half-smile of understanding reminded him that he had not lied.

"Sucks, doesn't it? A real shit sandwich."

Nick laughed. It was the perfect thing, the only thing to say. She knew what it was like. When was the last time he'd really talked to anyone? And the only one who understood, truly, right now, was the hostess of a juvenile gang bang. Grace raised her eyebrows, rolled her eyes. She shrugged. Nick knew the shrug.

"Nobody gets it," he went on, not altogether for her benefit. "You know what I mean?"

"Nobody."

"My mother died of cancer. How did yours die?"

"She didn't kill herself."

The hardness in her voice was unexpected, as was the direction the talk had taken. She had strayed from the shared grief, and he had to follow, at a polite distance. The conversation became an interview again, and Nick was sad for the loss of a companion, almost a friend. He regretted that he had to step back to his old role, as the nonjudgmental elder. It was a bore. He was afraid he would lose her, but he had to fall back to it, asking for what came next.

"I didn't say she did. Who says that?"

"My father . . . He said it, not to me. It was on the phone with somebody, but I was listening. She didn't. And she didn't love him. I don't even know if he's my father. My mom said he was, but she only said that when we came back to live with him. When she was sick. She wanted to die, she told me she did, and when she was in the hospital in the end, she told me to help, but I wouldn't. . . ."

A child again, crying and pushing her backpack over, crying for a full minute, two, then stopping all of a sudden. She wiped her nose clean with the whole of her skinny little arm, then looked at the snot, and made a face. She wiped the arm with the heavy blue curtain. Nick wanted to offer her something, but he wasn't sure whether it should be a teddy bear or a cigarette.

"Do you have a dog, Grace? Did you ever?"

"No. Why?"

He didn't know why. He hadn't believed her father when he'd said that he had a dog, but Nick was suddenly, strongly interested in the real reasons why Lopez had been in the park. That had been only months ago, but it seemed like ages. After all the failures of containment, the stories that spread like diseases, Nick had become less respectful of mysteries and boundaries. His new impatience had begun to work through other parts of his system, and it would have made him a better detective, had he a heart to match his cold curiosity. He wanted to know more, in case it made him care, even as he suspected it would not.

"I don't know, maybe a dog would be good company for you. . . . They're very loyal. . . . What was your mother sick with?"

"She had AIDS. She hooked up a lot, and she never used a condom. She had a hysterectomy after me, so she knew she couldn't get pregnant. I'm not like that. I'm careful. Believe me, I know how it is out there. Can we go home now? I have social studies and math homework left to do."

Nick was put off by the affectation of hard-won bar-whore wisdom, but he was impressed how she had recovered herself, had become practical and self-possessed again. He was unsure whether he was touched more by the tumult and justice of her tears, or by how she could stop crying and get back to work. He had forgotten to take her picture off his desk; maybe he would keep it there for a while. She slipped off the bed and hoisted the backpack onto her shoulders.

"All right, Grace, we can go. We'll take you. But what you did today? Please don't do that anymore. You could get sick or pregnant."

"I always use condoms."

"Well, that's good, I guess. But you could get hurt. Boys are stupid enough as they are, but when they're in groups, they're the worst things in the world. And a lot of people, they wouldn't treat you the same because of it. That may not be fair, but it's how it is. Did you tell anyone about being with boys before?"

"I was going to tell Sister, at school tomorrow. She's strict, but she's nice. She likes me, and I can talk to her."

"Let's hold off on that. Ready? Ready to go?"

"Yep."

"Come on, then."

On the drive home, Nick sat in the front. He didn't want to talk to Grace anymore, though whether it was because of her dark side, her bright side, or her freak side, he didn't know, and he didn't want to think about it. Nick called Napolitano, who said the boys at the hospital were fine. Scrapes, bruises, cuts. Even Ballsack wasn't so bad, just a couple of stitches, nothing permanent. His mother was still aggravated, mouthing off, until Napolitano explained what "cross-complainants" meant, and sex offender registries.

"Nick, I think we got it wrapped up here, as long as you can handle the father," Napolitano said. "He could still press charges against the older kid. He's not even too slow, like the mother keeps saying he is. He's just a little soft. His mother babies him. He got picked on at school, so she got him put in special ed. But he'll get locked up, if we don't square it away. How's the little hoochie?"

"She's fine. We're dropping her off in a minute. I'll talk to the guy, see what we can do. Keep 'em there. I'll let you know."

"Ten-four."

Nick asked the cop to stop around the corner from the address Grace had given. Dyckman Street, south of the park. Just a few blocks from where he lived; he was appreciative again of the privacies of city life, how you never knew anyone, if you played it right. Nick didn't want to draw attention to Grace, having her step out of a cop car in front of her house. When they arrived, he got out and opened the door for her. She fixed her glasses and hair, laboring under her backpack, and smiled as she walked away. Nick got back into the car and didn't say anything until they returned to the precinct. The young cop called over to him as Nick walked up the stairs, and Nick felt bad about his rude indifference to him over the past hour.

"Hey, Detective! All this work, all this running around—for nothing?"

"At best. I hope so. I'll let you know."

When Nick got back to the interview room, Ivan Lopez leapt up and tried to hug him. Nick pushed him away. Nick sat down on one side of the table and pointed to the far chair. Lopez began to protest, but he sat down. Nick told him he had to stop lying. Lopez became angry, yelling about the defense of honor, the defense of children, and Nick told him to shut up. Nick asked whether he had a dog. Lopez said that he never had one, had never said he did. Nick slapped him across the face. Lopez stood up and said he would sue, sue Nick's family, take everything away from Nick's children. They would have nothing when he was done. Nick slapped him again. Lopez started to cry, and Nick moved in close to him, saying Lopez had to tell him everything. *Everything?* Everything. How it had happened, with the mother. More tears, and Nick raised his hand again, then waited. He wasn't good with women, Lopez said. He had a brother, an older brother. He was dead now. The brother was with two friends. They knew a girl. They were drinking together, they could call the girl for Lopez. They went to the park, to Inwood Park. It was summer, and they drank together with the girl. Lopez drank a lot. He didn't know if they paid the girl or they dared her. Maybe both, a little of both, but it started good. They kissed, they started. He'd never done it before, and it felt great, and his brother and the other two cheered him on. And then she said she felt sick and wanted to stop, and he got mad, and the boys laughed at how he got mad. They held her down, and he finished. Then he got sick, too, rolling off her to throw up. His brother and his friends helped him home. He didn't see the girl again for a couple of months. Then he heard she was pregnant. He looked for her, and when he found her, she slapped him.

Lopez looked up at Nick, crying, to see if he was going to hit him again, too. Nick didn't.

"How do you know she's your kid?"

"I just know."

Maybe he did. It didn't matter. Nick had demanded to know more, and now he wanted to know less. He didn't want to know why Lopez walked in the park, what he wanted to remember, whether it was penance or pornography. Old times, old times. There was no reason, only rhyme. Nick told Lopez that they should all forget what happened today, that if he didn't press charges, none would be pressed against him. Lopez agreed. Nick left the room and called Napolitano, telling him that everyone could go home.

THIRTY-FIVE

Esposito was due back on Valentine's Day. All the predictable jokes were made about who would buy chocolates, where he and Nick would go for a romantic dinner. It was part of the ordinary back-and-forth of the Job, the guy-world of men paired, nearly literally, at the hip. Perez started on about buying roses, until Garelick glared at him, and Perez realized he might have trespassed into genuinely sensitive territory. Nick didn't hold it against him. As for Esposito, Nick had missed him for his own sake, but also because as one bad turn had followed another in those cold, dry months, Nick had come to believe in Esposito as a talisman, who would bring back warmth to the days, awaken the earth with rain. As for himself, Nick wasn't sure whether the other detectives saw him as someone under a dark cloud or as the cloud itself. He was eager for Esposito's return, and supposed Valentine's was more auspicious than April Fools'.

Luck was something not discussed around Nick. Napolitano had two stabbings in a row in which the perp dropped his wallet at the scene, leaving his photo ID in each case. He crowed that this was the kind of thing that happened to Esposito, but when Nick agreed, laughing, Napolitano turned away too quickly, as if the contrast were too painful to witness. Nick went out with Garelick to a DOA in a single room, an old man whose only company was a listless goldfish. When Nick picked up a gluey tube of medication to identify his ailments, he saw the instruction, "Apply twice daily to lesions," and flung it away. He scrubbed his hands until they nearly bled. When he tried to shake a few flakes of food into the fishbowl, the top popped off the container, burying the goldfish beneath a crust of crap. The fish didn't seem hungry. Garelick picked up the bowl and walked to the back, and Nick heard a toilet flush.

When the brick from the rooftop missed Nick's head by three feet, and Lieutenant Ortiz's by ten—the lieutenant had come out with Nick on a case, in a clumsily touching effort to probe for suicidal tendencies—Nick doubted the brick-chucker had intended him as the target. Whatever the circumstance, the lieutenant was satisfied by the scramble back to the car—dignity diminished but skull intact—that Nick's will to live remained avid. On the ride there, the lieutenant had asked him how he was feeling, had assured him he could call whenever, if he needed to talk. It was not the kind of conversation for which he had much aptitude, and Nick respected the effort, despite the odd tone of precondolence. Was that a word? On the ride back, the lieutenant shifted in his seat and looked out at the sky, as if the weather threatened lightning.

They had been right to worry about him. Nick had begun to try on the idea of not being there, and it fit him like a bespoke suit—the feel of it, the look, were unexpectedly becoming. He stared into the mirror and imagined no reflection; he liked what he saw. Not quite, not yet. Nick didn't want to kill himself, as such; he just didn't want to live. He was held in check to some degree by the taboo of it, but more because of a fussiness and laziness in dealing with the practicalities, and he put it off, like taxes.

The walk to City Island had ruled out cold water, and hanging had a copycat aspect after Maria Fonseca. He decided against the apartment, on the admittedly ironic terms that it was too depressing even for suicide. Days after, he would be reported as a foul odor and found in a bunk bed. The gun was obvious. That was the cop's way. It was always right there. That was that, then; the other details he could determine at leisure, or not. The sense of outright self-dominion was a novelty for Nick, and it pleased him, as did the irony of the inspiration, the little lamp of black light burning in the window. As he'd discovered with the recent interrogation of Ivan Lopez, he could accomplish more when he cared less.

This newly ruthless spirit of investigation prompted Nick to visit Michael Cole. Michael had also undergone a transformation, had become someone else. It would be good if they could talk. Could Michael explain his own causes and origins, his influences and metamorphic leaps? People could change, and maybe Nick hoped they could change more than once. He didn't see the harm in asking, or rather he was not troubled by the possibility of harm. And Nick was not motivated by curiosity alone. It would have made more sense had his concern been clinical, a desire only to capture a glimpse of something that he did not understand. But there was also a muddy impulse to make amends, in a vaguely twelve-step, check-the-box fashion. The impulse was not religious, in that his religion was not vague on the matter. There were no loopholes for contingencies, no points for saying you were sorry in advance. Killing yourself was the worst thing you could do, and you shouldn't do it. Nick was in a strange state, persisting in the idea that the answer could change the question. He was a missionary without a mission.

Nick wanted to say hello to Michael, say he was sorry, see what there was to be seen. He never thought that deep amends were owed Michael, on his own account; Nick had assisted in the delivery of tragic misinformation, but it had been wholly a homegrown, homemade catastrophe. Nick would apologize, but he wanted Michael to understand, for both to benefit from the larger perspective. He knew it was a stupid idea as soon as he knocked on the door. Michael would not explain himself like an exhibit in a museum. What were the missing museums again—Indians, coins, explorers, what else?

"Who?"

"Hello?"

A woman answered, older-seeming than Nick but probably not, hard-worn and maybe half-drunk. Her sour breath extended past the threshold, and she wore a new bathrobe of thick blue fluff, the price tag sticking out the neck, that made her seem bonier, the worse for wear. Because Nick disliked her instantly, he strained to be polite, appear interested, and she caught him in his effort. She looked at him as if he were a door-to-door salesman, shifty and shoddy. Which was only half-true, at best. And who was she to talk?

"What you want?"

"Is Michael here?"

"No. You police?"

"Yeah."

"What you want with Michael?"

"Just to talk with him."

"Yeah, right. When you people just wanna talk, people end up dead, in jail. You got a card? I'll let him know. . . ."

The request for paperwork made Nick realize his other mistake in visiting. There was litigation pending between him and the family, which would drag on for years. It would not be wise to document his interference. And then he smiled. Even as he was entertaining thoughts of annihilation, he was still afraid of a lawsuit, as if they'd dig up his bones to put them under oath.

The woman mistrusted Nick's smile as he shook his head, turned away. "He knows who I am."

A few nights later, as he was heading home, going up the stairs to his apartment lobby, a gunshot chipped the sidewalk. When the shot hit, Nick stopped for a moment. Yes, he does know who I am. A few pigeons lifted off from nearby roosts, wing tips softly flapping like polite applause; they were disturbed, but not much. Nick was nearly calm. He almost wanted to wave or give Michael the finger, but he resisted the instinct. He unhurriedly put his key in the lobby door and went in. Inside the apartment, he went to the kitchen, poured a glass of water, and sat down at the table. He took out his phone but hesitated before calling 911, savoring the company of his new problem. It was a good one: Could he be sure it was Michael? An assumption about a Cole brother was what had begun this whole crazy game. It had been far more obvious that Malcolm had been shot in the projects that night. There had even been evidence of it, with the ID. By comparison, this was sheer intuition, and Nick didn't place much faith in his instincts of late. It was not as if he couldn't have set extraordinary efforts in motion, by informing superiors that a fanatic had dedicated himself to the assassination of a New York City police officer. Maybe Michael was the one who'd graffitied "G-Had" in the lobby. A guaranteed attention-getter, that one was.

But only attention was guaranteed. A reaction did not mean a result, at least as desired. Nick could not control events, could not predict the consequences. There would be a big fuss, yes, but the only certain outcome would be that he would have to leave the apartment. The proof problems with this shooting were the same as with Michael's attack at Miguelito's funeral. Even if everyone knew, no one had seen, no one could say. Moving out was inevitable. The risk would be reduced, and the rule about living where you worked would be enforced. Nick wanted change in his life, but moving promised only headache, the same depression at five times the expense. He did not need new furniture, a view of another alley. Something would break soon, and it might not be him. Esposito would be back at work tomorrow; he would know what to do.

The strangest part was that Nick was grateful for the blundering ambush. He was flattered by it, in that Michael was one of the few people Nick could think of who thought he mattered very much. His first thought was that Michael knew what Nick wanted, wanted to help—*Penny for your thoughts?*—and his second was how funny it was to think so. His third thought was that he was glad Michael had missed. He had been tempted, tested; for now, with help, he had passed. An enemy had given him purpose, when friends and family had failed. Michael had made life interesting again. After that night, Nick took to coming and going through the alleyways behind the building, never through the front door. He would tell Esposito. Esposito would know what to do.

Esposito was greeted with cheers when he came back to the squad. Everyone stood and gathered around for handshakes and backslaps; he did a bounce-step from leg to leg to show he was fully healed, whole and ready. He looked better than before. He had lost weight and wore a new suit, a gray pinstripe; he had an eager, almost belligerent grin that sought to banish whatever doubts there might be about his fitness beyond the physical. Lieutenant Ortiz looked at him fondly, then peeked over to Nick with surreptitious hope. With the alpha here, the pariah might return to normal, and the pack would be restored to balance. The mood of festive relief lasted five minutes. Esposito sat down at his desk, and when he stood up, there was gum stuck to the seat of his new suit.

"Shit! Dammit! Who's the slob who did this?"

The guys crowded around as if he'd been hurt again, remembering it, maybe, or just chagrined that the homecoming had been spoiled.

"Ah, what a shame!"

"Alcohol will get that out."

"A new suit, too. What a pain."

"Ice works, too, I heard."

"All right, all right, enough already," said Esposito, shaking off his moment of pique. The attention was a little much, even for him. "Everybody, stop staring at my ass. What works? Alcohol and ice? Hmm . . . Can you think of a place where we can get both?"

He looked over to Lieutenant Ortiz, who waved him away. "Espo, take your partner and go out and get drunk. We'll hold down the fort. No sense in jumping right back in."

"You sure?"

"That's an order."

"Then, you won't have to tell me twice. Let's hit it, Nick."

Esposito picked up his overcoat with one hand and grabbed Nick's arm with the other, leading him out the door. "Good to be back, guys. Great to see you all."

They drove down Broadway to Coogan's. It was mid-afternoon, chilly, the sky pale and papery, and the darkness of the pub was consoling. When Esposito headed toward the bar, Nick steered him to a distant table in the dining room; there was a modest crowd at the bar, men alone and in pairs, predawn shift workers from the construction trades and casual alcoholics, opinions at the ready, anxious to share. Nick didn't know what he wanted to say, but he didn't want anyone to hear it. Esposito took a pint glass of ice and a tumbler of vodka into the bathroom, returning after five minutes. Passing waitresses were enlisted to examine the results of the cleanup. One suggested peanut butter. Another brushed his seat with her fingertips, then gave it a cheerful slap.

"Looks shipshape to me," she said.

"God bless your family," he called after her, watching as she walked away. He turned to Nick and smiled. "I'm back." He raised a glass, and Nick tipped his. *Tink.* The smile did not leave Esposito's face when he asked, "Are you?"

"I never left."

"Sure you did, Nicky boy."

"Yeah."

"What is it, your father?"

"Yeah."

"And your wife?"

"Yeah."

"And Daysi?"

"Yeah."

"That's bad about her, that's tough. Her kid, though—what else is she gonna do, you know? Family comes first."

"Are you kidding me?"

"What?"

The waitress was near—too near—and Esposito made a little circle in the air. *Same again.* He called after, "Plus whiskey! Two each! Irish!" He patted Nick on the shoulder, and they did not talk again until the drinks were delivered.

"Are you okay, Nick?"

"You're an Esposito."

"What?"

"Esposito, D'Amico, Donodeo. All of the names, I told you about. I got one now. The 'family comes first' thing—I'm an only child, I have no children, my parents are dead, and I'm in the middle of a divorce. It's not an outlook that does a lot for me. What's the Irish version of the name, O'Nobody?"

Esposito pursed his lips and considered. He raised his glass, and they drank.

"Sorry, pal. I guess I could have put it another way. But what's done is done. Your father, God rest him. Your wife? You know better than me, but it sounds like that's done, too. If you wanted to be with her, you'd be with her. You know where she lives. You could fight this, but you ain't fightin'. Past is past. But Daysi? Not past, not done, not in the hands of God. Your hands, and you still got a fighting chance there, Nick. Now that the ex is out of the way. What's he facing, ten years, at least?"

"Is it ten?"

Nick had avoided learning any of the particulars, but he surmised that an airport grab by the Feds was not for a misdemeanor. "Did you have a hand in that?" Esposito hesitated before he said no, and then realized the one word would not be sufficient. "No. The short answer is no. I didn't slip a bag of dope into his pocket before he got on the plane. But you and me both know how this works, Nick. Old files fall by the wayside, cases get dusty, warrants get accidentally deleted from the computer. Maybe by my asking around about it, making a couple of calls, it was brought up to date."

Nick considered the admission. He didn't like Esposito's intrusion, but it had been minimal and honest, a legitimate fix to a glitch in the system. Otegui's arrest had finished the relationship with Daysi, but the alternatives were worse. What if he'd arrived safely, what then? Would he have told Daysi she had to go back with him? Would he have tried to force her? He hadn't flown up to have a man-to-man with Nick, to tell him he'd better take good care of her, to be supportive and listen to her needs. No, Nick decided, there were no options but an ending, and this end was less bloody than the others. When he nodded, Esposito sighed with relief.

"I don't think you should just write it off, anyway. Give it a little time. Then check back in with her again. The snot-nose kid, he's still gonna be in the picture, but you're never gonna catch a break with teenagers anyway."

"No."

"Not even RJ. Boy, I know I'm in for a rough five years with him, maybe ten."

"No."

"You gotta get something out of this, Nick. You always do. You gotta."

"No. That's you, Espo, that's your line."

The eyebrows went up, alert to the possibility that the remark carried a hint of accusation; they descended again, in sympathy. Nick didn't like that either, but he knew he ought to take whatever he could.

"Yeah. It's my line," he said, "But you can borrow it anytime. Anything else going on, Nick? Not that you need any other reason, to be pissed off at the world."

"Matter of fact, there is. It doesn't bother me too much. It probably should. . . . Anyway, I figured I'd tell you when I saw you."

THIRTY-SIX

They were at Rikers Island within the hour. Esposito drove with one hand and held the phone in the other, not yelling, but his voice rising in volume from the brusque introduction—"Yes, this is Detective Esposito."—to subsequent demands to get to a boss, then dropping back down to sweet talk for the next round of secretaries. "Honey, don't I know you? Listen, you gotta do me a favor, it's important. . . ." All the hustle-muscles that had lain slack and fat for the past months came alive as if they'd trained for the moment. He made arrangements and rearrangements, talked his way past gates. It was late in the day for visitors, late in the day for unscheduled inmate movements. After months of neglect, Malcolm was not happy. He'd learned that Esposito had been out with an injury, but it was of small consolation. He had plans of his own. Like most informants, he saw himself as a partner more than an underling, and to be ordered here to answer demands had broken the illusion. No more covert ops and coded messages; this was a yank of the leash. He shot Nick a brief, baleful glance, reverting to his old role, as if Malcolm were still outside, king of the corner, and Nick was the dull constable ambling by. Nick couldn't say he liked the sight of him, either. Esposito did not trouble with any of the familiar banter.

"Malcolm, what's up with your brother?"

"Nothin'."

"No, not nothing."

"Like I said before, he don't visit, and I can't."

"What do you hear?"

"That he wants to kill y'all."

"Us? Me and my partner? Or any cop?"

"I can't say." He shrugged. "My guess, he has his preference, but he'd settle."

"Your brother could get killed for that, Malcolm."

Malcolm nodded, pulling on his lower lip; the gesture seemed more playful than pensive. "You know, that would bother me, and I'm sure it'd bother you both, him bein' so young. . . ."

Malcolm paused and looked at them, one then the other, as if they might want to take advantage of the break to offer condolences after his dry little elegy. He smiled when they said nothing, having put their pretensions to rest. "But it wouldn't bother Michael. It would not bother Michael one bit."

"He get religion?"

"He's playin' with it, I hear."

"Is he talking to anybody? Arabs? Is he connected to anything? Is he getting money?"

Malcolm laughed. "Like I said, I don't know. How am I gonna, in here? In here, somebody says they're Muslim, they don't go to court on Friday. Then they go back to Jesus when there's bacon Sunday morning. Muslim, Spider-Man, he just wants to be somebody else. My sister says he's on the Internet, lookin' up shit. When she comes in the room, he screams like he got caught jerkin' off, but he ain't. He don't go out much, barely at all. You know, the Dominicans, they only got to see him to kill him. Only, he got no place else to go.

"Anyway, the only Muslims I know, the Africans down the hall in the apartment building, all the girls got the sheets on their heads, all of that, they don't talk to nobody but other Africans. And Nation of Islam people, 'cross the way—You know them, right?—they got chased out, when they set up a fish restaurant and everybody got sick. And there's a guy on the corner sometimes, what's his name—Papa Israel, yeah—he's crazy. He says we're a lost tribe. He go down to the Deuce to scream at white folk, now and then. The Deuce, Forty-second Street, you know what I'm talkin' about? Yeah. I dunno if he says we're Jews or Muslims. I think maybe both. Even crazy Michael knows he's crazy. He wouldn't talk to him, not like that. But Michael—he's his own lost tribe. Who can say what's goin' on there, outside? People get funny ideas."

"What's your ideas, Malcolm? Are they funny?"

"Nothin' funny about jail. I think about gettin' out."

"That's good to think about. You will get out."

"When I'm old."

"Not too old."

"Old."

Malcolm had talked his way back from under the table to the other side of it; he was a partner again.

"I'm a convicted felon with a murder beef. What you gonna do for me, get me eighteen instead of twenty? Or you gonna pull strings on the inside, hook me up with double scoops of mashed potatoes? Get me to the front of the line, pizza night?"

"You talk about pizza and mashed potatoes. Then you talk about two years like it's nothing," offered Esposito, knitting his fingers, then gripping the sides of his chair, sliding it closer. "I never talked about years, about numbers. What are we talking about, Malcolm? What are you looking for? You want us to keep working together? You want to keep talking to me?"

Malcolm slid closer, too, on his own chair. "If I didn't, I wouldn't."

"Can you control your brother?"

Malcolm raised his hands, slid back, and smiled. "Yeah. But I couldn't even try, in here."

"What you thinkin', Mal?"

That might not have been his nickname, but Esposito had decided to make it one, his own. A new name, for the new circumstance. Again, there was no pretense of friendship, but neither was there anger in the question.

"Are you thinkin', or just playin' games?" Esposito asked.

"I think. I got time to think. I do it better now. All I needed was the practice!"

Malcolm backed up in his chair and examined his fingernails. The detectives waited for him to finish. "My lawyer said all you got against me is the tape, with my confession."

"Your lawyer might be right."

"He said if you didn't have the tape, I'd be a free man."

"Your lawyer might be right."

"Yeah. So?"

"Like the country music says, freedom ain't free."

"Don't piss me off with country shit, Espo. I know you don't listen to it, either. I see you as, what, a Sinatra guy?"

"Everybody loves Sinatra."

"Not me."

Esposito and Malcolm leaned in close together, and spoke in hushed tones. Nick stood up and walked around, mumbling what he remembered from the song. "I got the world on a string . . ."

"You want me to kill my own brother?"

That stopped Nick's breath, and his memory of the rest of the song went with it. He reached for the next few lines. "Sittin' on a rainbow . . ." No. This was not right. Another song. "Fly me to the moon, let me— Da!—upon the stars, something, something, something, Jupiter and Mars . . . In other words, hold my hand . . ."

"I could never ask anybody for that, Mal. But if you was to get out, it would be to take care of him. Take care of this. If all it takes is talking, talk. Think about it. Practice—for a week! That's the next court date, right? Maybe the tape can get lost. But lost things can always be found, if I gotta look. And I can make sure that they're found, even if me or Nick aren't around to do it. Especially if we're not, me or him."

Esposito extended his hand, and Malcolm took it. Esposito held on.

"Malcolm, I want you to know that I'm taking a risk."

Nick began to sing louder, in fear of hidden recorders, but also in disbelief of hearing what was being said. "In other words, darling, kiss me . . ."

"Me, too. I'm taking a risk," Malcolm said.

"No. You're not. You're an inmate lookin' at freedom. I'm a cop lookin' at jail. Not the same, not even close. It's the opposite. I want this on top. Look at this as the interest, or look at it as a show of good faith. Gimme three more, three more homicides, guys who got bodies we don't know nothin' about. Find out, work it. I know you can. I believe in you."

Esposito started to release his hand, but now Malcolm held on.

"Jail ain't all I'm looking at. Every time I talk to you, my ass is on the line. I could wake up with my balls cut off, somebody sees me. Forget about what they hear. Somebody hears, it's over. I don't wake up. That's snitching on strangers. Friends is worse. For that, they'd have some kinda party. I'd be the food. A brother? I don't think they invented what they'd do to me. So I'm glad you believe in me, and we got a deal, but don't give me any bullshit about risk."

In other words, please be true.

There was no singing on the way back, not much talking, either. Nick hadn't asked for this, and would have had no part in it, had he known how it would end. Did he know how it would end? Of course not, no. It had just begun. They had just leapt from the cliff. The bottom was far enough away for anything to happen. The law of gravity could be repealed before they were halfway down. It had been repealed. It was as if Esposito had cut the ground from beneath them and they'd been tossed loose from the earth, riding a meteor. Nick played the day in reverse. They should have stayed in the bar. They should have never gone in. He should have checked for gum on the seat. Should he have told Esposito about Michael? Of course, he'd had to tell him. What had he asked for? Nick had prayed for something to happen, a wish cast upon the waters. The prayers had been answered by the wrong god. Ellegua, maybe. He was known for playing tricks. It had been a while since he'd been in touch.

Nick knew Esposito meant to deliver on his promise, knew that this mad gambit had been undertaken on his behalf. He also knew that his partner was not entirely altruistic in his motives. He had been sidelined for months, and he wanted to get back into the game, to play it as it had never been played. He wanted to impress himself—Nick, too, as an audience of one—in full knowledge that the story could never be shared, the subject never discussed. That was the sad part, for Esposito, that this olympiad would be entirely underground, and if there were tokens of victory in any sheen—bronze, silver, gold—they would be buried in order of importance, deep, deeper, deepest.

"How's the kids?"

"Good. Great. They ask about you all the time. I lie to them, say you're doing fine."

Esposito saw through the ploy, and he didn't even try to ally Nick to his present course. He didn't need reminding that he had children—three of them, all alive—that he knew were bound to him, in whatever choice he made, in the near or far consequences of this hour. He took joy in this life, in the burdens and risks, joy that Nick might never know. Nick's own lost tribe, the three little girls, splashed in the shallows of the soft gray waters of limbo.

"How would you get the tapes?"

"They don't even make extra copies, unless somebody asks. The original's in storage. Maybe the defense lawyer has one, but he's not gonna give it up. I asked for one because of my well-known dedication and pro-fessionalism. So I have one, too. That's not a problem. It's insurance."

"It is a problem."

"Nah, it happens. C'mon. It happened last week! Didja read the pa-pers—with the dentist's wife, the hit man? You know how this goes. Two or three more times, they'll make a new procedure. 'Hey, why not make extra copies!' "

"It's a problem."

"Try harder. Tell me another one."

Esposito warmed to the challenge as they fell into their old roles, devil's advocate and—what? Nick didn't want to think about that. He had to think. This was not the adversarial system, not as he was accus-tomed to it. Not the friendship business, either, not one in which he was ready to invest. Malcolm would have said anything to stay out of jail. He'd already tried. How would it shake up Esposito, if he knew that Malcolm had called IAB, had said Esposito had tried to kill him, once upon a time? But there was no way for Nick to say that, without reveal-ing how he knew.

"You're already on the radar with IAB—more than that. They're gun-ning for you. A homicide case goes south, in a shady way. You don't think that won't bring attention, won't make 'em try harder? Won't they see something going on?"

Esposito laughed, too loudly.

"Number one, I'm the only reason Malcolm got locked up. It was never much of a case, and without me, it woulda never got this far. Why would I be the one to wreck it? Number two, it's a ghetto homicide, perp-on-perp, and nobody gives a shit. Three, it'll look like the DA's mistake, not the cops', and the DA and the cops are not gonna cooperate when they can point fingers at each other. Four, if IAB ever had anything on me, anything close to something, I'd be in a rubber-gun squad some-where already, delivering the baloney sandwiches at Central Booking. The Job doesn't have to be fair, doesn't even have to pretend to be. I don't know why the rats have it in for me, whoever it is at IAB, but I bet he never caught a real bad guy before, and he ain't gonna catch me. Because I'm not the bad guy! What else you got, Nick? C'mon, bring it on!"

Nick resolved not to let his jaw go slack at the summation, shrewd and rousing at once, the tack-sharp point-by-point rejoinder of fact, and the canny, roving, worldly-wise grasp of the politics at the far end of the island. Wasn't Lena the lawyer in the family? Didn't Nick have something to contribute here? Maybe a care package, with warm mittens and homemade cookies, vitamins, for his best friend, who was heading upstate, farther north than his usual destination. And who was inviting him to come along with him.

"Witnesses. Two witnesses to the statement."

"Try harder, Nick. The video guy won't remember. He's done a hundred of these since. He turns on the camera and thinks about lunch. The DA maybe, maybe not. This one practically had pneumonia. She barely remembered her name. And lawyers don't like to put their own people on the stand. Yeah, they could put me on the stand, and I'd say what Malcolm said. It wouldn't mean shit. Try harder, Nick! Records of visits here, to Rikers? I talk to everybody who'll talk to me, every bad guy who might do us some good. I didn't create the situation, but I will take advantage. That's my job. Yours, too!

"But with the tape gone, the case is down the toilet," Esposito continued. "The whole thing would stink to a jury. Either we look like mongoloids or it's all some kind of superconspiracy, Elvis lives and 9/11 and Area 51 all wrapped up into one. It won't float. Us—the DA—we lose cases all the time, even when we're trying our hardest, when we think we got everything nailed tight. Let's let the system break down to our advantage, for once."

"Breakdown," that was the word, Nick thought. Michael had saved him, in a way, and now Esposito might ruin him. He had been used to being part of the system; he hadn't thought of himself as such, a cog on a wheel, but he was a semi-significant functionary of a massive governmental organization. In the past, he had been frustrated by what it couldn't accomplish. What would it be like to fear what it could? He was not ready to learn. After he shook his head, Esposito continued soothingly.

"You weren't wrong to hold back and wait for me, Nick. Nothing could have happened to Michael aside from an interview, if you'd called it in right then. What does he say? 'Fuck you and goodbye.' And you woulda been gone, from your house. You know that. They woulda asked Allison if you lived with her, and she woulda said no, and you woulda been 'Out of residence during sick leave.' Guys get twenty-, thirty-day hits for that. 'Failure to report change of residence,' another ten days. You know why? The brass have to do something. They have to act like they did. And they pick the problem they can solve. The precinct, too. They'd never let you stay. Maybe you'll land back at the old place in the Bronx, where your old sergeant stole your best case for his buddy. Either that or they'd take your gun and send you to Psych Services, for not reporting it right away. The government, the police department, is not your friend. I am."

Esposito was his friend. He knew that. Nick hadn't betrayed him, even in a friendship born of betrayal, arranged in advance. Nick wouldn't go to hell for what he'd done so far. Not for that, not that circle, the lowest one, where the traitor Judas was locked in ice. Judas was a suicide, too, the one unforgivable sin. Which stop was on Judas's ticket, suicide or betrayal, when he took the downtown line to the terminal station? Enough, enough. Nick wanted to get off the train. He'd been assigned to Esposito because someone was convinced of his textbook corruption, the classic dirty cop stuff of finger wagging editorials. *A disgrace to the badge.* And even though Nick had witnessed vanity and arrogance, raw appetites and rough hands, nothing had come close to a real crime until Nick had inspired him to commit one.

"Don't do it, Espo. Not for me, not at all."

Esposito's tone was calming and adult, with a kind of bemused understanding—the bedtime story was frightening, yes, but he'd be in the next room if Nick had a bad dream. "Worse guys than Malcolm have gotten bigger breaks. Look what the Feds do for mob rats. Sammy the Bull. What was it, nineteen murders? And he did less than five years. Malcolm's done a couple of months already. I'm not waiting for somebody to die—me or you, especially—while the lawyers hash it out. Don't worry. Don't think about it. I got this."

Esposito laughed and patted him on the shoulder. The emptiness of whatever objection Nick might make was plain to both of them. Nick couldn't play father to the child, refusing to sign a permission slip for a school trip to an amusement park. Nick could do nothing to stop him. Esposito would have fun. Nick had been troubled lately by the sense that his life was not in his hands, and he had played with the idea of giving up, giving in. The sidewalk potshot had ended the game, had made real the possibility of extinction, and Nick had tightened his grip. He was not ready to cede control to an ad hoc committee of his partner and the Cole brothers. He didn't need his life to be that interesting.

It wasn't late when they got back, but Esposito drove straight to the apartment, slowing down a moment, then circling the block again. He pulled over and looked at the opposite side of the street, scanning the roofline, and waited for Nick to get inside before driving away. It was an escort's gesture; even on bad dates, Nick would walk the girl in, making sure she got home safe. The other detectives must have signed them out at the end of the shift, believing that they were out on the town, having the fine time that had been expected, ordered even, by the lieutenant. No one at the squad had called them back in, so Nick had to assume that the night had been quiet in their part of town. It was Valentine's Day, after all. Daysi must have been as busy as hell.

THIRTY-SEVEN

A tip, that was all it took sometimes. "Look at what's taped under the bumper of the green Honda, the third in from the corner." "He has another cellphone, and this is the number." "He's sleeping with his cousin's girlfriend, and if you confronted either, they'd give up everything." The momentum could be as important as the information, spurring one side to renewed commitment, the other to new mistakes. Sometimes, that bit of input was all it took to break a case, to break a man, the loose rock that became a landslide. Nick was intimately familiar with the experience. He was off balance, unsure whether his legs were unsteady or the earth were trembling, shifting beneath his feet. It wouldn't take much to push him over, and he didn't know which way he'd fall. You don't find this stuff out in church, as they said, but Nick didn't know how many times they could go to hell to get it and still come back.

Malcolm had begun producing information on a wartime footing, wholesale and piecemeal, good enough for the troops. The detectives chased bodies that lacked names, names that lacked bodies. They called around to different squads, putting together details—"Shot three times, outside, by two guys on a motorcycle"—with approximate locations. "There's a subway nearby, a block away, elevated? And on one corner there's a vacant lot. On the other there's a chicken place, and on the third corner, there's a nail salon? . . . No, I don't know what the fourth corner is. You're in Brooklyn—you tell me." Amazing how much of it there was, how easily obtained, like a subscription to *Bad Times*. It was also interesting to see Esposito work so hard on cases that weren't his, the answers passed to stumped classmates by the kid who cared most about how he did on the test. Nick didn't know whether Esposito had changed or only adapted, adjusted tactics for a larger, longer game. Malcolm was no longer just an informant for him but almost an oracle, dispensing cryptic wisdom from his guarded island. No, Nick thought, it was nothing as fancy as that. Malcolm was Esposito's new partner.

There was so much activity that Nick and Esposito barely had time to talk about where it all would lead, the other side of the bargain, even if they had had the inclination. Most of the information from Malcolm was vague, suggestive; enough was not. When Esposito announced one morning that he had to go to court, without further comment, Nick felt queasy. Had there been three solid cases from Malcolm already, three homicide collars? Had he already paid his ransom? It couldn't have been two weeks since they'd been to Rikers. Esposito had been out of work for months; Nick strove to believe that he must have had a backlog of court appearances. On the kidnapping alone, there must have been—no, nothing: Kiko dead on the street, Miguel dead in jail, the little brother dead in the apartment. Blue on red, red on red, exceptional clearances all, case closed. Nick knew how the next courtroom scenes would play. Malcolm's lawyer would ask for a copy of the tape, or another copy, and the DA would fail to produce it; there would be conferences, motions, maybe an adjournment; an angry judge would set bail for Malcolm, or release him without it. The system was designed for deliberation, engineered for delay, but it tended to mobilize into brisk efficiency when it was least convenient.

For that reason alone, Nick suspected that Malcolm would be freed imminently, if he weren't already at liberty. Nick wasn't ready for how fast it was moving. Tips from Malcolm, a tap on the levers of justice from Esposito, and *Voilà!* So far, it had been easy for Malcolm, and Nick wondered whether handling Michael would prove to be the hard part, or easier still. There were other systems at work, other forces in play, not subject to rules any of them understood.

Later that day, Ivan Lopez came in to the squad, uncharacteristically quiet. He had Grace with him, leading her by the hand like a blind child, and he began to cry as he started to talk. Grace seemed lost, blinking distractedly as she was led in, but she otherwise betrayed no bad feeling. She didn't seem to recognize Nick. She took her glasses off and put them on again, several times. When she placed him—"Oh! Hi!"—she seemed to gather herself together, to relax enough to exhibit some disdain for her father, suggesting that what was tragic for him was only embarrassing for her. Still, something was different; she was scattered but scared. Nick did not know which one to address first, who he trusted more for the baseline facts. Yes, he did, but he decided to speak with Lopez, so the man wouldn't feel disrespected. When Nick sat him down in the interview room, however, he wept. "The Sister, she calls me at work. She says Grace is absent. I come home. . . . *She is ruined*." Again? So soon? This time, Lopez wasn't angry, which concerned Nick. He brought Lopez a glass of water, some toilet paper to blow his nose, and left him to collect himself.

Grace was also shaken, Nick could see that, but it was hard to gauge how much she was affected by her father's hysteria. He led her to another room, and she shook off her backpack, dropping it onto the table with a thump. She wore her plaid uniform jumper. She didn't look at Nick, at first, but leaned down to check her pack, to see if she'd remembered a notebook. When she sat back up, she had a distracted, fidgety look. She chewed a strand of hair, counted with her fingers and mouthed the numbers *four, five, six*. Nick coughed to get her attention, and her look changed. She seemed older, wrongly wry; he had an image of her at a hotel bar, asking for "the usual." She swept her hair back and coughed in return. She did not need to wait for questions.

As she was leaving for school that day, there was a knock at the door. There was a man with a toolbox and the kind of dark blue polyester shirt that maintenance workers wear. He asked if her parents were home, and she said no. He said there was a leak in the pipes, he had to come in and fix it. Grace nodded and led him to the kitchen, where she took the milk and orange juice from the counter and put them back into the refrigerator. When she turned around, he stood close, smiling at her. She knew then there was nothing wrong with the pipes. He told her to get a beer from the refrigerator, and she did. This was relayed to Nick with the dull factuality of a book report, blunt and bland in the telling but earnest, determined to show she had done the homework on her own. Elaboration came at an odd point:

"'Get one for yourself.' That's what he told me, and I knew something was wrong.

"I go, 'I don't drink beer. I'm not old enough.' I did try it once, but I don't like it. I don't.

"He goes, 'You're old enough.' That's what he said."

Grace shook her head and went on. She started to walk out of the kitchen, but he pushed her back, not hard. He began to touch himself, and then he lifted his shirt to show the butt of a gun in his waistband. She went to the refrigerator and got a beer.

"I didn't like it," she said. "I only drank a little, and spilled most of it when he looked away for a second."

Had Nick been outside the interrogation room, watching and listening in, he would have walked away then. He knew what happened next. He could never imagine the evil she had encountered this morning, what it meant to her, but he was horrified that she felt it necessary to protest that she shouldn't get in trouble for the beer, as if she might get a ticket for it. She was litigating in her mind, what she could be blamed for, what she could not. To talk that way was diversionary, sometimes. One woman Nick had encountered could only complain about the muddy footprints in the house, when two men had broken in and shot her husband in front of her. But this was not quite that. Grace knew she was blameless in this, and she was attentive to any suggestion that it might be otherwise. She thought she had been lucky, in that she had not been killed, and she knew she had made a mistake in letting him in. But her father had opened the door for strange men who'd knocked, saying the landlord had sent them to spray for roaches, the meter had to be checked by the electric company. This was part of city life; the strangers had come and gone. Grace was citing precedent for her error, delving into issues for appeal.

"Well, what happened next, Grace?"

"What do you think? He raped me."

"There was intercourse?"

"What? Yeah, we fucked."

The harshness of her words shocked Nick, and she mumbled an apology for dropping "the F-bomb."

"That's all right, Grace. Did he hit you? Yell at you? Threaten you? Did he ask you or tell you to have sex with him?"

"He didn't say anything. He pulled my ear. We went to the living room. Like I said, he had a gun. I took off my uniform and lay down on the rug. It's the most disgusting rug. It's this ugly banana-green. . . ."

Nick was supposed to probe her about details, but he couldn't. They were crucial, but he didn't have the heart to ask, didn't have the stomach. What else did he need to know? Of course. "Did you hear about the guy who was doing this? The guy who was conning his way inside people's houses, hurting women?"

"Yeah, it was on TV. You think it was the same guy?"

Nick hated this. Her knowledge of the pattern was a complication, a reason for her story to be challenged. She was a problematic victim. She would be seen as such, Nick knew. He hated these cases. Ordinary bad men he could understand. They robbed banks for the money; shot people who threatened their dope spot; stabbed the guy who hit on their girl, or thought he did, when they were drunk or lost their tempers at parties. Bad impulses, bad days, bad ways of dealing with the world; none of it was entirely alien to him. There was always something you could find in the mirror. Nick knew there were risks to that kind of projection, but when you had nothing, you had to reach, try to picture why, work to connect. Not here. This kind of predator might as well have been from a cannibal island, a cult of cat-worshippers, for all they had in common. Just as he felt himself slipping back into his old habit of not wanting to know, it occurred to him that this case would be reassigned to Special Victims. It was not his case. This was rape—both kinds of it, the kid kind and the force kind, and a candidate for a pattern, to boot—and he would have nothing more to do with it, after the interview. Nick was relieved, mostly.

"I don't know, it may be. First we have to take you to the hospital, get you checked out. And then other detectives who are trying to find this guy, they're gonna talk to you, too."

"Does it matter if he's the same one or a different one?"

"No. Yes. It doesn't matter, because the guy who hurt you is bad, whoever he is. We want to catch him and put him in jail. And it does matter, because if he's the same guy who hurt other people, maybe you know something or remember something that can help us get him, and that can stop other people from getting hurt. You're smart, Grace. I know you are. And the people who want to talk to you are good people. So be honest, okay? Tell them everything you remember, even if it hurts to talk about it, even if it's a little thing that doesn't seem important. If you don't remember something, or didn't notice, don't say that you do. Don't say anything just because you think they might want to hear it. Okay, Grace?"

"Okay, Detective. What's your name again?"

"Nick."

"I like that name. It's my second-best-friend's younger brother's name. It's nice."

"Thanks, Grace."

Nick was glad she was able to take her mind off things for a moment, though it bothered him, a little, that she could. Her composure became more striking when he went in to ask Lopez if he wanted to come with them to the hospital, and the response was distraught sobbing. Nick told him to just go home, and he'd bring Grace back later. Lopez nodded, and didn't move. He would not be an asset to the investigation. Nick told the lieutenant what had happened, and asked him to make the notification to Special Victims. The lieutenant nodded. He'd have them meet Nick at the hospital. The drive was silent except for a remark Grace made at the end, as they parked. Nick opened her door, and she looked up at him.

"Detective Nick?"

"Yes, Grace?"

"That's a nice tie. Matches your eyes."

Nick strained not to shudder. He wasn't sure if there was a hint of flirtation in what she said, but there was something unconscionably casual. Her father's awful words—"She is ruined!"—came back to him, and he put them out of his mind before he could begin an argument with himself that he might not win. This was not his case, he reminded himself, and its imminent reassignment was now unreservedly welcome. He forced a smile and led her inside.

Two women detectives from Special Victims met them at the emergency room, and then two men followed, the pair they'd met at the diner, seen on TV months ago, from the task force for the serial rapist. Nick floated in and out of the room where Grace was being examined, leaving when the nurses asked for privacy, slipping back in when they were done. Grace wanted him there, and he stayed for her comfort, though he wanted nothing more than to leave. She was a candidate for victim number twenty-five in the case; sixteen attacks had been confirmed by DNA, and eight more were deemed part of the pattern by similarities of description and MO. When the task force detectives arrived, they thanked Nick with enthusiasm, and for the first time in months, he saw cops who looked at him like a found penny instead of a black cat. A big cop and a bigger one, one dark, one fair, the old binary pair. There was the customary blather, the "Sure-I-remember-you," and "How's-old-what's-his-name." "Give him my best." Nick almost laughed at the strategy behind their courtesies. They were on guard against him, concerned he might become proprietary, demanding a share in the glory, a place at the table. Esposito would have, at least before, and Nick was wishing they were working together again, when he remembered that they were. He didn't even feel like a found penny anymore, after the first real questions were asked.

"Did you ask if he ejaculated inside her?"

"No."

"Did you ask if she showered or washed after?"

"No."

"Did you ask if he touched anything in the apartment? Did you set up a crime scene, see if we could maybe get prints, DNA?"

Nick had not. He bristled at some of the questions, at the vague implication that he had to justify their summons to the hospital, the claim on their time. And he knew that he was right to spare Grace from multiple rounds of the same gruesome interview. But sending Lopez home had been flat-out stupid. Nick had done it simply to get rid of him, which hadn't been wrong—his emotional blowouts would have made it impossible to talk to Grace—but Nick's own lapse in judgment was a result of his disengagement, his desire to be done with the case. He'd held back, and then he'd rushed to finish. He'd meant to be kind, as well, but he hadn't done his job.

His dismay did not abate as the new team took over. The detectives were good, Nick thought, but their interview with Grace did not go well. They were thrown by her combination of confidence and innocence, her lack of tears. Though she had flinched and shivered at times when she'd first told the story, later repetitions had a cool, remote tone, as if the event had happened to someone she knew.

One of them asked, "How tall was he?"

Grace thought a moment before responding, "Short. Not really a midget, not a really tiny midget but . . . kinda like you."

Nick didn't blame them when they didn't believe her, not about the pattern. The similarities to the televised case were public knowledge—the plumber's helper bit, an approximate description—and the differences were profound. He had never stayed after the rape before, had never used a gun; he had never drunk beer with the victim, and he'd never said he'd call. Grace hadn't told Nick that; Nick hadn't asked. She also hadn't told him that the man had stolen a photo of her and her father from a table. The rapist had no history of taking souvenirs. The rapist hadn't used a condom with the others, and the detectives were unconvinced by the thought that she'd persuaded him to put one on. She'd even thrown away the beer bottles. At the hospital, the gynecologist said the results of her exam were inconclusive, which was often the case. Not enough science, too much story. Grace didn't make sense to Nick, either, but she inspired in him a kind of fearful admiration rather than skepticism.

When Nick withdrew from the room and told the detectives about her history of going missing, and the time with the three boys, they soured on her, lost interest. They'd just spent three weeks shadowing another self-declared victim of the serial rapist, a young teenager from a fundamentalist family who had finally admitted that what had really happened was that her first tongue-kiss with a classmate had been followed within hours by her first period. Knowing nothing about sex, she'd been afraid she was pregnant, and she'd decided she'd better have something to say. That was a tip that had wasted nearly a month of time.

The detectives told Nick that when they made an arrest, Grace would be welcome to view the lineup, but they would not, as of now, consider this part of the pattern. They already had twenty-four victims whom they believed, who had provided proven facts to work with and who depended on their efforts. As for Grace, they doubted even that any crime had occurred. When they left, one said, "She probably just wants to skip school. It happens. Sorry."

Nick wanted to correct him on the last point at least, but it didn't matter. It wasn't his case anymore. When they finished at the hospital, school was where Grace wanted to go. She calculated that if they rushed, she could make chemistry class; the teacher was doing an experiment today in which everyone would get to set something on fire. Nick walked her inside, and they went to Sister Agnes's office. When they sat down together, Nick told the sister that there had been a man in Grace's building who had frightened her, and she'd had to stay inside. After she'd first talked with the police, there'd been a concern that the man might be the serial rapist who had been on the news, and then other detectives had needed to speak to her. They should have let the school know sooner, Nick apologized, but the matter had been urgent. Sister Agnes nodded and studied Grace for any signs of contradiction to the account, changes in her face and bearing. Finding none, she thanked Nick and sent him on his way. As he was leaving, he overheard the sister say, "You're a good and brave girl, Grace. You make us very proud. Now back to class, and I will find out what lessons you missed, what you must make up." Nick envied both women for their sense of purpose, their place in the world, and wondered if he'd ever find either again.

THIRTY-EIGHT

There was never any argument between Nick and Esposito, but there was a chill—little fissures in the bond, like ant-eaten rifts on the edge of a leaf. Despite everything, Nick's refusal to assent to the scheme with Malcolm made him feel small. Since they'd begun working together, Esposito had yanked him along at any number of junctures. Always Nick had resisted, and always Esposito had been right—from the first dinner with Daysi, to staying with his family, meeting Lena, the children, and the rest. Nick would have known none of those experiences had he followed his instinct instead of his partner. Cowardice and conscience both held him back, as they had during his suicide idyll. As then, he tried the idea on in his mind, looked in the mirror to see how it fit him. He couldn't see it; the mirror was dark. It was the complexity that troubled him most, the excess of ambitions and the softness of assumptions; the plan was like an arcane financial instrument, with Esposito giddily speculating on murder futures, buying up options on fratricides. Nick lacked the math for it more than he lacked faith, though he hadn't an excess of the latter. He wouldn't give Esposito his last penny for the magic beans. Nick felt smaller still when he realized that he hadn't been asked for the penny; all he had to do was keep his mouth shut, his specialty. A small man but soundless, like a good child, not heard.

When there was a lull in work on Malcolm's leads, Nick and Esposito tended not to linger in the office. The distance between them would be noticed, and both became increasingly on guard against any kind of scrutiny, however well-intentioned. They took to driving around, looking for something to happen, for an adventure, a distraction. They listened to the police radio more often, ready to jump in on heavy street jobs. One evening, Esposito jerked the car to the side of the street. "Wouldja?" The old game they had, whether she was as pretty as the first glimpse, the first guess, believing before you saw.

"No," Nick said, out of habit, but also out of confusion—he didn't see a soul on the street. Esposito rolled down the window and took a mug shot from the glove box. Nick couldn't see who he was looking at. No one was on the sidewalk, no figure emerged from the lane of barren-limbed ginkgos. The block was desolate, eerily so for the time and place. Esposito just stuck the picture back into the box, crumpling it, and lurched back into the street, speeding ahead. "Nah, forget it." The episode was trivial, but the worry stuck with both of them. Esposito without an eye for this, shut out from his old luck, was not Esposito. Nick turned on the radio to a news station, so they could hear about traffic jams and gas prices, window-washers who had fallen from scaffolding.

As with Allison, when it started to go, there was a drift, and then it quickened. There was so much goodwill; the reserves were deep—so many debts back and forth that neither knew which account was red or black. For a while, there was a parody of elaborate deference, and whether the issue was whether to be tough on a shifty witness or where to eat, positions were quit at the first signs of conflict. Nick didn't have the heart to finish arguments, even if they were only in his head. Neither of them made a joke at the other's expense anymore; they didn't know if they had the credit. No one in the squad saw its degree. Or rather, they saw a change, but did not assume that things were so bad. Nick and Esposito worked with each other, day and night, and when one of them vanished, the other did, too, to keep up appearances. Nick grieved to see it. Esposito was his last and best tie to life, the living, but Nick would let go before he went along. If you're drowning, do you swim to a sinking ship?

Nick wondered what Esposito had done with the tapes. Magnets were supposed to work. He wanted to look it up on the Internet, but then he figured it was better not to have a record of the search. Substitution was easier, a distraction in the evidence room at the DA's office and a switch. Easier still if the DA asked Esposito to pick up the tape for her to view. The system was weakly defended against sabotage, challenge from within. Malcolm hadn't written anything down. The tape was all there was—a few feet of magnetic film, two spools, a plastic box. Micro-fine layers, millions of dots. In one arrangement, it's static, white noise. In another, it's *The Godfather,* the face of Pacino after he kills Fredo, even the music: Da, da-da-da, dot da-da . . . "Say a Hail Mary before you throw the line in the water. That's my secret. That's how you catch a fish." That was what Nick was thinking when they left a bodega robbery, grainy surveillance tape in hand. He wondered if they'd ever talk about it, when Esposito asked an unnerving question. "What's your favorite movie?"

Esposito had seemed preoccupied since the start of the shift, alternately smug and then cagey, waiting for the moment. Nick assumed there had been a pickup, a hookup with a new girl, and he wasn't sure he wanted to hear about it. Since he'd met Lena, he had understood that part of Esposito even less, since it was such a good marriage that was risked, upping the stakes even after he'd won the bet. But mostly it startled Nick to think that his partner had heard the *Godfather* music in his head, as if it were audible through his skull.

"What?"

"What's your favorite movie?"

"Are you kidding me? What's your favorite color? If you could be an animal, what kind would you be? Would you rather be able to fly, or be invisible? Espo, do you want to trade baseball cards after this? You wanna trade comics?"

Esposito laughed at Nick's sputtering protest, and Nick started to laugh, too.

"C'mon. What's your favorite movie?"

"You know. The same as yours, the same as everybody."

"Yeah, *The Godfather.* I know. Which one?"

"One and Two. They're the same story, the same thing. The third, it doesn't count. I like the first one better. It's more in New York. When they go away—Nevada, Havana—it gets harder. They deal with different people."

"Exactly. But your favorite movie, it might change."

Nick knew what was coming.

"There's a tape in my locker. It's labeled, *The Godfather, Part Six.* You might find another copy in your desk, same label, my handwriting, so it looks like a bootleg tape."

"So if I see it, I know it's not the real *Godfather, Part Six*?"

"That would be your first clue."

While Nick was dismayed to be in possession of incriminating evidence, he was relieved to find that Esposito was not clairvoyant, that his own mind was not so transparent. Not even a coincidence, really, given that thoughts about the tape led to thoughts about the movie, and Esposito had done the same, a few steps ahead, as was his habit. "Don't ever take sides with anyone against the family again. Ever." Stopping his partner now might have been beyond Nick's ability. It was certainly against the tribal code, and this was not just his tribe—it was his brother, bloodier than most. The wrong that Esposito had done had been undertaken with such an honorable spirit, and such magnificent talent. It had been done to save a friend who could not rise to the occasion of his own saving.

They drove around aimlessly for a while. Nick looked at the buildings, the five- and six-story brick apartment houses, sturdy and modest, none without some unpretentious classical ornament or variegation in the brickwork, zigzags of color and pattern. They were constructed with the subways, with them and because of them, in the teens and twenties, to relieve the sweaty densities of the downtown tenements, to make the city bigger and better, ideas that went hand in hand. There'd been a flow to it: Sandhogs had dug the tunnels for the A train, and Duke Ellington had finished the ride. New Yorkers of the midcentury, the American century, had grown up in more rooms than their parents had, with more possibilities. The can-do spirit. *Let's put on a musical, invent a vaccine.* Nick tried to recall what the mood had been when he had grown up here, if it had been invested with such confidence. He couldn't separate his own memories from the TV clip shorthand, the brassy newsreel voice-over announcing serial triumphs over breadlines, brownshirts, the moon. It didn't seem like that now. It didn't feel like greater heights awaited. If disaster could be averted, decay slowed, most would think it enough. They passed the Audubon Ballroom, another of the old vaudeville palaces, where Malcolm X had been killed before a speech. The assassins had been from the Nation of Islam, which he had left for Islam. The building had been an active synagogue at the time. What to make of that one? If those walls could talk, they wouldn't. Nick was reminded of nearer history, other chickens that might come home to roost.

"Any word on the guy?"

They barely mentioned the scheme with the Coles, but when they couldn't avoid it, they slipped into mobster obliquities, careful of microphones. It sounded affected, but it wasn't unwise. Nick considered whether it might have been better to be on speaking terms with IAB, now that real laws had actually been broken. But he could no more help Esposito with them than he could help Otegui with the Feds: the nature of his expertise made him suspect, his timing worse, like an enemy general offering to switch sides hours before the white flag is raised.

"The other one says he's down south."

"That's a little easy."

"Nothing wrong with easy, my friend. Everything doesn't have to be inventing the wheel."

Nick couldn't believe Michael would simply do as he was told, pack up and settle down amid the peach trees. Things worked out for Esposito, Nick knew, but this would have been ridiculously accommodating. If anything, Nick would have bet on another exceptional clearance, that the Dominicans would get Michael first. Miguelito's funeral would not be forgiven; Kiko's people would not let that pass unanswered. Nick knew he could trust their hate, but not their efficiency, and he did not know if he could wait. Still, there was something sly in Esposito's voice, something superior that incited Nick's curiosity even as his misgivings remained. It would have been hard enough to talk if they could have spoken openly, frankly, without the absurd codes.

"How long?"

"Can't say. I'm in touch, on top of it."

"I don't like it."

"Maybe it'll agree with him—the weather, the pace."

"People don't change."

"No? I've seen it happen."

Nick couldn't tell if there was affection or annoyance in the mild barb, if Esposito wanted to tease him into talking more, or if he wanted him to shut up. And if Nick couldn't read his partner, how could he hope to understand Michael? Nick couldn't picture Michael's mind any more than he could the rapist's, the furnace of alien hungers and hates. The mother's death had to have been the catalyst, but Nick had lost his mother as well, and it had not driven him to such galloping fantasy and fanaticism. And he had been younger when it had happened, when it should have been more formative. It had made him a little more solitary, a little more saturnine, sometimes a lot. Anything else? Not really, no. Grace, too, it must have changed her, even though Nick hadn't known her before. She found solace in homework and orgies, the scholarship slut. For what it was worth, she had the best take on death and disaster of the three of them, refusing revenge and despair. Nick pictured himself in a silken bed with Daysi and Allison, reading poetry, all of them feeding one another grapes. Esposito mistook his peaceful expression for a degree of reconciliation.

"Say a kid steals a car, gets into a crash," he began in a professorial tone, pleased with the opportunity to show off his thought. "The other driver runs away. Cops come, they find a body in the trunk of the second car. Do you lock the kid up?"

"Yeah."

"All right. Say it's not a body—it's a lady tied up, taped up, in the trunk. She's alive. The kid saved her life. He's a good kid, never been in trouble before. Do you still arrest him?"

Nick hesitated, resistant to accept the terms of the analogy. The role reversal was as touching as it was troubling. It showed how close they'd grown, how much they'd rubbed off on each other, but if Esposito could play the hypothetical game, Nick was all the less necessary. The theme of unintended consequences did not reassure him, and his answer was churlish.

"Nobody ever just goes out one day to steal a car, just once."

"This one did. It's my story, Nick. I get to say what happens."

Nick snapped back—"Do you?"—harsher than intended, brittle and volatile, but when he began to apologize, Esposito turned up the radio. He drove around the corner, found a quiet block—here, a school, closed for the day—and pulled over. "C'mon. Let's get coffee." There was no coffee shop where they'd parked. When they got out, Esposito put an arm around his shoulder, leading him down the street. More affectionate than usual, more intrusive. Reminiscent of more old mob movies, checking for the wire on the chest.

"You okay, Nick?"

"I don't know. I'm not crazy about this, Espo. You know that. I can see a hundred ways it can go wrong. I can't see one way it could go right."

"I know that. It's not what I'm asking. I'm asking if I can trust you."

Esposito slid his hand off Nick's shoulder, patting him on the side and back. Was he feeling for a microphone? Didn't he know they didn't do it that way anymore? Nick stopped walking, tossed his tie over his shoulder, and began to unbutton his shirt, offering his chest for examination.

"C'mon. You wanna feel? You wanna go swimming somewhere, so we can strip down, or you wanna go through the metal detector at the airport, X-ray my key ring to see if there's a bug inside?"

Despite his anger, Nick almost smiled at the irony. He had been trusted completely when he had been a spy, but now that he had severed that contact, his loyalty was suspect. Esposito straightened his tie and patted him again, shaking his head. He kept a firm hand on his shoulder.

"Stop it, Nick. I know. I know everything."

Nick looked blankly back at him, almost grateful to be exposed. Was it all over now? If he were in an interrogation room, he'd put his arms on the table, lay his head down, and sleep a guilty sleep. Almost grateful. He held back from any admission until the accusation was complete.

"I was a little mad you didn't tell me yourself."

The tone was too kind, nearly sympathetic, but maybe Esposito wanted him to lower his guard. Nick waited for him to finish.

"Lena told me about the miscarriages, the three girls. I understand, though—some things are just easier to tell a woman. With the rest of it—your father, your wife, Daysi. Too much. And I know you went to visit . . . that guy . . . in his apartment. Fuck it. Enough games. You went to see Michael, and Malcolm told me. He didn't know it was you, or why you went, and I didn't put it together till later. Not even really till yesterday. And I swear to God, Nick, I almost threw up at the thought that you were gonna say goodbye to Michael Cole and not me."

For a moment, Nick was sick, too. He'd expected the back of Esposito's hand, cursing at his treason; instead it had been held out to help him, magnanimous but unyielding in its grasp. He hadn't considered what harm it might have done to other people if he'd died—there hadn't seemed to be other people, then—only what suffering he might have spared himself. For the first time since they'd known each other, Nick felt like a man without secrets. All but one, and he almost felt clean. He just nodded, and Esposito went on.

"I know you don't like this play, this move, but I think it's gonna work out. It's you I'm worried about. You ain't the same guy I started with. I told you, you know about my last partner. I couldn't tell my kids—I couldn't face 'em—if you did something to yourself. You holding up?"

Nick nodded again.

"If you weren't, would you promise to tell me?"

Nick didn't answer, and Esposito put both hands on his shoulders, fierce in his grip, not checking for microphones.

"You're not going anywhere, unless I get a promise. I swear to you, I won't let you go unless you swear to me. Your word's enough for me, but I want to hear it."

"I swear it."

Nick nodded again, and he was released. After they went back to the precinct to sign out, Esposito asked him if he wanted to go out for a drink. It was late, and they had to be back early in the morning. Nick was afraid that his stunned gratitude would mix like whiskey with his beer. Three or four rounds in, if Esposito asked to borrow his gun for a bank robbery, he would not have refused. "Nah, but tomorrow, definitely." Esposito dropped him off at his apartment, without checking the rooflines or the street. Nick started to but caught himself, deciding to take his chances. Esposito had faith enough for both of them. For tonight, at least, it was more than enough.

THIRTY-NINE

Nick walked out of his apartment early the next morning, groggy after a restless night of half-sleep, to see two young cops at his lobby door, putting up yellow tape. They blocked his exit, telling him he had to wait, it was a crime scene. He looked at their faces and didn't recognize them; they had to be new. He was unused to this kind of arrival, this kind of reception. What occurred to him first was that he was in trouble, that IAB had found out he was living there, in the precinct. The petty vanity made him wince, but he decided not to say who he was to the cops at the door.

"What's going on?"

They looked at each other, a stocky Spanish one with a mustache and a spindly white female with librarian glasses. They knew they should detain witnesses, control the scene, alert their sergeant to suspicious persons and facts of potential significance.. They knew they should be wary about disclosing information to the public.

"There's been an incident, sir," said the female, in a country accent, somewhat Southern. What had brought her here, to do this? "Do you live here?"

"No."

The absence of further detail in Nick's response provoked both curiosity and irritation. The Spanish one stepped up to him.

"So, who you visiting? What's going on? Where you coming from? What's your name? Lemme see some ID!"

He started to reach to Nick's waist, to pat him down, and Nick pushed the hand away before the cop found the gun.

"It's Detective Meehan, kid. Slow it down."

He pulled his jacket aside to show his shield, which only the female cop saw. She grabbed her partner before he could react too forcefully to the push-away. Nick suddenly felt tense and dizzy; he wanted to run. He wanted to be somewhere else, do something else, be someone else. Part of his mind had taken in the situation, but it wouldn't share; he wasn't talking to himself.

"Easy, Juan. May I see some ID, Detective?"

She said "I" like "Ah." Kentucky, Ohio, Missouri, Tennessee. Indian names that were songs in themselves. Nick carefully angled his body, right hand raised, and took his ID out from his left back pocket. The Spanish cop veered between anger and embarrassment. As he stepped back, his partner stepped forward.

"Detective, you shoulda told us that, straight out," she said. "An unfortunate situation coulda happened, right here."

Nick considered the opinion and nodded. He clapped them both on the shoulders and walked them out of the lobby, talking fast to divert them, to divert himself from where his thoughts were headed.

"Yeah. You're right. So, what do we got?"

"We got a male shot."

"Likely?"

That was police idiom for the estimate of whether a person was likely to die. New doctors, new EMTs, were often offended when they were asked to make a bet on the fatality of an injury. New cops took no such offense, but they didn't claim any expertise, and formed opinions based on whether the man who was shot was angry about it or didn't move much.

"More than likely."

"Let's have a look, then."

The cops held up the tape for him, and he walked down the stoop. No one from the squad was there yet. A man on the sidewalk in a suit, face-down, briefcase less than a foot from his splayed hands. He had the look of someone running for a bus, on a vertical axis, down into the earth. Nick squatted down to examine the body, scanning it half a minute before he found the dime-size tufted circle equidistant between the shoulder blades. The fabric was too dark to show any stippling, but he guessed it was close range, an instantaneous death, clipping the spine and stopping the heart like a clock.

"What time we got for this?"

"Maybe six. Half hour ago, forty-five minutes."

"How'd it come over? Anybody see it or hear it, or they just find the body?"

"Guy heading to work, he hears it. Heard a shot a minute before, when he was around the corner, but he didn't see anything before he saw the guy. Probably happened right before he called it in."

Nick touched the neck. The flesh was warm, no cooler than his own. None of the pockets had been turned out or torn, and he felt a wallet in the back pants pocket. Not robbery. Robbery-homicides were bad cases, nearly impossible to find the random stranger with the impulsive finger. Not random, not this. Whose was this? Who was catching from the squad? Nick had been out of the rotation for a while, and he wasn't eager to jump back in. Not for this, right in his front yard, so to speak. He felt a chill, colder than the body would ever be, even when it went into the ground. He hadn't had coffee yet—that's what he told himself. That's why he hadn't thought it through, hadn't even begun to think, taking in the larger circumstances. He walked around and crouched down to see the face, knowing even before he saw that it was Jamie Barry. Jamie looked as surprised as Nick.

"Ah, Jamie, you poor bastard."

Nick saw the two cops looking at him, darkly collating his precipitous appearance and evasive remarks, his apparent relationship with the victim. What to say to them, to preempt a call to IAB? He hadn't the least idea.

When the squad arrived, they huddled around Nick. He was immensely grateful to see them, all of them, as they took out their notebooks for his terse recital of facts: Jamie Barry, longtime junkie recently rehabbed, shot once in the back, no apparent robbery. He could have been dictating the sparse newspaper clip. But he added that he knew him, as a neighbor, and didn't need it mentioned that he was staying in the building, had stumbled into the scene. He didn't need the aggravation, he said, and they nodded, knowing what he'd been through, what the Job could be like. Sympathy was immediate, and trust was automatic. They had to look out for each other. Napolitano, Garelick, and Perez fanned out for canvasses, taking plate numbers, looking for security cameras. Esposito remained, waiting for Nick to tell him more, to see if the story was altered or amplified for his more intimate audience. When it wasn't, he seemed almost hurt; there was always more, and he should have been the one to hear it. He pursed his lips and put his notebook away.

"The father's the super, right?"

"Yeah."

"So where is he?"

A fine question. At this time of morning, he was always outside, hauling the garbage from the alley to the curb, sweeping the lobby. By now, Mr. Barry should have been gawking outside the yellow tape, or standing inside, weeping. They walked to the edge of the scene, where one of the old Irish ladies was loitering.

"Where's Mr. Barry?"

"My God. It's not Jamie, is it?"

"No," interjected Esposito, sparing Nick the lie. "It's just that we'll be taking over the sidewalk for a couple of hours, in case there's any deliveries or whatnot. Is he around?"

"No. He's home, thank God. He'll be back tonight."

Esposito was confused, but Nick was not. "Home" was Ireland for his father or Mr. Barry, no matter how long they lived here, without intention to return. Nick wished he remembered where—Fermanagh? Tyrone?—to call him, to tell him not to come back, that there was nothing for him here, less.

"What happened, Nick? Thank God you're here. Still, I won't sleep tonight. . . . What was it? Should we stay inside?"

"I don't know yet. These things take some time to figure out."

If only that were true. If only there were some mystery or doubt. If Nick had been darker, shorter, fatter, with a ponytail, a different neighbor would have been mistakenly dead. What a privilege it should have been to catch a case like this. What a gift to a detective, to see a dead face and know who did it, with the certainty of a saint knowing what God has asked of him. But this was no gift, the lucid point amid the lurching shadows. Esposito took hold of his arm for some conference, but Nick pulled away, a sulky flinch like a girlfriend in a mood, to walk back to the body and crouch down again on the sidewalk. Jamie's eyes were half-open, dull and wasted. Nick had seen them a hundred times like that, but never so close. A cartoon image, windows with the shades drawn. Twittering birds surrounding him after the knockout punch, X's for eyes. Old folklore, old interrogation hustles, that the eyes would capture their last sight like a snapshot. But Jamie had been shot from behind. If the lie were true, his eyes would show traffic, a bus stop, a leafless tree. Dead and blind to who did it. Nick thought of Jamie hovering near, his unsteady spirit weaving like a drunk, not sure of his death, hustling for reassurance like for spare change. *Hey, Nick! It's me, Jamie! Got a minute? What's going on?* When Nick stood up, knees aching, he felt like he was brushing Jamie off again.

As Esposito led Nick away to the car, lifting the tape for him to pass beneath, he looked plaintively at his partner—*Yes? What now?*—and got a curt nod of the head in return. Time to go. You're being told to leave. The red carpet goes both ways, coming and going. Let me lift the tape for you. Bouncer or chauffeur? The *eruv*, the imaginary boundary that makes the outside the inside, letting the faithful say they were at home. It was Nick's work, his home, and he was being cast out. Esposito even opened the car door for him before getting in.

"Either way, Nick."

Nick nodded, unsure what he meant. Was that a threat?

"Either way, you got to get outta here."

Esposito started the car and pulled out of the spot, jerking a U-turn to take them back downtown. Nick waited for the explanation.

"Either Michael thinks he killed you and we gotta keep you outta sight. Or he knows he didn't, so we gotta get you outta here, so he don't come back at all of us, wandering around. We don't need anybody else getting killed over this. Shame you couldn't say you saw it."

Nick thought that sounded like a suggestion, and he paused, determined to consider the practical considerations first.

"Why didn't I call it in, take action? There isn't going to be a 911 call from me. I didn't chase anybody. It won't fly."

"Just thinkin' aloud here, Nick."

Nick slunk down in his seat, in accommodation to the idea that he should not be seen.

"Not for nothin,' " Esposito went on, "but even dead, the guy looked better than the last time. I saw him outside the church, at your father's funeral. He was shaking like a wet cat in winter. What happened, he straighten out?"

"Yeah. He's been clean a couple of months."

"That's a shame. Same time, he probably did ten things a day he shoulda got shot for when he was a junkie. Maybe he woulda slipped up tomorrow, taken his paycheck to the closest dope spot and shot the whole load up his arm. At least, you and what's-his-name weren't close. Whaddaya gonna do?"

Nick was incensed by the dull barroom philosophizing, and became increasingly worked up as he went through the reasons. There was the glib and flabby fatalism, suggesting that Jamie's time had come; the lowered expectations, permission to lose, granted in advance. Esposito would never have made the remark—"Whaddaya gonna do?"—about one of his own cases, and he would have had sharp words for anyone who offered them. Nick understood that Esposito was writing them both off, Jamie as victim and Nick as cop.

"Whose case is this? Who's up?" Nick burst out, "I want it. Tell the guys, tell the lieutenant, it's mine. Never mind. I'll tell them myself."

"You can't have it." There was no emotion or hesitation in Esposito's refusal; it was a flat statement of fact, as if one of his children had asked for a pony for Christmas, or a switchblade.

"Why not?" Nick was no less petulant in his protest than RJ or Johnny or Al would have been.

"One question on the stand, 'You were friends with the deceased, Detective Meehan, were you not?' "

Nick couldn't answer. "Yes" would have been a lie, but "no" sounded so shameful, stone-hearted. Still, he understood that it couldn't be his case, when it was his fault. Not his fault, but his failure. A conflict of interest, at a minimum. Nick wondered if Jamie's oblivious martyrdom might gain him some advantage in purgatory, when the accounts were laid out. Nick wondered if either of them had hope of purgatory, if there was something worth saving. God might have expected more from both of them than just a few good days.

"You see what I'm sayin', pal?"

"So whose is it? I don't want Perez or Garelick. How about Napolitano?"

"No, it's Garelick's. I was in the office before you. When I heard the address, Nick, I thought it was you. I was gonna tell the lieutenant that I wanted it. But then I thought about it. If it was you, I couldn't take it. The case, I mean. Believe me, it's for the best, having somebody on it who don't give a shit. He'll go through the motions, that's all. We gotta work this our way, Nick, off the books."

Our way. So that's what it was. Was that an invitation to join him, or an assumption that he had? Doing something about Michael had not helped. Doing nothing had not, either. Nick made an effort not to let his anger show.

"What about your guy?"

"I'm thinkin' he's a little late. He owes me a call."

Nick looked at Esposito as he drove, his heavy shoulders leaning toward the wheel so his arms would not have to work so hard to turn it, speeding down Broadway, cursing out the window since he could not hit the siren. The Roman nose in profile. Which Roman, what Rome—serving the city, or scouting the walls in preparation for its sack? Esposito saw Jamie's homicide as a setback, at most, a detour, and Nick hated him for it, but not as much as he hated how he himself had nothing better to offer, nothing better to say. It took enormous effort to control his voice when he posed the question, "You still think you did the right thing?"

If Esposito recognized an accusatory tone, he did not show it. "Yeah."

"Where is he now?"

"I'm gonna find out, soon as I drop you off."

Nick shook his head. He felt exhausted. When Esposito let him out at the precinct, he went upstairs into the dorm and slept more soundly than he had in a while, now that the world was crashing down, and he was safe again, in a strange bed. The guilty sleep, when fear is gone from your bones. He had a dream that Daysi lay beside him and told him she was pregnant, which startled him awake, transported him with a feeling of urgent joy. He sat up in the bunk, dazed, and his head swam. Tears pooled and fell. The sense of it, the belief in it, was so strong that he wanted to run down the block and kiss her, hold her, laugh and cry. He wiped his face. It was too much. It was as if he'd crawled from the desert and was given a slug of whiskey; good stuff, but not for this thirst. The only tears shed should be for Jamie, and Jamie deserved better, needed more than tears. Nick went to the bathroom to wash his face, and headed back into the office.

As he entered, Esposito raised a hand for him to stop, then put a finger to his lips and pointed to the locked door of the interview room. He waved Nick ahead, to the meal room, to acquaint him with the developments. Much had happened as he'd slept. When Esposito called Malcolm, he said that he hadn't known that Michael was back; no one had called from Georgia to tell him he'd left. The call woke Malcolm up, and he checked Michael's room. Michael yelled from behind the locked door that he wanted to be left alone. Esposito stationed two cops in the lobby, waiting for relayed calls, from Malcolm to Esposito, and they were waiting for Michael when he stepped off the elevator. They asked him if he lived there, and he took offense at the question. Esposito had warned them there might be a fight, and there might be a gun, but to try to be careful of the face, in case they had to do lineups. It had worked out well.

"Anyway, now we got him, for assault on a cop. He gave one of them a nice shiner. I guess he's learned how to throw a punch."

"Gun?"

"No. I got Malcolm tearing the place up for it now. I told him not to touch it if he finds it, that we might get prints or DNA off the clip. We got a shell casing for a .40 caliber by the body."

"Good. Do either of the Coles know what this is about?"

"No. I'm glad you were in the dorm when they brought him in. I want you in reserve. I'll talk to him awhile. Then you come in. See if he thinks you're a ghost. Not that we don't know already."

"Maybe, but we won't be any closer to locking him up for the homicide."

"Trust me. This one won't stay open for long. I let him keep his belt and laces. If we're lucky, he'll hang himself. Or maybe I'll flip him, like his brother, and we'll wind up as best friends."

Esposito smiled as he headed to the interview room. Nick regarded the return to the old swagger with mixed feelings, glad for his optimism, fearful of overreach. His partner did have a way of making friends. "Making" was the word. It was an act of raw creation, of breaking and rebuilding through force of will. Still, Nick found it hard to imagine Michael vulnerable to either bullying or charm. He was tougher than Nick, more honest, too. When he said he was going to do something, he meant it.

Nick opened the newspaper and turned on the TV to the news, glancing between them, paying attention to neither. One of the wars seemed to be going better, the other getting worse. Nick changed the channel to a nature show and turned the page until he found the crossword. He wouldn't talk to himself about this, at least for a while. An hour passed peacefully, until Esposito barged back in, his jacket off and his tie loose.

"That kid's an asshole."

Nick waited a moment before closing the paper; this could not be considered new information. Esposito seemed irritated by Nick's deliberate leisure, the lack of response.

"This prick is the toughest little scumbag I've ever talked to. He don't care. He is twisted and miserable, hard as a rock. I tell him we know, he nods. I tell him we have the gun, he nods, says, 'Bring it.' I almost wanna tell him his brother Malcolm works with me, we can work it out, I can work with anybody, things can be settled. I don't tell him that, but almost. . . . He sees I'm thinking, and he laughs. He says I should bring him upstate, he'd like to meet my family, too. I want to check under my car, to make sure he ain't hanging from the axle, next time I drive home. Nick, I never thought I'd meet anybody I couldn't interrogate, nobody I couldn't talk to, but this guy doesn't want anything I can give him, isn't afraid of anything I can threaten. I don't know where to go with this—there's no opening. Can you think of anything, Nick? You're a stubborn prick. Maybe you know the language. Can you help me here, or do you wanna go back to the crossword?"

The sting and the dare were well-aimed, well-earned; Nick doubted he could funnel his own frustrations into as useful an outlet. He ought to have something to offer, some insight into the fortress. What did he know about people who wouldn't listen? Nick thought for a moment, not much longer than that.

"Agree with him. Start talking, and then agree more and more. He's used to being fought with. He's ready for arguments against. Say he's right. He's never heard that before. I'll watch through the window. Put both your hands up, scratch your head when you want me to come in. That's the high sign. Set it up, somehow. Maybe say how problems happen when you do it all on your own, when you're a one-man show. You fall in love with yourself, you're blind to other people, other things, and can't anticipate every risk."

Esposito considered the advice, pleased. It had been a while since Nick had made much of a contribution. Esposito did not appear to catch the double meaning of the last admonition.

"Nice. I like it. Let's give it a shot."

Esposito turned and went back into the room. Nick waited for him to settle in, then made his way around to the one-way mirror, to watch. Esposito paced his side of the table, hands busy with elaboration. Though he stood over Michael, he made no overt attempt to intimidate;

he smiled more often than not and spoke at increasing length. Even though Nick couldn't hear what was said, he was almost persuaded by Esposito, his fluency and persistence, when his voice seemed to lift off in an anthem, or lower down to nearly a sigh. But he also saw that he might as well have been serenading a wooden Indian. Nick could only see the back of Michael's head, but his posture was eloquent, varying between church-pew stiffness and exaggerated slouch, elbows on the table. Mostly his arms were crossed, and he wiped his mouth often; sometimes a knee danced with a little nervous energy, but he'd catch himself after a few minutes and resume the rigid pose. After nearly an hour, Esposito sat down, leaning across the table, closing in the space between them. Michael tipped back, at first, then tilted forward, meeting him in the middle. Nick expected the face-off to continue, but Esposito suddenly withdrew and put both of his hands on his head, ready to rip out handfuls of hair. He looked like he would have much preferred to have them around Michael's neck, and Nick rushed around the corner to make his entrance.

Nick threw open the door and strode over to Michael, to amplify the presumed surprise with physical menace. As soon as he did it, he realized the mistake. Michael jumped back, knocking his chair from beneath him, but the reaction would have been the same had Nick tossed a firecracker at him. Nick was supposed to be testing for a single thought, not for the general health of his nervous system. Fortunately, Michael aced both tests, quick with his reflexes and his unfiltered remark. "You wore a vest, you faggot! Even at home, you got the vest on!"

Both detectives were astonished, at the candor of the admission and the brilliant idiocy of the take. *That's it. Nick must be bulletproof!* Nick started to laugh, so abruptly at first that he spat, which provoked Michael beyond restraint—*laughed at and spat on!* Michael lunged forward, swinging, knocking the table to the ground. Esposito knocked Michael back. His head hit the mirror and left a smear of blood from his nose, and he redoubled his effort when he turned again, but Esposito took hold of an arm and twisted it, taking him down to the ground and cuffing him. Esposito looked up at Nick as he locked the cuffs, baffled equally by his partner and his prisoner. Nick covered his mouth, and tears filled his eyes for the second time that afternoon. He raised two helpless hands to Esposito and stepped back quickly, trying to get out of earshot before he broke down in laughter again.

Nick staggered over to the meal room. The lieutenant observed the unsteady transit, and decided to remain in his office. Nick sat down and turned off the television, threw the newspaper out the window. He found some napkins and mopped his face, coughing out the laughter as if it were a bone in the throat. Not long before, Michael could have killed Nick with a Christmas card; a kind word from a man he'd wronged would have sent him to the river, the woods, a quiet place where he could have put the gun into his mouth. Instead, Michael had saved him with his hatred, with a gun—Twice!—telling him he mattered, he had a purpose and a place in this world. After a few minutes, Nick eased into a kind of punchy sobriety, as Esposito walked into the room.

"You know, he really doesn't like it when you laugh."

Nick smiled, and Esposito stood at the threshold, half-worried, half in on the joke.

"So, how many straitjackets do I have to order? You, I figure for a forty-two long. My buddy in there, a little less."

"I'm good, pal."

"I'm glad to hear it. Matter of fact, the other guy, he's calmed down a bit, too. I think he'll stay that way, as long as he don't see your face again."

"That's fine by me. Where do you figure we stand?"

Esposito exhaled heavily and sat down across from Nick at the table. Back to business again, a relief.

"I'm gonna have patrol take him to the hospital for psych shit. Observation. That'll buy us twenty-four hours, and then at least another day in jail. What he said in the room, that would be your classic 'spontaneous utterance.' He couldn't have been clearer if he'd put it on a billboard, but I don't know how it'll play to a jury. I don't even know if I'd want to use it against him, bring it up at all. There's a lot of noise he can make, if either one of us is involved. Especially with his lawsuit. He'll say we set it up. And I did set him up today, sure as shit. He can say he's persecuted, and the prick won't be lying. There's a lot of background to this, too much, and it's not just in the background. I don't want things to get too complicated."

Nick was glad he was already sitting down. *Too complicated?* Esposito seemed untroubled by the ironies. He had work to do, and he was doing it. That much, Nick had to respect, and he strained to emulate him.

"Now that I think about it," Esposito continued, "we're better off without the statement, better off without any long story. Skip the whole soap opera. As long as we get the gun, and we get DNA off it—it'll come in anonymous—the case is about a project kid from a family with a drug history who shoots a guy with a drug history. Why? 'Why' isn't our problem. If we get the evidence, we don't need to deal with the reasons. You follow me so far, Nick? It's not great, not terrible, but this is early, and we're moving along on this. I like how it's going."

Nick didn't know if he was genuinely persuaded, or was just desperate to believe the story could be finally contained. So many suppressions and exclusions, but that was how the system worked. He disliked the idea that Michael's confession—the one truth they had witnessed themselves—would never be heard, never factor in whatever justice was done. Jamie deserved a public reckoning, and Mr. Barry had a right to know. Shouldn't that matter more than anything? But what Esposito said made sense about how the case would unfold, and the end result was what mattered most. Nick nodded, thinking about what else was needed. "We got what he's wearing. It's good. The army jacket stands out. I'm sure he had it on this morning. You gotta take another picture, full-length, before he leaves. And we gotta cover every route between my house and his, see if there's video. If we put him on the street then, we're good. As long as Malcolm comes up with the gun, and we have workable ballistics and DNA. Then it could come together, but that's four 'ifs' I count, right there."

Esposito cocked his head slightly, allowed himself the hint of a smile. He strained to avoid seeming triumphal, but he needed Nick to believe in him again.

"See? If Malcolm was still in, we'd never have a chance with this. I know, it didn't stop it from happening, but maybe nothing would have. It coulda been you, another cop, but it was gonna be somebody. And not for nothing, I'm glad it was a junkie instead of one of us."

Nick didn't know what to say; it was true, but he couldn't bring himself to approve aloud. This time, the casual write-off of Jamie distressed him instead of provoking him. Had Jamie been only a junkie, had he stayed a junkie, he would have never been mistaken for Nick. Night sweats, withdrawal, daily temptations resisted. This was not the occasion for which he'd intended to rise. A knock from the interview room door drew Esposito back to it, relieving Nick of the responsibility of an answer. Esposito opened the door and half-stepped in to talk to Michael.

"Yeah, in a minute. Sit down. You'll go in a minute. I just gotta get some information from you, then you'll be on your way."

He waved to Nick, and then pointed to his jacket, making a writing motion, for pen and paper. Basic information, that was all they wanted. They knew Michael didn't have a criminal record or a driver's license, but they didn't have much to work with. Maybe with his Social Security number, email, they could find out more, something relevant from his military service or a murder-buff website. Nick felt slightly uncomfortable when he started to rifle through Esposito's jacket, the new gray pinstripe. The notebook was where it was supposed to be, on the inside pocket, but there was no pen. Everyone was always out of pens; you could leave gold doubloons on your desk and none would be taken, but you could lock your pens in a steel safe every night, triple-barred, and there would be one fewer of them the next morning. No one considered stealing them to be theft. Nick checked the rest of the jacket, and was not surprised to find keys, mints, a decent cigar. He was not shocked to find condoms, slightly repulsive to the touch, even in their cool foil wrappers. He had not expected to find flowers, two flowers, roses, red and white, each a boutonniere with a pin in the stem. Fresh, supple, with a faint moisture on the surface, like sweat on fevered skin.

"You got it?"

"Yeah."

Nick found one of his own pens and brought it over with the notebook. Esposito didn't look as he took them, concentrating as he was on the other side of the door.

"Thanks."

Esposito stepped into the room and shut the door behind him. Nick went back to the jacket and took out the roses, to touch and smell them, to make sure they were real in the daylight. Yes, the two of them, the red and the white, cut fresh today. Even with a homicide, Esposito had found time. Nick took the red one and held it, sat down at his desk to think. It was Mama Ortega who gave them, not Daysi, but Daysi was the only reason for him to go to the store. Not to say that he'd heard about her and Nick, and he was sorry, or he'd heard about her ex, and he wasn't really. Or to say both things, anything, just to get to talking. And there was only one reason to talk. Esposito didn't make goodwill visits to kiddie cancer wards or nursing homes. Nick had no claim to her, but Esposito had no business trying to stake one. There were millions of women in the city. Esposito hadn't created the situation, as he'd said before, but he would take advantage. After the intimacy of yesterday's conversation—making

Nick swear about saying goodbye—it seemed sharklike, sublime in its indifferent purpose.

Nick pinned the red rose to his lapel, but took the jacket off and hung it on the back of his chair. He wasn't sure yet how to wear his token, what it meant, only that he was ready to ride into battle.

The lieutenant came out of his office and walked over to Nick, who pretended to type.

"So, what do we got?"

"I think the guy who did it is inside with Espo."

"Good. We gonna lock him up?"

"Not today. Soon, I hope."

"What's the story?"

"Mistaken identity."

The lieutenant drew on his cigarette, then threw it onto the floor and stamped it out. He wanted to know, but not too much.

"They usually take a little more time to unravel."

"Espo knows somebody, tipped him off."

Lieutenant Ortiz nodded and smiled.

"Good. He's the guy for this. What are you doing?"

The question was casual but inadvertently profound. What was he doing? What was his purpose, his place? Nick slouched across his chair to cover the red rose.

"Shit, you reminded me. Notification to the family. Neighbors say the father's on a plane, coming back from Ireland today."

Nick went on the computer and found the number for Aer Lingus. He was forwarded to five or six people before he was connected to a retired Irish cop, a security consultant. Confidences were exchanged, sympathetic stories, bona fides. Mr. Barry's first name was James, Nick thought, just like his only son's. He didn't have a date of birth. Hang on, he could run him for the license, here it is, yes. Plus, he had an address. If the consultant could cross-check all the Barrys leaving Ireland today, it would be great, grand. He'd be happy to fax him something on official stationery, no problem. Seven-thirty, JFK airport. Nick remembered reading about what RFK said once, as he was flying in, "I wish they still called it Idlewild." An Indian name, for "a beautiful place." Those were the days, real brothers and real martyrs. It was five o'clock now.

As Nick stood up, Esposito walked out of the interview room. He came over to Nick, and threw his pad down onto the desk, to show him his latest gain. "Look, I have his cellphone and email address. You're gonna love this. It's 'G-HAD1.' He doesn't think we get the joke. We gotta get his computer, too, Nick. God knows what's gonna be on it. We can get rid of him now. I'll tell the cops downstairs they can take him. Hospital first. You know what's crazy? He doesn't know he killed someone else. He still thinks he's getting locked up for trying to shoot you. Anyway, you're right. We gotta canvass every possible street he coulda walked down. I'm gonna take a picture of him. Then we'll go. You ready?"

"Yeah, I'm ready."

Nick put his coat on, and Esposito saw the rose on the lapel. His eyes widened. The reaction was not as telling as Michael's had been, but it had revealed as much, and there was no need to fret over whether it was admissible.

"Ah, shit, Nick. Don't, don't read into this. Where you going?"

"I gotta go to the airport, pick up the father. I gotta tell him. I can't have him find out about it in the hallways, with the old ladies talking. It's what I owe him, given the circumstances."

"Ah, come on, lemme—"

Nick was out the door before Esposito could go on. He went down to the lot behind the precinct, took a car, and drove out to the airport. It was a slow drive, with bridge traffic, all the bridges, from Manhattan to the Bronx to Queens, island-hopping, down south to Jamaica Bay, the salt marshes. He got off the highway before the airport so he could walk around. An hour to kill. He had killed so many before, all of them, almost all. Esposito called several times, and there were more calls from blocked numbers. Allison or IAB? He was so tempted by both, for someone to talk to. Six calls, seven. He wouldn't answer, waiting for whoever it was to leave a message, but no message was left. Broad Channel, that's where he was, an island in the bay. Cops and firemen lived here, bungalow Irish and Italians, wary of outsiders. Little houses, some on stilts over the water. Tough people, living on sand that could be washed away in an afternoon. There was no one around. Nick put the car on the side of the street and headed toward the water. He found a sagging ash-gray wooden dock and walked to the end.

The sun had sunk to the horizon, glowing red like a banked fire, and darkness spilled out from the east. It was desolate here, but nothing was still. Crisp leaves shivered on scraggly trees, and breezes eased through the hummocks in silvery shimmers, brushing the grass back like the hair of a cat. An egret strode along the shore, and gulls wheeled and shrieked above. Nick thought about the last time he had walked to the water's edge, on the far side of the city, by Potter's Field. He'd wanted to walk in. He had walked in, though not far. Nick felt no such temptation now, though his life had not improved since. No, it was worse. He'd had Daysi then, and Esposito had been his trusted friend. Now they had each other, maybe. Maybe she was pregnant, with Esposito's kid; maybe that's what the dream meant. He'd woken before she could finish the sentence. *And we want you to be the godfather.* . . . Nick smiled, in spite of himself. A joke was better than nothing, even when it was on him. He tossed the flower into the water, watched it bob and drift away.

The sun was down to the last sliver when Nick turned and went back to the car. He drove slowly and parked in front of the Aer Lingus terminal, showing the airport cops his shield. He found the gate for the arriving flight, got a cup of coffee and waited. The phone rang again, from a blocked number. He hit the button without answering, waiting for the caller to speak. No one did, and he hung up again. No reception here, maybe. Passengers began to move through the gate, dragging luggage, looking irritable and relieved in shifting combination. Elderly couples in matching souvenir sweaters; young families carrying crying babies; practiced businessmen beelining for the cabstands, laptops in shoulder-strapped cases. More redheads than you would see on Continental or American. Toward the end of the crowd, Mr. Barry walked out, a shopping bag from duty-free in hand. He had a cowlick from sleeping on the plane, his sad old head nestled against an uncomfortable neighbor after a few breakfast Bloody Marys. He stopped when he saw Nick, pleased at first, but mostly confused.

"Nick! Hello! This is a surprise! Did you drive Jamie out? This is a treat!"

Nick shook his hand. He offered a curt, professional half-smile, shaking his head. He knew how to do this. He was even dressed for it, in a black suit. He was glad he'd gotten rid of the flower. Mr. Barry must have understood, but he resisted belief; he wasn't talking to himself, either. Nick realized from what the older man carried that he'd checked luggage. They'd have to spend time at the baggage carousel.

"I'm sorry, Mr. Barry. I have bad news."

Nick could have been reading a telegram. Mr. Barry's mouth contracted and made irregular ripples, as if it were a machine graphing sound waves, stress levels. He shook his head.

"I . . . Don't . . . Not yet."

It was perfectly clear to Nick what he meant. They walked without speaking to the baggage claim and waited. Nick stood just behind him, waiting for him to point out the bag. The black vinyl tread circulated, empty. It had the aspect of ominous ritual, and Nick pictured them waiting to meet Jamie's coffin, flag-draped, a casualty of a foreign war. The crowd leaned in, eager, mistrustful, and anticipating. Babies cried, and a middle-aged couple bickered, the man saying they should have driven to Florida, like before. Luggage began to spill out. A pair of young men with beards and sandals picked up backpacks. A stream of black suitcases and gym bags cruised through, and the passengers picked at name tags, appraising them as if it were an auction. Golf clubs, four or five sets. God, it went on, Nick thought. Mr. Barry the last passenger, his bag the last bag. Mr. Barry almost cried at the sight of his boxy old brown valise, and Nick seized it, leading them away.

At the car, Nick wasn't sure how to open the trunk. Was it the same key as the door, or the engine, or a different one? He put the suitcase in the backseat, and Mr. Barry got in beside, as if it were a cab. When Nick took the driver's seat, Mr. Barry leaned forward, put a hand on his shoulder.

"I knew it wouldn't last, Nick. God forgive me, but I knew it wouldn't. Did he slip up again? Is he in the hospital, in jail?"

Nick waited to answer. He knew that Mr. Barry was lying to himself, wishing things away. He must have gotten dozens of jail calls, hospital calls from Jamie, and Nick had never offered to intervene, had never been asked. He'd never have gone to the airport to get Mr. Barry, even if Jamie were dead, unless it were his fault. But Mr. Barry couldn't know that. He must have presumed there was more kindness, less culpability, in the gesture. Nick started the car, then leaned around, looking back.

"Mr. Barry, I'm sorry, it's worse than that. This morning, Jamie was shot outside of the building. He's dead. I can't tell you how sorry I am, Mr. Barry. He was doing so good. We'd talked a bit, lately, more than in the past. I thought he was doing great. . . ."

Mr. Barry put his hand on Nick's shoulder again and squeezed tight. A workingman's hand, and Nick tried not to squirm.

"Had he fucked up again, Nick? Was he back on the drugs?"

"No, Mr. Barry, he wasn't. He was innocent, he was good. He did nothing wrong."

"Was it the black people?"

Nick didn't know how to answer. His father might have asked the same question, the same way. The tone was more fearful than hostile, as if the matter were almost beyond comprehension, the difference not between darker and lighter neighbors but between transparent beings and opaque ones. Who did Mr. Barry think he could see through—white people, Irishmen? Not Nick, thank God. It wasn't black people who had done this. It was Michael, a singular man with a singular grievance. And Nick couldn't begin to explain, hadn't begun to evaluate how many recent murders—from Milton Cole's through Jamie's this morning—had arisen from a failure to discriminate.

Still, Nick hated to think what had shown in his own face, skeptical but incurious, when he'd first met Michael that night in the projects, ·bearing bad news. Assumptions that went not just with Michael's complexion but his address, the cheap furniture and the expensive TV. A disconnect between them before the awful connection, fighting in the hallway, and cursing each other's dead mothers. Not much hope that Michael and Nick could bridge the divide after that, like Malcolm and Esposito had. Wasn't that a fine model of cooperation? Nick wanted to tell Mr. Barry that racism was spiteful and wasteful, a shame and a plague, but that if he wanted true havoc, white and black men had to work together. Look at what had been accomplished today, with the plan to contain Michael, to spare Nick. Who knew what boundaries remained to be broken? Nick put the car in drive and headed to the exit.

"We haven't worked it all out yet, Mr. Barry. But I promise you, whoever did it will pay. Excuse me."

Nick's phone had rung again. He didn't know who was calling, but he'd talk to anyone.

"Yeah?"

"Meehan?"

It was a man, the one from IAB.

"Yeah?"

"So, you do answer the phone."

Nick didn't answer.

"You there?"

"I am. What do you want?"

"Slow down, guy. What do I want? That's not the question. The question is what do you want? I hear a lot of things are going on in your neck of the woods. We talked before, and maybe we can talk again. Pretty soon, nobody's gonna be interested in anything you got to say, unless it's a guilty plea. You wanna meet, you wanna talk?"

"Sure."

"Really?"

Nick was surprised by his answer as well, its suddenness and ease. He knew it was futile to hide, like a kid pulling the blankets over his head, so the boogeyman can't find him. And he told himself that he might learn more than he would confide, meeting the other side, face-to-face. If the mystery prick had been sitting next to him, right then, Nick doubted he would have told him anything. But he also knew that his life was hurtling toward catastrophe—he'd hit it, already—in ways that seemed not only unjust but unnatural, a train that had jumped the rails but was still picking up speed. And the prospect of moving—to a new apartment, a new precinct, a new partner—had become less devastating to contemplate. "You can put up with more than you think you can." That's what his father had said. It was true, but not true enough. To promise himself anything was to lie. By next week, he might not recognize the words, or the man who'd said them.

"Tomorrow?" the man asked.

"No. Next week."

"Listen, unless there's a death in the family—"

"There is," Nick said.

"Sorry. Um . . . I guess I'll call next week."

My God, Nick thought as he hung up the phone, this man had a knack for people. If he were a traveling preacher, he'd turn the pagans into atheists. Drifting from his lane, Nick nearly hit a car. Easy, easy, go down one road at a time. Mr. Barry took his shoulder again.

"Nick?"

"Yeah?"

"Can you take me there? Can I see him? I know it's late, but you're a cop, you can do it."

"Mr. Barry, I don't know if you want to see him now. Wait for the wake. It's better—"

"Is he bad? Was it the face? We can't have it open casket, the wake?"

"No. I mean, you can. And I guess I can take you there, if you want."

"Thank you."

Nick put on the lights and sirens, cut in and out of traffic. The phone rang and rang—he could feel it—but Nick didn't answer. The cars moved aside, mostly, and he and Mr. Barry got to the midtown tunnel in half an hour. Mr. Barry didn't ask any more questions. Nick looked back at him a few times during the ride. He was turning from side to side, nervous at the speed. Nick kept his window open. They sped through the tunnel, with its weird green-white fish-belly gleam, its muffled echo, and Nick went down the FDR Drive, then hooked back up First Avenue. He'd never tried to bring someone to the morgue after hours; still, he knew he'd manage something. Tonight, he'd manage whatever he needed. Tomorrow, he didn't know how he'd face Mr. Barry, how he'd take the sight of him, day in, day out, the dumb gratitude. He closed his window, and smelled something bad. Had Mr. Barry farted? It smelled awful, and Nick was almost offended. He pulled over at the morgue entrance on the side street and parked.

"Here we are, Mr. Barry."

There was no answer. Nick got out and opened the door for him, and Mr. Barry spilled out, almost falling onto the street. Nick caught him and pushed him back.

"Shit."

Nick held him up and looked at him. Was he dead? The face was as pale as the tunnel tile, green-white and still. The car stank of shit. Nick laid him down and closed the door. He turned the lights and sirens back on, put the car into reverse, backed down the street to the hospital. As he drove up to the emergency room, he hailed two EMTs who were walking out—strangers, thank God—and had them get a stretcher. They got Mr. Barry out of the car and wheeled him in. Nick found some paper towels, bleach, and latex gloves, and wiped out the backseat. Inside the ER, he took Mr. Barry's keys, so he could get into the apartment later. He needed to find phone bills and address books to locate relatives who could take care of arrangements for both father and son. In the meantime, he allowed the ER admitting staff to put him down as next of kin, as a nephew, so there would be no blanks on the necessary forms. As he drove home, it occurred to Nick that he might be called upon to make critical medical decisions for Mr. Barry. When the day had begun, he and Jamie hadn't even been friends; at the end, they were family, as much family as either had left, for whatever it was worth.

FORTY

race called the next day, in the afternoon. Nick asked how she'd gotten the number, and she said she had taken his card out of her father's jacket, a while ago, and kept it for herself. Nick didn't ask why; he didn't want to know. He had thought of her earlier, when he'd seen her picture on his desk. It would have been professional to draw her out on the matter, to subject her motives to a degree of scrutiny, but whether the theft of his business card had been inspired by a teen crush or telepathy, he didn't want to revisit the image of finding something in a pocket. Nick had barely spoken to Esposito since he'd found the flowers, but he'd spent much of the day out of the office, at the hospital and the Barry apartment. Mr. Barry's prognosis was poor, but Nick had found a phone number for a sister on Long Island, relieving him of his medical and funeral duties. "Thank God for you," she said. "What a blessing to have a policeman in the building." It had been a long day.

"What's up, Grace? How are you?"

"Good. Good, I guess. How are you?"

The question seemed devastatingly intimate, rudely direct.

"Detective?"

"Yeah. Sorry, Grace—I was distracted. Busy here today. I'm fine."

"Anyway, I was calling because you said the other detectives would call."

"Didn't they?"

"No. So . . . is it like . . . you, for me?"

She'd meant to ask if Nick had been assigned to the case, he knew, but he couldn't answer, the way she'd asked. Grace tried again.

"I mean, you're the one who has to get the one . . . for what happened?"

"Sure, Grace. Not just me, but I'm involved, and you can call to talk about it, if you have anything to tell me about it, anytime."

"That's what I figured. Anyway, the guy—you know, that guy—he came up to me last week, when I got off the bus, right by school. He said 'Hi!' "

"He said 'Hi'? Anything else?"

"No. There was a police car on the corner, and he walked away."

"Did you tell them?"

"No. I was surprised. I couldn't really think. I just ran to school quick."

"Next time, tell them, Grace. Anytime."

"Yeah, I know. That's why I called you. It happened again yesterday. He just popped up on the street, in the same place. This time, I was going to the bus—but I was leaving school. He said he wanted to take me out to the movies. I said I'd think about it. I said I couldn't go till Friday, because of school. Ugh!"

"Friday. That's tomorrow."

"Uh-huh."

"Sorry. Grace, are you at home now?"

"Yeah."

"Let me call you back in a little bit. I have to figure how we work this out. Did you tell your father about this?"

"God, no! He couldn't handle it. He'd *completely freak*! He's nicer now, but he cries a lot. . . . He doesn't bother me as much anymore. I kinda feel bad for him. You don't have to tell him, do you?"

"I will, at some point. He's still your father. Maybe not right now. Like I said, I'll call back soon. When does he get home?"

"Not for, like, two hours. I'm not allowed out, but it's okay. I have a lot of homework."

"Okay, Grace. Stay put."

"Okay, Detective. And thanks for talking to me. Bye!"

When Nick put down the phone, he walked into the lieutenant's office and closed the door. All he intended was to tell him about Grace, to ask him to call Special Victims, boss to boss; either team could work the case, but one of them had to get started. It couldn't float in administrative no-man's-land for another day. The lieutenant looked at him, then closed the blinds of the single window, so the rest of the squad couldn't see the conversation. As the blinds went down, Nick saw Esposito pick up his coat, tap Napolitano on the shoulder, and head for the door. Napolitano hurried behind. Nick was confused by the reaction, at first, then embarrassed. When someone went for a private conference with the lieutenant, it usually meant that there was a complaint to be made, an accusation that required the attention of the chain of command. This wasn't what Nick had intended, but he wasn't inclined to offer reassurance. What would he tell Esposito? *If I give you up, it won't look like this. You won't see it coming.* Lieutenant Ortiz took his seat and leaned across his desk, folding his hands, cracking his knuckles. From the lieutenant's pained, concerned expression, Nick saw the second misapprehension. His partner thought he was a rat, and now his boss was afraid he might kill himself. He could not object to the substance of the accusations, only their timing, their relevance to the issue at hand.

"Are you all right, Nick? If you need to talk, I'm glad . . . you're talking."

"Are you kidding me? No, Lou. This is what I got. . . ."

When Nick told him, he could see that the lieutenant was intrigued and relieved at the same time. He said he'd make a call, find out what was happening. Nick went back out and found the men staring intently at him, as if he were about to commence the reading of a will. Was Esposito in Mexico yet? He and Nick were now doubly divided, over the Cole machinations and Daysi. One was a major crime, the other a sneaky little indiscretion, but Nick wasn't sure which troubled him more. Yes, he was. He thought about calling Esposito, then held back. He went to his desk and sat down.

Garelick studied him before he ventured conversation, cautious in his approach. "It's supposed to snow tomorrow. Tough trip in for me. You, I guess it won't matter. You want coffee, Nick? I'll make a fresh pot. . . ."

It nearly broke Nick's heart not to laugh at him, but he gravely shook his head. "Not where I'm going."

"What? You want a transfer? Where?"

"The French Foreign Legion. Where we go to forget."

"C'mon, Nick."

"Nobody's got anything to worry about. Special Victims tried to dump a case on us. Now I want to steal it."

"Nick!" Garelick yelled, nearly trembling with relief. "I knew you were just an asshole! That's great! The best news! Still, I want a fresh cup. I might even take over the coffee club. It's such a disgrace, the way things have gone downhill. You know even the refrigerator is broken? The milk's on the ledge to stay cold, like my father did on Orchard Street, when he peddled fish. . . ."

"Your father was an accountant."

"Don't spoil the mood."

Garelick was pouring the coffee when Lieutenant Ortiz came out of his office. He was smiling, too. He had lost the argument with the lieutenant from Special Victims, and the case was not a case—it was nothing, as far as the other squad was concerned. Lieutenant Ortiz was welcome to waste whatever time, whatever manpower, he had on it. Garelick poured the coffee, taking in what was said. He didn't know exactly what was going on, but now he knew what wasn't. When the cups were full, he stepped out of the office, probably to call Napolitano, Esposito, to let them know they had nothing to fear. When they didn't return, Nick figured they didn't trust Garelick, either. He didn't care as much as he might have; he had Grace, someone to work for, the prospect of accomplishment, colossally simple, a snake he might catch without jumping into the snake pit.

Lieutenant Ortiz drove down with Nick to pick Grace up from her building, and they circled the school, noting exits and entrances, where the bus stop was, the possibilities of escape and approach, residential buildings and commercial ones, which had wide windows, where someone might watch, where someone might run. Grace was interested by the mechanics of the operation, excited that she was part of the plan. When she told the lieutenant that he should grow his hair longer, that it would make him look younger, both detectives flinched and didn't answer. The lieutenant didn't even turn around when they stopped, but Nick got out of the car and opened her door, an escort's gesture, he knew. They were around the corner from where she lived, so neighbors and worse could not see.

Nick told her that she should go to school tomorrow, she would be safe, they would make sure that nothing went wrong. He thought about giving her his cellphone number, then decided against it. It could be taken the wrong way. The lieutenant drove back to the school and parked the car. He did not make a movement that indicated he might get up. Instead, he settled in his seat and looked over at Nick, lighting a cigarette.

"Nick, do what you gotta do. I've done too much police work for one day. This kid—I got daughters her age. My God! Do you believe her?"

Nick nodded.

"Yeah. Me, too. I can't believe how she's keeping together through this. I can almost see how you'd hold it against her. How somebody might. Stupid, but I can see it happen. God forbid . . . And you have to let the father know. You want me to take care of that, Nick? You want me to make the call? If he won't let her go, he won't. We can work it out without her, just cover the school."

Nick knew at once that he had no intention of telling Ivan Lopez. Not telling him was what Esposito would have done; maybe they had rubbed off on each other more than he was willing to admit.

"Nah. I got it."

"Plus, you let the sister know that we'll set up here tomorrow. We'll be outside. The school day should go on like normal for the kids, everyone else. Everything should seem like it usually does. Did I ever tell you, Nick, that nuns scare me?"

When Nick saw Sister Agnes in the hall, she regarded him sternly, then beckoned him to follow her to her office. En route, she stopped a group of girls as they jogged down the hall, in basketball uniforms. One of them was singled out, and the rest were sent on; Sister Agnes accomplished the separation with a wave of one hand, then a flick of the fingers. The outlier was culled from the herd with astonishing economy. The girl trembled, at first, then sulked.

"What is this you have around your neck?"

"A medal, Sister."

"I see that. What of? I apologize. Let me rephrase. Of what saint is this a medal? Whose image is cast about your neck, in bronze?"

"Saint Barbara, Sister. And it's gold."

"Perhaps electroplate, but it is no concern, the surface. Did Saint Barbara have red eyes? Were they made of rubies, this saint who you believe to be your friend? Who is Saint Barbara?"

"I dunno, Sister."

"No, you do not. And since you do not, and cannot, please do not wear this jewelry. A crucifix, the Miraculous Medal, Our Lady, many things mean something. Saint Barbara does not."

"Yes, Sister. But my moms gave it to me."

"Tell her, then, to look up Saint Barbara, and your mother will find she does not exist. Saints are to help us find God. God does not find us— even—*especially*, when we try to look pretty, in a foolish, unladylike way.

Such as with makeup, as you wear. Go to the bathroom and wash your face, please. Right now, so I will not ask you to stay after school tomorrow, to write an essay about modesty."

When the girl had been dismissed, Sister Agnes explained that the legend of Barbara was from the time of the early Christians, during the persecution of the Romans. Her cruel pagan father had her killed for her faith, after which he was struck down by lightning. Sister Agnes continued the lesson as she led Nick to her office. "The Orthodox Church still allows her cult, but we do not. So you see, if a Greek girl wore the necklace, or a Russian, it would be merely silly. But for many Spanish people, from the islands, Barbara is a disguised saint. They use her as the Christian face of one of the pagan gods, from slavery. The war god, of all things—because of the lightning! Can you think of a deception that is quite so repellent? Can you, Detective?"

"Not offhand, Sister."

"If I wanted a thousand gods, I could have stayed in India."

They sat there in silence for a moment, each distracted by private reverie. Sister Agnes seemed mournful. Did she miss her childhood, its crowded heavens? Nick looked away, in furtive deference, unwilling to intrude, reluctant to be caught staring. He felt terrible for poor Barbara, cast out from the communion of saints. What a harsh accusation, the worst possible insult: not unimportance but nonexistence. Nick sympathized. Then, he remembered.

"Actually, there is something worse, Sister. That's what I came to see you about."

"Yes, forgive me. Please."

And Nick told her what had happened, what he wanted to do. He did not tell her that Grace had been raped, only that she had been followed by a man Nick believed to be the rapist. He assured her that he did not mean to interrupt the routine of the school; in fact, he needed it to continue without interruption. Sister Agnes considered what was said, flexing her fingers.

"I might suggest the tower, on the southwest, as convenient. Quite a bit of the surroundings are visible, and it is rarely used."

"Convenient for what, Sister?"

"If you need to shoot him, of course. From a distance. With a rifle."

"Thank you for offering. I think other plans . . . are, um, being planned."

"Very well. We are at your disposal."

Sister Agnes rose from her seat, indicating Nick should do the same, and led him down the hall. She stopped for a second, then continued walking, as if something had occurred to her, but she did not want to reveal her sudden thought. "We have a very fine lady here, a counselor. Do you think that Grace would benefit from speaking to her, in the event that she has experienced any . . . difficulty or confusion?"

"It's always good to have someone to talk to. . . . I don't know if Grace is more confused than anyone else her age. Less, in lots of ways."

"I see. . . . Ladies!"

Sister Agnes had spotted the basketball team again, as they clustered in a hallway corner. One of them had seen her, and she had spurred the girls into jogging again with a desperate elbow, amid fits of giggles. Sister knew there was some clandestine activity afoot, likely innocent, but nonetheless worthy of her notice. "They must be watched, always. Otherwise, it would be bedlam."

"Bethlehem."

"I beg your pardon?"

"The word comes from 'Bethlehem,' Sister. From a mental hospital in England, called Bethlehem. It was the way the local people said it."

Sister Agnes stopped abruptly. "That may be true, Detective, but it is nonetheless impertinent. I shall see you tomorrow, of course, if necessary. But I hope it is not."

Back at the squad, the plans were laid early in the evening, for the next day. Grace would be watched as she walked from her apartment to the bus stop; one of the detectives would be on the bus when she boarded. The rest of the roles required costumes, or at least props, and Nick was impressed by how they were fought over. They could use a groundskeeper, a phone company man on the pole, maybe a derelict. Could there be a hot dog vendor? No, not in this cold. And snow, heavy snow, was forecast for tomorrow. Esposito had hung back from the meeting, and Nick thought he seemed sullen. He usually wanted the lead, and usually he got it; now he said nothing. Garelick wanted to be a priest, but Lieutenant Ortiz had vetoed the request.

"That's just prejudice, plain and simple," Garelick muttered, his affront unfeigned.

The lieutenant was unmoved. "I'm the priest, and what I say goes. Whoever doesn't have a bit now, they're in cars, two in a car, on side streets, ready to move in. Nobody gets to be the milkman, nobody gets to be the chimney sweep, whatever. This is not a goddamn high school musical!"

In the end, the assignments were made, and Esposito and Napolitano took one of the catch cars, staying off to the side. The lieutenant was wrong. This was a play, and it was high school. Grace alone had undertaken her role without fear or fuss. The men had argued in the office about what her signal should be if she saw him, whether it should be to blow her nose or take off her glasses, and Nick tried to remember if she was in the habit of doing either. It had to be subtle enough for the detectives to recognize, at a distance, without the rapist noticing, up close. Less than doing jumping jacks, more than yawning or blinking, touching her nose. Nick told the lieutenant he'd work it out, and tell them later.

"And you told the father, Nick? What did he say?"

"A lotta cursing in Spanish, a lotta crying. He's the father. You know how it is, Lou. But he knows this is the best chance to get the guy, so he's on board."

Nick thought he had lied beautifully, but he caught a flicker of wariness in the lieutenant's eyes, so he went on. "The one thing he says? He says, 'Make sure there's not a trial. The animal, he doesn't deserve it.' I told him we'd do what we had to do."

The lieutenant was satisfied with the answer, and went home soon after. When Nick called Grace again, it was from the lieutenant's office, with the door closed. He hoped her father wouldn't pick up the phone.

"What kind of shoes do you wear, Grace?"

"Regular shoes. Ugly. Uniform shoes. But tomorrow it's supposed to snow, so I'll wear my new boots. They're really nice, and—"

"You'll have boots on, in the morning?"

"Yeah. It's supposed to snow. My father got 'em. I can't believe it, but they're really nice."

"Okay. Wear them tomorrow, even if it's sunny. And if you see the guy, I want you to drop down, pretend to tie your shoe."

"But there's no laces."

"I know. It's so if you drop down to check, it's not for that. It's so we'll know he's there."

"Won't he know, too?"

"No. I don't think so. Most guys don't pay much attention to shoes. He's smart, but I don't think he's that smart. Were, um, you wearing shoes when he was there before? Was he really interested in them? Did he touch them, or did he say anything about them?"

"Nah."

"Okay. Just check something in your shoe. Pretend something's stuck, there's a rock in it, whatever."

"Okay."

"All right. Good. Also, since they're new shoes, would you walk around in them tonight for a little bit? I don't want you to stub your toe, and everybody jumps in, scaring him away. Tell you what— Never mind, let's think of something else, another signal—"

"No, Nick. It's okay. I get it. They fit fine. My father has a shoe store. He doesn't know much, but my shoes fit. Anyway, I'm gonna march around my room, just to be safe, so it feels right, for tomorrow. It's gonna be hard to go to sleep tonight. . . . And I can't tell my father, right?"

"Right."

All of these melodramatic secrecies were awful, maybe illegal, but the alternatives were worse. Lopez could only get in the way. Grace called one last time, later that night, just before Nick was going home.

"Detective Nick?"

"Yes?"

"Do you promise to get him?"

The temptation tore at Nick, but he could not say the one word she wanted. He grasped for an answer that would give neither of them frostbite.

"I can't make guarantees like that, Grace. But I promise you, if he shows up, I'll do what needs to be done."

"Okay. Mostly, I just wanted to say thanks. Also, that I feel sorry for him. That guy. He must be so . . . I don't know. But can you imagine what it's like to be him? I feel bad. . . . Is that weird?"

Nick was speechless again, as he had been when she had first called that day. Then, he had feared she had seen through him; now he was afraid he would never see her, never begin to comprehend her wild gift. She hadn't forgiven the rapist, but she felt for him, tried to understand. There was something devastating in how she did that, even now— especially now, on the eve of another ordeal—that there was a place in her mind for compassion, a thought for someone else. It was almost offensive in its generosity. She was the true mystery, not the degenerate who pursued her. Brutality and need were natural, not this. Nick was humbled, grateful that he had the chance to work for her.

"Do you think it's weird?"

"A little, Grace, but we're all a little weird. You're all right, though. Get some rest."

"Okay. See you tomorrow."

"We'll be there, even when you don't see us."

Nick looked at her picture on his desk one last time before he went home, in the silly pose, the ghastly, trashy getup. He wished he had another, like Napolitano's communion pictures of his kids, the sweet piety not at all false despite the canned emotion and hokey costumes. Then he thought this photograph was a better icon, just as it was, a reminder that things were not as they seemed.

FORTY-ONE

A cold night, a cold dawn. It was barely sunrise when Garelick and Nick set up on a rooftop with binoculars, and they remained for two hours before Grace left her apartment, across the street. No one expected anything to happen during the morning, but rehearsal would limit the risk. An older undercover had been borrowed from Narcotics to keep watch in the lobby, singing sentimental songs, sipping brandy. Perez was the passenger on the bus, but he was forbidden the use of hidden microphones, which might have tempted him to have sustained conversations with his sleeve. He had been instructed to remain aboard for several more stops past the school—two, no five—just to be safe. Garelick and Nick would have the sleeve-mikes, earpieces concealed below wool caps. It was late morning when the two of them walked onto the school grounds, in green coveralls. Sister Agnes was waiting at the gate. She did not acknowledge Nick as he passed. The air was fierce and frigid, with sudden gusts that approached gale speed, and the snow had begun to fall. That would have explained why Sister Agnes's eyes were so red.

The sister couldn't stay there; she was too visible, too effective in her pose of warning. Nick didn't want to approach her, equally wary of countersurveillance and of her fiery eyes. He had to tell someone, and he found the priest, pacing on the edge of the pallid lawn. Lieutenant Ortiz wore a cassock of the old style, the black robe with the long row of buttons down the middle, thirty-three of them. When he saw Nick, the lieutenant tapped him on the shoulder, beckoning him with a nod to follow around to the side of the school. He shivered, the white skullcap on his head offering little warmth. Nick was appreciative of the efforts he had taken, until it occurred to him that only the pope wore the white cap.

Nick stared at it until the lieutenant noticed the scrutiny and responded with a hint of petulance.

"Garelick gave it to me. It's a yarmulke from his family. He wanted me to have it today. For luck. I felt bad that he didn't get to do the priest bit. God damn, I want a cigarette."

They withdrew farther into the grounds until they found an alcove in the walls, a hidden garden in the gap. There were four bare rosebushes, a plaster saint, three girls huddled around a single unlit cigarette. Lieutenant Ortiz strode in among them and snatched it out of their hands.

"Gimme that."

He slapped his chest, his hips, where he might have expected to find his lighter in ordinary clothes. The cassock had no pockets. He took the matches from one girl's hands and lit the cigarette, ducking down and blocking the wind with his shoulders. He could have done it at sea, during a typhoon. He drew deeply on the cigarette, twice, then passed it back to the girl.

"Thanks."

The girl blinked, then nervously returned it. Lieutenant Ortiz took the cigarette and winked at her before turning to lead Nick away. Nick could hear them as he left: "What's up with Father? He's so *ghetto*. . . ."

The snow fell more heavily, started to stick to the ground. Though Lieutenant Ortiz was calm again, a cigarette dangling from the corner of his mouth, Nick fumed at the needless risk of the encounter, the attention it could attract. Yes, just another day in the convent, nothing to see here, nothing at all, just the pope bumming smokes from schoolgirls in a storm. They walked to an outbuilding, a shed that held some landscaping equipment, some tools. Nick stepped inside to assess the possibilities—a bit of a workshop, a bit of a clubhouse. It would do. The shed was almost warm, and Nick calmed down. The lieutenant waited at the door, looking outside.

"You have to tell Sister Agnes to go back inside," Nick said.

"I'll tell her. We might as well hole up here for a few hours, till the afternoon. I'll call the other guys, tell them to set up again at two. Have them pass by, every half hour or so, see if somebody's lurking around. The weather's on our side. It doesn't feel like it, but it is. Here comes Garelick—looks like he's got some supplies. Good. Don't complain about the hat, Nick. You'll hurt his feelings."

Garelick came inside and closed the door after him, stamping his feet like a Yukon trapper back at his cabin. Nick had doubts about whether he was up for it, if he had the heart or the strength for the labors ahead. Garelick cared about Nick, not the girl or the perp. When Nick had shown him Grace's picture, on the rooftop earlier, he'd barely glanced at it. Garelick carried a brown grocery bag in his arms, and cleared a table of oil cans and paintbrushes to lay out sandwiches and coffee. After the meal was arranged, he shook out the bag, and two packs of cigarettes and a lighter fell out. Lieutenant Ortiz smiled. If he'd had doubts about Garelick, they had been laid to rest.

"Hang tight," said the lieutenant. "I'm gonna have a talk with the sister. Back in five. Don't eat without me."

With that announcement, he strode back into the storm.

"What's up with him? It is cold out, dammit. . . . Nick, are those shoes waterproof? You really should— Anyway, I brought coffee. I'm having mine. I'm not waiting. They're all black. I got cream and sugar on the side. Real cream, Nick. I know you like that."

Garelick stamped his feet again, and unzipped his green coveralls. He was wearing a suit underneath, dark blue, with a white shirt and a yellow checked tie. He might have bought it on sale twenty years before, he might have worn it once a week since, but the effect was elegant, as if he had crawled up through the surf at a moonlit tropical beach, shedding his wet suit for a tuxedo, monocle, and martini. He fixed Nick a coffee and made another cup for himself, lifting it in casual salute. How old was he? Was he sixty? He couldn't be much more, but he wasn't less; today he had come here, slipping through a blizzard, in disguise, trying to help snatch a serial rapist. He had semi-contemporaries who were Sunbelt evacuees, arguing over shuffleboard scores, nudging someone else's widow in the diner nearest to the golf-condo townhouse community. *I don't care about my pressure. Would you give me the dessert menu?*

Even as Nick had begun to recast him, sloughing off old assumptions, Garelick raised a hand with unexpected authority; he put his coffee down, and Nick felt obliged to do the same.

"Nick, let me tell you this as advice, as a friend. Before the lieutenant comes back. No one has more than one stomach. You can't eat twice. Do you follow what I'm saying?"

"No."

"This fight with Esposito. I don't know why you and him hate each other now, but I don't know why you connected in the first place, let alone got so close. You were the only one who ever really got along with him. Not for nothing? Nobody really got along with you, either, Nick. You were a putz; he was a prick. But it worked! Now, both of you, you're driving everyone crazy. Everybody can feel it. Nobody has fun anymore. And there's more than hard feelings at stake. On days like today, you don't need the distraction. Somebody could get hurt.

"Don't say anything. I wasn't looking for an answer. I didn't ask a question."

Nick understood and agreed, though the desert wisdom of the two-stomach bit was still obscure to him. Lieutenant Ortiz came back inside. He found a seat on a stool and hiked up his cassock, taking a cigarette and coffee. He had jeans on beneath his robes, which somehow seemed indecent. As they ate, they worked through the possibilities. When the rapist had first attacked Grace, conning his way inside her house, was the gun real? Was he from this neighborhood, or had the next meeting been by chance? At this stage, the perp appeared to be a planner, a strategist. He knew where she went to school, how and when, that she walked alone. Nick remembered what he could about the pattern. Most of the victims were young, suggesting that there was a preferred target, which meant selection and study. The rapist didn't just knock on random doors. But a third of the victims were middle-aged and beyond. What did that mean? That he made mistakes, but he didn't mind when he made them. Everything was good for him, each one a win. When Nick asked the lieutenant if he knew anything else, he replied that his counterpart at Special Victims had brusquely informed him that the details were confidential. It would be sweet for Lieutenant Ortiz if his squad carried the day.

When they finished eating, conversation dropped off. The lieutenant took the one good chair, and Garelick shaped bags of grass seed into a bench. Nick went to the window to check the snowfall. Sodden flakes began to pile up; the noontime sky could have passed for dusk. The lieutenant was right, the storm was on their side. Whoever was out there couldn't see them, and no one could see through them, to their lesser motives. The boss wanted revenge on a rival lieutenant; Garelick wanted to show he could work, when it mattered. Nick wanted to believe his luck had changed, that his heart still beat. That he could be a powerful help to a child who needed him, and accomplish something without his partner.

What mattered was that they were here. But Garelick was right, too. Differences had to be put aside to focus on the matter at hand. Nick called Esposito.

"Hey, Espo."

"Hey."

Garelick and the lieutenant both stirred when Nick spoke, then took pains to appear as if they hadn't noticed. It was awkward enough as it was, and Nick stepped outside.

"What are you up to? You in the office?"

"Nah . . . have to meet somebody. Quick trip."

"Anything going on . . . with that? Either brother?"

"Haven't met him yet. . . . The connection's kind of bad here."

The connection was fine. Esposito didn't want to talk about it on the phone, and he was right to remind him. The Cole brothers didn't matter as much to Nick today, somehow; not Jamie Barry, either. Today was for possibilities, not the past.

"Yeah. How's the driving?"

"Not too bad yet, but it's getting there. When we set back up again, it's gonna be tricky to find a spot, to make sure we're not stuck when your guy shows up."

"Yeah."

"Listen, Nick? Let's go out tonight, get something to eat, have a couple of drinks. I'm not gonna drive back upstate in this weather. I mean, after this wraps up, however it goes. This guy, maybe he forgot his galoshes, you know? Maybe he puts it off today . . . Maybe he's not even the same guy from the pattern. Besides, the kid—she's a little off, isn't she?"

"No, she's solid. And he'll be here."

"Okay. I'll check back in a bit. You someplace warm?"

"We got a roof over our heads. Catch you later."

At first, Nick was glad they had talked. Dinner would be good. They might clear the air. Maybe Malcolm hadn't panned out. He couldn't control his brother, or he wasn't trying, or there was no need. Nick could talk Esposito into "finding" the video for the DA, letting the case work its way through court, getting Malcolm a lenient plea for his cooperation. Maybe there was an innocent explanation for the flowers in the jacket—two of them meant that he had seen Mama, not Daysi, after all. Let the past pass. Nick was astonished to realize that it was work that had made him this happy, that vitalized him, called him back to life. And it was the thought of work that bothered him about the conversation with Esposito. What was wrong here? Nick was planning the capture of the most wanted criminal in New York, arguably the worst man out of eight million, and Esposito was planning dinner. Maybe if it wasn't his case, his collar, he wasn't much interested. Leave it alone, Nick thought. Stick to work. Work and weather.

Nick grabbed a shovel that leaned against the wall, telling Garelick and the lieutenant that he was going to give the grounds a once-over. Garelick pointed out a snowblower in the corner of the shed.

"These make it a lot easier, Nick, trust me. I got one, and I don't even use it. I pay the neighbor kid. Shoveling is not fun. You wouldn't know. It was a shock to the system when I had to do it, when we first moved out of the city—"

"The snowblower might be better, but it's a lot louder. I'm not gonna have an engine roaring next to me, if I need to talk or listen. Don't worry. You can wait here for now."

Garelick made a sour face, considering the manual labor that awaited him. He stamped his feet again, knowing they would get colder still. When they looked at the lieutenant for a decision, they knew the answer. The shovels were the better tactical option, and the lieutenant would not have to lift one. He extended a hand and traced a blessing in the air. Nick went out into the blizzard, and shut the door behind him.

The snow was an inch deep, a little more, on the path from the garage to the school. It was coming down harder, and Nick pushed the shovel ahead, skimming the powder and slush from the path, scraping against the concrete. He could see fifty feet, maybe, but he was looking at buildings and trees, not trying to make a face in the crowd. At the school, he followed the path to where it angled out to the gate, the street. An iron gate, with the chain wrapped around the center bars like a garland, pretending to be locked. Nick took off the chains and walked off the grounds, closing the gate after. The bus stop was farther up the block, closer to the shed. How could he pick out Grace in a crowd of girls, if any of them knelt down to check their shoes? Nick couldn't wait far from her, couldn't wait here. The shed would have been perfect in other weather, except for the stone wall that blocked the view of the street. Nick cleared out a narrow trail from the school to the gate, a single file walkway. It took him fifteen minutes, and he was soaked in sweat. He looked at his watch—quarter to one. Sister Agnes must have sent the custodial staff away for the day. No, she would have gotten something out of them, had them mop and buff the assassination tower. Nick should have looked into that, so the detectives could have blended in with the staff instead of taking over their work. No, this was best; no one would react, ask questions, show a break in the routine. His back ached, and he trudged back inside to the shed, to rest for the last hour.

Nick closed his eyes for a few minutes, lying down on Garelick's sack bed. It was surprisingly comfortable, and he only woke when he slid off the side of the plastic. Jolted, Nick looked around. The lieutenant was on the phone with Napolitano or Esposito, confirming their position in the catch car. North and west were parkland, steeply sloped and thickly wooded. They couldn't cover that, shouldn't need to. Was there coffee left? No, yes, it was cold. Don't need it. Did Nick hear right? Perez would be walking around, in plainclothes. What kind of clothes? Nick jumped up and grabbed his shovel. Garelick looked doleful as he got up. Nick checked his watch. Quarter to three, dammit. He'd overslept.

The lieutenant stopped him with a hand on the shoulder.

"Put some rocks in your pocket."

"What?"

"Rocks in your pocket. Slow down. Wait for it to happen. Don't run, don't push. It's up to him now. He'll come. This is your day, Nick. Things are turning for you. I can feel it."

"What?"

"Rocks in your pocket. Trust me."

Why were Garelick and Lieutenant Ortiz speaking to him in rustic fables? Two stomachs, lucky rocks, like he was a peasant boy who needed references to simplest nature in order to comprehend the wider world. Still, Nick understood, and understood both men to be right. When he looked at the lieutenant, he almost didn't recognize him. His advice was unassailably wise, and his regalia forbade any dissent. Had he offered his ring, Nick would have kissed it, kneeling. Instead, he took a breath and waited for Garelick to get a shovel.

They slipped down the path toward the school, but when Garelick started to shovel, Nick pulled him away, told him to keep walking. Whatever sudden reverence Nick had felt for the lieutenant, he did not feel obliged to clear his way for a triumphal procession. They started digging out the sidewalk in front of the gate, rough and sloppy, good enough for civil servants on loan. Nick's long underwear was soon cold and wet beneath his coveralls; he didn't want to think about Garelick, with his suit beneath his suit. Snow, snow, snow falling down. How Nick had loved it when he was young. Everyone did. Did Grace, today? A bell rang. The girls must have been dismissed. Nick dug faster, hoping Garelick would follow. The detectives moved toward the bus stop, and they were halfway there when Garelick fell.

Garelick began to yell in another language, bitter and foreign. Nick thought he was making it up at first. The words were like coughing—spitty, gargling sounds, like popcorn cooked in his lungs. Garelick's face went gray, his color not much darker than the snow. A man walked down to them from the bus stop and leaned over, asking what was wrong. He was dressed for the cold, well-prepared—a blue down coat that almost reached his knees, a bulky black knit cap. He also carried a shopping bag. He looked familiar to Nick.

"Ees nothing. He drunk."

Nick did a bad Russian accent, haplessly inspired by the Slavic-sounding noise. Nick jerked his head away from the stranger and leaned closer over Garelick, fanning his face with his hands. The girls began to walk through the gates, all of them at once, the whole school. No one would stay late today, for sports or clubs. Nick and the black-capped by-stander looked over to them at the same time, and then Nick looked down again, so he wouldn't be caught staring.

"Good luck," the man said. "*Vaya con Dios.*"

The man in the hat walked away, across the street, then turned and waited. Nick spoke into his sleeve, calling for help, pressing buttons, and when he did not hear an answer, he called 911 from his phone. It would take a while for an ambulance, in the snow. The hat waited in the middle of the street for girls to come to the bus stop. He knew no cars would come. There would be almost no traffic today. He could wait and watch. Nick knew him, but couldn't place him. Again, the halves of his mind were not yet speaking. He couldn't leave Garelick. Garelick twitched, and Nick touched his face. It felt cold, but everything else did, too. Nick looked over to the man in the street—hat man, his man—and saw that he was speaking with someone else. The second man came over—Perez—as the first began to pace, agitated.

Nick tried to keep his voice down as he asked, "What did you say?"

"What happened? Is he all right?"

"No, I called an ambulance. What did you say to the guy?"

"Who?" Perez was baffled. "What guy?"

"In the street, the guy you just talked to?"

"I said I came to pick up my daughter, she was crying. She said something bad happened at school. I said I was afraid it was one of those crazy school things, like from Colorado or Virginia."

Perez had conjured another damsel, but the distress appeared to be actual and widespread. One girl screamed, then another; two fell in the snow.

"Stay with Garelick."

The man in the cap began to move through the packs of girls, who were slipping and falling, laughing and throwing snow. Nick got up and slipped, got up again, moving in toward him—thirty feet. More shrieks—terrified or delighted, the same to the ear—girls falling over, bending down to fix their shoes. Bedlam, bedlam. The girls thinned into smaller groups, heading toward different bus stops, the train. The man began to pace, going back and forth, approaching one group, another. Nick slipped again, hit the ground hard. The wind was in his eyes when he got up. He couldn't see the man, still couldn't place him. Another context, not this. A scream again, not delighted, very near. Nick couldn't see where it was coming from until he saw a girl who looked like she was dancing, swatting at her boot with each frantic kick. This was the signal, the sign. Twenty feet ahead, Grace and the man in the hat. He pulled her free arm, and she pulled away. He saw Nick coming, turned to her and slapped her face. "You liar!" It shocked Nick as if he'd been slapped, too. The man was not only enraged, he was wounded, hurt to the core, as if he had offered only love and had been betrayed. He dropped the bag and ran. Nick was close, but both of them scrambled on the sidewalk, neither gaining ground.

When the man broke off to the street, Nick saw a figure in black striding forward, his robes flapping back. He was bellowing into the winds as if he commanded them. A car rounded the corner, sliding as it turned, hitting the curb and skidding again, gaining traction. The catch car, with Esposito and Napolitano. It rocketed forward, then slammed into a hydrant on the far side of the street. The lieutenant marched ahead, slapping his hips, then yanked apart his cassock, buttons spraying, to get to the gun. Grace cried out, "Shoot him! Father, shoot him!" He did, but he missed.

The man stopped, stunned, then began to run. He lost traction for a second, then adjusted his stride, skating over the snow. Rocks in your pocket, just the thing. Nick followed after, pushing with a side step, sliding forward, and by the end of the block, where the park began, Nick was almost within reach. That was when the catch car almost hit him, swerving near, fishtailing as brakes were slammed. Nick dove to the side, and as he lay in the snow, he was racked with so much pain he thought the car had not missed. He heard sirens. *That was fast.* Not for him. For Garelick. How was he? Even as the thought formed in his mind, Nick knew it wasn't first among his regrets, and he was afraid he might cry. As he struggled to stand again, Esposito and Napolitano crouched over him, one trying to stop him, the other trying to help him up. Nick didn't know which was which, but he saw that Esposito had tears in his eyes.

"Shit, Nick, are you—"

"Go."

"Are you okay, Nick? Can you move?"

"Go! Nappy, go! Get him!"

As Napolitano lumbered off, Esposito stayed with Nick. He grabbed a shoulder, and then quickly released him, fearful a bone might be broken.

"Nick! Can you get up?"

"Yeah."

As Nick regained his footing, his ribs, his back, and most of his muscles ached. Was all this pain from the chase, the snow shoveling, a spill? He was still wondering when he saw Napolitano trudge back from the edge of the trees. No, that wasn't why it hurt. Nick collapsed back down in the snow, sitting down, face in his hands, and only looked up again when Lieutenant Ortiz seized his arm, struggling for breath. "Did we do it?"

The particular form of the question almost sounded vicious, reminding Nick of the scope of the disappointment. He dreaded seeing Grace again, and tried to figure out what to tell her. But the thought of her moved him past self-pity, spurred him against reacting as her father had, wailing about ruin and loss. It wasn't his own head he needed to hold in his hands.

"No. Yes. I know who he is. Where he lives. We need a lot of people, to cover the perimeter. We need dogs here."

FORTY-TWO

Cops had begun to descend on the location in volume, six or seven cars, lights flashing. Perez was beside a stretcher that bore Garelick into an ambulance, and joined him inside as the door shut. A uniformed cop had secured the shopping bag the rapist had abandoned: a six-pack of beer, a nightgown—for a little girl, pink, full of princess frills—Vaseline, duct tape. Sister Agnes led Grace back toward the school, an arm around her, cooing reassurances as the girl wept. The sight of her in tears almost made Nick tear up, for its own sake, but also because it made vivid in his mind his promise to her, about doing what had to be done. She managed a weak smile as she walked past and said, "Sorry. . . . I know you tried."

Nick scanned her face for glimpses of irony or rebuke; there were none, only a kind of broken tenderness. He had been pitied again, which made him ashamed. He tried to separate the natural disasters of the day from the man-made ones, and he couldn't manage it, couldn't even decide which events were disasters. If Garelick hadn't collapsed, the man wouldn't have come over, and Nick would never have seen his face. If Perez hadn't made up his batshit story of the girls being at risk, the man wouldn't have rushed in. What had the man imagined, a school shooter, a gas leak, that had made all the dropping bodies and yelling seem part of a catastrophe instead of a holiday? This was the lesser fantasy, modest tricks of color and light in the fun house mirror in the rapist's head; far stranger was the picture of himself, as Grace's rescuer. No, there were benefits to both incidents—God forgive him, he hoped Garelick was all right. The only unmixed non-blessing, Nick realized, was when his partner had almost run him over. That would take some time to work through.

When Nick walked past one of the cops, he overheard him say, "Man, that Esposito is something else. Shit really happens when he takes 'em down!"

Before Nick could react, the lieutenant waved him over as he closed his cellphone. Esposito was beside him, and he stepped back a pace when Nick walked over. The lieutenant was excited. "Finally, a break! One of the K-9s—the bloodhound—they're finishing a job in the Bronx. They should be here within the hour. They asked, do we got something from the perp? It'll make it easier for the dog to track him. I said no, but maybe there's something in that shopping bag he left. I can't even remember, was he wearing gloves?"

"It doesn't matter," said Nick, tapping Esposito on the arm. "C'mon. Let's take a ride."

Nick looked around for an undamaged car they might use—"There's one"—and Esposito handed him the keys with a look of self-reproach so profound that Nick laughed. The misery in his face cheered Nick beyond what was conscionable; still, now there were angles to work, tactics to plan, an occasion for hope.

"Stop it, Espo. You drive."

The lieutenant's phone rang again, but before he answered, he warned them, "Don't be long."

Esposito got behind the wheel. He couldn't look at Nick, not yet. They rolled down the hill, braking and releasing, more cautiously than even the slick road warranted.

"So . . ." Esposito kept his eyes on the road with such distracted determination that Nick wanted to make him pull over, take a deep breath.

"So . . ." Nick began haltingly. "So, what do you feel like for dinner?"

"I feel like eating my gun, Nick."

That was not what he wanted to hear. Which one was who now? Nick didn't even want an apology, not for this. Not for anything; Nick just wanted things to go back to where they were, whatever they were. Not this, and no one dead, neither of them. When they passed 181st Street, Nick saw Esposito turn his head toward Daysi's shop, and he realized that Esposito was still waiting for a response.

"If I believed you, I'd have to take your gun from you."

"I don't know, Nick. I never messed up like I did today. I mean, I know you know that it was an accident. Otherwise you wouldn't be busting my balls. And I appreciate that, you being a shithead in the old way. But it's different, and I don't like it. I don't have a sense of things like I used to. I do, but it's wrong. Yesterday, last month, last fall— whenever it was, when we were the goddamn kings of this—if I'd hit you with the car, you woulda landed on top of the rapist, knocked him out with your thick head. That was our luck then. Now . . . Well, today we weren't even partners. I was in the car with Napolitano. It wasn't right. I know why you're pissed at me, but . . . This ain't the time, I know. Where are we going, anyway?"

Nick took a breath, took it in. His ribs ached but his head was clear again. Esposito was right. It should be talked about, and it had to wait.

"Make this left, then right on Broadway."

A car sliding across the opposite lane distracted him; both vehicles moved in slow motion toward each other, gliding toward collision. The detectives tensed up, but when the cars coasted back into their lanes, they relaxed again. Nick's phone rang, from a blocked number. Nick didn't know what would happen later, if he and Esposito would still be talking, so he took advantage to ask, "What's up with the Cole brothers?"

Esposito shook his head, more despondent still as he hunched over the wheel. "I talked to Malcolm today. He got the gun. Forty caliber, same as the one from your friend Jamie Barry. He's gonna meet me later, but he sounded different. I don't like it. I don't know. He said he doesn't think he can talk to his brother."

This was no good. Esposito might have been better off with less confidence, but neither of them could afford for him to lose faith altogether. Esposito's voice almost broke, angry and uncertain. "I told him that wasn't good enough. I gave him a chance, and he ain't takin' it. . . . The leverage I got, he still don't understand. . . . Where are we going?"

"You know the place."

It was a gift to put it as a riddle, to make Esposito think of something else. Esposito puzzled it over for a while, raised a hand as if giving up, then thought again. Nick pointed, and they made the turn and parked. Fortunes had shifted on this block for them several times before.

"You're kidding me."

"No."

"Shouldn't we wait? I mean, he can't be back home yet. Did he see you? Did he recognize you? Does he know that we know—that you know—who he is? Nick, I know this is your case, your call, but this is basic. This is his hole in the ground, this is where he hides. Do we want to close it off right now, or let him come home?"

Esposito was right, but Nick didn't care. Tactics and plans, the best they could do with what they had—that had been done already today. They were still cold and wet, angry and tired. They were still empty-handed.

"Let's go in."

"All right."

They stamped their feet in the shabby lobby, leaving clumps of snow. They went upstairs one flight, to apartment 2B. Nick listened in at the crack of the door. The TV was on. Esposito turned the knob, and it opened. When he was in, he took his gun out but stepped aside to let Nick pass, to let him go first: His case, his risk, whatever else might come. Nick ran past, gun drawn, down the hallway.

In the living room, there was a girl of maybe fifteen, sixteen, sitting on the couch, knitting. There was a white wool blanket on her lap, and she was making—Nick didn't know. It was a square. He didn't know what it would become. She didn't move. Nick didn't. Esposito cleared the apartment, the bedroom, kitchen, and bath. She looked Mexican, looked just like her sister, who rested in an unmarked grave. Nick didn't point his gun at her, but she dropped her knitting and pushed the blanket from her lap. She raised her hands.

"*Tranquilo, tranquilo,*" Nick told her. "*Policía.*"

She didn't move. She didn't seem comforted to learn they were with the government. Nick looked over at the wall, where Esposito had drawn a mustache on the mother's picture. It seemed a little blurred from the cleaning.

"*Donde es Raul Costa?*"

She didn't move.

"What's your name? *Cual es su nombre?*"

Nick knew what she'd say, even though she didn't answer.

"Your sister, where is she? I know. Do you? *Tu soror, donde esta? Maria Fonseca?*"

She was stunned that Nick knew the name. Could they be Immigration? Nick saw her try to think it through. They were said to hit farms, poultry processors. Sometimes they hit restaurants. They hit jobs where they had illegals in numbers; not houses, not little ones, not somebody's sister's boyfriend's house. Nick didn't want her to figure it out yet, and yelled the same question. She looked back, more baffled than fearful, and he believed she was honest in what she said. "Factory. Massa-*choos*. How you say, *Massachusetts*. Maria, she good. She make computer."

"No."

"No?"

"No. You are . . . Mercedes?"

"*Sí, Mercedes.*"

Now she was more afraid. Esposito smashed the picture on the wall, punching through with his fist, all the way through the sheetrock. Nick was glad he still had a glove on that hand. Nick kicked the television over. Esposito threw a chair through the window. Costa would not come back here. They would burn him out, burn the hole. That was a figure of speech. Still, it felt good to do it, to tear down his home. Maybe he would feel it in a corner of his mind. Nick saw Esposito punch another hole in the wall, and he punched one, too, indifferent to whether his hand would break. Mercedes started to cry, which made Nick recover himself. Esposito did as well, and he knelt down by the couch to try to calm her. Nick went into the kitchen to find a plastic bag, and then he went to the bedroom, looking at the stray clothes on the floor. Little red underpants. That would do. Nick picked them up with the bag, then turned the bag inside out. Esposito had been speaking Italian to Mercedes—*L'uomo chi abitare in questa casa, dov'e*—and the near sense of it seemed to calm her down. They told her to put on her coat, pick up her solitary backpack of possessions, and then they escorted her down to the car. Nick wanted to ask her when she'd gotten here, if anything had happened to her with Costa, what she knew about him. He didn't ask anything, didn't even try. Nick wondered if Mercedes had ever seen snow before.

When they got back to the school, Nick brought Mercedes onto the grounds. He rang the doorbell at the main building for a few minutes, and when no one answered, he looked around. There was a light in the shed. An old man was inside, trying to start the snowblower, yanking on the cord, adjusting the choke. It coughed and started, then failed. Nick started to explain things to him, faster, then slower, to blinking incomprehension. Nick took his arm and put Mercedes's hand in his, told him to bring her to Sister Agnes. Nick said the name, Sister Agnes, and the man seemed to know what to do.

When Nick went back to the street, he asked the lieutenant about

Garelick. The cassock had been exchanged for an overcoat, grudgingly, Nick thought, but it made for better access to the holster.

"He's alive, he's okay. They have to do tests."

Even this middling news had a sanguine effect. When the blood-hound finally arrived an hour later, their spirits rose further. The K-9 handler stepped from the driver's seat and went round the back; he had the appearance of an aide attending to an ambassador. The hound regarded its audience with deep-set weary eyes, and emerged from the car with a heavy step. In the snow, the hound's tread lightened, and it cast its head back and forth; it was untroubled by the weather, whatever had gone wrong today or might yet still; it was ready to begin what it had been born and bred for. Nick led the entourage down the block, to where the trees began, where they had lost Costa. The dog was in a harness, on a long lead; the handler stood over the hound, fixing it in place with his knees, and took the bag of underwear from Nick. The bag was placed over the snout with a rude suddenness, and the dog shuddered. The handler gave Nick the bag back, and Nick accepted it reluctantly. The dog and handler began to crisscross ahead, finding the trail. Nick looked out through the little wilderness, the darkness in the woods, the bright swirling snow, the sun that was setting somewhere. The dog lunged forward, straining on the leash, and the detectives clambered down the hill after them. A few of them had flashlights, and the beams danced crazily ahead like woodland sprites.

At the bottom of the hill, the highway barred their way, and the dog led them south a few hundred yards before cutting back up the slope. Soft curses broke out from the party as they considered the climb, but they quieted when the dog bayed and put its paws up on the frost-slicked trunk of an oak; they jolted to a halt, peering into the tangled shadows of the branches, and several cops drew their guns. Had he been treed, so soon? No. The handler reached up, and took a black wool cap that hung from a twig. It was handmade; Nick wondered which Fonseca sister had made it. The handler offered it to Nick, and he stuck it into his pocket. They made their way back uphill on a low diagonal, breathing heavily, freezing and sweating. Several blocks later, they were at the top of the ridge again, at a break in the fence. Most of the party were glad to be back on level ground, but when Nick looked over at Esposito, he looked disappointed at the change of venue. Blizzard, bloodhound, the forest primeval, and a quest for a beast; even with the botched operation, only an hour in the past, this beggared the dreams of boyhood. Nick smiled; he had a partner again.

The trail led them on streets more than sidewalks, usually on the side, close in to the parked cars. They were a motley bunch—a few in uniform, some dressed for office work, one or two bundled up sensibly for the weather. Nick still had his groundskeeper coveralls. It might have been better to have a car take them behind the tracker, warm and dry, resting for the next event, but no one was willing to admit they were tired, and no one wanted to separate, in the event they had to leave the road again. In the child wonderland of the storm, now in the early evening, the snow drifting a foot high in parts, the manhunt was less of a spectacle. No one seemed to notice them. Passersby trudged along, determined to get home, or they ran and threw snowballs, hoping it wouldn't end. The men followed the hound down to Broadway, where the plows and salt trucks had begun to clear the streets. The handler fretted about the dog's paws with the salt, but he said it wouldn't damage the trail. Nick's fears were different, and he felt a wave of nausea when the dog stopped, turning north and south, before leading them back uptown.

Esposito clapped him on the back. He understood what it meant: Costa had not gone back home. Not a mistake, then, not yet, burning that bridge. North again, block after block, past the precinct and beyond. Who did Costa know? No one was left at the precinct to run computer checks; calling anyone else would have brought Special Victims into the game. The lieutenant would not let them share in the prize, when they seemed so close and had suffered such loss. When Nick looked over at the lieutenant, he worried there might be a second cardiac casualty. The lieutenant caught the concerned eye and waved a hand; he was fine. The march went on, getting closer to Nick's apartment. What could they know about where Costa might run? Not that the computers would offer much. Nick knew Costa had no real criminal record, nor would he have intruded in the vast databases of mortgage applications and tax liens. Friends, family? No, and maybe. He was alone with his mother in that picture Esposito had vandalized. Twice. No. Costa was not a man with connections to people; it was why he had to force them, as he had. These were the footprints to track, the ones they followed now. Terra incognita, the white spaces on the map.

They cut west again, off Broadway, toward the park. Nothing but apartments, Nick knew—no restaurants, bars, or movie theaters, where a stranger could come in from the cold for an hour. All of them were getting tired, except for the dog.

"Whaddaya think, Nick?"

Esposito had put a hand on his shoulder.

"I don't know. We don't know shit about him, and I don't want him to make sense to me. I don't know."

"You wanna know what I think?"

Nick did.

"I think it's kinda funny that I'm glad we're not sitting down having dinner. I pictured it for a second—steaks, drinks, pretty broads, dry clothes—and then I thought how much better it was here. Am I out of my mind? This is the night. This is gonna happen. This is on. Tomorrow? That same dinner, only better, because we're gonna be celebrating."

The words could have come over the wireless during the worst hour of the Blitz, as the planes droned and the bombs dropped, nearly hilarious in their contempt for any result but victory, inevitable, absolute, and very soon. It cheered Nick; it cheered the hell out of him. Faith or fantasy, it didn't matter. Not just for the cause, the case, but for the friendship; all the fires had been rekindled, all at once, and they blazed. No warmth but this, and not much more light, but for a while Nick forgot the cold and dark and kept walking. His side ached when he laughed. The only doubt Nick had about Esposito's vision for tomorrow was that he knew he'd have a hard time moving in the morning. They cut back east, to Broadway.

Nick didn't know what private jokes, what doubts or desires, were in the others' minds when the dog rushed forward to the subway entrance and down the stairs, but all his newfound fellowship and focus dissipated with the new direction, down and out. The company jumped over turnstiles as the attendant pretended not to see, and then spread out across the concrete platform. The A train had just left the station, downtown-bound, lights and noise dwindling in the tunnel. The men kicked the snow off their shoes as the dog stopped, circled, stopped again. Nick knew that Costa, with his head start, had probably left four or five trains before. This is where it ended. Nick hadn't caught the man in the case he'd stolen, the case in which he'd found himself, at least for a few hours. The magic of the night ended at the bottom of subway stairs.

King for a day, and the day was over. Costa had gone to ground, and when he came up, he wouldn't be Nick's to capture. Nick looked at the lieutenant, who shook his head, and sat heavily on a bench.

"This kills me. This was our shot. Now I gotta tell that prick we were right. It's their show now. Sorry, Nick, I really am. I coulda sworn things were breaking right for you on this."

The other cops offered condolences as they followed the K-9 handler upstairs. Nick felt like he was at his father's wake, receiving the line of earnest two-handed handshakes, shoulder pats, nods of understanding. Esposito stepped aside for a private phone call, and returned a few minutes later.

The lieutenant stood and stretched his legs. "Well, I might as well wait for the next train, get down to the hospital and check on Garelick. It'll be fastest. Nick, you have to put in the 'wanted' card on this guy, in case he gets picked up for something, tonight or whenever. I know the last thing you want to do is type, but we have to cover the bases. Shit, they're gonna want all kinds of paper on this—shots fired and car crashes, men down—I think I ought to just check myself into the hospital with chest pains, get a night's sleep before I have to deal with it."

"Do what you gotta do, Lou," said Esposito. "Fuck 'em. Let the paper wait. I'll go back with Nick. We'll take care of everything. I know you were kidding, but you ought to get yourself checked out. Don't take this the wrong way, but you don't look your usual healthy self."

The lieutenant laughed and lit a cigarette. Esposito seemed impatient, eager to leave. Nick didn't see the point of rushing, and he was almost sorry to hear the arriving train. The lieutenant stamped out his cigarette, and the three of them boarded. Nick and Esposito got off a stop before the lieutenant, by the precinct, and they shook hands again when they parted. The gesture had the gravity of ritual, as if a treaty had been signed. The lieutenant felt that his men were functional, honorable, and cohesive, which he had not fully believed the day before. They had attempted something exceptional, and deserved more than they had accomplished. Nick almost agreed, almost believed him. What he didn't believe was that Esposito's plans had anything to do with typing.

FORTY-THREE

When they came up from underground, back into the blizzard, Nick started to head up Broadway toward the precinct. Esposito took hold of his arm.

"C'mon."

"What?"

"I need you here."

Esposito led him west, along 181st. Nick had questions, but he didn't know where to start. They slipped and stomped through the snow. As they approached Ortega Florist, Esposito began to cross the street, but Nick stopped him. This was not how he wanted to end the night, but he couldn't move on without knowing, without closing one case, at least. He'd have an answer, as Esposito would have, were the shoe on the other foot.

"Nick . . . It wasn't like that."

Nick waited, looking at him, without having to feign coldness. The snow was bright in the streetlights, the crazy uncaptained flight of each wide, wet flake skidding through the air, landing where it would.

"What was it like?"

"I didn't even see her, Nick. I just stopped by."

"Why?"

"C'mon, brother, you know me—"

"Yeah, I do."

Esposito nodded. "I'm sorry. She's just so goddamn hot."

That was it; it was that simple. There had never been anything adult about his adultery. Human, but not even that.

Bad dog! Why did you jump up on the dinner table?

I like meat.

Just beasting. Motivation really wasn't the issue, Nick supposed, but it was satisfying to hear it put plainly. Nick considered whether there was anything else to be said, whether his own traitor's heart had any right to demand more. No, let it go. Maybe he'd have a better claim on purgatory if he did, and he'd be in less of a hurry to get there.

"All right."

"Yeah?"

"Yeah. Just . . . don't . . ."

"I swear to you."

Esposito's relief was genuine, as was his contrition, but he hadn't understood Nick at all. "Not for me, Espo. Not just for me. Not even mostly for me. You're chasing your own tail. What happens when you catch it?"

Esposito seemed almost stunned; he had gambled on forgiveness, but he hadn't counted on compassion, the possibility or the need. Nick hadn't intended any insult, but he knew the terrible recognition, when you take off your hat because your head's a little hot and a stranger drops a dollar in it. Esposito blinked and shook his head, rubbed both hands through his hair. Nick smiled at the recollection of the high sign from Michael Cole's interrogation, the cue to break in on the interview. The smile was another dollar in the hat. Again, he didn't mean it.

"C'mon, Espo. Let's go where we're going. Let's do what we gotta do."

Nick took his shoulder and pulled him along. Esposito stepped unsteadily.

"Let's see this through. Everybody thought it was my night tonight. Everybody felt it, the change of luck, the way things seemed to line up. It was my time, my turn. You know what? Today wasn't a complete disaster. We broke the case. We didn't get him, but someone will. He's done. Now that everybody's got their head out of their ass, me and you both, let's do what we gotta do. Throw away the rabbit's foot and tell me what we got, how we can finish this."

"Gimme a minute."

They walked west, clumsily through the snow, uphill and down, toward the river. Esposito marched forcefully but without speed, determined to move his mind away from himself. As they approached the covered walkway that bridged the railroad tracks, Esposito put his arm out for Nick to stop.

"He's got the gun for me, Malcolm does. That's what he says. But I don't trust him. Yesterday, it was like pulling teeth. Today, he talks like he's room service—'Absolutely! Right away! Is there anything else?'"

Nick looked at the footprints leading across the walkway, down to the river. There were a few more coming toward them than leading away, reasonably fresh. What was he, an Indian? Stop it. Stick to what you know.

"Are we early or late?"

"Early. I told him two hours. Less than an hour since I talked to him. Quiet here, private, especially now."

"You ever meet him here before?"

"Shit. Yeah. Mostly here."

"So, you think Malcolm's renegotiated the deal. With who?"

Esposito checked his phone for missed calls and shook his head. He kept the phone in his hand, at the ready.

"I'm afraid that them being brothers, it might mean something after all."

The tribute to sibling unity was not what it might have been, under other circumstances. They walked over the bridge, over the dry concrete, then back into the snow, the steep slope down to the river. Nick slipped, and Esposito tried to grab his shoulder, and both landed on their asses. Neither of them could quite manage a laugh. Help was not help here; a hand was not a help. Nick tried to remind himself to trust his eyes, not his luck. They staggered to their feet, and then down the path, to just above the river, above the boulders by the feet of the bridge. They'd had a beer here, in better weather, after that day with the santero, the death and the rescue, maybe for atonement. Nick had last spoken with Daysi not far away. Esposito had chosen this place for other confidences and ceremonies as well. A kind of rhyme there, yes, but before Nick could dwell on that, Malcolm called out. Nick didn't like that he was ready for them, that he'd seen them first.

"Hey, Espo! You're early."

"Hey, Malcolm, there you are! Am I early? Moving around in this shit weather, I thought I was late."

"Nah, you know. Maybe it's me. Was gonna call you, but I lost my phone. For real!"

Nick was glad that he wasn't obliged to join them in the small talk.

Malcolm and Esposito were better actors than he was, but the lines were terrible, halfhearted excuses, lies that were as shameful for their laziness as for their deceit.

"You got that thing for me?"

"Yeah."

Malcolm handed a package to Esposito, which he held and weighed, unwilling to expose its contents to his touch or the elements.

"So . . . you got your partner here. . . . What's up, Meehan. Haven't seen you for a while. Glad you're feelin' better."

Nick didn't smile, didn't try to. Esposito must have told him that Nick had been sick, missing the previous meets. Malcolm extended his hand, and Nick shook it. Esposito pushed past the civilities.

"And you didn't handle it yourself, right? Good. You hear from Michael? He call?"

"He didn't have to. I saw him at the house. You guys are messin' with his head. It's bad. What he do? What you tell him he did?"

Nick was impressed by the control of information Esposito had shown. Clearly, he'd told Malcolm nothing about Jamie Barry. And he was surprised that Malcolm had accepted the lack of disclosure, that he hadn't asked how Esposito knew that Michael had come back. Nick was also taken aback that Malcolm had agreed to find his brother's gun without asking how they knew one was there. Malcolm sounded entertained by it all, and that bothered both detectives. The way he talked wasn't a bluff of nonchalance but the bemusement of a spectator, a man who didn't have a stake in the game. In jail, Malcolm had told them he didn't care about his brother, and Nick had believed him. Esposito must have been right; Malcolm had gotten lazy once he'd gotten what he wanted, once he'd gotten out of Rikers. No, that didn't quite fit, either.

"Shit," said Esposito. "Michael's out already? What he say?"

Nick wished Esposito had tried to bluff, had kept the worry out of his voice. There was no fear in Malcolm when he answered.

"He says he shot your partner—you, Meehan—but you musta known it was coming. And you, Espo, tried to send him to the nuthouse. The problem with Michael, like I tried to tell you, is he's always right. So when things don't work out, it's because there's big-time CIA shit going on. You can't talk to him. You're either stupid or you're in on it. I was gettin' ready to leave when he comes in, all shook up, more pissed off than ever. It takes me back. I gotta remember, this was his first night in jail.

I been fucked with by the police my whole life. I know what goes and what don't. I know you got high-tech cameras, I know you tap phones, you got tricky shit goin' on. Me and you, Espo, our shit is the trickiest! But when he starts tellin' me he's gotta figure out how you stayed so still when you hit the ground, Meehan, I just laugh. Oh, man, was that the wrong move, does that flip him out!"

Nick knew how that might happen. He noticed that Malcolm slowed down for the last part of the story, told it less like a joke about a stranger. He was sad about how it ended. That made some sense, but not enough.

"He comes at me. I take him down. I hold him down till he gives, even though he don't say he gives. He could never fight, and I still got the big-brother shit going on. But I let him go, and he runs in his room, slams the door. I'm glad I didn't have the gun on me, his gun. I wasn't shittin' you, Espo. It was hard to find. I only got it when I went to the freezer today, see if there was something to eat. I pick up this box—brussels sprouts. Nobody, nobody in my house, would ever eat that shit. Plus, it was heavy. I gotta give him that. It was a good way to keep everybody from messin' with it. Anyway. I was thinkin' about headin' back down South myself, settin' things up, like I said."

Malcolm's accent followed his itinerary, drifting down across the Mason-Dixon Line. "Ah" for "I." *Like ah said* . . . Nick thought Malcolm was moving a little fast.

"So, Espo, you think we're good now, with the tape of—"

"What tape?"

Nick could see Esposito tense up. The baroque avoidances in their own conversations on the matter might have been extreme—"That thing with that guy, and the other one"—but the only reason to speak of a tape would be for the benefit of a tape. The three looked at one another, unsure what could be said, whether they were past talking. Hands shifted in pockets—dodgy movements, menacing and feigning menace—jacking up alarm. Had Malcolm really given Esposito the gun, any gun, and did he have another? They couldn't see one another, which might have been a blessing, buying a moment. Everything Nick had warned his partner against, all the code-red contingencies, now threatened, and the only way out of the hole was to dig deeper. Nick could not go further, could not go back. What next? Snow swirled down, and he tilted his head back, opened his mouth, to catch snowflakes on his tongue. One, two, three, all of them sweet and clean.

A man lumbered down the path, taking small, reluctant steps, heel heavy, guarding against slipping down the hill. There was an odd tempo to his respiration, once he was in earshot, up and down, fluttery breathiness, then low, labored moans. He was heard before he was seen in any detail. He fascinated the three of them, as a distraction and a grateful delay, but also because he was all mismatch—tan overcoat, too dressy and light for the weather, holding something dark by his chest and a newspaper over his head like a rickety awning, unready and unwilling to be here.

"Malcolm! Meehan! He's got my gun! Tell him I'm a cop!"

Nick didn't know the face, but he knew the voice. Esposito knew neither. Malcolm knew both. The man was not alone. Michael was behind him, and it was he who spoke first, firm and ready, as if bringing the meeting to order.

"Get down. Hands out, hands up, everybody."

The man sank to his knees, and Michael pointed the gun at Nick, at Esposito, before returning the barrel to the back of his hostage. They obeyed out of amazement, hands still in gloves, unready to shoot. Michael addressed his brother.

"You left your phone."

So Malcolm had told the truth; Nick had even gotten that wrong. Michael held it up in his free hand. He flipped it open and pressed a button. Seconds later, there was a muffled ring from somewhere within the IAB man's coat. The man looked up at Nick, pleading in his eyes. The mystery prick, revealed. Younger than Nick had thought, thin and red-haired, pale and sharp-featured, practiced in expressions of severity, not this. Eyes, mouth, cheek muscles seemed like they wanted to have nothing to do with each other, bits of his face all trying to leave at once, to be first to the exits. A camera was around his neck, with a long lens. How long had he taken pictures, until he'd felt what he thought was a gun to his back? Nick guessed Michael didn't have a gun, until he'd taken the IAB man's. The man had descended with the newspaper over his head, as if his mother were in his ear, telling him to mind the cold and the wet. An Irish mother, maybe, waiting at home for him, supper on the stove. The redheaded man looked to Nick. "Tell him, Meehan! Tell him who I am! You know!"

"Don't lie," said Michael. "He's dead if you lie."

"He's a cop," Nick said, though he suspected that the truth would not spare the man, that it might not spare any of them. The suspicion was what kept Nick from smiling at Michael's deluded idealism, his insistence on the perfect fraternity of all policemen.

"No shit, he's a cop," said Michael. "I followed my brother here. I knew I'd see at least one a you here, maybe two. This one was spying in on you, I figured, but I was only sure when his phone rang. It was the last call my brother made. This gun I got? It's his. I'm glad it's a cop's gun. Still, Mee-han, I wanted to hear it from you."

Michael shot the IAB man in the head. The head went forward, stop-action quick, frame to frame, here then there, and the torso tilted after. Bodies in motion, bodies at rest. Michael shifted the gun back to Nick with a fluidly mechanical movement, like the hand of a clock. His head darted back and forth among the three hostages before fixing on Nick.

"Wanna laugh now?"

Nick did not. Michael had wiped the smile from Nick's face, as intended.

"What you did to my brother—"

Malcolm strained not to yell when he interjected, "Michael! These guys didn't have anything to do with Milton! Stop this. It's crazy!"

"Shut up! I'm not talking to you! I'm talking *about* you."

Even in the heated first words of the outburst, Michael still looked at Nick, as if the sight of his brother were unbearable.

"I shoulda known when I found out he got to see Moms at the funeral home. I shoulda known when he got out, came home. You people. What you done to my moms—at least that was quick and clean. With Malcolm, how you turned him, what you turned him into, that's sick and disgusting, the lowest of the low . . ."

Michael had practiced for the moment, had seen it a thousand times in his mind, maybe never as richly fulfilled. He raised the other hand with the clarity of a semaphore signal, holding Malcolm's phone, and the thumb moved among the buttons, knowing which to press.

"Well, that was the last call. Who was the call before that? There's all kinds a calls to this number, back and forth, like they were in love. Why do I know whose phone's gonna ring? Who made my brother a traitor? You know how I know? Because it's always the quiet ones; those are the ones you gotta watch."

As Michael glared at Nick, holding the gun in one hand, the phone in the other, trying to maintain the bravura posture, another phone rang.

The sound was slightly stifled, but its source was plain enough, and not expected. Michael looked flustered, no longer so sure of himself. When Esposito held up his phone—his case, his call—Michael's arm sagged, and the gun dipped down. Everything had been perfect before this, better even than planned. Nick and Esposito were slower than Malcolm, who rushed forward—"Fuck this shit!"—and tackled Michael, grabbing for the gun. It went off, as guns do, and Malcolm howled and fell back, angrier still, taking Michael with him, both of them twisting in pain. The gun waved in a two-handed grapple, and Nick dropped onto it, knee first. He snatched it up and rolled away from them—"Got it!"—then he rose and looked over. Esposito had grabbed Michael by the collar and belt, as he shrieked, flailed, and kicked. Malcolm roared, rolling and holding his leg. "Kill that prick!" And Esposito cursed senselessly before flinging Michael aside, as if he just couldn't stand to touch him anymore. Nick never knew if it was intended, to throw Michael over the drop, to the rocks, to the river—or just away. Michael was the quiet one, the quietest, after that. The others didn't speak, but they heard one another breathing. The snow still fell, and Nick tasted it on his tongue.

After a minute, two, ten, Nick got to his feet. Malcolm packed snow on his leg, the mid-thigh, not near the femoral artery, not bad. Esposito had his hands on his knees and was peering down the slope, watching for movement. He stood up slowly and then turned around. He looked at Nick, then to the ground, at the IAB man, the redhead in the red snow.

"He knew you, Nick. By name. Malcolm, too. He didn't ask for me to help. I'm guessing he knows who I am."

There was nothing accusing in his voice. Esposito leaned down and took the camera from the body. Nick handed Esposito the gun, a 9mm semiautomatic, that had just passed through too many hands.

Nick felt cold, and stuck to a kind of cold truth. "I've never seen him before in my life."

Truth at its coldest, the element in its solid state; you could warm it to liquid, heat it to gas, but it was too dangerous to breathe. Esposito nodded.

"Guess we know who he was, though."

Nick needed to say nothing to agree.

"I still can't for the life of me figure out why these guys try so hard, why they want me so bad."

The words themselves could have seemed boastful had the voice not been joyless—confused, almost afraid. But Nick understood what the IAB man was after.

"He believed in you, Espo. He never doubted."

The simplicity of the observation startled both of them. No one else had held Esposito in such esteem, had thought him so limitless and singular, that to watch him was a privilege, worthy of consecrating all working hours, if not all waking ones. Even as Esposito's faith in himself had been shaken, and Nick had lately struggled, skeptical of all purpose and virtue, this last disciple had remained defiant in the lion's den. Esposito could not exult in the loss of this man. Nick did not want to stay.

"I'm gonna go, Espo."

"All right. I gotta have a talk with Malcolm. I'll take care of it."

As Nick mounted the path, his footprints obliterating those of one, maybe two, dead men, it occurred to him that his partner's assurance could have meant anything—two things, itself and its opposite—a guarantee of Malcolm's safety or his silence. *I'll take care of it.* . . . Nick listened for another gunshot, but he heard only the wind, which rose as he did, more steadily. Before he entered the walkway, he waited; the tunnel caught the wind in its mouth, made it rumble and growl. He didn't look back, but watched as the snow seemed to fall upward in the squalls. Not fall but fly, hovering then darting, chasing or chased. Moths on fire, drawn to themselves, blinded by their own light. Unnatural nature, forgetful of its own laws. Nick waited a little longer, then kept walking.

FORTY-FOUR

As he headed east on 181st Street, Nick turned his mind to what to do next, in the simplest, most practical terms. He could go to the precinct or go home. He wanted to get out of his clothes and shower, but he didn't keep extra clothing, a toilet kit, and towel in his locker, as everyone else did, because he lived so near. He was afraid that when he warmed up and dried off, he wouldn't go back out. All he really needed to do was a few computer checks, fill out a form, to raise the alarm on Costa. And the rest? His hands had begun to shake. His body began to stiffen and seize up. The day's labor, the night's cold, both had cost him. The task of typing a sheet of paper seemed monumental, physically daunting; paperwork of any kind seemed lunatic and make-believe. What would his memo-book entries for the last hour read: "Seventh circle of hell inspected, all apparently normal." When he realized that if he went to the precinct, he would see people he knew, people he liked, who would ask him radical, unanswerable questions—like "How are you?" and "What's going on?" He knew he could not do it, could not face them. He went down to the subway, where an uptown train took him home.

As Nick walked up the stoop to the lobby, he realized he wouldn't have to worry about his youthful pursuer creeping up behind him. Nor would he have to try to avoid the grief-ravished old man who would thank him so kindly for his help. These were yesterday's guilts and fears. All done. How to replace them, with what? He fumbled for his keys at the door, and his phone rang. The number was blocked. Well, at least he knew who it wasn't.

"Hello?"

"Nick? What's so funny? It's so wonderful to hear you in a good mood."

"Ah, you know, it's just one of those days. Unbelievable at work, just getting home. I can't . . . tell you how happy I am . . . that it's you."

Allison's voice was so welcome that real pleasure filled him, masking the cracked irony.

"Don't tell me you've been out in this mess."

"I have, all day, and I'm soaked and frozen. I'm right outside the door. Do you mind if I get a shower and thaw out? Can you call back in half an hour? I'll call you. Are you just checking in, or is there something else?"

"A little of both. . . . Are your teeth chattering? You poor guy! Please, go in and warm up. Call me when you're room temperature."

"I will."

Inside, Nick began to tear off clothing as he walked down the hall, tossing away gun, shield, and cuffs. The picture of Grace was still inside his pocket, inside his notebook, and he took it out gingerly to put it on the kitchen table, not yet ready to look at it again. He couldn't manage his boots yet. The laces had congealed and fused, and his hands were numb. He found himself naked with bound feet, peeled like a banana, with heaps of coveralls, pants, long johns, and underwear knotted around his ankles. He laughed and wished Allison were here, how she would laugh at the sight of him, and the thought nearly warmed him. He turned on the shower and trudged to the kitchen for a knife to cut his laces, his legs still bound by his clothes. Clambering into the tub, he liberated himself beneath the hot water. After feeling had returned to his limbs, he left the whole mess behind him in the shower, boots and all. What did Allison mean, something else? He dressed and went to the kitchen. What did he want, whiskey or tea, to set him up for the talk, the night? After he put on the kettle, he found he was out of whiskey. Best that way, he thought, to keep the head clear. Clearer, anyway. Would you look at that, he thought. He'd managed to look on the bright side. Even the idea of a woman, this one . . .

"Hey, it's me."

"Are you warmed up? What were you doing out there? Tell me!"

And so Nick told the story of Grace, as well as he could manage, starting with bits of the day and then stopping to go back, their serial encounters, how talented and sweet she was, how brave, the episode with the three boys, which made Allison recoil. He was glad he never said how Grace reminded him of Allison a little, when she was a schoolgirl, but he felt defensive at Allison's occasional hints of disapproval. He looked at Grace's picture on the table, knowing how much more there was to her.

"I know it's an odd thing to say, but the nonsense with the boys, even though I wish she hadn't done it—it kind of inoculated her against this guy, Costa. I mean, what he did was unforgivable, how he hurt her, and I don't want to make it sound like it's not as serious a crime to rape a slut, but think about what it would have done to . . . a little girl who was more sheltered."

"It would have destroyed me," said Allison, shuddering.

"Me, too. For her, it was like stomach flu. Awful at the time, and she'll be more careful later. Not like that, I know—but the sight of him didn't send her running away, screaming. She helped us, held up like a soldier the whole way through."

"I don't know what to say, Nick. 'Good for her,' doesn't really sound right, does it? 'Lucky' doesn't work, either. . . ."

But Allison had thought both of those things, as Nick had, and he was touched and grateful to hear them. He was desperate to talk, to tell—some of it, at least—and he wished he was sitting next to her, lying next to her, now. Did he dare say that, ask or make the offer? No, not yet, and he went on with the story, Sister Agnes, the lieutenant in the cassock, the girls with the cigarette. Allison laughed and gasped, asked questions and made comments; the story flowed between them, back and forth, and Nick almost felt as if they were holding hands. He could picture the way she rolled her eyes, her version of it, a quick up and down, and he remembered the way she covered her mouth when she laughed suddenly. On to the school dismissal, Garelick's collapse, the near recognition of Costa, the signal with the snow boot, and the fired shot. At times, it seemed to Nick that he was talking about someone else; he couldn't believe it had happened today, and it wasn't the half of it, not even close. Years had passed with little incident of real meaning for him; today, events of life-shaping significance had arrived with the regularity of rush hour trains. He went on to the foot chase, almost being hit by the car.

"Hold on a minute. Don't get ahead of yourself. Your partner, is he all right?"

Nick didn't understand the interjection. Why should she care? How could she possibly even be aware of Esposito? He didn't want to think about what had just happened with Esposito, what might have happened since. And he started to feel a lunatic anger at the idea that Esposito might have arranged to cross paths with Allison, too, when he realized she was talking about Garelick.

"Nick?"

"Sorry. I guess the brain's still a little frozen. He's okay, I think. They're still doing tests. I got confused because he's not my regular partner. My regular partner is the one who almost ran me over. I don't know who felt worse about it. Not that it mattered, really, who felt what, next to everything else. What was I saying?"

"Nick, I have no idea," said Allison, laughing kindly, sympathetic and baffled, delighted to hear more. "I don't know if you do, either. God, though, it's good to hear. I don't know. . . . All I know, right now, is that my day has been a lot less exciting."

"What did you do?"

"Lay in bed. A snow day."

"Ah, Allison, good for you. You make me jealous."

Allison didn't answer for a moment. Nick saw her resting in their old bed, maybe drifting off, both of them drifting off together, like old times. The pause was suffused with love and regret, and he waited for her to say something. When she didn't, he worried, and she must have, too, because she pushed ahead to fill the dead air.

"So . . . Grace. Does she know?"

"Know what?"

"That you tried?"

"Allison, what does it matter that I tried?"

Both of them were silent, struggling to hold back from obvious comment, frustrated with each other's demonstrable and stubborn not-getting-it.

"Gimme a minute, Nick."

"All right."

They heard each other breathing on the phone, calming themselves.

"Nick, I love you, but you're five kinds of idiot. Let me give you the first two. One, it does matter that she knows you tried. I know what matters most to you is getting the guy, but what matters to her is that she's safe, she's not alone. Where is she now? Does she know what's happened, with all of this?"

"Is that the second one?"

"Yes."

"No."

" 'No,' means you don't know where she is, she doesn't know what's going on, what to watch for? Does her family know what to look for, how they might help?"

"No."

"So you just took a swing at it, you missed, and went home? 'Sorry, I lost.' And you said you grabbed this case—stole it, even. You took it for yourself. Well, fine, but isn't there supposed to be more of a package for girls like this—social services, supports, all kinds of things?"

Nick dreaded to hear what the other three stupidities might have been. For a second, he thought she was bluffing. There could only be one more, two at most, that could be laid out so cogently. Best not to ask; these were enough. At the same time, he was delighted to hear Allison talking to him like that, holding him to account, holding him tight. It was a little rough but not mean, and he liked it.

"You're right. I should go. I should go now, straight there. Allison, thanks—I should . . . We . . ."

"Good. But hang on, Nick. You didn't ask me how my day was."

The comment was haggardly marital, tediously needy in a way that Allison never had been when they were together. He was unused to it, didn't like or understand it, but he played the muffled husband in perfunctory response.

"You're right. I'm sorry. How are you?"

"You're scaring me. Was I ever like that? Don't say it like that. I was kidding, almost. I didn't have a day. I was in bed. I want to see you. I want to talk more—this was so nice. I was afraid at first! But I want to see you. Can you come down? Are you working tomorrow? It's Saturday."

Nick hesitated, then ventured a joke, to test her patience for him. "I just want you to know, I'm not backing down on my alimony demands. I got used to a certain standard of living, and I aim to keep it."

"God, Nick, you can be an ass! Oh, it hurts to laugh. . . . I've got a little . . . back problem lately."

Nick was so relieved to hear her reaction that his eyes teared.

"Nick?"

"No. I mean, no, I'm not working, and yes, I'll come down. Do you want me to come down now?"

Now it was Allison who hesitated. "No, Nick. Go to the girl's house. Take care of that. You got me so caught up with the poor thing! I'm so tired, I'm going to fall asleep soon anyway, and I think I'm going to have good dreams. Besides, the way the day's been going for you, you'd probably hail a cab that's in the middle of some terrorist plot."

Nick smiled at how right she was, though she only knew half of what had happened. And he kept smiling, thinking about seeing her tomorrow.

"All right. Good night, babe. See you tomorrow."

"I love you, Nick. Good night."

Allison hung up quickly, afraid Nick would be too slow to say he loved her in return. So many thoughts came to his mind right then, and they seemed to align. She loved him, a day in bed, bad back, good dreams. She had something to tell him, but it had to be in person. He'd dreamt this, just two days ago. It was a delirium and a delight, a heartbreak that might make his heart whole again. Except that was just a dream, and it was with another girl. So what? To hell with Daysi. Let Esposito have her, if he wanted. No, this was so much better, if it were real. Nick was convinced that Allison was pregnant. Had it been five months? She hadn't said much, but she couldn't hint too heavily or he'd catch on, and if he pushed her to tell, she'd be unable to resist, and she wanted to tell him in person. . . . Paranoid reasoning, he knew, paranoid in reverse—a benevolent cabal, with clandestine actors and energies laboring on his behalf. Nearly six months since he'd seen Allison. Her pregnancy would show. He went back to the bathroom and washed his face. He believed it, truly felt certain. Everyone had said, everyone knew, that tonight would be his night, that his luck would change. Nick caught himself, realizing that it would kill him tomorrow if the door opened and he saw a skinny woman whom he still loved.

FORTY-FIVE

After he hung up the phone, Nick walked around the apartment, looking for shoes. He had shoes. He wanted boots, dry ones, but he had only the one pair, in the bathtub. What time was it? He checked his father's closet, found a good pair that fit. Nothing had been touched, the two suits, five shirts, a few shiny ties. He had planned to give them away. Lucky for him, he'd been delusional and catatonic, incapable of dealing with minor matters of wardrobe disposal. What else might fit? No, leave it. *Move on, move out.* He laced up his boots, piled on a jacket, a hat. Gun, shield, and cuffs, the picture of Grace from the table. He slipped it back into the notebook, and put the notebook in his pocket.

As soon as he walked out the door, he found he couldn't think about Allison, Jamie Barry, or even Grace, though he was headed to the Lopez house now. Yesterday's guilt and fear, they had come back. Five men had met by the river; how many were still breathing? What would the living say, the dead tell? How to chart the congress of conspiracies? It was a bedouin saying, that the enemy of my enemy is my friend. This must have been why the Arabs invented algebra, just to keep track of this kind of thing. As he feared, Nick couldn't begin to reckon this yet, couldn't even write the equation, let alone solve it—the double crosses of Esposito by Malcolm, of Malcolm by Michael, of Nick by Esposito with Daysi, Nick triple-crossing IAB with Esposito. Was that odd or even, in the end, and did the mutuals cancel each other out? The irrational numbers preoccupied Nick because he'd have to get them down before he could do the simpler math for what had happened—one man definitely dead by the river, probably two, possibly three. Nick had been more than a bystander, fighting Michael, giving Esposito the stolen gun. And if any of that came to light, the spread could look like two-to-six, five-to-ten for Nick, depending on how much the judge wanted it to count.

The walk was not long, even in the heavy weather. When Nick entered the lobby, he realized he didn't know which apartment Grace lived in. He'd never been inside the building, and hadn't written a single official line about her, in any of the cases—when she'd been missing, with the boys, and with Costa. Nick had always carried her off the books, so to speak. At the mailboxes, he saw there were three Lopez families, two on the sixth floor, one on four. He'd work his way down. He hit the elevator button and listened as the machinery ground and halted, ground and halted again. Rusted gears, frayed cables, it didn't matter; there would be no stair climbing for him today. The thought of it made him stretch his legs as he waited, the calves and hamstrings. The elevator finally opened, a narrow brass-fitted box the size of a phone booth, and it lifted him reluctantly to the sixth floor.

When Nick knocked on the first door, a gigantic-sounding man bellowed from inside, "I didn't call no police! We don't want no police here!" Nick was satisfied with the response. At the second door, around the corner of the U-shaped hall, no one answered. What to make of that? Nothing, yet. He expected them to be home, but it was Friday night, not a school night, and there was a better possibility they were out, alone or together. He didn't know what Grace had told her father, if anything, and what Ivan Lopez would do if he knew. Yes, he did, at least the last part. He'd march down to the precinct and demand to see Nick. If he had, there would have been no one in the squad. They'd all be at the hospital, with Garelick. Except for Esposito. Maybe. Where was he? Nick should call, find out about both of them. One fiasco at a time.

Nick walked to the stairwell after the second apartment, and as soon as he opened the door, he heard salsa music blasting out at tooth-loosening volume from a lower floor. He felt a headache at the first note, and it flipped multiple aggravation switches in his brain. Dat, da da, dat, da da, dat—it was epilepsy with trombones. The rising irritation raised his spirits, and he was ready to let the people blasting the music have it before he visited the Lopez apartment with his canned apologies and social service referrals. But when he turned the corner of the fifth-floor landing, he saw a man waiting in the stairwell on the fourth floor, peering out through the opened door. Nick recognized Costa, even though he saw him from behind, and knew that Costa wouldn't hear him as he approached.

At first, Nick wanted to crack him across the skull with the butt of his gun, but he decided against it. Nick needed him awake, to talk. He kicked Costa behind the knee that held his weight, and pushed the back of his head with the heel of his hand, so he'd fall forward. It worked, except for when the gun went off. Costa's, into the linoleum, before it bounced down the hall. Nick hadn't even seen it, but he stepped on the gun hand, put his own gun to Costa's head. Nick began a bloodthirsty speech, telling Costa he would shoot him, that he could, before he realized that since the music had drowned out the gunshot, his rhetoric might be limited in its effect. This was the best party Nick had ever been to. He should call the police to complain that it wasn't loud enough. He cuffed Costa and picked up the gun, pulled him to his feet.

Costa hadn't seen who'd arrested him until then, and he must have assumed it was an elite squad of snipers, an armored battalion, satellite guided commandos. His disappointment at seeing Nick, alone, was so profound that Nick was tempted to tell him about the bloodhound, the manhunt, the task force. Maybe later. They walked down the stairs, into the lobby. Nick was going to call 911, to have a patrol car come, even though it would take a while—ten minutes, twenty, unless he said it was an emergency. And saying that it was an emergency would invite a lot of cops to come. Maybe even Special Victims, who would be more than happy to take Costa away from him. Nick had come too far to be satisfied with an honorable mention in the case. He hesitated before calling, hesitated even to take off his glove to dial the number, when Costa spoke first.

"God, that was loud, wasn't it?"

Costa was casual, as if it were natural how they met, inevitable how it ended. Nick spoke in the same tone, though his was a very different sense of relief.

"What a fucking headache!"

"They're Dominicans. They're the worst. Try living in my neighborhood. Believe me . . ."

Maybe they'd both think of this as inevitable, later in life. It was an ordinary tendency to rewrite one-in-a-million crapshoots as manifest destiny. But Nick was ashamed, when he considered the actual arithmetic. Costa was at the third place on the planet where Nick knew that he had been before. They'd covered the school, where he lived, but Nick had been stumped by the complexity of counting to three. What would Costa have done with Grace? Or Ivan? Who would he have killed, who would he have kept, where would he have gone? Nick decided he ought to ask about that, later on, when they got back to the precinct. Whenever, however that happened.

And he didn't just worry about how long it would take for a cop car to arrive. There would be the cop questions that came with the car. *You did this alone? Where's your partner? Where's Esposito?* And since Nick didn't have an answer—there might have been two bodies to deal with, maybe three—he didn't call 911, or the precinct desk. He called Esposito, got his voice mail without a single ring. Nick was exposed, in more than one sense. Adult male detectives shouldn't make solitary and informal visits to underage rape victims. And he shouldn't be waiting there, in the lobby. Grace and her father might pass through at some point, and this was not the time or place for a reunion. He walked Costa to a corner of the lobby, pushed his face against the wall, and walked away to leave an urgent out-of-earshot message with Esposito—this is the address, get here right away, with a car. "We'll be in the basement." He took advantage, as Esposito would have, grabbed Costa by the coat, pushed him ahead to the stairs.

The basement was a warren of drearily uniform little rooms, brick walls and concrete floors, all painted battleship-gray. A storage room, padlocked; a utility room that was not, with mops and buckets, white plastic jugs emitting chemical smells, a box of glossy black plastic garbage bags. No laundry room, no superintendent's apartment, which was good—no visitors or interruptions, no witnesses. Nick caught himself. What was the matter with him? This wasn't a secret, let alone a scandal. It was perfectly legal, laudable, a good thing, even great. This was a matter for the lieutenant, the police commissioner, the whole city to know. This was not how Nick should live, in fear of exposure, flinching at the thought of it like an abused child ducking every raised hand. Still, for now, it was best to avoid any public interference. A boiler room with a couple of milk crates, that would do.

Nick had Costa face the wall again as he searched him, patting him down, then going from pocket to pocket. A second gun was unlikely, but a knife, a razor blade, was not. Wallet and keys, a dirty handkerchief, two pens. Good. Nick needed one. A cherry lollipop. Who was that for? He could ask. He would. Talking would pass the time, and talking was the next task. Nick wanted a confession, of course. Did he need one? He didn't look forward to a long night of conversation. As it was, he had Costa on the one rape and the attempted kidnapping during today's misadventure. The rest of the pattern would be locked in with the DNA—all science. The stories didn't matter. Even if none of the victims could identify him, if half of them decided they couldn't go forward, Costa was done for life. Nick dreaded the idea of spending hours with him, attempting to connect. But he knew he needed to—there were almost certainly more rapes, unreported—and he had to try to get to him, have a peek inside his head. Would he need a flashlight, or sunglasses?

Nick saw Costa tense, lower his shoulders, begin to crouch. Nick stepped back to avoid a kick, hand on his gun.

"Easy . . ."

"I can't take this! If you're gonna do it, just do it!"

Nick hadn't thought about how all of this might have seemed to Costa, with his vastly different preoccupations and assumptions. His day had not gone as planned, either. He had no more expected for it to end here in the basement than Nick had, but he'd drawn an entirely different conclusion about what would follow. Costa had been shocked on the landing, disappointed on the stairs, resigned in the lobby, and now terrified in the boiler room. Quite a circuit, but Nick didn't know which feeling would most dispose him to talk, alone or in their cocktail combination. Nick turned him around, refusing to show any emotion in his own face, as confusion was added to the mix in Costa's.

"What's happening?"

"We're waiting here, until a ride comes. Sit down."

Nick pointed to a milk crate and backed up a few paces, so he was near the other. They could sit and talk awhile, pass the time. The boiler was an old hulk of steel piping and grimed-over gauges. The room was warm and smelled of diesel and disinfectant.

"Are you kidding me?"

"Are you in a rush?"

As Costa kicked his milk crate, Nick reflected whether shooting him wasn't such a bad idea, after all. No, no more conspiracies, not after today. Nick had to decide how to come at him, considering the approaches. Man of Authority, Scary Weirdo, New Best Friend. A catalogue of them, available for the modern inquisitor. He slid his own crate so that it sat squarely in front of the door, and eased himself down onto it.

"Don't sit, then. Suit yourself."

The crate was more comfortable than he'd expected. It was a relief to sit, and Nick didn't want Costa to see how tired he was, how weak and sore. Costa held his wary stance as they looked at each other, breathing heavily, and then he righted his crate with a foot. When he sat, they resumed looking at each other, sizing it all up. No staring contest for Nick, no eyeball-to-eyeball challenge. When Costa tried one, Nick looked away, then down, pretending to think. He was thinking. You couldn't pretend that, after all; even pretending to think was thinking. Should he take out his notepad? Not yet. They should start talking first, about something not quite to the point. The boiler gurgled and groaned, let out a hiss.

"Do you remember me?"

"Do you think I'm stupid?"

"Do I think you're stupid? No, I don't. I answered your question. Will you answer mine?"

"Why should I?"

"I answered yours. It's fair."

"This is fair?"

So this was how it would go. *I know you are, but what am I?* Five minutes in, Nick was exhausted, by the pettiness as much as anything else. Costa hadn't showered or changed, but he wasn't shivering; he didn't seem tired, even though he'd walked as far as the detectives had—exactly as far, to the step, at the subway.

"What do you think is unfair about it?"

"You grabbed me, for nothing. And your partner wrecked a picture of my mother, like some vicious retarded kid who has no respect for nothing. You think I did something? Prove it, shoot me, or let me go. You think I'm gonna talk to you, you're stupider than you look."

"I don't need you to talk. There's DNA."

"You can suck my dick."

"That would work, but we usually just swab the cheek."

The little tantrum, the school yard slur, maybe they weren't so bad. Costa was rattled and humiliated. If the approach to take was to break him down instead of building him up, Nick's indifference to the insult was a worse insult than Costa's. Nick read him the Miranda warnings in an apathetic mutter. "Now that I've read you your rights and whatever, are you willing to answer questions?"

"I'm gonna sue you. I'm gonna have your salaries. I'm gonna be rich."

"It's gonna take a lot more than my salary for you to get rich."

Nick took out his pad, flipped to a clean page, pretended to write. It was better when Costa feared the worst. Just like the last time, the first time in his apartment, when detectives had come in to not-catch him. He'd gotten cocky then, too, disbelieving his luck before concluding that luck had nothing to do with it. *It must be that I'm just that good.* If every criminal was by definition an optimist, reckoning they wouldn't get caught, Costa must have believed he could move mountains. It was time to bring him back down, keep his mind on the little things, take the first steps.

"What's your name?"

"You know what it is. You think you do."

" 'Raul Costa.' That's the name I'm putting down, for the paperwork. If I'm wrong, you should correct me. Otherwise, it'll look bad. For your lawsuit."

Costa considered the possibilities, and nodded.

"Your address, date of birth? Like I said, if you're suing, if this is all a big mistake—our big mistake—this is basic stuff. I don't know what happened. I know what you're going to be accused of. You can talk about it or not. I know you know your rights. You've seen TV, you can talk or not talk. I got my own problems with the guy I work with. Bigger than yours. Why do you think he wasn't there with me? It's a long story—anyway, I don't trust him. You saw him maybe once. I have to see him every day. I'm not just saying that, as a game, to play you. You're smarter than that. I wouldn't try it on you."

"Is he coming?"

"God's honest truth, I have no idea where he is."

Nick was both disappointed and relieved that Esposito wasn't listening by the door. Esposito wouldn't have minded the line of argument so much—he'd try it himself, if he thought it might work—but he would have been discomfited by the depth of feeling, the lack of acting in the method. Still, it had broken the ice between them. This was progress. Nick asked for his address again, how old he was. All business—height, weight, Social Security number, scars and marks, next of kin. Nick dutifully wrote down the information supplied, but for the last question, there was no response. Nick looked at Costa, and he looked back; he was tough again. This was regress.

"Nobody?"

"No."

"No brothers, sisters? Mother?"

The corners of Costa's mouth dropped, and his eyes concentrated darkly. "No."

The mother lode, the mother line. Before Nick could venture another word, Costa rolled his eyes and spat on the floor. "You just said you don't get paid enough. Now you wanna play psychiatry, go deep on me? C'mon! Are you lockin' me up, or can I go?"

"Like I said, this is just basic information. I'm not your enemy, I'm not your friend, I'm just doing the paperwork. And you are locked up. Didn't I tell you that? Sorry if I didn't."

Nick remembered the last talk with Malcolm at Rikers. If the man on the other side of the table knocks you down ten feet, you should dive another twenty. If he wants to keep talking, he has to come get you, he has to reach, and now you've got his hand in yours. Nick scribbled his own name, the date, the time on the pad, so he wouldn't have to see so much space on the page.

"What am I being arrested for?"

"Do you mean today?"

"Don't mess around. Don't play games."

"No, Raul, I won't. Right now, it's kidnapping and rape. Attempted kidnapping, for today, my mistake. But also burglary. I forgot that."

"What? I never stole nothing in my life!"

"I didn't say you did."

"Why you saying it, then?"

"What burglary is, Raul—your lawyer will tell you the same thing—under the New York State Penal Law, is to trespass with the intent to commit another crime. Mostly, you're right, it's guys breaking into a house to steal something. I didn't say you did that. But what your lawyer will tell you is that you're being accused of going somewhere you weren't supposed to be, to do something you aren't supposed to do. That's what burglary is."

Let him chew on that for a while. No, let it choke him. It had been such a long day. Nick shouldn't have spoken after that, not even a vowel.

After ten minutes, he did—only two letters, one consonant, one vowel, nothing more. But it showed Nick was more eager than his opponent.

"So."

A mistake.

"Are you kidding me?"

"About what?"

"That's the best you got? All of this, this is a joke. You're a clown. This is a game. Nothing happened. It's all a lie. They all lied. You're lying to me, too. You're not even as good as your partner. He's just a regular retard, but at least you know where you stand with him. I do. Do you? You stabbed him in the back in two minutes. You're the one who's gotta explain. Not me. Nick? Is that your name?"

Nick had given him real emotion, knowing Costa could taste it like blood in the water. To separate from Esposito had been tactical, an opportunity in the conversation. Nick didn't care that Costa knew his first name. He didn't care if he learned his last name. If Costa found out where he lived, he'd have to get in line with the other half-assed assassins. Well, he could move to the front of it. So what? Nick put his chin in his hand and nodded, philosophical. What would Esposito say? He'd say, if you're still talking, you've won. That was hard to keep in mind, at the moment.

"Yeah, my name, you picked it up. I asked for yours, so it's fair. Raul, Nick—Nick, Raul. I should have introduced myself at the beginning. And I should have apologized. My partner shouldn't have drawn a mustache on your mother. And for hitting you. But you were out of line, too. One thing I don't get is that you think this is some big 'Gotcha!' when I was the one who told you in the first place that I don't like him. So what? Maybe tomorrow, I'll put in a request to shift my cubicle. You know how it is at work. What do you do for a living, Raul?"

"I have asthma. I get a check. But also I work in groceries, sometimes."

The topic of employment seemed to depress him, so Nick pushed it.

"Yeah, so you know! All the lifting, all the long hours, the bullshit with the boss, the people. Anyway, it's just a job. You're just my job today. It's nothing personal. Somebody says this about you, you can fight it in court. I'll go home to my girlfriend—she's Dominican. She's hot, but it's complicated. I'll push her over to get half the bed. First she's gonna complain, then maybe I'll get laid, but probably I'll get slapped. In the morning, she'll probably leave me a sweet little note. You know how it is."

The show of barstool camaraderie seemed false to Nick, but there was nothing he wouldn't try. Costa's body seemed to droop as if it were a plant cut off from the root, but then he sat up again and spat, "Call the cops again. I'm sick of this. Let's just go."

Nick was thinking the same thing, but since Costa had suggested the course of action, it was no longer possible. The indifference was the real insult. Nick knew how that worked. He stood up and stretched, as if to rub in his freedom of movement. He thought of Grace, the broken promises that he hoped to repair. Her last words to him: "Sorry . . . I know you tried." Maybe she was with Special Victims now, looking at mug shots. The case would not be his for much longer. Maybe Ivan was with the lieutenant, telling him about how Nick had lied, that he never knew about the sting at school. Maybe a lawsuit there, maybe a transfer. And depending on how things went with Esposito, this could be Nick's last real night on the Job. Yes, he would see this through, unsure whether it was pride or despair that roused him, whether he was striving for triumph or begging for pardon.

Nick forged ahead. There were appeals to Costa's vanity, how clever he was to have avoided getting caught for so long. The media would be all over it—he'd be the lead story in every paper, on every TV station. Costa saw through the flattery, and while it clearly pleased him, he was content not to share his satisfaction. Inspiration struck, and Nick lied. "We found all your clippings from the paper about it in the apartment." Costa's dismissal was weak. "A lot of people were interested in . . . that guy." Suggestions that there might be a psychiatric defense offended Costa; exhortations to be a man about it bored him. The irony of the appeal to manhood escaped both of them at the time. Every time Nick was tempted to quit, to leave the basement, he reminded himself of what awaited him outside—maybe nothing good, nothing good enough. "I know you tried." Onward and forward and backward, over and over. Proofs and persuasions, offered with feeling when he could manage, faking it when he had to. Nick delved into Maria Fonseca, who'd killed herself; Mercedes Fonseca, who would want to, when she learned the truth of who he was, what had happened. Nick didn't know enough about the pattern—the two dozen others—to work with details, but the ventured gibes about Costa's lack of endowment or endurance seemed to make him proud. Worse—the upper lip lifted in what must have been a grin, vain and simpering at once. He spread his legs, pushed out his crotch, and laughed.

"You know that's bullshit. You even seen what I got. Remember the pictures, when you came? You know!"

Ah, yes, the stack of snapshots in the bedroom drawer. A candid, you might call it, ankles hoisted. The one that followed the snapshot with Maria at the beach. That was still on Nick's desk, folded in half so he'd be spared the sight of Costa. Nick tried to console himself with the idea that even if the picture hadn't been folded, the face still wouldn't have meant anything, even if he'd looked at it every day. What bothered him more was how he'd tossed away the other pictures in disgust after he'd seen the naked one, when there might have been more evidence in the pile.

"Thanks for reminding me."

"That's the best you got?"

No, there was always more. The prospect of prison showers, an angry God who saw all things. Costa gave him the shrug. That was all? No more fire, no more fear? The shrug, how well Nick knew it, the fleeting sympathy, the bored refusal. Even talk about DNA didn't rattle him, as if he'd made an agreement with his molecules not to cooperate. This was over. He was in Nick's handcuffs and would wear others till he died; the city was safer, the victims would take what comfort they could. That didn't matter. It did, but the taste of it was not as it should be. The last duel had been fought to a standstill. Nick and his nemesis, sticking out their tongues at each other. They were so tired, both of them. Where was the third?

Esposito was still not there, still had not called. What was he doing, weighing bodies down with rocks? And how long could that take? Stop it, stop. You can't cry that no one is helping, when you want to brag that you did it all yourself. Nick stopped. Two stomachs, lucky rocks. Was that the best he had? There had to be something better, or at least something worse.

What was the worst thing Nick could say? Was there a list, a world record for the worst things anyone had ever said? A wayward thought. More and more of them would come until he slept. Another one, more wayward still. When it struck Nick, he knew it was a revelation, a true one. But it didn't feel as if scales had fallen from his eyes. It felt more like he could now see in the dark; he could see better in the dark, without the distraction of daylight. He realized he'd barely spoken about young Ms. Lopez Santana. Which was a strange thing—at a minimum—given how she had brought them together, how much she'd meant to both of them. He'd be a different man if he pursued this line, he knew. When Nick did, Costa could see the change, and he was intrigued. Nick was smiling. He felt a little sick. He did not know whether he was casting out demons or calling them to come.

"Yeah? What is it?" Costa asked.

"Raul, this is over now, between us, the business part. I think that's the first question you asked me, and I'm gonna tell you. I mean, we're done here, so it doesn't matter. Man-to-man, I know you're not all bad. You weren't bad to Grace, never roughed her up—she never said you did. I know. She tells me everything. She's something, isn't she? Special, that one—a little wild. Unbelievable! I mean, she can be kind of a pain in the ass, the way she insists—condoms, condoms, condoms. You'd think she owned the rubber company. Shit, is it worth it, though. . . . I want you to know, she's in good hands now."

Nick never looked at him as he spoke, casting his eyes farther up the wall, so they seemed to envision a private bliss. A leer spread across his face, then faded; Nick wiped his brow, smiling, wise to the ways of the world. He went on. "I don't kid myself. She picked me up when she dropped you. One day she's gonna drop me for somebody else. Still, while it lasts . . . Would you look what she gave me? I asked her for a picture, and she got dressed up special, had this taken for me."

Nick walked over to him, holding out the picture, and Costa's body sagged as he longingly took in the trashy image. His head sank down. When he lifted it again, his shoulders wriggled, as if he needed to extend his hands, to gingerly reach. Nick drew the picture back—*Nuh-uh*—to let him know that only one of them could touch. Costa began to cry. Faintly at first, struggling against it, before he surrendered to despair. He bawled and shook, blew his nose on his shoulder. Nick had sickened himself with his own performance; Costa's brought him to the edge of vomiting. He felt cold again, as if he had the flu. Costa didn't look at Nick when he raised his head, finding his own spot on the wall where the pictures would play for his private show, the last before the curtain went down. A pendant of drool hung from his lip, swinging back and forth.

"You know what got me about her? All the other ones, they screamed and cried. I know they were lying, but still . . . Grace, she got into it. You know what she said when I left?"

Now he looked at Nick. The drool descended, dropped.

"After, she fixes her hair—you know how she does it—straightens her uniform. Looks at me. You know? She says, 'All you had to do was ask.' That's how she got me. That's how I knew. And she broke my heart. . . ."

Costa's head went down again before he could see Nick cover his mouth, with both hands. He wanted to cover his eyes, his ears, too, like all three monkeys. The jag resumed for a while, until Costa stopped, suddenly, disgusted with himself. Now, suddenly, here was the revulsion, little and late. Nick didn't want to guess where that small island of self-reproach might lie, if it was that; he had gone far enough, and now Costa was coming out to meet him.

"I'll tell what—how it was. The others, it didn't happen like they said, what was in the papers. And Grace! That wasn't in the papers at all! You know why? It was love . . . a love story. You know. They don't care about that. I can write down what happened. Just give me a minute. Would you let me clean myself up? Leave me alone. Get these off my hands. . . ."

Nick nodded, stood, and walked out of the room. When he was out of sight, he rushed down the hall to the utility room and threw up in the slop sink. It felt like an exorcism, getting rid of whatever was left inside him. When he finished, he wondered how he'd arrange it, to uncuff one of Costa's hands. If they'd been at the squad, Nick would have done that already, cuffed the weak hand to the waist-high steel bar, so he could write. He would have rewarded him with the tidbit of freedom for some minor conversational breakthrough. Not here, not alone, even though all of Costa's defenses had been breached. If there were a fight, Nick was determined to keep it unfair. But it was over. There was no fight left in Costa. Nick wouldn't be careless, but he could let him have his hands. He wanted the story, whatever it meant, wherever it led.

When Nick returned to the boiler room, he told Costa to lie down on his stomach, next to the wall. Compliance came without question or protest. Nick placed Grace's picture on the ground beside Costa's head, so escape would not be his first thought. As Nick transferred the cuffs from Costa's hands to an ankle and a sturdy floor-level pipe—tight, but it fit—Costa's respiration neither sped up nor slowed. His body remained limp. He rolled over and sat on the milk crate when he was directed to do so. Nick tore out the pages that had writing on them, and handed over the pad with a pen. Costa began to write, and Nick withdrew from the room. He waited just outside the door for a moment, then went back to the slop sink to throw up again.

Every few minutes, he'd quietly look in on Costa, who never seemed to notice or care as he wrote in rapid script, inspired. Nick washed his mouth out at the sink, felt in his pockets for a mint. The only thing he had was the lollipop he'd taken with Costa's wallet and keys. He rinsed out the remnants of his vomit from the sink, gargled repeatedly. No message on the phone, still, and Nick and decided he had to call the desk, even 911, no matter what. He was suddenly starving, light-headed with hunger. But when he began to dial the precinct, it didn't go through; no reception, underground in the concrete bunker. Nick didn't think it was too risky to step upstairs for a minute, but he checked the boiler room one last time, just to be sure.

There was Costa, hanging from the wall. Before Nick ran over to him, he put his gun on the floor, both guns—Costa's, too—in case it was a trick, an ambush. He stopped ten feet away, half-hopeful, half-afraid. The notepad was on the floor, as was the pen. No, no tricks. The legs were in an odd knock-kneed position, the arms slack, shoelaces around his neck, affixed to another pipe. The face had a blue cast, like snow in the moonlight. Nick knelt slightly to hoist Costa up; he was heavier than expected. But when Nick slid his knee underneath Costa for support, he felt the hard-on with his thigh. That was supposed to happen with hanged men, he knew, but Nick jumped back, revolted. Costa slipped down again, went back to dying. *Such* an asshole. Nick lifted him up as he had before, wondering how he could cut the noose. When the shoulders twitched, Nick almost dropped him again. Costa still didn't breathe. Nick took his keys from his pocket and sawed where the laces were frayed. Not blue, the face, more purple. A dozen scrapes with the key, but the laces did not break. Nick held Costa up, waiting for him to inhale. Face-to-face, Nick could see spit caked at the corners of Costa's lips, a nub of brown food between the teeth. Eyes rolled back, half-open. Twenty seconds, fifty, without even a last spasm from the reptile brain. Nick held him, chest to chest, and could not feel a heartbeat other than his own, but his was a jungle drum. Resuscitation was a necessity, the last of lessening chances, but he hadn't even cut through the shoelaces. Mouth-to-mouth was out of the question. It just wasn't going to happen. Nick hadn't killed Costa when he might have, he'd tried to save him when he could, but he would not kiss him back to life. Another minute, two, and Nick gently let Costa go.

FORTY-SIX

Nick moved his milk crate into the hallway and sat down. He didn't know how long it was before Esposito appeared, running.

"You got him?"

Nick nodded.

"He's in there?"

Again, yes.

"That's amazing!"

That it was. Nick was tempted to begin explaining, but he didn't have the heart for it, or maybe it was the absence of another organ, lower down. When Esposito saw Costa, he cocked his head to one side, then the other, in an oddly parrot-like motion, before he went into the room. Nick didn't see or hear him for a few minutes. When Esposito returned, he began to gesture in tentative palms-up circles, reaching for explanation, until his arms dropped.

"Nope. Nothing. I got nothing to say," Esposito managed.

Nick raised his hands. *Comprendo, señor. Exactamente.*

Esposito collected the other milk crate and sat down beside Nick. After a while, Esposito coughed. "You wanna ask me how my day was?"

Nick laughed at the echo of Allison's question. It reminded him—no, another time.

"I do, I do want to know. How it turned out."

Nick's apparent bemusement reassured Esposito, and though he began his story with a halting caution—"When you left, it took me some time, some time just to try to figure out what to do."—soon after beginning, the momentum gathered, and there was excitement in his voice, not the old proud delight in an escapade, a feat, a win, but a humble awe at what had happened, almost as if he hadn't been there. For a long time, he talked about looking down at Michael, to see if he moved, listening for a cry.

"Finally, Malcolm says, 'You gotta help me. I gotta go to the hospital.' I look at him. 'I gotta help you?' "

Esposito blinked and made a face, less displeased than curious, looking out at some imagined distance, and did the parrot head-cock again. Nick had never seen him do that before, but he guessed it was not the second but the third time he'd done it that night. Nick hoped never to see it again. He felt cold despite the dank heat of the hallway, and though he didn't want to speak, he knew he had to ask.

"So where is he now?"

"St. Luke's," said Esposito casually, oblivious to Nick's trepidation. "You know, with all the shit he put me through, I was thinkin' about taking him to a hospital in Brooklyn, the Bronx, the worst, biggest take-a-number-maybe-we'll-get-to-you-by-Tuesday joint I could think of, and make the prick limp back home. You know that wasn't the first time Malcolm talked to that rat? When I was huntin' him—back before—he called IAB, said I took a shot at him. Can you believe these people, what they believe?"

"I don't know what to say."

"Me neither. St. Luke's is fine, and he wasn't going to Columbia, at least not with me. Half the Detective Bureau is there, with Garelick. Had to take my own car, and he bled on the seat. Anyway, I was pretty pissed off at him, not tellin' me that the guy had called again. They met a couple of days ago, and the guy gave him a tape recorder. Malcolm told me he didn't tell him anything, but he figured he ought to cover his bets. Today, the guy calls, Malcolm plays it cute. 'Maybe you should be there, when I go to meet somebody, by the bridge.' "

"You don't think he told him about the other tape, with his confession?"

"Would you tell him about the tape?"

Nick worked on that for a while. "No, but I'm trying to get away from the 'What would I do if I was him' kind of thing. Matter of fact, I gave it a try, not too long ago."

Nick inclined his head deliberately toward Costa, determined not to mimic the parrot head. Esposito returned to the circling palms.

"Yeah, but—see? Nothing's different. Malcolm made a move on me, behind my back. Fuck him, but so what? We're both still goin' in the same direction. It's all the same now, and it's done. I took the tape recorder out of his pocket. Into the river. Plus the camera. I dropped Malcolm off outside the hospital and told him to lie to the cops till tomorrow. Not to lie, just not to talk, not yet. 'Uncooperative.' And he's gonna stay uncooperative until somebody asks him about Michael and the other guy. Once it's out in the open, he breaks down, tells them the truth."

"The truth."

"The truth. Not everything! Enough though, and all true. This ain't— They won't ask—for some kind of . . . encyclopedia. Whatever, you know? I told Malcolm to say what happened. And what happened was that he went to meet the IAB guy, and his crazy brother followed him, and Michael killed the IAB guy because he thought he was killing a real cop. And there was a struggle, and Malcolm got shot, and Michael went over the edge, hit his head on a rock."

"Is that what happened?"

"Yeah. The gun Michael killed Jamie with, that's next to him now. Malcolm's gonna tell 'em about that, too. So's the other gun, that he took from the IAB guy. It's all together."

"I don't know, Espo. There's always something you didn't see. . . ."

"Yeah, Nick, I know. And no, there isn't. I do this for a living. You, too. For one, there isn't always something. Some cases just won't break, no matter how good you are or how hard you try. This isn't one of them. My phone? I paid cash for an extra one, just for Malcolm's calls. It won't come back, not to me. It's in the river, too. Whoever catches this won't be as good as me—I'm not bragging; it's just the way it is—but I gotta expect they're professional. Has to be. It's a cop killing, after all. And they're gonna solve it, almost all of it. They're gonna find out what went down with those three guys, but the picture they get is a close-up. It leaves us out. The IAB guy must have been freelancing, too, breaking rules. They don't do one-on-one late-night meets like that, with guys like Malcolm. It's basic safety, basic sense. He went way over the line trying to get me, and it'll show. Incompetent. Maybe obsessed. Will they look for more? No. I wouldn't, honest to God. You look for more when you don't have enough, or it doesn't fit. This is an exceptional clearance. It's closed."

"There's always . . ."

Nick couldn't finish. He had no words left in him. Yes, he had a few, but he couldn't speak them. There was already something that his partner didn't know; he hadn't factored in a major variable from the beginning, and Esposito's predictions were less persuasive when Nick considered the past. Their shared past, the reason for it. Nearsighted of Esposito, you might say. Nick looked at Esposito, as tempted by confession now as he had been by any prior sin. Did Esposito know already, seeing or not-seeing? They were not in the friendship business, he'd been reminded before. Nick nodded, yes, then shook his head, no. He smiled, helpless. What to say? Esposito knew what to say, what had to be done.

"Did you know his name?"

"Who?".

"The guy. The dead guy. You know the one I mean."

"No."

There was nothing defensive in the denial, as Nick knew it was almost a technical question, a request for specifics. The substance was already known.

"No, never did. Never asked. Never met him, like I said. Never told him anything but the truth, until you sprung Malcolm. And I never told him anything after."

Nick couldn't watch Esposito as he spoke. He was disgusted with himself, even as he was relieved by speaking. The post-purgative solace. He waited for a reaction, and when he didn't hear one, he went on. "I was stuck where I was, in the Bronx. Pissed off and going downhill. After a real bad day, this guy I know—not a bad guy—says 'Be a field associate, you can go back home.' Didn't know it was you they were looking at. Didn't really realize till we partnered up. Couldn't tell you after. Here we are."

Nick had heard the song before, from others in the interview room— the daisy chain of reasons, how the boss yelled at you when it wasn't your fault and the bus was late and the ketchup squirted on your favorite shirt, and that was why the dog got shot. *An accident, really, and mostly just a shame* . . . Every asshole has his reasons. Nick kept his head down after he'd finished. Like choosing a blindfold before execution, he thought. The next words hit him like a pistol shot.

"You poor guy."

Nick looked up. He hadn't heard any sarcasm, but he needed to see to be sure. Esposito seemed as confused as he was, struggling to explain. The palms again, circling, head cocked.

"If you banged my wife, I'd kill you. But if you didn't even think about it, not once, I wouldn't understand you. You never hurt me, Nick. You hurt yourself, trying not to. Your word is good enough for me."

Nick smiled and closed his eyes, tilted his head back. Waves of grievous relief passed through him, and he nearly fell asleep. Was it just because of tonight, this day and this night, that this most fundamental of betrayals appeared no worse to Esposito than a bump in the road? Nick had to think so. Last Tuesday, next Wednesday, it would have likely rated better than the fourth- or fifth-biggest surprise. Esposito cleared his throat.

"So whaddaya wanna do with this shithead, the one on a string?"

"Call it in. I guess I got to."

Nick just wanted it to be over. Esposito shook his head, not to dissuade him but in deepening dismay, foreseeing the fallout. "Your case, your call. But this is bad, Nick. You catch a bad guy, a guy you know, you take him into a basement for a couple of hours, and he winds up dead? The DA, they're not big on the vigilante shit. The Job? I don't know what they'll do, but they ain't gonna give you a medal. Not anymore. Lawsuit, too—forget about it. You know there's family somewhere, and they're gonna say you killed the guy. You'll win in the end, I know. But Nick, this is America, this is New York. They'll put you through shit for years even if you don't get locked up."

Esposito didn't look at Nick as he spoke. Nick watched him weigh the options and consequences, spelling them out as clearly as if he had chalk and a blackboard. Something of a teacher to him, in his lesson's belabored simplicity; something of a doctor, delivering bad news. The logic was flawless, and Nick felt his stomach tighten and sink.

"What I done, with the Cole brothers? You could look at it two ways. You could put me in jail, or not. That's it. I get caught, or I get away with it. No medal, no attaboy, nothing. I knew that going in. Now I wish I'd listened to you, even though it worked out, even though I still don't see any other way I coulda done it, keeping you safe, keeping things the same. But you, you do everything exactly right, all official, by the book, except for the very end. You work your ass off, you work smart, and I don't even know how you got him, Nick, but I know you got lucky after that. On top of that! Grand slam! A straight flush! You shouldn't even get a medal for this, Nick. You should get a parade. And now? Now you're fucked."

Esposito the philosopher, tracing the paths that had taken them to this moment, the path that led away—cause and contingency, randomness and inevitability. The convergence of choice and chance. Nick shook his head again. He didn't know if he could bear any more wisdom, any more truth, even at the barest, coldest solid-state minimum, but his partner went on.

"Like I said, your case, your call. Isn't it funny, Nick, how when you start, you picture all the great things you might do, and in the end, you wind up wondering what you can get away with?"

When Nick rose from his crate, his calves began to cramp. As he clutched the wall, Esposito jumped up to steady him, seizing an arm. After the pain passed, Nick limped back inside the boiler room, for a last look at how he'd solved his last case. This was how it all ended. No, not everything, only the good part. He could conceive how a kidnapping charge could be made against him, at least how the arguments would be framed. *The law says it's when you take a person against his will, not a "good person," and a cop of all people should know better....* Maybe they'd go easy on him, in the end, but he wouldn't be a cop anymore. His career was over. Was that so bad? He looked at Costa, the kinked neck, the darkened face. Nick wished he could have been proud.

Esposito still had his gloves on as he picked up the notebook, and started to examine the pages. "Shit, Nick—you broke him? He even wrote it out for you? He wrote this?"

"Yeah."

For a second, Nick did feel pride, if only in the narrowest aspect of the contest, that he'd cracked a code, found a way in. He almost didn't care what Costa had to say. All had been revealed, and Nick assumed that Costa's final disclosure had been equally candid and complete. The story would go where it would, and Nick would make no further effort to spin it, stop it, shove it along, no matter what.

"What did he say?" Nick asked.

"You're not gonna like it."

"What?"

It hadn't occurred to Nick that there might be something other than truth at the end of the ordeal. He tried to take the notebook, but Esposito held it away from him, in his gloved hand.

"Hang on. Wait, don't touch. I hate to break this to you, Nick, but there's pages and pages about how if he's a rapist, you are, that you're no better than he is. She'll never stay with you, blah, blah, blah. Plus, a lot of sex stuff."

Nick stepped toward Costa's corpse as if he were about to punch his lying dead head, when Esposito stopped him, grabbing the collar of his coat.

"Are you kidding?" Nick's voice nearly cracked. "This guy blames me?"

Esposito shook his head, then nodded. No and yes.

"Easy, buddy. It is what it is. He says everything was going fine for him, till you showed up. That's the gist of it, yeah."

It seemed like sacrilege to erase a man's last words, even this man's, but Nick could not let them be heard. "Throw that shit out. Burn it. That is just not—"

"Easy, now. Would you let me finish? There's a lot here, a lot of cross-outs and starting again. But look at the first page. Just don't touch."

Esposito held the pad in front of him. "I, Raul Costa, have done NOTHING wrong. It is NOT my fault." That was it? Nick found it hard to concentrate on the pages that followed, found it hard even to think of it as a confession, with all the shrill denunciations and mopey platitudes. As if Nick should have expected more.

"Shit. I mean, I know it doesn't mean anything, but I wanted a real statement from him. For him to just admit what he did."

Esposito's laughter perplexed him.

"Don't you know what you got? Leave it to you to see the downside. . . . I love you, pal, but you got this wrong. It's perfect. Just the first page. Nothing about getting arrested, nothing about you yet. It's all whiny bullshit about how life is unfair. Don't read it like a confession. Read it like a suicide note. It is! I'm gonna put it back in his pocket, just that page, not the rest. Let's get out of here."

Esposito shook his head, smiling, and Nick realized how well it worked, how it would make the lie true. Was it that? The words had not changed, but they now said something else. They had been translated by circumstance. Or maybe they had become hostile witnesses, repudiating their prior testimony. But their meaning would not settle and fix, not as intended; the story would go on, with or without Nick. Maybe it was time to just get out of its way.

Esposito asked if he'd searched him, if Nick had anything from the body. Nick handed over the wallet, keys, lollipop. Esposito said he'd take care of the warrant, so that when cops found him and ran his ID, they would know who he was, what he had done. The story would arrive with the body at the morgue, shaping the understanding of what had happened. This walking depravity had finally been overtaken with remorse, had fallen prey to his own hatred. Which had happened. It was what had happened. True enough, close enough. Let's finish and be done. Tomorrow, a fresh start.

Neither of them spoke after that, until they left the basement. Esposito took the wallet, wiped it down, slipped it into Costa's back pocket. Keys in the front. There was a momentary hesitation at touching the body, but Esposito pushed on, did what he had to do. He unlocked the cuffs from the ankle and pipe and handed them to Nick, who rubbed them on his leg, as if to get the Costa traces off before putting them into his pocket. He remembered Esposito's revulsion at the morgue, and thought how hard it must have been for him to touch the body. Nick was glad he hadn't disclosed the details of his last, nauseous proximity to Costa's mortal arousal. Esposito shuddered when he finished, brushing his shoulders as if there might be flecks of death on them, like dandruff. Upstairs, Esposito circled the lobby, checking for cameras, but Nick waved him on. He knew there weren't any. Someone had checked it for the stakeout earlier today, when Grace had left for school. They were in the clear.

Outside, the chill air tasted as sweet as mint, and snowflakes fell like flower petals in the lamplight. So beautiful, all of it was. As Nick looked north to the park, remembering how it had started, he felt dizzy. The magic landscape seemed to circle and buck. How it all goes round and round; maybe Ivan Lopez would find this body, too, just like at the beginning. No, there was no going back. It would be another story tomorrow, about someone else. Nick felt steady again, almost strong.

Esposito had walked ahead of him, was already at the car. He opened the door and was about to get inside, stamping the snow from his feet.

"I'll give you a lift home."

"Nah. I'll walk. Clear my head."

Esposito looked doleful, uncertain. His face could have been Nick's face from yesterday, hours ago, most of his life.

"See you tomorrow?" Esposito asked.

"No."

Esposito looked bereft, alone. Nick knew that face, too, and he spoke quickly, careful of his emotion, fearful of the breadth of its spectrum.

"No. We're off tomorrow."

True enough, cold truth, the coldest, in its solid form. No promises and no lies. He'd see Allison tomorrow, the old wife, the old life. No, he'd see what was new. Tomorrow, after he woke, he'd see soon enough, he'd know what he'd dreamt, which dream had survived the daylight. Husband and father; neither and nothing. All in the air. Nothing was fixed yet, settled, as things were in the basement, down by the river, on the rocks. Three dead men, men of agency, of ambition and resolve, who had known the world was against them and had proved their own truth. Rapist, killer, and rat, the hell with all of them. Nick recoiled at the presumption, the lack of charity. Had he already forgotten—wasn't it only minutes ago, when he'd last been forgiven himself? As if he were outside of the process, as if he wished to be. He walked over to Esposito, touched his cheek, tousled his hair. Not quite right, the contact; something distant and paternal to it, when he was neither. Esposito took a glove off and shook Nick's hand. That was better. That would do. No desolation in Esposito's eyes, not that Nick could see, now that his own sight was unhindered, unhelped, by the wilder lights. Tomorrow would tell, enough to keep him interested. He was not a hopeful man at heart, but he would manage. Nick turned and walked away, out of the deeper snow to the road, shaky-legged but thankful that he didn't have far to go.

ACKNOWLEDGMENTS

Abiding thanks to my agent, Jennifer Rudolph Walsh; Laura Van der Veer, Michael Mezzo, and, most obviously, Julie Grau at Spiegel & Grau; early readers Elizabeth Callendar, Amanda Weil, and John Driscoll; and last-minute Spanish proofreaders, Eduardo Castell and Rafael Estrella.

ABOUT THE AUTHOR

EDWARD CONLON is a detective with the New York City Police Department. A graduate of Harvard, he has published articles in *The New Yorker* and *Harper's Magazine* and has been included in *The Best American Essays 2001*. He is the author of a memoir, *Blue Blood*, a finalist for a National Book Critics Circle Award, a *New York Times* Notable Book, and a *New York Times* bestseller.

ABOUT THE TYPE

The text of this book was set in Palatino, designed by
the German typographer Hermann Zapf. It was named
after the Renaissance calligrapher Giambattista Palatino. Zapf designed it between 1948 and 1952, and it
was his first typeface to be introduced in America. It is
a face of unusual elegance.